The Safe House

The Safe House

by

AnnMarie Reynolds

Published by

begin a book Writing Services & Independent Publishers

First paperback edition published in the
United Kingdom, December 2024.

ISBN (Print) 978-1-915353-32-0

ISBN (eBook) 978-1-915353-33-7

Cover design: AnnMarie Reynolds (some elements AI generated)

Publisher: begin a book Independent Publishers

www.beginabook.com

For Mum, Dad and Susannah

This book was conceived and written during one of the most traumatic times in my life.

My parents and sister were with me every step of the way.

I can never thank you enough.

Books by the same author:

- **When Foundations Crumble**

- **Resurrection** (sequel to When Foundations Crumble)

When Foundations Crumble and *Resurrection* will be re-released as 2nd Editions in December 2024. 1st Editions are no longer available.

Acknowledgements

It's been six years since I published any work of my own and, to be honest, *The Safe House* wouldn't be out there right now if it wasn't for the help (and friendly jostling) of a few people.

Kerry, who, over breakfast every morning (whilst feeding my disabled son), patiently listened to me reading every single chapter aloud. Her reactions and belief in the story were instrumental in convincing me that publishing *The Safe House* was a good plan!

Les Ellis, my 'Alex' sounding board. I felt it necessary to seek the objective opinion of a sensible man to tell me if Alex was plausible, but the only person to hand was Les so ... only joking. Les has also been chief 'pusher' when it came to making me get on with publishing this, so thank you also for your faith in me and this book.

Frances, whose generous offer and support means *The Safe House* stands half a chance of being an audiobook one day!

All of the wonderful authors I have had the great privilege of working with and publishing under *begin a book Independent Publishers* over the last four years. Not only are you all incredibly talented writers, you have supported me during some turbulent times and been understanding when I've hit unforeseen bumps in the road.

My friends Sue, Fan, Maria and Rachel. You have been there for me with tissues and hugs, coffee and sympathy. I am so grateful to have you all in my life. Your support of me as a writer, businesswoman and friend means more than I can say.

Elwyn. You had faith in my business from day one. Without your early encouragement, *begin a book* would not be where it is today.

My Mum, Dad and Sister. You know how much you mean to me. I love you with all of my heart. You embody the essence of family.

To my incredible sons, Byron and Lochlann. You are my world. You are unique in your own ways, and I am beyond blessed to be your Mum. I will never stop loving you and advocating for you both - you're kind of stuck with me. Sorry about that!

And finally, a huge thank you to everyone out there reading this book. I cannot tell you how much it means.

Thank you all.

AnnMarie xx

Chapter One

THREE YEARS EARLIER

Seasickness is the plague of the wealthy.

I don't know who said that but I remember hearing it as a child. I think it might have just been something my parents told me so they could condition me to our lifestyle.

"Expect to be seasick; we spend half our lives on yachts. Seasickness is the plague of the wealthy".

I'm lucky, though; it doesn't plague me. I don't know if this is because my insides are made of iron (ancient folklore) or because I have spent so much of my twenty-two years at sea. My family is rich. I have been brought up on the ocean. We have sailed to every imaginable destination accompanied by staff who know our every whim. We have a mansion in rural England, which is far too large for the three of us. There are numerous rooms in our home yet we live in only four. This is my life. It is the way it has always been, and to me, there is no other world.

I am lounging on the top deck of our yacht, *Cassiopeia*, with the sun dipping below the horizon. This is our fourth trip of the year, and the weather is perfect. It is mid-July, and I can think of no place I would rather be, particularly as my boyfriend Alex has joined us. Well, I say he has joined us, but he has spent more time hanging over the side of the yacht than he has with me. He assured me that he was experienced on the sea so I am finding it a little odd that he is still succumbing to the most basic of sea-faring ills. We have been on board for three days now.

Alex and I have been dating for six months after meeting at a red-carpet event. We had that 'eyes across the room moment' and have been together ever since. He is easy to talk to, good-looking, only two years older than me and understands the pressure that comes with our lifestyle. Alex's family is also wealthy, though his parents are 'new' money as opposed to my family, who have been rich forever. One of my long-deceased paternal ancestors struck oil in America and brought his relations across to England on the profits. By the time it was my grandfather's turn to inherit, the oil business had diversified into engineering, and thanks to a breakthrough invention - my grandfather was a bit of genius apparently - our fortunes continued to be secure.

Alex's fortune is from a lottery win, scooped before he was born. Alex was the product of his parents' champagne-fuelled celebration party. He has no siblings, which, in my experience, is often the case in our circles; I am an only child, too. Alex thinks the pressure of wealth and continuing to secure his lifestyle through investments is a hardship. I disagree. At least he has something to do on a daily basis. My life, by contrast, is vacuous. Whilst many would think I have it easy, I do not. Every day I am pressured to look a certain way, to act a certain way, to eat a certain food, to attend a certain party...it is exhausting. And, as I am beginning to realise, it's false. There is very little depth to my friends; a challenging conversation can be hard to come by, and I am often lonely. I am not suggesting you should feel sorry for me; simply pointing out that I and my peers should not be judged until you have walked a mile in our shoes. Even if they are Louboutins.

Alex seems to understand how I feel which is why I invited him on this trip. We are currently on anchor, in distant view from the coasts of an archipelago of British territory islands, yet his equilibrium hasn't adjusted. I know it can't be helped, but I am a little ticked off that any romantic intentions I have cannot come to fruition. Though I have to meter my frustration; it is hard to be intimate on a yacht in any case, especially with my parents and several crew members on board.

I look again at Alex, still leaning over the side a short distance from where I lie.

"See any fish down there?" I call, laughing at my own joke as Alex turns wan features my way.

"Very funny, Aurora."

I laugh some more.

"It's alright for you," he says as he takes a brief break from studying the clear blue waters below, "you're used to this."

"And who told me they were too?" I ask smartly.

His answer is swallowed by another lurch over the gleaming white fibreglass. After a moment he raises his head.

"Is there nothing I can take?" he pleads.

I shrug. "You've had every travel medication on board. Short of finding you a doctor…"

His blue eyes pierce mine, tired and worn from the endless retching.

"Can we?" Alex asks hopefully. "There must be a doctor

on the island…" he gestures towards the mounds of land highlighted by the setting sun.

"I guess," I say, "I'll ask the crew."

He nods before bracing his forearms on the metal rail and dropping his head. Standing there - as he is - Alex could be Adonis. Or something close. His silhouette is framed by the warm orange sunset glow, which in turn illuminates his muscular chest. He is fit by anyone's standards, and I know how lucky I am to be his girl of choice. Currently.

Where Alex is tall and lean, I am short and curvy. Endless hours in the gym followed by juicing and dieting have never eradicated the areas of which I am most conscious, and whilst I know myself to be pretty enough with my heart-shaped face framed by soft blonde curls, I am not 'the body' most men of my acquaintance desire. I am wife material. That's what my mother has always said. I am the one rich men marry knowing my hips should be capable of producing heirs whilst they parade their wealth and passion with statuesque and nubile models. Even now, in modern society, I see women being dumbed down. It remains the belief of some that we should not have thoughts or an opinion, especially when we become the 'chosen one.' When that happens, we are to be grateful for the opportunity to continue our life of luxury and simply produce the required heirs. Several men of my acquaintance have suggested as much to me, and I have discouraged their advances. I have a brain. I intend to use it.

≈≈≈≈

When I was twelve, I attended an after-school business club at my private school. I was the only girl. The tutor spent most of the time frowning at me whilst directing his comments and ideas to the boys. It was blatant sexism which society had supposedly outlawed. At the end of the class, the tutor pulled me to one side.

"Can I ask," he'd begun in his plum English voice, "what made you think to attend this club?"

"Because, Sir, I will take over my father's business one day."

The tutor had laughed. "Will you now?" he'd asked. "Does your father not have a male heir?"

I had shaken my head. "No sir, just me."

He'd nodded. "And what, may I ask, is your family business?"

"Engineering," I'd begun, "my grandfather designed a safety component used in modern diesel engines and now every single engine has one..." I'd felt myself warming to the theme as a passion for my grandfather's achievements shone through, "...what it does is..."

The tutor had held up his hand. "Enough," he'd said, "I do not wish to know what this component does, nor do I wish to hear any more from you. If you take my advice, you'll marry well, let your husband take over the business, and you will bear his children."

I had stared at him for a moment, willing my twelve-year-old brain to understand. Why? Was the only thought I'd been able to form. Why? It's not like we were living in the dark ages.

"Well, girlie," he'd said with a wave of his hand, "that's all. Oh, and I don't want to see you in another business club again. Got it?"

I'd left the room on trembling legs.

Some years later, I'd understood him to be an ignorant pig.

≈≈≈≈

Like I said, it's often fake, and Alex is the first person I have met who understands this.

You might wonder why I have continued with this lifestyle when it would appear I abhor it but let me be clear: there are only some parts I find distasteful. For the most part, I have been brought up in a loving family with parents who have supported me and my childhood has been happy. I'd have loved to have a sibling, someone to play with, share clothes with and talk to late into the night, but that never happened. I don't know why. I don't remember the subject ever being spoken about, and eventually, I gave up hope. I had the pony, of course, and the dog and all manner of other luxuries, but one thing I'd realised I needed from a young age was human company, and of this, there was no shortage - if you counted the staff. Real human company was rare which is why I grabbed onto Alex with both hands. Alex, I believed, was my forever.

The sunbed to my left dips as Alex levers his body onto the soft, green cushion.

"Feeling better?" I ask as I turn my gaze to the side.

"I think," he says, "that if I lie really still and don't talk, I'll be okay."

I laugh. "That's impossible. You are the only person I know who talks more than me."

Alex offers a weak smile. "True."

I rotate my head back to the centre and focus on the darkening sky. It's clear; there will be stars. A beautiful moonlit romantic backdrop. For a moment, I experience a feeling of complete calm. It's perfect, and it is how it should be. Caught in the sensation, I extend my left hand towards Alex and run my fingers down the lines of his abdomen. I feel softness peppered with the occasional coarse hair as I journey across his chest. Alex tenses beneath my palm, and I smile. I understand why he is tense because I am tense too. Alex and I have yet to make love.

"Stop," he says after a moment as he tenderly grasps my hand with his, "we can't."

"Oh shush," I chide as I interlace my fingers with his, "there's no one around."

"I know," he responds, "but the crew and your parents…"

"…are at the other end of the yacht. We're on the top deck; no one even knows we're here."

The top deck of a yacht is both enchanting and frightening in equal measure. Our yacht has three upper and two lower decks, which means Alex and I are currently resting at least ten metres above sea level. It feels like we are flying in our own private world, the stillness broken only by the distant lapping of waves against the hull. This is the beauty of the top deck, yet that beauty can be snatched from your grasp in seconds. All you have to do is look over the rail to realise how small you are and how big the ocean is. I am amazed Alex has been able to do this for such a long time, especially when he has told me he cannot swim. Fate, though, has offered him no option, and I love him all the more for choosing to be here with me when he could be in our cabin resting. I appreciate that more than he will ever know.

"So…what do you say?" I ask with just the right intonation, "I can't think of anywhere more perfect for our first time."

Alex's fingers grip tightly onto mine, the pressure increasing as I ask my question.

"We can't," he repeats, "what if someone sees?"

I laugh. "Seriously, Alex. Have you never taken a risk? I'm sure I'm not the first girl to suggest an al fresco session."

Alex doesn't echo my laugh. "Honestly, Aurora, your language is so basic sometimes."

I frown and turn to face him again. "Session?" I query.

"Yes," he asserts, "referring to the act of making love as merely a 'session' cheapens the whole meaning."

"Okay," I respond lightly, "what would you prefer I say?"

He snorts and untangles his fingers from mine. "I'd prefer we didn't discuss the subject at all."

Again, I frown as I feel the loss of his fingers from my hand.

"That's crazy; we've been together six months; why would we not talk about it?"

Alex stands and paces three steps forward. It's an annoying subconscious habit of mine that I count everything, so I know he has taken precisely three paces. *Arithmomania.* It has a name. My parents were delighted when I was diagnosed at the age of ten. I don't think they liked having a daughter who counted everything for no apparent reason. Once it had a name they felt able to talk about it, which was good, I guess.

Alex has stopped far enough away to be out of reach but not so far that he cannot hear. I take a moment to admire the glorious planes of his back, dappled by the rising moonlight, as he shoves his hands deep into the pockets of his shorts.

I wait. I don't know what else to do. I am in unchartered territory, though this behaviour is not entirely unusual for Alex. Sometimes, he will insist I only eat what he wants me to and, should I stray from his very prescriptive list, I will be ghosted for at least twenty-four hours. So far, I have been subject to forty-eight hours of ghosting.

"I'm not ready," he says finally, "I'm not ready to make that kind of commitment."

I laugh, snort and choke all at the same time. "What kind of commitment?" I manage eventually.

He turns allowing me a slow perusal of his perfect form.

"Making love," he says, spitting the words as though they are distasteful.

I shake my head. "I'm lost."

Alex sighs. "It's simple. I am not ready to make love with you, Aurora."

"But..." I splutter, "Why not?"

He inclines one shoulder. "I just think it's something to be saved...for the right moment."

"You mean after we're married?" I ask, only half-joking.

Alex moves towards me. "What makes you think we are going to be married?" he asks.

"Whoa," I hold both hands up, palms outwards, "I wasn't being serious."

"Good," he nods. "Good."

Silence descends, and for the first time in six months, I begin to wonder what I see in Alex. It's a strange thought process. Mere minutes ago, he was an *adonis* who could do no wrong; now, I am considering his worth...but the way he has just spoken...

"It's not that I don't want to get married," he is clarifying, "I do, of course, I do, and it may well be to you..."

I'm almost tempted to say thank you. Almost.

"...but we're still young," he continues, "and this life," he gestures around the yacht with his left arm, "it's all fake. You know we agree on that. I need to find out what is real. Where I belong."

I nod. In some respects, I hear him, though that still doesn't explain why he doesn't want to be intimate with me.

"Is it because I'm fat?" I ask and then immediately berate myself. I've not used that expression for a very long time. I've educated my brain to consider my shape curvy, not fat, yet I appear to have defaulted.

"What?" Alex asks as he runs his hand through his hair. I love Alex's hair. It's this tawny gold colour, short on the sides and precisely long enough on the top to allow some curl. "Is what because you're fat?"

I baulk. Has he just agreed that I am fat?

"Why you won't...you know..."

He sighs. "No, Aurora, it is nothing to do with you. I simply believe in waiting until everything is perfect."

"But nothing is ever perfect," I state, "we both know that. We live this outwardly perfect life, which is little more than a facade. How can you ever know when life is perfect?"

"I will know," he asserts, "I will know when the time is right."

This conversation is going nowhere, and I get the impression that no matter how long we talk, I will never understand. I know that Alex is not a virgin, nor am I, so beyond the fact that he's not attracted to me, I cannot find another rational explanation. Unless he's gay.

"Are you gay?" I blurt out.

His expression had been one of mild irritation, now it morphs into fury. He leans closer to where I lie on the luxurious sunbed.

"For fuck's sake, Aurora. No, I am not gay. Just because I do not want to sleep with you right here and now does not make me gay."

His voice has risen, and I take a second to reflect on his words.

"And you said my language was basic," I mumble.

"What?"

"My language," I repeat, "you said it was basic, yet what you've just said…"

He paces away again, this time taking four long strides. I sit up and adjust my simple strapless dress before swinging my legs off the bed.

"Look," I say, "I'm sorry. This was supposed to be a nice break, a time for us to get closer to each other…I'm not sure why we're arguing, but let's not. Okay?"

I watch his shoulders rise and fall methodically. I wait. Again.

He breathes out a sigh. "Okay."

I go to him. It takes me six steps, not four. Carefully, I place my hands on his back, just below his shoulders and drop a gentle kiss on his spine. He stiffens, and I withdraw, but then he spins around to face me, and our gazes lock.

"I'm sorry too," he says.

He's close enough for me to kiss him. To close the distance

and blend our lips, but I don't. The atmosphere has changed.

"I think it's being so sick," he says, "it's messing with my head."

I smile. "It's okay. You need your rest. Maybe if you're feeling a bit better, you can get some sleep."

Alex nods. "Yeah, I think you're right."

He lifts his arms and brings them around my waist, tightening the hug into an embrace, and I drink in his scent. He smells like home though I couldn't tell you what that was if I had to create a perfume. I guess it's just his smell. His Alex smell.

After a few moments, he places a kiss on my forehead. "I'm going to the cabin," he says, "I'll see you there."

I nod. I could offer to go with him but I need some time to collect my thoughts. "See you in a bit," I reply.

With a final kiss, this time on my left cheek, he breaks away and begins the descent from the top deck to our cabin. I watch his departing form as I mentally replay the last few minutes and try to figure out what the hell just happened.

≈≈≈≈

A loud shot raises me from my slumber. I have fallen asleep on the sunbed on the top deck. I don't remember returning to it after Alex left, but I must have done. A second shot rings out, and this time, I encourage my brain to engage. Where has that come from? We are a distance away from shore and the only yacht currently on anchor. I spin my head around, looking for fireworks, an explosion, anything to explain the sound I have just heard. I see nothing.

Cautiously, I rise from the bed and tiptoe towards the steps that lead down to the lower deck. I expect to see the crew or my parents as I begin the descent but all is quiet. They must be asleep.

My bare feet have just touched the wooden board on the upper deck when another shot sounds, and this time, I identify it. It is a gunshot. And it has come from inside the yacht.

I pick up my pace and run down to the main deck, halting at the glazed sliding doors which lead to the sky lounge. There are no curtains to mar my view, and I see Alex standing with his back towards me, head down. I drop my chin to follow his gaze, nausea pooling in my stomach as I recognise the prone forms of my parents. On the floor. They are not moving. Alex must be trying to help them. I clutch my neck and scream.

I have never screamed before. My throat rips and burns as the sound escapes into the dark, silent night. I cover my mouth in horror, and Alex turns towards me, no doubt alerted by my screech. I look into his eyes, thankful, grateful that he, at least, is okay. And it is because I am grateful and because I cannot process the scene before me that it takes a while for me to realise what I am seeing. I look deep into his blue gaze. I expect to see hopelessness or fear reflected, perhaps even horror, yet his gaze is empty. Nothing. His right arm raises forward as if to point towards me, and finally, my brain catches up.

Alex is holding a gun.

I scream again, rooted to the spot, watching in slow motion as he begins to run towards me. I don't know what to do. I don't know where the crew are, but I suspect that no one is left to help me. I cannot understand what is happening, why my boyfriend is holding a gun over my parents' bodies and why he is now pointing that same gun at me, lurching in my direction like a crazed madman.

I want to go to my parents; I want to see if they are okay but I cannot. I know this with absolute certainty.

Two more paces, and Alex will be able to open the sliding doors. In the back of my mind, I am aware he could have shot the gun through the doors, so perhaps I am to be saved...but I don't have the luxury of chance. I don't know who this man is any more or why he has committed such a heinous crime. My fight or flight instinct kicks in, and I run to the side of the deck, where I clamber onto the metal railing, which provides the final barrier between the yacht and the sea. It's a hell of a jump, and the ocean whirls menacingly beneath me. I cannot think of a single reason why I would voluntarily launch myself off this yacht until I hear Alex behind me, shouting to me, threatening to shoot me too, telling me not to jump, that everything will be okay and I know I have no choice.

I take a deep breath and let the railing go.

≈≈≈≈

Thankfully I have entered the ocean feet first so I am barely winded. Beside me, something falls into the sea and when water kicks back I realise Alex is shooting at me. It takes every ounce of strength I possess to swim in the direction of the islands. I don't know how far away they are, I don't know how deep the water is, I don't know whether the current is safe, I don't know if I have the energy to get there, but, when I risk a glance back at the yacht I know I need to keep going. Alex stands on the bow, feet planted firmly on the deck, gun raised in my direction.

And I know at that moment there is one thing about which he has been truthful.

Alex cannot swim.

Chapter Two

PRESENT DAY

BRISTOL, ENGLAND

Sodden cardboard sticks to my back as I roll over. My hand encounters thick, wiry fur, and I smile. Rex is still here; he hasn't left me.

I don't actually know if Rex is his name. He picked me up in the town centre underpass a while ago and appears to be as homeless as me. Given a choice, he's not the kind of dog I'd keep - but the luxury of choice is something I no longer have. He stands, shakes his small brown form and sniffs at my face. Gently, I push him away. I enjoy his company, but I draw the line at face licking. I've seen where he puts his tongue.

I groan as I test my toes and fingers for sensation. It has been another cold night, and my meagre clothes do little to keep the chill at bay. Not for the first time, I reflect on how I ended up here, but as soon as my thoughts go in that direction, I order them to stop and re-route. All I have the energy to focus on now is survival.

Though I'm not entirely sure what the point of survival is.

We are in the doorway of a coffee shop, and it's early. The sun is rising, but I doubt it will warm us enough. It's late Autumn, and I'm heading towards my second winter alone on the streets. I wish I could be a tortoise or a squirrel and hibernate until the warmer weather arrives, which would mean missing the trauma of winter nights out here, but I am not. I am a human, a deeply damaged human who requires food and shelter in order to survive.

Survive. That word again.

Rex stretches his paws in front of him and yawns. I am responsible for an animal I neither sought nor wanted. I have two mouths to feed.

Feet appear in front of me, brown loafers, and I recognise them instantly.

"Hey," I say as I stand and move away from the doorway. Brown loafers lead to no socks, tight black jeans and a black puffa jacket.

"Alright?" he replies. He has a friendly face, scarred from teenage acne, dreadlocked brown hair tied in a ponytail and green eyes. I guess him to be mid-twenties. His name is Colin. I know this because it says it on his name badge. Colin works in the coffee shop. I like Colin. If it's not busy, when he opens up, he lets me inside for a few minutes. Sometimes, I get a cup of something warm and a slice of toast. He's one of the only people who doesn't appear repulsed by my appearance which is something I quit caring about aeons ago.

"How many steps today?" he asks, and I laugh. He tests me every time I see him. I'd asked him once if he knew he'd done precisely fifteen steps from the doorway to the counter. Colin had shaken his head. Now, he counts them himself and takes the odd detour to throw me off. It never works. Arithmomania. It's a curse.

"Seventeen," I reply.

"Dammit," he says. He has left the door open, an indication that I can enter, so I do, Rex trailing at my heels. It's warm inside.

Colin places a bowl of water on the floor, and Rex licks at it greedily. The water is joined by a few slices of bacon. I watch the dog's face transform into pure ecstasy. Often, the dog is treated better than me.

"What do you want?" Colin asks.

I shrug. "Whatever you can spare."

A moment later, he produces a mug of steaming coffee and a bagel. I try to eat delicately, but I am starving. I can't remember if I ate last night or yesterday at all.

"You want one for the road?" Colin asks.

I nod. He passes me a paper bag which I know is our cue to leave. Paying customers will be arriving soon, and we cannot be in the shop when they are. It's an unspoken rule.

I smile at Colin as Rex and I take our leave. We have another whole day to negotiate, but at least we are no longer doing it on an empty stomach.

THREE YEARS EARLIER

I swim until my lungs threaten to burst.

The rocky mound rising from the sea seems further away

instead of getting closer. I can feel the strong current pulling at me, and I know it won't take much to be swallowed up, another victim of the yawning ocean. Saltwater stings my eyes. I am desperate for a drink. My skin itches, and my light sundress feels as if it weighs a ton. It is dragging me back, so I stop and tread water to remove the offending garment. I am not wearing a bra, but I don't care. I'll worry about decency if I make it to land.

Without my dress, progress is easier. I look behind to see that the *Cassiopeia* is now a speck in the distance. I have not been followed. There have been no further shots. I am alone.

I have lost all sense of time when, eventually, my feet touch the seabed, and I realise I can stop swimming. My legs are jelly. I stumble as I try to gain purchase on the ocean floor. It takes a few moments, but eventually, I right myself before walking slowly and carefully towards land.

PRESENT DAY

Rex and I are sat on our usual bench in Victoria Square. I like Victoria Square because it leads to Clifton Arcade and one day I want to shop in Clifton Arcade. I've wandered the rows of unique shops and admired its Victorian architecture but I have never stepped inside. I am no longer fit to grace these establishments. But I will be. One day.

When it is dry, I spend my days on this bench watching people who have purpose as they come and go. I love the diversity here. The eclectic mix of boutiques attracts all walks of life and it is one of the only areas I don't feel out of place. Occasionally, passers-by will stare, some will offer me a sympathetic smile, others take a wide berth, and there are the few who toss me some coins. I don't beg. I don't have a cardboard sign; I simply sit in my worn and dirty clothes and let the world judge me.

If you'd told me eighteen months ago that this was what my life would consist of, I would have laughed. Loudly. This existence I endure every day could not be further from the luxury into which I was born, and I marvel at my ability to survive with almost no skills.

When I first made it back to England, I looked for a job and a place to stay, but I had no identity. I was in an unfamiliar city with no roots to ground myself to. I had left the *Cassiopeia* that night wearing only a sundress and knickers, no passport, nothing to prove I even existed. The shocking events of that night barely made the news back in England or, if they did, it had peaked and dipped by the time I returned. It had taken a long time to get back home, and when I finally arrived, I knew I couldn't go back to my old life. As soon as my feet touched home soil, I was engulfed in an aching loss and crippling loneliness that was so deep I feared I might never survive. I had been away for eighteen months - a lifetime - and the woman who returned was a shadow of the girl who had left on a dream holiday alongside the love of her life. Everything I thought I had known that day had been stripped bare, taken apart piece by piece, until the events of my final weeks before returning to England destroyed all my remaining belief in the decency of others.

The Aurora of old had perished on the same fateful night as her parents, and thus, when I spent my first night on the streets of Bristol, sleeping on the bench in Victoria Square, I discovered an odd security in being no one. I became invisible and after a while, I learned to enjoy it. So, I buried Aurora and remained invisible.

I don't know what happened to the yacht. I don't know how the crimes Alex committed were discovered, nor do I know where Alex is or if he is even alive. I went to the library once to flick through the newspaper archives. The report noted that Cassandra and Andrew Foster's daughter, Aurora, had not been found and, after several unsuccessful search dives, had been declared lost at sea. That was it. No mention of Alex or the crew. The photo of my parents had been taken on the yacht the day before, smiling deep into each other's eyes, Mum's colourful birthday banner strung across the sun deck behind them. It was all I could do to hold it together as I stared at the faces I knew so well. I ran out of the library, back to my bench and cried until I had nothing left.

≈≈≈≈

One of the problems with modern society, I have realised, is that we are scared to help others. We don't know if a stranger's erratic behaviour is genuine pain or need or if it is the result of a manufactured high. We are also wary of being physically abused should we offer help; or being sued for assault or some similar misdemeanour.

On that day, the day I cried my tears dry, only one person stopped to see if I was okay. His name was Father Derek Brown. He took me to his parish church, made me a cup of tea and gave me some clothes from the lost and found box. He told me that God would help, that all would be well and he encouraged me to talk.

I tried, I really tried because I believed in his sincerity… but I couldn't. The Bible might say that good will prevail if we trust, but how could I trust when the two people I loved most in the world had been cruelly killed by someone I thought was my soul mate? At that time, I didn't think even God could help, so I thanked Father Derek Brown, changed into the oversized clean clothes and walked out of his church.

THREE YEARS EARLIER

I have made it to land. Before me stretches golden sand streaked by moonlight. There are stars in the inky night sky. I knew there would be. I was right. I laugh.

I laugh because I remember thinking this was the most romantic evening ever. I laugh because I remember thinking this would be Alex and my first time together. I laugh because I am wearing nothing but a pair of lace knickers. I laugh because I am exhausted. I laugh because I have gone beyond the point of grief. I laugh because…there doesn't seem to be anything else to do.

I half walk, half stagger in the direction of sound. A discarded beach towel lies to my right, and I make a diversion to collect it. It is a child's beach towel, bright pink with flowers and a hood. I think someone is missing this towel but I am glad they have left it behind. It covers me enough for decency.

The volume increases as I make my way towards a trail of twinkling lights. They run either side of a pathway framed by palm fronds and remind me of Christmas—of happy times, of times when I believed Santa to be real, of times when my parents were alive.

I choke down a cry as an overwhelming urge to vomit hits. I don't know how far I have swum, but I am certain this and the onset of shock are causing the nausea. I have no choice but to head into the palm fronds and empty my stomach. I lean my left hand against the trunk of a tree and close my eyes. I see Alex as he leans over the side of the boat. I watch as he moves towards me and sits down on the bed next to me. I hear our conversation, the way he dismisses my advances and I watch his beautiful form as he walks away. And then there is nothing other than my blood-curdling scream.

At first, I believe this to be happening in my mind, but when I open my eyes, it is apparent I am actually screaming. My voice is forming words around the screams and gulps, but I don't know what I am saying. My eyes blur, and I sink to my knees in the soft sand. I don't want to be here. Why should I be here when my parents are not?

I decide that life isn't worth living and that the pain is too much for me to bear. My survival instinct has gone.

I lie face down in the sand and try to forget to breathe.

PRESENT DAY

It is, as I predicted, a beautiful winter morning. Before I became invisible, the weather was something that simply happened. If it rained, it rained, and if it was sunny, it was sunny—that was it. Now, it is crucial to my everyday survival, particularly as the days and nights turn colder.

Rex snuggles next to me on the bench, lets out a deep sigh and drops his head to his paws. I stroke his rough head with my left hand and watch the familiar daily activity.

Across the first swathe of grass, I see Roseanna bustling towards her place of work. She is a short, round woman with a huge smiling face and terrible dress sense. If ever she walks my way I get a whiff of strawberries and talcum powder, an odd yet comforting combination. I think she is probably in her mid-fifties and walks quickly, twenty steps to cross the park before disappearing into Clifton Arcade. Like Rex, I actually have no idea if her name is Roseanna. It is part of my entertainment to give each regular a name based on what I believe to be their personality. For some reason, all of the names I assign begin with R.

The man in the suit I have called Roland, and he enters the park with clipped strides. He is always smartly dressed in a three-piece pinstripe of varying colours. He carries the same battered brown briefcase every day and is usually talking on his phone. He is mid-thirties, at a guess, with sandy-coloured hair and a square face. His eyes are close together, which disrupts the proportions of his visage. Of the two, you would think Roseanna would be the one to notice me, but she never does. Roland, though, always walks directly by the bench and throws me some change, and every time, I thank him. We have never exchanged words, mostly because he is often talking to someone else, but he smiles. Every day. Without fail. Except for weekends. Weekends draw a different crowd.

Rex raises his head to acknowledge the jangle of metal hitting the ground as Roland's money lands by my feet. It is two one-pound coins—enough for lunch. Roland will never know how much his simple act of kindness means. I thank him. He smiles, and that is our interaction for another day.

As the world moves on around me, I ponder my future. I have been lucky to survive this long on unforgiving streets. Fitting into this life has been far from easy; days are spent scrounging, picking up leftovers and trying to keep warm; nights are the same, except they are governed by fear. In inky darkness the streets come alive, not only with those like me but others too. Real people. Those with a home and money to spend. Revellers. Destroyers.

To them, it is a game to kick and spit at me, knock over my

carefully constructed cardboard room, and throw burning cigarettes my way. They are drunk and often high. They laugh hysterically as they watch me putting my meagre life and pitiful belongings back together.

Then there are those who are after more than a good time. They see a woman alone and figure she is fair game. They shout obscenities and ask things of me no one has a right to. Sometimes, they have knives. I curl up as small as I can and remain mute.

My upper-class accent has offended my fellow street dwellers, and I have often been ostracised. I have been beaten for sleeping in the wrong doorway or scrounging at the wrong restaurant. They believed I didn't belong, and they were right. They said I must have a home and should go back to it and to my life of luxury.

I could. There is nothing stopping me. Though I don't know what has happened to my home, there must be money somewhere. I could get a DNA test to prove my identity, and I could reclaim my life. It wouldn't be easy, but I could. Yet here's the rub. I don't want to. For all the challenges and fears I face daily, I feel more at home here than I ever felt before. I like that I have no responsibility; no one is telling me what to wear, or how to speak, or what to eat. And I like the anonymity - this is especially important. If I go back, if I prove my identity and reclaim my birthright, then I will be out there again, traceable, and that cannot happen. If Alex is still alive, then I refuse to be found. I refuse to be hunted. I refuse to give him any more of my life than he has already taken.

≈≈≈≈

"Hey, baby girl."

I turn my head to the sound. Astrid is walking towards me.

I didn't need to recognise her voice to know instantly that she was approaching. Astrid jingles as she moves, courtesy of a myriad of bangles and bells which adorn her person in an eighties hippy way. Astrid is, quite simply, beautiful. We have hung out and looked after each other for a while now. Astrid was the one who put me back together after the last time I was beaten, and she showed me the ropes. She's an old-timer who's been on the streets more than she's been under a roof. I don't know her story, nor do I ask. Not because I am not interested but because I do not want to share mine.

After eleven strides, her tall, loping form reaches the bench, and I look up to meet her clear green eyes. Astrid is clean. She doesn't do alcohol or drugs; she is like me. She has the most glorious copper-coloured hair, which falls in long braids to her waist, and is as slender as she is tall. Like I said, Astrid is beautiful, and it is a mystery to me why she isn't a model. I have told her countless times to walk into an agency and try her luck, but she won't. I think she's stuck in the same way I am. Neither here nor there, existing, surviving and wondering.

"Hey," I reply.

Astrid reaches down to tickle Rex under the chin. He licks her hand in greeting.

"He is so cute," she says in her south-western twang. "I wish I had a Rex."

"You can have mine," I offer, "he's just another mouth to feed."

Astrid nods. "True, baby girl. True. How's it going today?"

I open my palm and show her the two coins from Roland.

"Lunch?" She asks, and I nod.

"We can get a maccy deal and share if you like?"

"Yeah, cool," Astrid replies. "I don't think I've got anything else on."

I laugh. I cannot remember the last time I had the need to consult a diary or a planner. The only way I know what day it is by reading discarded newspapers.

"Gonna be a cold one tonight," she says as she settles on the bench beside me. "Where you going?"

I shrug. "No idea yet. Usual place, I guess."

Astrid is quiet for a moment. "I've heard of a new place I was thinking of trying. Wanna join?"

"What kind of new place?" I ask. I am always careful where I sleep.

"It's a shelter, I think. Denver told me about it. Said we can get a hot meal, too."

Denver is in his fifties and popular in our community. He is eager to tell anyone who will listen about his investment banking days - before the crash. The story changes each time he recalls it, though, but I have no doubt he believes what he is saying. He spends a lot of his time alone, singing quietly, and I sometimes wonder if he lives in our world.

"And how does Denver know it's okay?" I ask.

Astrid shrugs. "Same way any of us know anything, I guess, baby girl."

"Right," I reply, "someone told him."

"I don't know," Astrid says, "but it's not like we've got a night booked at the Ritz, is it?"

She has a point. We fall into silence.

THREE YEARS EARLIER

Big fat drops of rain splash onto my face, and I turn my head to the side. My gaze connects with a gecko who is watching me, eyes wary. I blink and then instantly regret it as dried sand combines with wet, rendering me unable to see. I lift my right hand from where it is resting in my makeshift bed and rub ineffectually. Out of my peripheral vision, I watch the gecko saunter away.

I am alive. I realise this at the same time as I register the blue sky above. The rain has stopped almost as soon as it began and fronds of sun are now weaving their way through the palm trees. I have slept where I lay, face down in the sand. Now, it is morning.

A bird shrieks in the trees above, and a faint smell of cooking reaches my nose. It takes a moment for me to fully remember, to recall the horrendous events of the last twenty-four hours, but when I do, they hit me afresh, and I watch the scene as if it is once again unfolding before my eyes. The pain of the loss stabs at my stomach as my brain whirs out of control. I cannot process any of this. I need it not to be real. I think I am still in shock. No. I know I am still in shock.

I push slowly to my knees. I did not want to be alive. This was not the plan. As I rest back on my heels, I realise I am sat in prayer and at the irony of this, I send my gaze skywards. I search for something, anything, a sign to tell me how I am supposed to live, but there is nothing save miles of sky. The hopelessness of my situation begins to override the shock, and as I kneel, looking for answers, I make myself a promise. One that I will live by until it is no longer time to do so.

I promise that I will never again trust a living person.

I feel my mind retreat like it was battling for me to listen, to give me strength, to tell me I could do this and I would be okay but now it realises the war is pointless. I am empty. My soul is waving a white flag.

As a child, I remember being fascinated with the mind, the fact that it was never still. I believed it was impossible not to have a thought at every single moment because my mind was always busy and full. As a teenager, I tried meditation because it was the cool thing to do, but I was hopeless because I couldn't quiet my mind.

Today, though, for the first time in twenty-two years, my mind is quiet. It has no thoughts, nothing for me to consider, nothing for me to address; it has simply shut down.

I drop my eyes to my lap and adjust the child's beach towel, which has begun to gape. I recognise that I need to move, get out of here and do something, but I have no idea what that something is. Part of me understands that a heinous crime has been committed and so I must report it to the authorities, but I realise I don't actually know which authorities. We are anchored in the Caribbean Sea, and the yacht is registered in the US. Does that mean the laws from here, where I have landed, apply or should it be the US authorities? Then again, everyone on board was British, so should I contact English Customs, or Transport Services, or Coastguard Services…

I drop my head to the sand as a frustrated yowl escapes my lips. It is too much to think about. I want my parents found so they can be properly remembered, and I need Alex to pay for what he did, but I am terrified and alone. I am not used to having such weight on my shoulders, and I realise I am ill-equipped for any life other than the one I was born into. I genuinely feel as though my brain will burst, so I take a few deep breaths and inhale the salty ocean air, along with a faint smell of food. I cannot cope; I do not know how to survive in this other world. I have no money, no passport, no clothes, no identity...it is too much.

I close my eyes again. Maybe this time, God will take me, too.

PRESENT DAY

Astrid leads the way as we walk towards our new home for the night. We have skirted the town centre and are now crossing the river to Spike Island. It is here, Astrid says, that we will find the shelter.

I have not been to this part of Bristol before, so I am curious as to my surroundings. The area appears to be heavily industrialised, although there are a few houses and residential streets dotted within. Immediately I get the impression of art and culture. Victorian structures have been carefully and sympathetically remodelled, and I read the names of several museums and galleries as we pass. The air smells fresh, washed clean by the winter breeze blowing in off the channel. I decide I would like to know more about where I am, for it feels safe and comfortable.

It is dark, but instead of pangs of fear, I feel warmth, like the darkness enveloping me in a cloak. I am used to being on my guard, wary, watching my step, looking out behind me, yet that has lifted since we crossed the river. I don't know what it is, but there is something special here.

We stop in front of what appears to be a disused warehouse. I can tell this is Victorian, too, from its structure and design. It is only one storey, but the roof is way up and partially engulfed by a large chimney. I love seeing old chimneys; they remind me of a time when I believed life to be easy, when manufacturing was at its peak, when families led simple lives, when the men went out to the factories, and the women looked after the home. I know this goes against everything women have fought for - me included - but for some reason, I romanticise the times before equality and rights. I cannot tell you why.

Three large arched windows grace the side of the building. These are heavily leaded in a chequerboard pattern. From within, I see a welcoming glow.

"This is it," Astrid says.

We walk towards a pair of large, heavy oak doors. Rounded on top, they reach almost to the roof. Astrid pushes one side open. It creaks as it scrapes along a hard tile floor. As we enter, we are assailed by warmth, and hurriedly, I push the heavy door closed behind us. There is a long iron bar, which I can see fits across both doors to form a locking system, but I leave this where it is in case anyone else needs to enter.

"Wow," breathes Astrid, who is a few paces ahead of me.

We walk into what I can only describe as a wartime military hospital. Rows of bunks line the sides and centre of the room. The interior is vast, stretching further than I can see. Off to the right is a small room set apart from the main area. This is furnished simply with a table and two metal chairs, and it is from this room we are greeted.

"Come in, come in."

Astrid enters but I pause on the threshold, I need a moment to process this. I hear a scrape as Astrid takes one of the metal chairs adjacent to the desk. On the other side I see our host. He, I note, is seated on a black faux leather office chair. I know it is faux leather because it's shiny. For a second I think of my gorgeous real leather jacket, long and flowing, autumn red, exceptionally expensive and so soft to the touch. It was an eighteenth birthday present from my parents and one of my most prized possessions. Where had it ended up?

His gaze is fixed on me, dark eyes penetrating as he waits for me to sit too. I stare him out. I am not as gullible as Astrid. I made a promise to myself that I would never again trust a living soul and to go from the streets to this…it doesn't feel right. It's not a five-star hotel by any stretch but it is warm, dry and there are beds, which is an improvement on my bench or the cold hard pavement. I can smell onions or maybe its leeks. This must be the hot meal that Denver mentioned. I half spin in the doorway and count thirty people milling about. Why, I wonder, is this place not packed? Anyone living on the streets would literally kill to be here. Even if only for one night.

"What is this place?" I ask as I return my attention to the small room and the man with the penetrating gaze.

He shrugs. "Somewhere safe."

I nod.

"It's amazing," says Astrid. Her voice has become breathy, a mixture, I presume, of excitement and desire. Desire because our host is not unattractive.

"Used to be a warehouse," I comment.

"It did," he replies. "Won't you join your friend?"

He extends his hand towards me and drops it down to indicate the other metal chair. I hesitate for a moment longer before deciding I have nothing to lose. I sit in the second metal chair, surprised to find comfort from its worn but padded seat.

"I'm Rich," he says and I laugh.

"What?" His dark eyes look directly at me again. I cannot decide if I am challenged or unnerved.

"Rich?" I question.

He nods.

"How can you call yourself Rich when you're in a place like this?"

He watches me and then slowly nods. "You're being cute," he says, "I like that." A soft accent accompanies his words, yet it is not one I can place. "My full name is Richie, but most people drop the 'i.e.'. It's easier."

Astrid nods eagerly. I remain still. That's rubbish. There's hardly any difference between saying Rich and Richie and barely anything in the writing of it; but who cares? Definitely not me.

"So..." Astrid says as she leans forwards. Everything jingles, and I get a waft of her flowery scent. We cleaned up a little in the bathroom at Maccy D's earlier, and Astrid found a discarded perfume bottle in the bin. There was a little spritz left so she'd used it, liberally. "How does this work?" She asks.

Rich mirrors her, leaning across the table until there is barely any space separating them. I try not to gag.

"You're so pretty," he observes as he looks at her.

She smiles and a blush creeps up her cheek. I watch the primal mating ritual begin. If you're the kind of girl who 'puts out' on the street then you become something very different. I have not gone down that road and nor has Astrid; we would rather starve. Watching her flirting now - it's a novelty.

"I can't believe you're not a model," Rich continues as he reaches out and tucks a tendril of Astrid's hair behind her ear. "I might be able to make that happen."

I snort, and again, dark eyes pierce mine.

"Problem, Bambi?"

I cannot hide my anger. "Bambi was a foal," I say as I stand and push the chair away. It clatters to the floor behind me. Rex hunkers down in fear. "Bambi was weak and inexperienced in the ways of her world. I am not like Bambi. I don't care what this place is, but it feels like some kind of mindfuck. I'm outta here."

"Whoa," Rich pushes his chair back and holds up both hands. "I meant no offence."

"No?" I spit, "Then I suggest you work on your repertoire. Come, Rex."

My faithful companion sniffs at my heels as I stomp back the way we came. I hear Astrid's call and heavy footsteps behind me but I don't care. There is no way in the world I will allow myself to be made a fool of. Again.

The door looms ahead and I reach for the circular iron handle, twisting and pushing but it refuses to open. I can see that the iron bar has been dropped into place so I begin to lift this but it's stuck fast, padlocked to its shackles at both ends.

"What the hell?" I ask as I whirl to confront Rich. "Let me out of here."

"Sorry," he glances at his wristwatch, "we always lock the doors at this time of night, prevents over-crowding."

"Well, if you let me out, then another person can come in," I state, but Rich shakes his head.

"It doesn't work like that."

Above, I hear the spitting and buzzing of a fluorescent light bulb. For the first time I notice that the vaulted ceiling is completely covered in these, each one hanging down from a metal wire and forming a neat row. Like the beds.

I laugh. "Seriously?"

He nods. "Totally."

Rex sighs and drops to his haunches.

"Nice dog," Rich comments, "what's his name?"

"Rex."

"Good name."

I consider how to play this. I know it's odd to think of passing up the chance of a hot meal and a bed for the night, but my issues of trust run deep. Rich is tall and good-looking with sandy blonde hair that flops over his brow to meet the dark eyes I've already encountered. He's wearing jeans and a tight jumper which I know is not by accident. The tighter the garment, the more defined the abs. Alex used to dress this way. These are not the clothes of a street dweller.

"What's your name?" he asks and again I get that lilt, the accent I cannot place.

I shake my head. "No," I say, "you don't get to do this, just let me the hell out of here."

He is frowning at me and I understand his confusion. He has done nothing to warrant the extent of my reaction - except lock the door - but I don't have the inclination to explain. Though he is different to Alex, he could also be the same and regardless of the luxury he is offering for the night, I do not wish to spend any time in his company.

Am I being irrational?

Absolutely.

Do I care?

No.

I learned eighteen months ago that the only person I could count on was myself and I will do whatever I can to protect the fragile shell that passes for my existence. Rich is too dangerous.

This is something I simply just know.

Chapter Three

THREE YEARS EARLIER

My outcry of despair is louder than I intended, and it's not long before I hear voices. I understand enough to know that I am about to be discovered, so now I must make the choice. Do I let them?

I am emotionally empty. I have asked God to take me twice, but he hasn't. I have prayed to be reunited with my parents, yet I am still alone. Why? Is there some sick path I am supposed to follow?

The voices grow louder, and I identify one as male and one as female. They are talking about me; about the sound they heard about someone being in trouble. I don't have long. If I am going to continue to run in the hope of achieving my mission to leave this world and be with my parents, then I must get up now. I flex my ankles. They are dead. I have been resting my weight on them for too long. I lunge forward onto all fours and use my hands to push to standing. My ankles protest as pins and needles prick in anger. I am dizzy. My head is pounding. I have stood up too quickly, or perhaps it is not that at all.

I can see feet now, two pairs wearing flip-flops. I notice corns on the larger of the two; the smaller pair are decorated with blue nail varnish. Both sets are deep brown so I figure these belong to locals. I look at my feet. They are pasty white. I am not a local. I am not anything anymore. My identity has been stripped from me in the cruellest way.

I test moving my right foot. The pins and needles are subsiding, so I step forward, relieved when both feet cooperate. I don't know where I'm going, but I know that I don't want to think anymore. I want to be in a vacuum or a bubble maybe, where thought is irrelevant and feelings cannot be touched. I want to be in heaven with my parents, safe in the knowledge that Alex is in hell.

"Hey, you okay?"

The voice comes from behind; my getaway has been foiled.

Later I would reflect it had been a half-hearted attempt. I had neither run nor hidden. Maybe I had made the decision to stay without realising. I turn my body to the sound.

The feet belong to a man and a woman. Unsurprising given their relative size and condition. They are local; it is obvious in the way they are dressed and their overall appearance. They both have long dark hair, though his is tied back roughly with some kind of band. He has simple clothes, lightweight baggy trousers, brown in colour and a white cloth top which hangs off his bulky frame.

She wears a dress similar to his top in style, loose and flowing, but here and there, I see dots of bright pink colour. Closer inspection reveals these to be flowers. Their skin is dark, courtesy of the Caribbean sun, I imagine; their lips are full and red as if they have just bitten into some juicy strawberries, and their eyes are kind. Twinkling. Engaging. Smiling. Both sets are warm brown, though his sit deeper and are further away from his slightly crooked nose. Hers are delicate and I notice crinkle lines at their outer edges.

"No, I don't."

"Which hotel are you staying at? Do you know how to get back there?"

I shake my head. "I'm not staying anywhere. At least, I don't think I am. I don't have a key..." I glance down at my body, covered with only a child's beach towel and a torn pair of lace knickers.

"I don't have any pockets," I offer and then immediately dissolve into fits of laughter.

I was demonstrating that I had nowhere to keep a key, but for some reason, pointing out the obvious to Yarrick and Clarice tipped me over the edge. I have now officially arrived at insane. I know I don't have a key; I know I have no pockets; I know I am not staying anywhere, and I know there are no friends. There is no one. Just me.

And Clarice and Yarrick.

Clarice and Yarrick. Even their names are hilarious. Who calls their baby Yarrick? It's such a grown-up name. I picture Yarrick's imaginary parents cooing at him, calling him in those cute, annoying voices that all parents adopt.

"Yarrick, oh yarrie, yarrie..."

That's it, I am gone. I have now departed sanity. The laughter in my ears sounds manic as I sink back to the warm sand. I should care, but I don't. Maybe insanity is the key. Maybe this will unlock the door to my parents and the life I used to know.

With tears streaming down my cheeks, I look up to the deep blue sky, laughing in the face of God or heaven or whatever the hell is up there. And then I am floating. Upwards, leaving my body, looking down upon a curled-up form dressed in rags. As I gain height, I begin waving to the parents and children on the beach below, whirling around in the breeze and pull of the fluffy white clouds. I am nearing my next destination. I can feel it as everything slows and time ceases to exist. I have arrived. I am in a place of no pain, no fear, no...anything. It is a place of nothingness. I look around. I also cannot see anything. Am I blind?

There is blackness. Stark in contrast to the blue conduit that brought me here, and I wonder if I am dead. I close my eyes and allow the last of my senses to shut down as I once again hit the ground.

Am I dead? I hope so.

PRESENT DAY

Rich reminds me of Yarrick—not in physical appearance but in stature. Yarrick had that air of authority Rich possesses, although, in the former, it was softened. I don't believe Rich to be soft. We are still in the hallway, staring at each other, waiting it out. Who will crumble? Will Rich open the door and leave me be, or will I admit defeat—the lure of a warm bed and hot meal too much to overcome?

I sigh.

Rich holds out his hands, palms facing forward. "I won't hurt you," he says, "I promise. Just stay. It's pointless going out there now." He nods his head towards the solid wooden door.

I watch for any sign of disingenuity but there is none. I'll give him that. Even if he is lying, it is not apparent in his features. I don't respond. In the distance, I hear the familiar jingle that can only belong to Astrid.

I'm not surprised she is coming to find me. Us.

Us.

Me and Rich.

Ugh.

Why does that thought simultaneously repel and excite? I have only just met him. And I know I don't like him yet I'd be lying if I didn't acknowledge the increased rate of my heart. It's only slight, but when you live on the streets, you become attuned to your body in a way most people will never understand. Is my heart communicating anxiety? An emotion with which I am wholly familiar. Or am I out of breath? I walked here quickly, taking short, rapid steps, some ten more than I had walked to reach the office from this hallway when we entered. Or is it something else?

Rich's eyes are regarding me. He hasn't blinked, or if he has, I haven't noticed. Why is his gaze so piercing? Why does he want me to stay?

"Why?" I ask.

"It's warm in here, and there's food." He points out the obvious.

"I ate at lunchtime. And I have my clothes." I gesture at the rags hanging from my body. These are from the church lost and found from the day when the good reverend took pity on me. I have worn them until they are barely more than threads.

Rich smiles. "I know, and I know that you are more than capable of looking after yourself, but honestly, it doesn't make sense. You're here now. Just one night. Stay warm. Fill your belly."

His voice has softened, and I wonder at my earlier comparison of him to Yarrick. Perhaps there is a softer side, but I could never trust him. It's in his eyes—something lurking there. Something I thought was passion when it lurked in the depths of Alex's eyes. An expression I identified as pity and warmth when I saw it in Yarrick's eyes—though look how that turned out. And in the eyes of Rich...I don't know yet. I simply don't know.

"Ra?" Astrid appears in the hallway, and Rich turns to the sound of her voice. But not before he's allowed the two letters of my adopted name to whisper from his lips. "Ra..." he repeats.

What the hell?

"Are you coming in?" Astrid asks, "it's okay. Denver knows this place."

I'm not scared. Not of being here anyway. I don't understand why I'm running away. I tell myself that it has something to do with Rich. He seems...smarmy. No, that's not the right word. I think it's just that I know instinctively I cannot trust him. But then again, I don't trust anyone.

"I...okay," I nod, more for Astrid than Rich. "It feels odd," I say, "being somewhere warm with no expectations, I guess I just panicked." I am trying to convince myself as much as my assembled audience.

Next to my feet, Rex yawns and lets out a whimper.

"Excellent," says Rich, and I get the feeling he was never in doubt that I would stay. It's crazy. My reaction to this place and to him. I've been here less than ten minutes yet it's pulling me in a way nothing has since that fateful night. I cannot decide if it is a good pull or one from which I should be running, but I won't know until I spend some more time here. And a hot meal will be greatly appreciated. Suddenly,

I realise just how tired I am.

"C'mon, let's go and do the paperwork stuff, and then we can get you both a comfy bed and something to eat." Rich leads us out of the hallway and back towards his office.

"There's paperwork?" I ask. I don't like paperwork. I have avoided it ever since I decided to become invisible. That was kind of the point. I don't want to be found. If anyone knows what happened that night, if Alex is still alive...the thought sends shivers through my entire being.

Rich laughs. "It's nothing to worry about," he says as he guides us both into the small room and indicates the two metal chairs. We sit.

"There's funding," he continues, "and to keep everyone happy, I have to record who comes and goes, that's all."

"What kind of funding?" asks Astrid.

"Like a grant," Rich replies. "We have investors, people who are interested in helping street dwellers like you."

"Then why is it a secret?" she continues.

I turn to my friend. "This place is secret?"

Rich laughs. "It's not exactly a secret, but we have a limited number of beds," he indicates to the long room beyond his office door, "and only a few volunteers willing to help us out. We can't afford for it to be common knowledge otherwise, we would be overwhelmed, and then we would have to close. No one wants that."

"How can you possibly control numbers once word gets out?" I ask.

Rich looks directly into my eyes. "People only turn up here if they've been given the tip-off by someone we trust.

In your case, Denver."

"How...?" I look at Astrid, who shrugs.

"I told him we knew Denver," she said.

Considering how long we were in the office before I walked out, she made quick work of telling Rich that piece of information. Not that it matters.

"Still," I counter, "if this place is as 'brilliant' as you say, warm bed, hot food...yada yada...even with only the select few being aware, word would still get out. We do talk to each other, you know."

Rich nods: his eyes are still piercing into mine, and I'm beginning to feel uncomfortable. "It's like a...loyalty programme..." he says. "Everyone who stays is logged," he indicates the forms on the desk in front of him that we have yet to complete, "and each person gets a certain number of nights."

I laugh. I can't help it.

"A certain number of nights? Jesus, what the hell is this place?"

Astrid swivels to her right. "It's safe," she says sharply, "so if I were you, I would shut the fuck up before we both get thrown out."

"Whoa," I hold both hands up towards her, "what's with the attitude?"

"You," she huffs as she points her index finger in my direction. "I haul your ass off that cold, damp bench and bring you somewhere decent - I didn't have to, you know. I could've brought anyone. And ever since we walked through that door, you've been a total bitch."

I recoil. She's right. If you'd asked me three years ago how I would have reacted to someone speaking to me that way, I couldn't have told you. I guess I would've curled up and cried. In my pampered world, I had been untouchable. Now, I've learned the hard way, though. I understand what my former self could never have done. That life is shit. Yes, that's right, shit. I've learned to swear, too.

"Sorry…"

Beneath my feet, Rex grumbles in agreement.

Astrid's shoulders drop. "It's okay," she sighs, "I get it."

She does? Well, that's great cos I have no clue. All I know is that Rich affects me in a way I can't name, and I'm not entirely convinced it's good.

Speaking of, he has been watching our exchange with interest. I can feel his gaze glued to the side of my face, and I wonder why me. Why not stare at Astrid? She's stunning. She's stare-worthy. I'm not.

As if by unspoken agreement, Astrid and I simultaneously pick up the forms from the desk. Rich holds out two pens, one for each of us.

"You can both write?" he asks.

I almost laugh. He has no idea.

"Yes, I can write."

Astrid chooses not to answer, fixing her attention instead on the flimsy paper we're being asked to fill in. I drop my gaze towards the form I hold, skimming the scant few lines. It's pretty simple. Name; Date of birth; How long have you been on the streets; Do you have any dependants; Do you have a drug/alcohol/abuse problem?; Do you have any dietary requirements? What the actual…?

"Dietary requirements?" I ask incredulously, "Are you having a laugh?"

Rich…laughs. "Yep, gets them every time."

"My dietary requirement is food," Astrid says, "does that count?"

"It's not a serious question," Rich counters. "We want you to feel at home here, and having to fill in forms is not the best place to start. So, we figured we'd shake it up a bit. Have some fun."

"Lame," I say under my breath. But he hears me.

"Yeah," he shrugs, "perhaps, but it always gets a reaction. Even from the most damaged ones."

His statement, so matter of fact, draws me up short for a moment. 'Even the most damaged ones.' Yeah. I guess there are those more damaged than me. Than us. But I'd never know because there's this unspoken rule in our community. It's the one that says no one actually gives a shit about who you are or what you've been through. All we want to do is get from one day to the next. Which is odd and something upon which I often reflect. Why the hell do we want to get to the next day when we're done living the crap of the day before? It's a circular argument and, thus, entirely pointless. We strive to live so that we don't die. We want to die, but actually, we hope that someone will save us. So, we strive to live. Hence, entirely pointless.

"You're a thinker," Rich says, and I know he's talking to me. I don't need to find his dark, all-seeing eyes to realise this. In any case, Astrid has moved out of the office, having dropped her form back on the desk, so it's just me and him. And Rex.

I shrug. "Aren't we all?"

He shakes his head. "Not necessarily. But you are. I can tell."

"Not much else to do out there," I nod towards his window, noticing for the first time that it's one of the arched ones I saw when we came in. There's history in this room, in this building. Ironic. It was built to create something, to form an object from nothing, to deliver a service or goods to those in need and now…now it's a shelter for those of us fortunate enough to have the key. To be given the nod. To be deemed worthy. Even now, on the streets and in the darkest of days, the hierarchy still exists. And no one gets to choose. You're either in, or you're out. You either had a job, or you didn't. You either had a family and a home, or you had the streets. In the time since this vaulted warehouse was constructed, little has changed. I can't decide if I am sad or completely disinterested in this conclusion.

"See," Rich says, "I lost you again."

I drag my eyes from the darkness outside and focus once more on him. He speaks well with a hint of an accent, European perhaps.

"What was this place?" I ask.

He shrugs. "A factory back in the day. Part of the ship-building empire until manufacturing moved North. Cheaper. Then it was used for storage, anything and everything that came into the port. Fish, a lot of fish. And now…now we get to enjoy it."

I'm surprised. Rich seems well-educated, or he has at least done some research. "Who do you work for?" I ask.

"I don't; I'm a volunteer, like everyone else."

"Your day job then?"

He smiles. "This is my day job."

"But how do you live? You must need money; otherwise, you'd be on this side of the desk with me."

"I live in," he says, gesturing towards the main area, "like a hotel. Part of the deal with the investors. I live here, on call whenever I'm needed, keep everything running smoothly, and they pay my expenses. It's actually pretty simple."

It's been a while since Astrid left the room and I'm starting to wonder what she's doing, though I'm surprised to realise I'm in no hurry to find out.

"How long have you lived here?"

"Two years. It was my job to open the place. Get it up and running. Seemed like the perfect opportunity."

I nod in agreement, but it makes little sense to my old mind. The one I would have used before. The one that had plans and ambitions. The one that wanted more for me. The one that my parents, my upbringing and my education had cultivated. Two years he's been here. I lost my old mind longer ago than that. Now I have a new mind. One that is naturally curious but has no interest in pursuing any answers. It's one that lives in the here and now with only one function. To keep me alive. So that I can enjoy the never-ending roundabout of 'do I want to live' or 'do I want to die'.

It's a ride and a half, I can tell you.

Chapter Four

THREE YEARS EARLIER

I am not dead.

This becomes apparent when Yarrick and Clarice kneel down and start prodding me. Gently. Like my mother used to. Checking to see if I'm okay.

Bugger. I'm really not dead.

I turn to the side. Clarice's face swarms into view. It's a kind face. Warm and welcoming, and in those dark brown eyes, I read concern.

"Are you okay?" she asks, which is a ridiculous question. Of course, I'm not okay. Do they often find half-naked women covered with a barely adequate children's towel lurking in the palm fronds?

I shake my head.

On the other side, I feel Yarrick move, and it's not long before his face joins Clarice's.

"Do you know who you are?" he asks. "Do you have a name?"

Do I?

Well, I do. And I know it's Aurora. But somewhere in my mind, where there resides the last vestiges of sanity, I realise it's not a common name. And, once Alex's crimes are discovered, it won't take long for people to figure out who I am. I don't think I want people to know who I am. I think I need to be someone else. But for the life of me, I can't think of anyone I'd want to be. I shift onto my knees and look around. There's blue sky, palm trees, flowers, water and … sand.

"Sandy," I say, "my name. It's Sandy."

"Good, good," nods Yarrick. Clarice looks at me approvingly as if I've just completed an incredibly complex puzzle. I guess I have.

"So, Sandy, do you know where your friends are?" Clarice asks.

"No," I reply, "in fact, I think it might be just me." As the realisation that it really is just me settles again, tears spring in my eyes.

Yarrick frowns. "Don't cry," he says. "It's okay; we'll find your friends."

"No," I shake my head, "you don't understand; it really is just me."

The two of them exchange a glance. One that says, 'What the hell have we just found?'.

"How did you get here, petal?" That's from Clarice.

"On a boat," I shrug. I don't know how much I want to tell them, but I don't want to reveal anything close to the truth. I also don't know if I want them to stay or leave. In my previous pampered and almost obscene life, I never faced this kind of confusion. My brain has no reference point.

"Okay," they speak and nod in synchronicity which would be amusing if I had anything other than desolation in my being. I've done the insanity moment; that's how I ended up on the ground again. Now, I'm in a sombre and depressing state, which I think I might prefer. This feels numb. I like numb.

"Was it a big boat?" Yarrick asks.

A big boat? You've just found someone who has clearly taken leave of her senses, barely dressed and caked in sand, and your first sensible question relates to the size of the boat?

But then again, maybe that's a good question. If I've arrived on a big boat, I guess they know where to start looking.

I glance out to sea, wondering if the *Cassiopeia* is still bobbing around out there. A floating graveyard.

"No, it was small." I hold out my hands and move them close together to demonstrate. I don't know why. I'm sure these people are perfectly capable of understanding what small means.

"Ah," responds Yarrick as if suddenly the whole world makes sense. "That dinghy." He turns to Clarice, who nods.

"We wondered what happened," she says. "It's not often we get dinghies washed up ashore. Most visitors come from the big boats, those fancy yachts out on the water. They have these speedboats that churn up the swell and frighten the children."

I'm guessing she's not a fan of the fancy yachts and speedboats.

"Well," says Yarrick, "now we know what happened we need to get you somewhere safe. Do you have any clothes?"

They know what happened? Well, they're one step ahead of me. I have no bloody clue. Clearly, the minuscule piece of inaccurate information I've provided has given them all the answers they need. Brilliant. Saves me a job.

"Clothes? No," I say, "this isn't even mine." I gesture at the towel. Of course, it isn't mine. Why would anyone of my size and shape wear a bright pink flowery children's towel?

I'm amazed at my calmness. Whilst I have far from forgotten what happened, it's like I've entered an alternate universe. I am watching and experiencing my life from somewhere else. It's a place of no pain, of numbness, as I've said before. It's a good place to be. Previously, I would've only thought to get here using illegal substances, but it appears that watching your wonderful boyfriend kill your parents and then point the gun at you achieves the same result. Who knew?

"Come on," says Clarice, "I'll help you up."

I take her proffered hand and scramble to my feet. The towel slips. All the way down. Yarrick has the grace to look away.

"Sorry," I mumble.

Clarice pulls me into a hug. It's warm and squishy and feels safe.

"Don't worry, petal," she says softly, "there's nothing we've not seen before."

I don't know if I like her response but I can't be bothered to care. She's making me feel safe which right now is probably the best option. Assuming I decide to live. I've still not figured that one out.

We leave the palm fronds with my makeshift covering back in place and cross the top section of the beach towards a row of wooden huts. They're the kind I would've stayed in once upon a time. The ones that sit on a long pier stretching out to sea. Each one further into the water, providing ever more exclusion. Tourist huts. Family huts. Honeymoon huts. Ones I would've envisaged staying in with Alex. Now, they look like ugly blots on a beautiful deep blue palette. I think we're actually going to these huts as we get closer to the pier, but no, thankfully, we turn away just before the water line and skirt a dense woodland of palm trees which leads us back inland. If you ask me, this seems a convoluted route, but (a) I have no clue where we're going, and (b) I lost any right to sensible thought when a madman killed my parents and turned his gun on me.

We've now reached the end of the beach and are approaching some grass-covered hills. Not luscious grass like we have back in Britain, but scorched, prickly grass that hurts my feet as we negotiate the base of the first hill. Oddly, I don't care. Up until today, I would have considered myself a lightweight. Though I lived a life of luxury I was never a great fan of the beach, preferring instead to stay on the yacht or in some secluded woodland with a gurgling river nearby. I always found the beaches to be overcrowded, noisy and full of pale bodies that really shouldn't have been in public view. I also hated walking in bare feet, especially over stones.

Today, I am a very different person. Today, I feel the sharp spikes of the harsh grass, but I couldn't care less. The pain in my feet feels lesser than the pain in my heart, thus I don't waste energy focusing on the soles of my expensively manicured lower limbs.

I find it odd that neither Yarrick nor Clarice have spoken since we began this walk. They've shared glances when they thought I wasn't looking, and Yarrick has helped me over some of the rough terrain, but beyond that, it's like I'm not here. I realise I am comfortable with this observation.

The base of the hill opens to my right, revealing an inlet with a narrow dust track. We turn onto this track to be almost immediately confronted by a ramshackle cabin. Nestled amongst an array of tropical foliage, it looks odd and totally out of place. There are two floors, and the first one looks bigger than the ground. It's a kind of upside-down shack, and for a moment, I amuse myself by wondering if it could topple over or if the builder was blind.

That's an unkind statement. I'm well aware that such a thought is a symptom of my upbringing where to frown upon those less fortunate is 'de rigeur'. For a second, I think about my home in England and compare its grandness to the simplicity of the house in front of me, but that is too painful. When I think about home, I think about my parents, and I know that if I am to survive, I have to put those thoughts in a box on a shelf inside my mind and label it 'do not open'.

Though I mention survival, it is a state I am still considering. At present, I don't see any reason to continue my pathetic existence, but there is one niggling thought that won't go away, and that is why I have dutifully followed Yarrick and Clarice. I am thinking about Alex. And how, if he's still alive, then he should pay for what he has done.

And, to the best of my knowledge, I'm the only one who can make that happen.

PRESENT DAY

Astrid and I have been shown to our beds for the night. Rich has 'people', it would seem, and for this job, it's a spotty, gangly kid who can't be more than sixteen. He walks hunched as if apologising for his existence and glances furtively around. He must know he's safe here - according to Rich - so I can only assume he has some kind of mental challenges. He is yet to speak, merely indicating two beds on the left of the warehouse before shuffling away. His clothes tell me he's a street dweller, but his blond hair is tidy, cut in a modern short style, and his skin looks clean. This is at odds with most of our kind, but I can't be bothered to ponder it. He's a kid. And he's helping Rich. That's basically all I need to know.

The beds are narrow, more like bunks, but the sheets are fresh and smell of lavender. Adjacent to each bed is a small cupboard on which stands a green metal lamp. And that is the extent of our accommodation.

Though they are next to each other, the second bed (which has been indicated as mine) is tucked a little back from the main row in a small alcove. It is forty steps from here to the communal kitchen and then a further twenty from the kitchen to the shower facilities. Beside me, Astrid is squealing.

"Can you believe this?"

I shrug. I don't know if I can or not. But I guess it's real because we're here.

"Fucking Denver, he kept this a bit quiet," she says. I hear several jangles as she lifts sheets and crawls into their starch warmth.

"What the hell's wrong with you?" she asks. Which I accept is a decent question. "You've been so bloody miserable since we got here. This, my girl, is five-star fucking accommodation. Anyone'd think you've been shoved in the dankest doorway around."

I have yet to move from where the spotty kid left me. I am looking at the bed, and I am seeing it. I am smelling the fragrances from the kitchen, I am hearing the chatter of other guests, and I am feeling the warmth of a well-heated warehouse, but for some reason, I am frozen. Rex licks at my feet, reminding me he thinks this is pretty cushy, too. Adjacent to my alcove bed is a dog blanket and water bowl. Nice touch.

Rex licks at my feet again, and this time, I move towards the bunk and sit carefully on the edge. I have disturbed the fibres of the sheet, and they release a burst of lavender. I like lavender. I look across at Astrid and shrug.

"Sorry, I just…" I wave my arm in an arc as if that will explain my mood, but clearly, it does not. "I guess it's just…a surprise. Maybe too much. I can't remember the last time I saw a bed, let alone slept in one."

That is a blatant lie. I remember every sordid and painful detail of the last full-size bed in which I slept. In the upside-down shack.

Astrid tilts her head to one side, reminding me of Rex. I look down at my battered friend, who immediately tilts his head in exactly the same way. For the first time in a very long time, I laugh.

"Fuck's sake, you two."

Astrid smiles. "Just chill, babe. It's all good."

I nod. I want to believe her; I really do. It's just…

"Ladies…"

Rich. He's my problem, and now he's standing at the foot of my bed.

"Hope you like our little home here?"

Astrid jangles out of bed and throws herself into his arms. Even at my best, I don't remember ever being that demonstrative. The last person I willingly embraced was Alex, though sometimes I did enjoy Clarice's warm, squishy hugs.

Rich is giggling as he lifts Astrid and whirls her around. He's obviously not bothered that we both still stink.

"I'll take that as a yes," he says as he puts her down. The pair of them high-five.

"What about you... Ra, isn't it?"

I nod. "Very nice. Thank you."

"Very nice, thank you?" he mimics. "This is the fucking Hilton, and that's the best you've got?"

"What do you want me to say?"

Astrid sends me a sharp, sideways look. "Ra..." she says, "Seriously?"

I glance into her eyes and realise for the first time that I'm being selfish. This isn't just about me. This is about Astrid and Rex, too. And it's only for one night. It doesn't matter what I think of Rich; it doesn't matter that my gut is telling me to get the hell out of here; it matters that Astrid and Rex have a bed and a full belly for the night. Damn what I think.

"I...thank you...," I manage. "Seriously."

Rich regards me; his face is set, closed, whereas when he'd looked at Astrid, there had been an openness. Joy even. I feel bad. I have no reason to doubt this man, I have, after all, only just met him. And so what that I've got a gut feeling? Perhaps that's where I've been going wrong. I had zero gut feeling about Alex, and in hindsight, my stomach should have been jumping out of my throat.

Men are not all the same. I know this, and I understand this, so maybe it's time for me to give Rich the benefit of the doubt.

It is only for one night.

I look at the bed with its welcoming sheets, soft pillow and lavender scent - the latter of which has now reached the depths of my senses and I feel my limbs begin to loosen. I'm relaxing. It's working.

And then I remember the upside-down shack.

And I am reminded once more that men are never to be trusted.

≈≈≈≈

We're in the kitchen, which evokes memories of everything I hated about school. Though the smell is welcoming, the rest leaves a lot to be desired. Steel surfaces stretch around the perimeter, each containing four large serving platters set into the units. I am in the middle of the queue, behind Astrid, and we shuffle obligingly forward like soldiers, a neat line of down-and-outs waiting to be served.

Behind me is an old man. His clothes are more threadbare than mine, their stench stronger than the aroma of the hot food. His manners have deserted him, and I feel my personal space invaded as he gets closer to me, his rancid breath hot on my neck. I swallow down the bile that has rushed to my throat. His lips graze my ear, and I shudder.

"Scuse me, darlin'". He's reaching around me for the uniform plastic tray, which he doesn't need to do. He can wait, like everyone else. I step back and deliberately sink my heel into footwear I instinctively know barely covers his undoubtedly swollen feet. He yelps, and I smile. I'm a bitch. I don't know when I became that person, but I am now proud to own it, and those who judge me for it - well, they want to walk a mile in my shoes.

"Oops, sorry," I throw over my shoulder. There's a grunt and then the welcome feel of cool air on my neck as he retreats to a safe distance. Message received loud and clear.

Astrid is handing me a tray, and I take it from her, noting how jagged the edges are and how wet its surface is. Everything is exactly the same as school: wet trays, jagged edges, and lumps of indefinable gloop.

"Isn't this amazing?" she whispers as she grabs a plate and begins ladling gloop from the first of the four pans onto her plate.

I nod. The gloop turns out to be peas, which I am assuming are supposed to be mushy.

We shuffle to the next tray and the next and the next, each time helping ourselves to a variety of different coloured mounds of congealed food until, at the end of this first section, we have something that passes for bangers, mash, peas and carrots. It looks hideous but there's no denying how good it smells, and my stomach rumbles in appreciation.

"Who do you reckon does all this?" Astrid asks as we move to the next section.

I shrug. "Rich probably has people."

She sends me another warning glare. I'm getting used to these now.

"Ra...I thought you were going to drop that whole Rich thing."

She's right. I did promise to let my animosity towards the oh-so-saintly Rich go. Astrid knows nothing of my past, of Alex, of my parents, or of the upside-down shack, and I'm not about to enlighten her. My reaction to Rich is mine and mine alone. I cannot keep bringing Astrid to the same pity party.

"Soz..." I reply, and this time, I smile, a curving of my mouth that actually reaches my eyes. It feels strange. I remember being told once - probably in an incredibly boring Biology lesson - that it takes forty-three muscles to frown but only seven to smile; thus, smiling is less effort. The point, I presume, was to make us become a class of happy little pupils on the basis that teenagers always take the path of least resistance. I don't remember being impressed with this fact at the time - odd that it's chosen now to revisit my conscience. I toy with telling Astrid this little nugget, but I realise it would indicate an education of which she is ignorant. And that could lead to questions which I never want to answer.

She returns my smile with genuine warmth and I feel a rush of emotion, the complete opposite to everything I felt when Rich smiled at me. I've been lucky; I know I have. I could so easily have become another statistic, another sad and lonely has-been, washed up in the gutter of life, so to have someone like Astrid in my corner... I need to appreciate her more.

I have an urge for human comfort, and without conscious thought, I reach forward and drop my head on her shoulder. It's bony but oddly safe, and I breathe in her unique Astrid scent. We still haven't showered, but unless you're like the old guy behind me, we don't notice our lack of cleanliness—not anymore.

Astrid drops her head on top of mine, and we stay there for a moment, two lost souls in the middle of a homeless shelter soup kitchen, taking what we both need. And in that moment something precious passes between us, and I know she feels it too. A bond. An understanding. A guarantee. A promise - that we will always be each other's comfort.

It's the closest I've felt to home in a very long time.

THREE YEARS EARLIER

I don't know what I was expecting. My brain is stuck on the *Cassiopeia* with its opulent luxury and has yet to catch up to the dimly lit, basic accommodation into which Yarrick and Clarice lead me.

The lack of daylight is the first thing I notice as we enter the ground floor. It's a simple abode: one room with an assortment of chairs in various states of disrepair leading to a kitchenette at the rear. I realise why there's no light when we get to the back of the room—this house is set into the hillside, and the only windows are at the front of the property, which is a hundred paces away from where I now stand. I wait for my eyes to adjust.

A tiny shaft of light from an unplanned gap in the wall highlights the dust motes that our feet have kicked up. It's just enough for me to determine a few pots and utensils hanging from the roof above the kitchenette. There is a cooker, basic, like the rest of the house, and it is to this that Clarice now goes with a pan full of water. I look for the sink and taps but I don't see them. I want to find them. I need a drink.

"Water?" I croak and point ineffectually at the pan under which Clarice has now lit a gas flame.

The residual gas odour lingers for a moment before it burns off and is replaced by an earthy, musty smell that increases in strength the deeper into the room I walk.

Yarrick nods and takes my hand. At first, I resist. I am still wearing only a beach towel and torn knickers; I need both hands to protect my modesty, but I am no match for his big paws and strength. Awkwardly, I bunch the towel in my right hand and allow my left to be drawn towards an alcove I had not previously noticed. A surprisingly modern sink is nestled in this alcove complete with a long-headed tap promising liquid refreshment. Above the silver of the sink are two cupboards hanging at a curious angle and it is one of these that Yarrick now opens. Absently I survey its interior, noting that even though the cupboard is far from straight, its contents are neatly stored and very much upright. I don't have the energy to consider this conundrum now.

Yarrick's large hand grasps an earthenware mug, which he fills with water from the tap. I take it from him and drink greedily, even though drinking a cold beverage from a mug feels strange. Cold drinks go in glasses, hot drinks go in mugs - and then the idiocy of that thought lands. I have nothing. No clothes, passport, money, identity…I don't think it really matters what receptacle I use anymore. Nothing matters.

"Better?" he asks, and I nod. "Help yourself whenever you need to," he continues, "all the mugs are in that cupboard," he indicates the place from which he removed the heavy cup mere seconds ago.

"Thank you."

I don't know what to make of this place or of Yarrick and Clarice. They seem kind; they have generously allowed me into their home - though how long for I don't know - but I am still in a dilemma. I want to go back to England, to familiar places, to grieve and mourn and figure out what the fuck just happened, but I'm also liking this anonymity. This feeling of not belonging. Of being free. Of having no expectations and no one to be accountable to.

"C'mon," Yarrick nudges me back towards where Clarice is presiding over the pan of water.

"Tea?" she asks as we pass. Yarrick answers for us both. "Strong and sweet," he says.

To the far left of the kitchenette is a set of wooden stairs that ascend in a higgledy-piggledy fashion towards the first floor. They look as undecided as me—should they ascend in a straight flight, or would they be better forming a climbing cone? In the end, they do both, and I find myself moving as much from side to side as I do upwards, yet there are still only thirteen of these steps carved into the cool, damp hillside.

Compared to the ground floor, the space into which the stairs spill is practically ablaze with light and significantly larger. Off a main corridor, there are at least three doors to rooms unknown, and above my head, the roof is glazed, like a conservatory, which accounts for the light. I blink in surprise.

"Tinted," Yarrick says as he points to the expanse of glass, "to help with the heat."

I incline my head but don't answer. I don't think he was expecting me to.

I follow his not-inconsiderable bulk along the landing until we turn a slight corner to the right, where we are immediately confronted by two more doors adjacent to each other.

Yarrick leans on the left one, pushing it open, and then gestures for me to enter. I squeeze past his solid form and find myself in a bedroom—a surprisingly pleasing bedroom.

Against the right-hand wall is a single bed supported by a wrought iron frame. A sumptuous-looking sheet and pillow rest on the mattress, along with a brightly patterned quilt adorned with intricate flowers in shades of yellow, pink and green. On the far wall leans a large wicker drawer, set directly beneath a generously proportioned circular window. The glass in this window is stained in the same yellow, green and pink as the quilt, and several rays of patterned light dance off the white walls and polished wooden floor. My feet are still bare and I notice immediately that this floor is bereft of dust, unlike everywhere else we have walked.

To my left is a wardrobe in the same wicker as the drawers. This is tall and large, with three-opening doors. It joins onto a desk, which has a small wicker chair tucked beneath it. The final piece of furniture rests in the left corner. This is a matching wicker pedestal that has an ornate bowl and matching jug standing upon it.

"For freshening up," Yarrick points. He must have been following my eyes.

Though basic, this room is beautiful and has a totally different smell and presence from the rest of the house. It feels fresh. Lived in. Loved.

"You can stay here," he continues, "no one uses this room. Until we find your friends."

"Thank you." Two words which feel hugely inadequate.

Yarrick nods at my beach towel. "I'll find you some clothes," he says and walks past me to the wardrobe, which he opens to reveal several lightweight dresses. "Choose whichever one fits," he indicates the dresses before opening the top drawer of the unit beneath the window. This appears to contain underwear, new and still in their packets, which strikes me as odd.

"It's all new," he says, and for a moment, I wonder if I've spoken aloud. "We were going to rent this room out, you know, for someone like you, and figured it would be welcoming to have some basics."

I've stayed in many hotels over the years; most have been the height of luxury, willing to accommodate every guest's whim - but never have I been anywhere kitted out with a complete set of women's clothes. A shiver runs down my spine as an unwelcome premonition reaches my conscience. What the hell have I walked into?

"It probably seems a bit strange," he says gruffly, and again, I wonder if I've voiced my thoughts. "But we don't have shops on every corner—this stuff can be hard to get hold of, so when a cargo ship beached a couple of years back, well..." Yarrick's arm encompasses the room. " I didn't want it to go to waste."

I release the breath I've been holding, relieved that my premonition is unfounded. Growing up in a world of luxury, I forget that we're not all granted the same access to basic needs such as clothing. Of course, they would take advantage of a cargo ship's demise. Yarrick smiles, and I notice how even and white his teeth are. I'm surprised. He doesn't look like someone who would have good teeth.

A noise brings our attention to the doorway. Clarice stands on the threshold holding two steaming mugs. She passes them both to Yarrick. "I'll bring up the rest of the water," she says, "for you to wash," and departs as quickly as she came.

"Towels are in the bottom drawer," Yarrick says, handing me one of the mugs. "Make yourself at home. Maybe rest awhile. Later," he pauses, "we'll see about your friends."

Clarice re-enters the room with the saucepan of water, which she proceeds to pour into the porcelain bowl in the corner. "Give it a minute," she instructs, "and it'll be fine."

With a nod to each other, they leave the room, small Clarice and large Yarrick, an unlikely pairing who have saved me from myself.

The door clicks, and I am finally alone. I drop the towel, remove my knickers and walk to the washstand. Clarice has left a bar of soap and a cloth, which I use to rid myself of sand and grime. The water is brown by the time I finish, and I stare into its murky depths. It looks like the sea when I jumped from the *Cassiopeia*, dark and unwelcoming.

I browse the dresses and draw out the first one that looks the right size. It's a floaty confection in hues of aquamarine with a buttoned front and belted middle. I feel like a giant peacock.

I investigate the rest of the drawers, finding toiletries and a hairbrush, which I attempt to pull through my tangled locks. It hurts, but I like it. The pain reminds me of what I have been through, and this is something I must not forget. I have to remember what happened to me every single minute of every single day because that is the only way I will find Alex and bring him to justice, or better still, learn of his deserved demise.

I allow myself to dream of Alex falling into the ocean, screaming, squirming, and reaching out for a lifeline before finally becoming silent. Human-shaped flotsam journeying with the tide.

My bones ache. My heart aches. My brain aches.

I climb into the soft bed and pull the patterned cover to my chin. My sleep is fitful, plagued by the last images of my parents and then Alex's evil grin as he stands over them.

I am holding a gun. I raise it as Alex faces me.

For a moment, his eyes register surprise, but then he, too, lifts his gun, levelling it at my heart.

It's a duel of the highest stakes. Who is the more competent? Who is the fastest? Who has the best aim? Who can hold their nerve?

I squeeze the trigger, eyes fixed on Alex's hand. Watching. Waiting. Barely breathing.

And then I awake. I am gasping for air. I am looking at the patterns of light changing, swirling, and bouncing from wall to wall. I catch my breath. I am once again calm, once more dead inside.

I remember where I am and why I am here.

I remember my dream.

But I do not know which one of us won.

Chapter Five

PRESENT DAY

Someone has taken my clothes.

I'm still trying to decide if I care as I pace back towards my bunk for the night. My modesty is protected by a large blue fluffy towel, which I found in place of my clothes as I exited the shower. I am naked underneath, which reminds me of the time when all this began—when I had nothing but a children's pink coverall on a paradise island.

It occurs to me that I should probably be more appropriately clothed, but I have no idea where my ragged garments have gone. It's weird; though I am in a place full of people whose motives are likely to be questionable, I feel no fear. I am not concerned that I am sparsely covered. I feel safe here. I am not sure why.

Rex wags his tail as I approach the bed. I move into the gap between mine and Astrid's bunk, which gives him the chance to nuzzle and lick my bare feet. It tickles, and I jump away. Astrid is already ensconced between her sheets and laughs at my attempt to avoid Rex's dribbling attack.

"Have you got any clothes?" I ask, pulling the towel tighter around me.

Astrid nods. "They were on my bed when I got back from the shower. You'll have some, too. Rich told me it's part of the 'experience'." Her wrists jingle as she air quotes the last word.

"New clothes?" I ask as I cast around my immediate surroundings for anything that looks wearable.

"I don't know if they're new, but they're clean," she says.

I shake my head. "I don't see anything. What am I looking for?"

Astrid shrugs. "Loose trousers, maybe. Hoodie."

Again, I shake my head.

"Try looking under the bed; perhaps they've fallen off."

I kneel down on the small rug which has been thoughtfully placed to protect our feet from the bare concrete floor, and peer under the simple metal bed. Nothing.

"Nope," I say as I sit back on my haunches.

"How odd," Astrid comments.

I scan the room. There are twenty-eight bunks besides the two that Astrid and I are occupying, arranged in neat vertical rows from the entrance door all the way to the kitchen and showers at the back of the warehouse. It's hard to tell if they are each taken - people are still milling about eating, showering, talking - but I know that no one has entered since Astrid and me.

Because Rich locked the door.

The shower was heavenly. Nothing compared to those I was accustomed to in my former life - barely more than a hot drip from a rusty raised head - but it's incredible how far my standards and expectations have dropped in such a short time. There are eight showers, each situated in its own cubicle. They run along one wall which has been clad in light blue tiles, not dissimilar to those at the private gym to which I once belonged. Each decaying nozzle is separated by a flimsy wooden divider and has a slatted door, like an old Western saloon, which is held in place by one tiny bolt. If anyone was so inclined, they could easily intrude on another person's shower, but I imagine we're all of the same mindset. Why bother?

That mindset has been for me, the biggest adjustment to my new life. I was so used to caring about things, people, animals, objects and yet now, I care about nothing. Not even myself. Every day is mind-numbingly the same, so I understand why Astrid is so pumped about being here. It's different. It's new. It's warm. It's clean. It's comfortable. It's full of other people. We've eaten a good meal, and it's a million times better than my usual bench. But I still have no clothes.

A pair of feet appear next to my knees. Large feet encased in black trainers adorned with two white stripes on their outer edges. For a moment, my heart stops as I think it's Rich - there is no doubt the feet are male - but as I glance cautiously upwards, I'm relieved to see they belong to another male. Someone I've not yet encountered.

Though I am on the floor, it is obvious to me that he's not the tallest guy in the world, which seems at odds, given the size of his feet. He looks a little older than me, mid-thirties perhaps, and has a solid build, on the cuddly side of lean. He is smiling down at me and I automatically return the gesture. Years of good breeding. He has an open face, eyes of the clearest blue which sit close to his nose, a wide smile set into a coarse, ruddy complexion and a shock of bright ginger hair. I like him on sight.

"Ra?" he asks, and I nod.

"Sorry, I thought you'd be longer in the shower." He places the bag, formerly held in his right hand, onto my bed. "Nothing special but better than what you had."

"Clothes?" I acknowledge this to be a rhetorical question.

He inclines his head and holds out his hand. I'm not sure if he wants to shake my hand or help me up, and as I don't entirely trust the towel's protection, I ignore his outstretched offering and scramble to my feet with as much dignity as I can muster.

"I'm Spencer," he says, arm still pointing towards me. "I'm one of the helpers here."

"Spencer?" I knew a Spencer once. Back in college. He was nothing like the one standing in front of me now.

"Yup," he nods a little too vigorously, and I'm reminded of the kitsch-nodding dogs that were all the rage for a time. In my former life.

"Thanks." I incline my head towards the bag and he nods again. Rex lets out a whine, and it is only now that I realise we have an audience. Of two. Astrid and Rex are watching our exchange with barely concealed interest.

"Get you, baby girl," says Astrid, "no one delivered my clothes in person." She winks, and I throw her what I hope is a 'fuck off' look.

"Ah… you weren't here when your clothes were ready…" Spencer interjects. A wave of red washes from his forehead to his neck, and I wonder at its cause. Astrid? He wouldn't be the first male to succumb to her not-inconsiderable beauty, which, when you're trying to blag a meal on the streets, has its advantages. Bewilderingly, Astrid remains unaware of just how beautiful she is, preferring to believe we 'get lucky' every time a googly-eyed male hands over a few meagre coins.

She laughs. The sound is warm and rounded, like a good, full-bodied red wine. "I'm only messing."

Spencer looks relieved. "I hope they're okay," he says as he finally drops his outstretched arm, and for a moment, I feel bad. I should've taken the trouble to at least shake his hand and introduce myself properly. But then I remember where I am. We don't do that. Not in this world.

"If they're clean, they'll be fine. Thanks again."

He inclines his head briefly before turning on his heel and walking off in the direction of Rich's office. It takes him fifty steps until he is out of sight. Why I watched every single one is beyond me.

"You've pulled," Astrid giggles, and I throw her another look.

"Fuck off."

She laughs harder.

"It was you who embarrassed him," I point out, "he was fine until you spoke."

"I still think you've pulled," she says, and I ignore her, going instead to the bag Spencer left behind.

Inside, I find navy joggers, a white T-shirt telling me to 'Choose Life', and a grey hoodie. There are also some socks, underwear, and a pair of black trainers like the ones Spencer wore. Though it's hardly designer or on trend, everything has the same lavender smell as the sheets and zero holes.

I feel like I have come up in the world as I do my best to

wriggle into the mismatched assortment beneath the flimsy protection of my blue towel.

Eventually, I am done, and for a moment, I revel in the feeling of cleanliness. There is no grime, sweat or foul odour on any of these clothes and all that was on my person has been washed away by the shower. It's been a long time since I felt this comfortable, so I allow myself to relax - just for a second - and recline on the bed. The smell of lavender is heavenly. I breathe deeply and close my eyes.

I am asleep. I know this because I am dreaming, yet I am somewhere between both worlds. My mind is playing a movie of my life in full colour, yet my ears and body are aware of Rex nuzzling into my side. It's a trance-like state, and I allow myself to stay there. It's a state that many of us sleep in when we're on the streets. Half asleep, half awake. A learned behaviour, perhaps, so that we may be ready to run from the ever-present danger. It gets us through. It's got me through.

My life movie has reached that final journey on the *Cassiopeia*, and I am on the top deck watching Alex as he retches over the side. I am examining his form more closely now. I am scrutinising his every movement in a way I did not when this time played out in reality.

I see the moonlight bounce off his back as he leans over the railing. I see his feet encased in rope-soled deck shoes and his legs covered by the latest style of shorts. He is wearing a belt, a black one, with a large silver buckle, and it is the first time I have seen this. In my trance-like state, I frown.

Why do I not remember the silver buckle? But then, why the fuck does it matter? I conclude it does not.

He is talking, asking me about doctors and telling me that he is still feeling ill. He's berating me. His tone, I realise now, is far from gentle, and again, I am aware that this is the first time I've noticed this. Watching your 'life movie' on repeat is definitely enlightening.

I am telling him that I will find him a doctor, that I will ask the crew and I am smiling at him. He leans over the side once more, and I hear him being violently sick, emptying every last particle from his stomach. The moonlight shifts from his back, and for the first time, I can see beyond Alex through the clear plastic of the barrier over which he is leaning. I see his head upside down, mouth agape, and I watch in almost morbid horror at the sight of him being sick. Yet, there is something wrong.

I look more closely. I zone in on his mouth. I hear the sounds of his stomach roiling up into his throat, but his mouth… there is nothing leaving his mouth.

I keep my gaze penetrated on this orifice, the place through which so much bile has passed over the last three days, and there is nothing. Not even a spit of saliva.

Alex's stomach and mouth are giving two different accounts of the same event, and as I watch my former love, the man, the beast who murdered my parents, hanging over the side of the *Cassiopeia*, I realise, with devastating clarity, that he was never actually sick.

It was a ruse. An act so blatantly obvious that not one of us noticed.

Alex lied. He wasn't seasick. Ever.

I open my eyes, and a tear trickles down my cheek. I'm back in the real world. In the warehouse with Rex by my side. The lights above me are bright, but I stare unseeing, unfeeling.

I am numb.

I have uncovered yet more of Alex's twisted mind, and as I start to process, I recognise fear settling deep into the pit of my stomach.

Alex lied about being sick.

What else did he lie about?

I now understand that he was nothing of the man I thought him to be, but there is only one thought that terrifies me. One thought that is beyond bearable. One truth that could so easily have been a lie.

Could Alex swim after all?

Fuck.

TWO YEARS EARLIER

We have a routine, me, Yarrick and Clarice. It's simple, and it works.

Every morning, Clarice brings me a mug of hot sweet tea. In the early days, I told her I didn't like it sweet, but I've been here a long time now, and she's never made it any differently, so I've got used to it. Clarice is the kindest person I've ever known - and that's including those I would have called friends over twelve months ago.

Her very presence makes me smile as she bustles about her daily chores. After I've washed and dressed, it's customary for me to help out in the house, sweeping, cleaning and cooking - I don't mind; I've learned a lot - before the three of us sit at the rickety table in the front, underneath one of the only two windows on the ground floor, and eat a breakfast of fresh fruits and baked pancakes.

I have no idea what time any of this happens. I've become used to watching the sun moving across the sky, which gives me a rough gauge, but as every day is the same and I have nowhere else to be, the time is immaterial.

At first, Yarrick went out every day looking for my friends. Of course, he didn't find them because they didn't exist - but I could never tell him that. I stuck with my story and gave only the smallest of necessary details whenever he asked me for information.

I had been on that dinghy, I say. The one they'd found at the same time as me. It came from one of the big yachts, I tell them, and I was in the dinghy with some friends. I don't know what happened. I came to in the palm trees. I think there were three of us, maybe four, but I couldn't be sure. I guess we were drunk and had capsized. Somehow, I'd made it to shore.

I'd lost everything in an event so traumatic I sometimes wondered if I'd dreamt it. But then I'd wake up in the brightly coloured room at the top of Yarrick and Clarice's home.

At first, I didn't know what to do with myself. Women on this part of the island, I realised, worked around the home. Yarrick took time educating me in their customs and ways so that I would learn to fit in. He was kind, and I liked that it was important to him for me to have a place. Both he and Clarice urged me to call their small abode home, and I never wanted for anything. Except my parents.

It transpired that I had swum to one of the smaller islands in the archipelago and now find myself living - which is a very loose term for those first couple of months here - on Añaposta Island. Having previously only seen the islands from the luxury of the *Cassiopeia*, I had no idea there were so many or that some were of US territory as opposed to British. In total, Yarrick informs me there are thirty-six islands. Only sixteen of those comprising the British archipelago are inhabited. I think it amuses him to share facts with someone like me who, under normal circumstances, would be considered to have a greater intellect. I don't mean that to be derogatory; it is simply a fact based on the differences in our education. Though I have discovered schooling to be compulsory here and a priority, higher learning has only been accessible in the last twenty or so years, which, according to Yarrick, means that neither he nor Clarice were fortunate enough to attend.

The more time I spend here the more refreshing I find the culture. Far from there being any class or gender divides, which I had wrongly assumed existed, men and women are valued equally, though the division of work would be considered sexist in England. The small community of which I have become a part exists around the women remaining at home to educate the younger children whilst the men leave each day for roles in management or similar. I have no proof of this, of course, but equally, I have no reason to doubt the hierarchy Yarrick describes. There are many women and many children, each of whom seems happy and content - even if some of the youngsters appear a little old to be still schooled at home. In many ways, though, this is part of the appeal of the life I now live. The flexibility. The movement away from rigidity prescribed by societal norms. Yarrick is clearly popular and, from what I can tell, spends a good amount of time helping each family to the best of his ability.

After I'd been here a while, I wondered at his source of income. He laughed when I asked, telling me that I didn't need to know. I was safe, happy and healthy, which was all that mattered. It still bothered me, though, so I pressed, and eventually, he revealed the huts on the pier to be goldmines. Honeymoon couples mostly.

I work alongside Clarice every day. We go first to the gardens where we tend and pick the luscious crops, and then, if there are guests in the sea huts along the pier, I take fresh fruit and linen to them. It is a novelty to me, having a purpose, and I am enjoying it.

Seeing the wealth of those occupying the luxury huts was difficult at first. If I was cleaning and found a discarded toiletry item of a high-end brand, one that I knew well, it took all of my strength to keep the memories of my parents and previous life at bay. But I had made myself a promise: one day, somehow, I would make Alex pay for his crimes, and if Alex had died alongside my parents, then I would simply find his family, and they would pay instead. Each time I came across reminders of my former pampered existence it steeled my resolve and hardened my heart. The promise became a mantra, and the mantra became my law.

Now, our routine works. Yarrick maintains the sea huts and small boats that are afforded to each of the huts. Clarice and I clean them and stock up their provisions. In our spare time - of which there is little - we mix with Yarrick and Clarice's friends, who have welcomed me as one of their own. We dance, we eat, and we laugh with an abandon I have never before experienced. I cannot remember the last time I wanted or sought an internet connection; it is like the world beyond this small island has ceased to exist.

I no longer wear make-up; my clothes are simple and practical. My skin has a permanent golden glow and my hair is long and healthy from a diet rich in fruit. I have grown accustomed to the heat and enjoy the silence of the night when I retire to bed. Aurora has become Sandy. The transition has been almost effortless, and some days, I forget I have lived before.

But then I will remember. I will see the prone form of my

dead parents when I close my eyes, and I will know that Sandy cannot live forever.

And I will realise that somehow, Aurora must find her way home.

PRESENT DAY

Torturing myself about Alex's aquatic abilities is pointless. I have given that excuse for a human being enough of my head-space in the last three years, though my realisation that he faked his sickness has been tough. It feels like a fresh punch in the gut at a time when I am beginning to heal.

Not that the healing process means I've forgotten my promise of course, far from it. Alex or his family will pay - make no mistake - and if it takes me the rest of my time here on this mortal coil, then so be it. I have all the time in the world.

I slept surprisingly well. The bed was narrow but comfortable, and though I am in an open room with many others, I found my peace remarkably undisturbed. Even Rex is relaxed, snoring gently in the crook of my arm as we enjoy the last moments of rest.

It is early. Shafts of warm red light emanate from the arched window above where I sleep. I don't know what time it is, and I don't particularly care. Somewhere in the distance, I hear a pigeon coo, and I smile, safe in the knowledge that when it empties its intestines, the contents won't land on me. To date, I have been the recipient of thirty-seven deposits of white goo, falling on my unsuspecting form as I sleep. I don't believe this to be lucky. Not after thirty-seven.

Rex lets out a sigh, and I scratch his head. His warm tongue seeks out my palm. I recoil. I don't want his slobber on any part of my skin, which makes me wonder again why this dog has attached itself to me. I'm not a dog person - I never have been, but for some reason, he's here, and I guess we're stuck with each other.

I shift onto my side and scan the large open space. Most of the bunks are occupied by bumps of all shapes and sizes, though none are moving as yet. Astrid is asleep facing my bed so I take a moment to admire her beauty as she lies in complete relaxation. I am reminded of something my mum used to say. She would tell me that no matter how old I got and how grown up I became, when I was asleep, I would always be her baby. That's what Astrid reminds me of now. An innocent child, untarnished by the harsh realities of life and I'm almost saddened that she will wake up.

My bladder makes its presence felt, so I gently shift Rex to one side and make the short journey to the toilets. No one would ever call these facilities luxurious - they are utilitarian at best - but they are clean, hygienic, warm and therefore a damn sight better than a hole in the ground. And they have toilet paper. To me, this is the definition of luxury.

I wash my hands, splash my face with water and run damp fingers through my hair. There is a cracked mirror above the sink and I dare myself to look into it.

Not that I'm afraid of what I will see, nor will I be repulsed, but I simply have no need of the vanity this exercise will undoubtedly birth. I will start pinching and poking at my face, twisting my hair, making it tidy and for what? I decide to ignore the internal dare and leave the room.

Rex trots to my feet, his stumpy tail wagging, paws clicking on the bare cement floor.

"What's up, boy?" I whisper, reaching down and running my palm across his wiry back.

There is little movement from any of the other bunks, but the smell of bacon reaches my nostrils, and I breathe deeply.

"Mmm..." I remark to Rex, "you smell it too, huh?"

He nudges my hand as if in affirmation, and we walk back to the bed. Though someone is clearly in the kitchen preparing breakfast, I have no idea what the protocol is, so I figure we're best-off waiting until the routine becomes apparent. I don't even know how long we're allowed to stay. Astrid said it was one night, but I have no idea what the definition of night is here.

I rummage around in the carrier bag that Spencer dropped by my bed last night. Finding the navy hoodie, I pull it over my head before lying back on top of the bunk. I can still smell lavender, even though I have slept in the sheets for a good few hours.

I stare at the ceiling, wondering what I should do now. I'm no longer tired and feel the need to do something, yet I have no job or purpose anymore. On the streets, it's easier. I'm constantly on the move from place to place, bench to bench, doorway to doorway, looking for food, shelter and protection. Here, I have all of those things, so there is literally nothing for me to do.

Oddly, I find this hard.

A noise to my right alerts me to the imminent arrival of Rich and I groan. When I said I wanted something to do, I didn't mean a conversation with him, but it's clear he's heading my way, so I'm going to have to suck it up. Great.

"Morning. Sleep well?" His voice is quiet in deference to those still slumbering.

I nod. "Yes. Thank you." I have shifted my position so that I am sitting on the side of the bed rather than lying prone. I would have felt at too much of a disadvantage had I remained where I was.

He nods and looks down at Rex.

"Him?" he asks.

I shrug. Does he really expect a report on how my adopted dog has slept? My traitorous companion has other ideas, though, and after stretching on his belly until he's at his full length, he gets to his feet and patters over to Rich. I am then forced to witness a bizarre ritual as Rich drops to his knees and scratches Rex under the chin whilst murmuring something I cannot hear. I'm not bothered. I have no desire to know what he's saying. After a moment, Rex rolls onto his back, and the two of them engage in belly rub adoration. It's both comforting and unnerving.

"Did you want something?"

I interrupt their love fest, and Rich raises his eyes to mine. The smile he held in place for Rex slips almost immediately.

"Yes," he says, "can you come to the office? I don't want to talk out here."

I frown. "Why?"

Rich shakes his head and gets up from the floor. Rex returns to his former position by my feet.

"I could ask the same question," he responds, "but I fear I'm unprepared for the answer."

My frown deepens. I am more confused than ever.

"Just come with me," Rich states firmly, "it won't take long."

I glance at Astrid, who still sleeps soundly and wish, for a moment, that I could be her. I know that she has a shit life, too, and I have no idea where she came from or how she got to be on the streets, but she seems to have it all together, and I…well, I don't.

With a deep sigh, I leave the scented comfort of my bed and follow Rich's departing form through the corridor of bunks and into his office at the front of the building. The clickety-clack behind me confirms that Rex has come, too.

I sit in the same metal chair as last night, waiting for Rich to close the door behind us and settle in his oh-so-superior office recliner.

"You're smart," he says without preamble, and I widen my eyes.

"What?"

"You heard."

I shake my head. "You ordered me in here to tell me I'm smart?"

"I didn't order, I asked."

"Semantics," I state. Rich smiles.

"Precisely my point. There aren't many street dwellers who would know that word even existed, let alone how to use it."

I shrug. "So, I have an education. What of it?"

"You could be useful to me," he says, and I snort.

"I don't even like you. Why the hell would I want to be useful to you?"

Rich drops his head to one side and looks at me as if considering something.

"Have you wondered why you don't like me?" he asks after a moment.

"Nope. And I have no intention of wasting valuable brain power on such a ridiculous exercise."

He laughs. "You," he says as he points a finger towards me, "are priceless."

I don't respond.

"You're different," Rich observes after twenty seconds of silence have elapsed. Obviously, I've counted.

"We're all unique."

"That's not what I mean." He leans forward and places his elbows on the table, hands forming a temple. "You're not meant to be here. Are you, Ra?"

"Denver…"

He shakes his head. "Quit being facetious. You're too clever for that. On the streets," he clarifies.

I shrug as the pulse inside my temple begins to pound. Rich is the first person to make such an accurate observation. Somehow, he knows that I should be living another life. But how the hell does he know that? I have to stick to my story. I cannot risk being found. Not yet.

"I don't know what you mean." I attempt disinterest.

"For fuck's sake!" Rich slams his hand on the table, making both Rex and I jump. "Sorry…" he runs the same hand through his hair as he sits back. "Sorry."

I have no clue what the hell is going on here, but I know that my gut instinct about this man was spot on. He's crazy. I need to leave.

I scrape the chair back and stand up.

"No, wait."

I shake my head. "Not a chance. I'm getting the fuck out of here. Right now."

"Just a second..." his attention is snagged by the sound of the door opening. Automatically, I glance in its direction, expecting to see Astrid's beautiful presence framed in the gap. But it is not Astrid who has entered.

I swallow. What the...?

"You two know each other," Rich states unnecessarily.

I am mute. Struck dumb. I cannot process it.

Rex is not experiencing the same difficulties and rushes towards the visitor. Dog and man share a moment. I swallow again before realising I need to find my voice.

"Colin?" I manage eventually. "What the hell are you doing here?"

TWO YEARS EARLIER

It is low season. The huts are occupied to a lesser degree, which means there is less work. Yarrick continues with the seemingly endless maintenance, but Clarice and I are turning our attention to other duties. We garden, we cook, and we sew.

I discover that I am not the only one to benefit from Clarice's generous nature as she teaches me the basic skills I need to help her sew clothes for some of the poorer children. I'm not great at this, but she encourages me to keep going, and eventually, I manage to put together a few simple smocks. I'm almost embarrassed at the pride I feel at such a menial achievement. Clarice laughs when I voice this thought.

"You've done good," she says, "nothing small about what we're doing here."

I think she's being too generous, but if she's happy, then who am I to argue? We spend most of our time outside the shack, sitting in shaded areas where there is enough light to sew while being protected from the glare of the sun. Even though this is low season, the sun continues to shine relentlessly—a far cry from the climate in which I grew up.

As the months roll on, I am shocked to realise I've been here well over a year. In some respects, it feels like forever and in others, only yesterday that I jumped into the swirling waters below the *Cassiopeia*. I don't feel homesick any more, though I know I won't see out my days here. I have too much to do back home, and I am reminded that I need to figure out how to achieve a return passage. Twelve months is a long time in anyone's memory. I should be safe to go home now. There will be minimal fuss or questions, I am sure. If the story of that night ever made it back to my home, then I'm certain it will have long since been dismissed, and I, just another casualty. A victim of the floating graveyard.

I broach the subject with Clarice.

"I think I'm ready to go home," I say. We're sitting on the top of the hill above the shack, enjoying the view and the last rays of the sun. It's late in the day, and I know Yarrick will be back shortly.

"Okay," she says and begins bustling about, tidying her sewing and organising her bag.

"No," I laugh, "I didn't mean home, home. I meant home.

Where I came from. England."

Clarice looks at me, and I see her eyes narrowing. I presume she's squinting against the sun. "Oh," she says and then falls silent. This was not the response I was expecting.

"Do you know how I could do that?" I press.

She shrugs. "Yarrick will know." Her eyes regard me in a way I've never experienced, almost as if she's weighing me up, seeing me for the first time.

"Are you okay?" I ask.

Clarice closes her eyes briefly, and I wait. Something has shifted, and I have no idea what.

"Yes," she responds eventually, "we were just not expecting…" Her sentence drifts to no suitable conclusion.

"It's not that I'm not grateful," I say, "far from it. Please don't ever think I'm not appreciative of all that you've done for me. This place," I gesture expansively with my hands, "has become home. But I do need to go back one day. I have to."

Clarice picks up her bag and begins the short walk down the hill without any further acknowledgement. I scramble after her.

"Did I say something wrong?" I ask.

I see her shoulders shrug as her form continues its descent ahead of me. "We'll talk about it later. When Yarrick is back."

"Okay."

I've never seen this side of Clarice, and I don't know what to make of it. She's always been the warmest, kindest, most welcoming person, and yet now there is a definite chill which has nothing to do with the early evening mist. We arrive at the shack in silence.

I go straight to my room. I don't know what has happened, but I sense that Clarice needs some space, and to be honest, so do I. Arriving at the decision to return to England was huge - emotionally - and I am frightened of what I might find when I get there. Is Alex still alive? Does anyone know that the *Cassiopeia* was the scene of such a gruesome act? I'm sure there must be some knowledge - the crew would have family and friends noting their absence if nothing else.

I lie on the bed and stare at the familiar ceiling, watching the myriad of lights that play through the window as they bounce from ceiling to wall. When I first slept in this room, I didn't like these lights. I don't know why, really, except they always seemed to be doing a happy dance, and I was far from cheerful. After the first few weeks, I learned to enjoy their presence though and began to look for patterns, counting the rays and colours as they shone into my sanctuary. Every day brought a new show, orchestrated by the height of the sun and the clouds as they momentarily blocked the rays. I found I could lose myself for hours watching, counting, meditating, wondering.

My train of thought is interrupted by a knock at the door. I respond, unsurprised to see Yarrick. His bulk fills the door frame, and I move from the bed to the desk, choosing to occupy the chair that sits adjacent instead of my previous location. For some reason, it feels more appropriate. Yarrick closes the door and perches his not-insignificant rear on the spot I have just vacated. I wait.

"Clarice says you're leaving," he begins.

I shake my head. "Not at all. I've simply been thinking about returning to England, but I don't know how that's possible. I asked Clarice if she had any ideas."

Yarrick nods. "I see."

"It's not that I'm not grateful," I add, painfully aware that I've already said the exact same thing to Clarice, "but England is where my life is. Was," I amend.

For the first time since we met, I am struggling to read Yarrick's face. Like Clarice, he has always been open, jovial and welcoming. Though there is no hostility now, I feel the same chill that I felt when I first mentioned my thoughts back on the hill.

"Why?" he asks.

I frown. In some respects, it should be obvious why, but then in others…I'm happy here; I have a new life, so yes - why?

"I guess…I guess I want closure. I need to know what happened. To my friends." I have to remind myself to be careful. We no longer talk about how I came to be on Añaposta Island, so I must stick to my original story.

His dark hair flops over his face as he leans forward, bracing his elbows on his knees. I notice streaks of grey beginning to form. He sighs before raising his eyes to me once more.

"It can be arranged," he says. He speaks slowly, enunciating every word.

"Okay…"

"But" he rubs his palms together, "you don't have a passport or any identity. How would you board a plane?"

"That's why I asked," I respond. I am watching his face; the craggy lines that have become so familiar to me seem more deeply etched. His eyes are the same warm brown that they've always been, but I see something different in them. A coldness, perhaps.

"As I said, it can be arranged as long as you understand that we would need to obtain suitable identification for you."

I nod. "Well, yes, of course."

He tilts his head to the left. "I have to say, I wasn't expecting this. I thought you were happy here."

"I am, I am. It's just there's a part of me that's missing, and I want to feel whole again. I have to find out what happened. To my friends."

Yarrick studies me before allowing a small smile to grace his lips. "Very well."

He stands as if indicating that our conversation is over, but I am none the wiser. Both Yarrick and Clarice's reactions have been off, and I have to know why.

"It's not personal," I say softly, "I love being here with you, and you've been so kind…"

Yarrick slashes his hand in the air, effectively cutting me off. "Save it," he says.

I frown. "Why are you being like this?" I ask, "I don't understand."

He takes two steps towards where I sit. His large form looms over me. "We didn't expect you to leave," he replies, and though he's simply repeated his earlier comment, this time, I sense more than just coldness in his tone. This time, I sense malice.

"I'll come back," I say, "once I've sorted everything out back home. I just need some answers."

Yarrick's gaze is unwavering. His eyes bore into the depths of mine, and I wonder again what the hell is going on.

"Don't bother," he replies before turning on his heel and

heading towards the bedroom door. "Oh," he throws over his shoulder as he pulls on the handle, "it will be arranged, but you will need to pay."

"Of course," I reply, although I have no idea how I am expected to pay. I have no money to my name and no access to any bank or accounts.

Yarrick looks back at me, and, as if reading my mind, he clarifies. "Not with money."

I shake my head in bewilderment.

"You'll understand," he says and, with a final, blank stare, leaves the room.

I remain where I am, frozen in time, rigid, confused and frightened.

Yes, frightened.

Because that look he gave me, the final stare, was cold and malicious, but in its weight, I saw so much more than that. I saw... revenge?

A shiver runs down my spine, and I wonder what the heck I am doing here - a thought that hasn't troubled me since the early days. My place of safety and sanctuary, whose pleasures I have enjoyed and thrived upon, has, in the space of a few minutes, been sullied, damaged beyond repair.

Why on earth would Yarrick want revenge?

And I guess a more relevant question is, how the hell does he plan to achieve it?

Chapter Six

PRESENT DAY

Colin has yet to answer my question; he is just smiling awkwardly.

"Well?" I press. I have no right to address Colin in such a brusque manner, for he has only ever shown kindness, but his being here is off. It feels like more than a simple coincidence.

He swallows and takes three paces into the small room. I see his Adam's apple bob. "I didn't know you'd be here," he responds, and I frown. What the hell kind of answer is that?

"Ditto," I say before belatedly realising this word has a meaning I do not wish to imply. Courtesy of a big movie from a life I barely remember, it can be considered an endearment, a declaration of love, so I speak rapidly without censure in an attempt for clarity. "I could say the same thing," I declare, "and in fact I did. I asked what the hell you are doing here?"

Rich moves from his position behind the desk, circles us both and closes the door. "Keep your voice down," he says, "the others are still asleep, and we don't need any more interruptions." He indicates the two metal chairs, the sight of which I am beginning to hate. Rex, my ever-loyal yet traitorous companion, is already snoozing in the corner. It would seem that he has no immediate plans to leave.

Colin takes one chair and pulls the other towards me. With nothing better to do, I sit. Again.

"Colin is one of the volunteers here, " Rich begins, "and today is his day for volunteering."

Beside me, I sense Coffee Man nod.

"Okay," I respond. I don't see any point in wasting my breath on anything more profound but it does strike me as odd that Colin, the one good guy I've met, is here with Rich, a guy who I instinctively dislike. I still have no idea why my reaction to Rich is so intense, but I don't intend to wait around and find out.

"Yes," Colin says as he turns towards me. "I'm really glad to see you here. I wanted to tell you about it, but…" he trails off.

"Like I said last night," Rich picks up, "we have to be careful about who we tell and when. The facilities are not luxurious, make no mistake, but compared to your usual abode …"

"Excellent. Well, I'm not going to pretend this isn't a little freaky," I gesture between Rich and Colin, "but whatever," I shrug, "I'm leaving so … "

Rich smiles. It's that half-smile. The one I don't trust.

"Have some breakfast," he offers. "There's no rush. You don't need to leave right away, and your friend isn't even awake yet."

"I know, but the sooner I go, that's one more bed. Another person in, another good deed done."

Colin is watching me. I can sense the warmth in his stare.

It is oddly comforting.

"You can wait a bit longer," Colin says. "I'll get you some breakfast and Rex, too."

The dog lifts his head, connects gazes with Colin and the two engage in some man/beast love.

"Great," Rich says, slamming his hands on the table as if it has been decided. Like in a boardroom. A major deal done. "Why don't you take Rex and get started?" he addresses Colin, "I need a moment with Ra."

The chair to my left scrapes, and I know it will be mere seconds before I am alone with Rich again. I don't want to be alone with him, but at the same time, I realise I have no choice. Sometimes, you have to give up the fight. Choose your battles. This is a small battle, little more than a skirmish. I need to keep my strength up for the big fight. The one I promised myself I would engineer, even if it was the last thing I ever did. I hear the door close behind Colin and Rex, the thud of boots and the clickety-clack of paws on the concrete fading into silence.

I remain mute. Rich clearly needs to say something. Let him begin. He clears his throat, and I raise my eyes to his. For someone who appears outwardly in control, this seems a strange, nervous gesture.

"I ..." he begins, then shrugs. "Okay," he tries again, "I'm just going to be honest."

"That would be novel."

"Quit being so prickly," he says, "we're the good guys here."

I laugh. "Really? You do realise good guys don't exist?"

Rich shakes his head. "I have no idea - nor do I care to know - why you have arrived at that conclusion, but one of these days, you will have to lose that chip you are determined to carry on your shoulder."

"Why?" I ask, "And why the fuck does it matter to you?"

He shakes his head. "Prickly," he says, almost to himself. I sigh. We're getting nowhere. I remind myself that this was one battle I wasn't going to fight.

"Go on..." I say eventually, "You were going to be honest."

"Are you ready to hear me out?" his eyes bore into mine and again I am left with that disconcerting feeling that he can see inside my soul.

"Shoot." I cross my legs, one over the other and shift back into the relative comfort of the padded metal chair.

"I know about you," he says. My eyebrows arch in alarm, and he raises his hand to prevent any riposte that I might have been considering - which is just as well. I have no response, just sheer panic that my cover has finally been blown. That they know who I am and they know I have a home and that I don't and never did belong. "Colin recognised it in you," he says, "he could tell you were educated, but beyond that," Rich shrugs. I frown in response. "There aren't many who come through here with what you've got," he continues, "and I think we could help each other. I can offer you a permanent place in exchange for your help with certain - duties."

The bile rises in the back of my throat as the face of a man older than Rich swims in front of my eyes. Yarrick. He asked for my help so that I could pay for my passage back to England. The passage was necessary, but the trade-off was in no way an equal exchange.

Sickness rises automatically from the pit of my stomach, and I feel my throat constrict. That time with him and

Clarice, those months when I was securing my return to England, when the machinations were being put in place for my transport - those memories have haunted me night after night. I have had to distance myself from those thoughts, though. Otherwise, I would not have survived. They have been locked in another box on a shelf inside my mind with a label which reads, 'The truth of my return to England'. It sits next to the one holding the pain of the *Cassiopeia*. I have no desire to open either of them, yet Rich's choice of words threatens to breach the locks. He doesn't have the key, but it is a stark reminder that I must remain strong, that I must keep my thoughts clear of that shelf inside my mind. I cannot slip up. I cannot reveal my past. I can only live for today and then, perhaps, tomorrow. I need to stand firm and remember my promise to never trust another person. Nothing has changed.

I direct my attention back to Rich. He cannot possibly know that his words have triggered something. We are a million miles away from Añaposta Island and the life I left behind. But that doesn't stop the nausea as my brain fashions several interpretations of his meaning, of the duties I would be required to perform. None of my ruminations are pleasant.

"Duties?" I almost choke on the word.

Rich nods. "Helping around here, in the kitchen, making the beds - that kind of thing."

"You don't need someone with an education to do that," I reply before instantly realising how snobbish that sounds. If I have learned nothing else during my time on the streets, it is that we are all equal. We may dress differently, we may speak with accents, we may use words that confuse others, but that's just window dressing. Beneath it all, we are humans, and we are all the same.

"There's some admin stuff, too," Rich says, and I am almost

angry that he has not challenged my previous statement. He should be defending those less fortunate than I, not allowing me to get away with my privileged and derogatory crap.

I wait for a beat. "Why do you want me to help? There are so many like me. So many out there who would kill to be given this opportunity."

"I've been waiting to meet you," Rich replies cryptically, and I watch as he shifts in his chair awkwardly like he's uncomfortable. "Colin ..." he shrugs, "let's just say he sees something in you, and now that I've met you, so do I."

I laugh. I can't help it. Rich just watches me, gaze steady, eyes intense.

"You know what's more worrying?" I ask as I compose myself. "Some people actually believe that crap."

He shakes his head. "You're something else."

"All part of my charm. Now can I please get some food, my dog and get the hell out of this place."

His eyes connect with mine, and it is me who looks away. I don't like the way he stares right through me. He is dangerous. This I know though I have no substance for such a thought.

"Your loss," he says finally and raises his hand towards the door. An indication that I am dismissed.

In my previous life, the gesture would have riled me. I believed myself to be above most and would never respond to such an impersonal and rude prompt. But today, I have none of those hang-ups. Today, I am relieved. I get to leave this office. This tiny, sparse, functional space from where I instinctively know no good can come. I don't hesitate. I scrape my chair back, watching with satisfaction as Rich almost flinches, the noise loud in the still silent halls.

"People are ..."

" ... sleeping," I finish. "I know." I have my hand on the doorknob.

"You really are a bitch, aren't you?" he addresses my back.

I don't reply. Maybe I am. But if that is true, I know it is not because I am inherently cruel or uncaring. It is because I have been conditioned to be that way by men – men I thought I could trust.

I leave the office and head towards the enticing smell of bacon cooking. I need food, I need my dog, and I need my anonymity.

Anonymity that only the streets can afford.

TWO YEARS EARLIER

It is the day after 'D-day', though I am not referencing the war. 'D-day' in my world means 'disaster day' because it is the day, on reflection, when everything changes.

I have slept fitfully, which is unusual. Since I've adjusted to life here on Añaposta Island, I have found myself sleeping soundly, yet I have spent most of the last night awake, watching the light play through the coloured window glass and reflect on the walls, much as I did in the early days.

My stomach is in knots. Though I don't understand what has changed I know that something has, and that my request to find a way home has shifted the balance in our comfortable routine. I remember Yarrick's eyes as he spoke to me last night. The words he said when I asked if it was possible to find a way back to England. He was ... angry, and perhaps I can understand that, for he and Clarice have given me so much, but it was the other emotion I saw that troubles me. It was only in his eyes for a split second, but that was long enough for me to see it. Revenge. And my mind has played that moment over and over as I have struggled to understand why. I still don't, but what has caused me the greatest turmoil is that I suddenly feel unsafe. Though this is not my home, I have come to love it in a way. I have become part of the community here, and I have felt the kindness of others. Not once have I felt scared or frightened, and I have almost forgotten that feeling, putting it to the back of my mind as I have done with everything else I saw on the *Cassiopeia*. But it has returned and that, I know, is why I have lain awake.

The reflections on my wall reach halfway to the ceiling - it is time for me to get up. One thing I have enjoyed most during my time here is the lack of modern trappings. In the days before Alex (for that is how I have decided to refer to that time), I could not imagine having no watch or phone or internet. To have no idea of what time it was or who was wearing the latest fashion would have sent me into a panic, yet here it has ceased to matter. I look at the sun in the sky, and that tells me all I need to know. Once I got used to it, I found it freeing and refreshing, and I think that when I do find my way back to England, I will not go back to the level of dependability I had before. Once I have achieved my goal, I will allow myself the time to simply live. Live for myself and for my parents without fear of being uncool. Having nothing, watching your life dissolve in front of your eyes, is a great leveller, and though I always thought my previous existence shallow, I now understand the depths of that shallowness - and believe me, it's barely a flicker below the surface.

There is a knock on my door, and I swing my bare legs out of bed. I stand slowly, testing their stability before walking towards the door and opening it. Clarice stands on the other side, a mug of steaming tea in her hands. This is normal. This happens every day. Automatically, I reach for the receptacle.

"Thank you," I say, and she nods. I wait. Usually, Clarice is chatty yet this morning she says nothing. She shifts from one foot to the other as she pauses on the threshold. She is uncomfortable, and the nausea in my stomach responds. The tea is normal, but this version of Clarice is not.

I watch, one hand holding the mug, the other on the door handle, wondering if I should just close it. Clarice has her eyes fixed on the floor.

"Thank you," I repeat as I begin to push the door back into its frame. I don't like seeing Clarice like this, and I feel the fear from last night return.

"Wait," she puts her hand on the door and pushes it lightly back towards me. "I have to talk to you." She glances furtively behind her before shuffling into my room. It occurs to me that I haven't invited her in, but it is her house. The door closes. I retreat to the bed and sit as Clarice paces from the door to the window to the wardrobe and back again in some kind of weird triangle. I have never seen Clarice like this.

"You shouldn't have asked," she says finally, and I snap my eyes to her face. I notice that she looks drawn, her eyes large and hollow. She looks nothing like the Clarice of yesterday.

I say nothing.

Clarice stops pacing, and it takes a moment for her luminous patterned dress to finish swaying. She is wearing yellow today. Bright yellow. Sunshine yellow. It does not make me feel happy.

"He is angry," she glances again at the door. She is nervous, but it seems more than that. She appears ... afraid?

I shake my head. "I need to go home," I say. "I have to find out what happened to my friends." Just in time, I remember my cover story. "Why has that made him angry? You always knew I would need to go back."

Clarice is pacing again. "I don't think we did. Not really."

I frown. "I don't understand. When you found me on the beach that day, you knew I had unanswered questions."

She nods, and her round, comforting form comes to a stop in front of me. "Yes, but we thought you would stay once you'd adjusted. We thought this would be your new home."

Again, I frown. "It is. You've both been so kind to me, everyone here has been, and in many respects, I don't want to leave, but there are things that I really need to know. I have to go back. Surely you can understand?"

Clarice glances again at the door before settling down beside me on the bed. Her eyes drop to the floor. "You are our family," she begins, "and family don't leave."

A shiver runs down my spine. Though her voice remains warm, Clarice's choice of words feels less than. "I will always be your family," I say, "but I have family in England. Friends. They will want to know that I am okay."

"That cannot be." She turns her head towards me. "You cannot go. He will not allow it."

I take a deep breath, watching her eyes, waiting for her to become the Clarice of whom I am so fond, but that doesn't happen. Where usually there is a twinkle of love and affection, now there is nothing. Her expressive orbs are emotionless. If she weren't speaking, I would be concerned she was no longer alive. My belly curls, and I shift a little down the bed. Further away from her.

"You must realise there is a price to pay," she continues, "and you have to pay that price."

Yarrick had said something similar last night, yet when he'd delivered those words, there had been a menace in them which had brought fear and unrest. Clarice is simply stating facts. There is no emotion. I am lost for words. I don't know how to handle this.

Over the last months I have grown to love these two people who were my saviour. Their gentle kindness has helped me to heal from a situation so sickening, so raw that I didn't ever think I'd stop bleeding - but I have. Slowly, they have shown me love, kindness, and tenderness, and I have become part of their family. Clarice is not wrong about that, but I had thought they always understood this would only ever be temporary. But even if they hadn't, the way Yarrick reacted last night and now Clarice ... I no longer feel safe. I feel like I am a stranger again. A stranger to myself and to them.

I had become Sandy. I had embraced Sandy, and Sandy had grown to become a person. Perhaps only half a person, for she could never be whole - not until she knew precisely what happened that night - but she was a person all the same and had started to find joy and comfort in the simple community life here. I had almost begun to think of Sandy as my best friend or maybe my twin. The other side of Aurora. The pure side. The side that had not witnessed the atrocities that night. The side that could allow herself to be reborn.

In many respects, Aurora had died that night, too, and Sandy represented her soul - but that didn't mean she was content. Sandy had the same questions Aurora did and now that she had healed, Sandy wanted answers. Maybe I would never be Aurora again. Maybe I would always be a hybrid of but we were in agreement now. Sandy. Aurora. It didn't matter. On this, we were interchangeable.

Aurora had to find Alex, or at least satisfy herself that he was dead too. Sandy had to find answers, know what happened to her parents, and grieve them properly. We both had the same goal. To get back to England. For there were no resolutions to be found on Añaposta Island.

Clarice shifts beside me, and I turn back. Her eyes are still watching, cold, emotionless. Instinctively, I reach out to her and place my hand on her thigh, hoping to find the Clarice of before. She looks down, shakes her head and then gently covers my hand with hers. I feel the familiar warmth, and a rush of love begins to battle the fear; maybe it will even defeat it. We stay like that for countless minutes. Heads bowed; hands locked. I want to speak, but I have no idea what to say. I know that I must wait for her cue.

Eventually she removes her hand from mine and then gently pushes up from the bed. Her eyes, when she looks at me this time, are full of unshed tears.

"I'm sorry," she says, and I watch as a single tear escapes and plops onto the floor. My eyes search hers, looking for something, anything that will tell me what has changed. Slowly, she shakes her head and shuffles towards the door. She is defeated, and I have no idea why.

She turns to look at me one final time. "I will try, Sandy," she whispers, "I will try to protect you, but ... " and then she's gone, leaving nothing in her wake save her unique flowery aroma and a million questions.

I sip my tea. It is cold and bitter. For the first time since I have been here, Clarice has not sweetened my tea. Perhaps it is an oversight, but somehow, I know that it is not.

I close my eyes, picturing her tortured face as she left the room. I don't understand anything yet I feel as if the unsweetened tea is important. A message?

My legs wobble as I instruct them towards the sink. I no longer like unsweetened tea. I cannot drink this, even if it does mean something. I lift my arm to pour the contents of the mug away, alarmed to see the piece of solid earthenware fall from my hands. It crashes onto the side of the ceramic sink, shattering into fragments that dance as they succumb to the force of gravity. Rainbow lights highlight their journey, and my head spins. I grab for the sink but it is no longer there.

My knees buckle, and it takes less than a second for me to fall amongst the remains of the broken mug. I have no control over my body. I am weightless. I am without sensation. I watch the colours dancing on the ceiling, bouncing over the walls, and then I feel my eyes close. It is sub-conscious. I do not instruct them to do so. I see Clarice's face in the back of my mind. I see the dead behind her eyes. I see her unshed tears and then I hear her saying sorry. Over and over again.

And then I see nothing. For like that night on the *Cassiopeia*, I have once more lost everything and am shrouded in deepest, darkest blackness.

PRESENT DAY

When I find them in the kitchen, the Rex/Colin love-fest is in full swing. Rex almost looks adorable as he gazes up at Colin. Colin is smiling, laughing, holding bacon up high, and then asking Rex to sit nicely. It's like I've walked into an alternate universe—a place where normality reigns, and people are kind to animals and others.

It is still early, and despite my show of petulance in the office with Rich, I have made sure to tiptoe past the beds as best I can. It isn't fair to wake others simply because I detest that man; my job now is to fill my tummy, grab my stuff - what there is of it - and leave.

"Here she is," Colin says to Rex as I enter. His voice is softer and smaller like you would use with a child. It is oddly endearing. "We've been having fun, haven't we?" he asks. My canine friend inclines his head to one side. These two have definitely bonded.

"Would you like to keep him?" I ask, gesturing towards Rex. "He's not really mine anyway."

"I'd love to," Colin shrugs, "but no pets. I'm in rented."

I nod. Back in the day, when I was Aurora and lived in an overly large country house, we had pets. I am a cat person, but my parents loved all animals. My father had a 'hunting' dog, which was a family joke, for dad never went hunting. The dog grew old and fat in front of the fire.

"Where do you live?" I ask suddenly and then wonder why I want to know.

Colin leans against the steel counter and drops the final piece of bacon to the floor. Rex gobbles it noisily before sighing deeply and stretching himself across Colin's feet.

"Just over the river, about a mile from here. It's a house share."

I nod again but say nothing. It's not like I know Bristol. I simply ended up here, and my knowledge of the city is essentially limited to benches and doorways.

Silence descends as I look around the utilitarian room.

"Oh," Colin suddenly pushes away from the counter, "you wanted some breakfast?"

It's a question but he doesn't wait for me to answer, busying himself instead with a frying pan. "Toast?" he asks.

"Yes. Please," I respond and Colin glances at me over his shoulder.

"Always so polite," he grins.

It is infectious, and I find myself smiling back. "Why did you tell Rich about me?" I ask after a moment.

Colin turns from the stove. "What do you mean?"

"You told him you thought I was educated. Why? Why were you even talking about me?"

Colin resumes his activity with the frying pan. "I knew that Rich was needing help here and I don't know," he shrugs, "I just got the feeling you'd be a good fit."

"But you never mentioned this place to me," I counter, "how could you even know I would find it?"

"I didn't, but I'm a big believer in what's meant to be. I figured if you were meant to come here, then you would. And you did." He smiles as he slides a plate across the metal counter that separates us. "Here. Better than I can usually offer."

I look down. He's not wrong. Instead of the odd dry bagel from the coffee shop, Colin has served up six slices of bacon, four pieces of toast and a mountain of baked beans.

"Are you trying to fatten me up?" I ask.

He laughs. "No, that's a standard portion. We like everyone to leave here with as much as we can give, though you could do with putting a bit of meat on your bones."

I shake my head as the first mouthful of bacon hits my taste buds in the most satisfying way. "Not often I've heard that," I remark, almost to myself.

"No?" Colin has heard me.

"I've always been what you'd call 'curvy'," I say, "so this," I gesture to my frame, which has undoubtedly slimmed down during my time on the streets, "is a novelty."

Colin watches me, his green eyes clear, and I notice, not for the first time, that he is far from unattractive. "Why are you on the streets?" he asks quietly, and too late, I realise I have dropped my guard. I have given him an insight into who I was rather than who I am now, and that is something I cannot afford to allow anyone. I drop the unfinished bacon onto my plate and call to Rex. It's time to leave.

I have covered twenty-two paces and am almost at my bunk when Colin reaches my side. He takes hold of my right arm and pulls me gently to a stop. I shrug free, but he is persistent, and though I know I have revealed too much to this man, I also trust my gut - and my gut is telling me that this guy is okay. That is the only reason I allow him to take me to another room off the main area, one that I've not seen before. It's a second office, one much like Rich's, but situated at the far end of the building as opposed to the entrance. Here, there are only metal chairs, five of them set in a semi-circle. No desk and no luxury faux leather chair. Rex trots behind me, and when Colin indicates for me to sit at one end of the moon-shaped row while he sits at the other, Rex has to decide where his loyalties lie. He chooses me, and his warm, wiry form covers my feet as he sighs deeply.

Colin leans forward, arms resting on his knees. His long hair is flowing loosely today; the dreadlocks have gone, leaving behind a mass of untamed curls. I can't decide if I like this style or not. He turns his head sideways to look up at me.

"I'm sorry," he says, "it's none of my business."

"You're right," I agree, "it isn't."

He nods before swivelling his head back to the centre and regards the floor. There is nothing remarkable about the floor; it is the same as the rest of this place. Concrete, dull, utilitarian.

We lapse into silence. "Thank you for breakfast," I say eventually, and Colin half laughs.

"You hardly ate any of it."

"Still ..." I reply, "thank you."

He nods. Silence. Again. I want to ask Colin why I am here, why he stopped me leaving - and then my mind goes to Rich. Is this all part of the grand plan? Has Rich asked him to make sure I stay?

"Why am I here?" I decide it's easier to simply ask rather than wonder.

"I don't want you to get the wrong idea," he replies. "I want you to know that I understand."

"Understand what?"

"You," he says. His hands are clenched together between his knees, and I see his fingers idly playing with a ring. It's a large silver ring, chunky, with a rotating band and it is this he is spinning.

"I don't understand me," I say, "so how the hell can you possibly claim to?"

"I'll rephrase," he responds. "I don't mean that I understand you so much as I understand your journey. I understand where you've come from."

My hands begin to sweat, and I recognise the symptoms of a panic attack as a wave of emotion sweeps downwards from my head. It is not a pleasant emotion. It is fear. Fear that perhaps somehow, in a way I can't even begin to comprehend, Coffee Man knows who I am. I remain mute. I cannot process an appropriate response.

"Your accent," he continues, "I recognise it. I hear the education in your voice, I see the way you carry yourself with a pride that cannot be learned. I came from that place," he reveals. "I had an education and money, and though I can't pretend to know how you ended up here, I do know what it's like to leave that kind of security behind."

The panic has reached my belly but as I process Colin's words, it dissipates a little. He doesn't know who I am. That much is clear. It is something else he recognises in me, something that he, too, claims to have known.

"But you work in a coffee shop," I say, which, on reflection, is an illogical response.

He smiles. "Like I said, I know what it is to leave that life behind."

"You had money?" I ask.

"Yes. I didn't always look like this. I was what you would call a 'regular public-school boy'."

I am shocked. Though Colin is by no means scruffy, the hair, the nose piercing and his general demeanour would never have suggested a private education. Then I realise I am applying Aurora's old prejudices and judgements. I am no longer her. I am Ra. And Ra has no such opinions.

"I got into skateboarding," he continues, "which was not an accepted activity. At first, my parents humoured me; they thought I'd get bored in time, but the opposite happened. I didn't realise until I stood at the top of a run for the first time just how much of a prison I lived in. When I flew down the ramps, I felt alive, and I knew I had found my true home."

I shift slightly on my chair, angling my torso towards him. I have not had anyone open up to me since I returned to England, and though I have chosen to remain invisible, being seen now in this room feels good. Warm. Like I belong.

"Anyway, I started competing," Colin says, "and by the time I was thirteen, I was racking up the wins. The fact I was winning meant my parents were okay with it. They could tell their friends about their talented son, even if they did gloss over the details of what I was actually doing." He shakes his head. "I have no idea why they couldn't just be honest, but appearances meant everything to my parents. I was sixteen when I took my first serious spill. I broke my collarbone and wrist. I couldn't skate for a while, but I wasn't interested in studying either. I knew what I wanted to do with my life and it wasn't something I could learn from textbooks. That's when the rows started. At seventeen, I had another spill, and this one was big. I was a real mess. I was in hospital for a month and then rehab for even longer. I didn't realise it at the time, but that spill signalled the end of my skating career, and once that sunk in, I couldn't see a reason to live." He looks across at me from beneath hooded lashes. "I overdosed. My parents found me in time, but once I'd recovered, they kicked me out. I was no longer their son who was achieving great things; I was this burden, and they were ashamed. Ashamed of what I had become and what I had tried to do. It was tough to believe that their love for me was less than their desire to be accepted. Anyway, I ended up on the streets. Just like you."

I have not spoken or moved whilst Colin has been speaking. I have watched as he's revealed the bare bones of his story and I have seen the play of emotions. I recognise them, every single one, and I recognise the glitter of tears in his eyes.

"No one chooses this life," he says softly, and I lift my head, allowing our gazes to connect. "But when we are offered help ... we need to know to receive it."

I feel the dampness in my own eyes and watch a tear drop from the end of my nose. It lands on Rex's dark fur. He doesn't notice.

"No one cares how you got here, and no one needs to know, but you don't have to be alone. Not anymore. I'm offering you help. Please ... take it."

I press my lips together as I stifle a sob. I am containing a myriad of emotions which I cannot begin to identify. I don't know if I even want help, but I recognise myself in Colin's story, and I see the sincerity in the depths of his steady green gaze. He has been through his own trauma. He has fought his own Alex, and now he is sitting here with me and my scruffy dog, offering us support.

Can I do this? Can I allow someone to help me?

The wounds run deep and the scars are still forming. I stand by my promise that I will never again trust another person, but then I remember that my original promise had a caveat.

And that caveat was that I would never trust another person until it was okay to do so. In my mind that time would come when I had settled my score with Alex or his family, but perhaps in that I was wrong. Perhaps it is okay to trust someone before I find Alex or answers.

I take a deep breath. Colin is watching me, and I know he is waiting for me to respond.

It is a monumental effort, but eventually, I nod. Just once.

"Okay," I say. "Okay."

And as I release the emotions and give myself permission to drop my guard a fraction, I hope and pray that I have made a good choice.

Because I know that I do not have the strength to come back from another betrayal.

Chapter Seven

TWO YEARS EARLIER

I wake to find myself in an unfamiliar room. It is dark and cool, and I can smell the unmistakable tang of wet earth. I must be somewhere beneath Yarrick and Clarice's house, deep within the mountain upon which their humble abode is built. A few candles light the walls, ensconced in small grey earthenware pots, much like the mugs we use. I look up. There is a round hole in what would be the roof, no larger than a dinner plate yet enough to allow in oxygen and a sense of time. That's why the candles are able to burn. There is a small supply of their lifeblood. I pull myself to a sitting position as I glance down at what has been my makeshift bed. I am surprised to see it comprises a good deep mattress. For some reason I had expected to be waking on the floor. There is little else around me, and as I stand, I register the cold, damp earth beneath my feet, which are bare. I am wearing one of the white-flowered nightdresses from my bedroom and nothing else. I run my hands over my legs and up my torso, confirming that I have not been allowed the decency of underwear.

My head is throbbing and I am certain that is due to whatever Clarice laced into my tea. I knew my tea was doctored. I think I knew before I even sipped, but perhaps

I didn't want to believe it. Now, though, as I look around at my current abode, I know I have not ended up here by accident. There is some plan, some destiny for me, which is somehow mixed up in my request to return to England.

Oddly, I am not scared. Whether the drugs have yet to fully wear off, I don't know, but I am surprisingly calm as I pace thirty steps before reaching another smooth, cold, earthy wall. I continue to walk, and within minutes, I have determined the room to be nine hundred square paces in size. I have also discovered a small alcove set back from the main area which has the rudiments of bathroom facilities. A roll of sumptuous toilet tissue hangs from a single string suspended from the roof. I laugh at this oxymoron. The accommodation could not be more basic, and yet I am afforded luxury bog roll. I also have a limited supply of fluids courtesy of a large clear bag filled with what I can only assume is water. This, too, is suspended from the ceiling and has a small plastic tap fixed into the bottom of the bag. Experimentally, I lift the lever and watch as a single trickle of water drops to the earth by my feet. I have, it would seem, the necessary requirements for survival: oxygen, water and light, but I have absolutely nothing else. If I thought I had lost everything on the *Cassiopeia*, I now realise that I was completely wrong.

As I stand in my earth hut and begin to piece recent events together, I conclude that now I have nothing. Though I cannot yet make sense of why I am here and what this place even is, I know instinctively that any shred of dignity I had left has evaporated. Gone, leaving nothing but posh loo roll in its place.

When I saw my parents fatally injured, when I stared straight down the barrel of a gun, when I leapt into the swirling ocean, when I came to live with Yarrick and Clarice - of course, each of those events stripped away some part of who I was but during all of those times I still had one thing I could hold onto. And now I don't even have that.

That one thing?

Hope.

PRESENT DAY

We are back in the kitchen. Several others have awoken, including Astrid, who is bouncing up and down on the metal bench affixed to the tables. It is here we are eating breakfast. The tables are also metal, and for a moment, I amuse myself with the thought of a lightning strike or an electrical failure. It wouldn't take long for a spark to arc throughout this whole warehouse; such is the extent of conduction material. Then I remember Rich and his faux leather chair. The fact that will be less of a conduit dampens my mood.

"God, I slept soooo well," Astrid says as my rear end bounces in time with hers. I know I have lost weight; it hurts every time I land. I literally have no padding.

"Good," I mumble. I have yet to contribute much to our conversation simply because I cannot work out which words to form. When Colin and I left the second office room, we had an understanding. He had revealed part of his life to me, and in return, I had agreed that I would stay for the next twenty-four hours, but only if Astrid could, too. Colin hadn't hesitated to meet my terms—thus, Astrid hasn't stopped bouncing.

"And..." she continues, "we get another night! Woo hoo! Another whole night!"

I nod. I know this because I am the one who made it happen, but I also know this because she has reiterated it at least a dozen times. In many ways, I find it humbling that this has had such a big effect on her. Though I cannot pretend to be upset about missing another night on the streets, I have in the past been used to substantially more luxury than this, so I very much see it for what it is. To Astrid, though, it could well be The Ritz, and I begin to understand more about the life that others who have been on the streets for longer than me have had to lead.

"No scrounging for food today," Astrid sings as she drops another piece of bacon to Rex, who has barely stopped salivating. I have lost count of how many pieces of pig that dog has eaten, which is a worry. Not because I am concerned for his welfare but because, for the first time in my life, arithmomania has let me down. I have often considered it a curse, yet now I am without certain facts I am actually finding it disorienting. Another shift in my excuse for an existence.

"Do you think," she asks as she turns towards me, "we could even wangle another night after this one?"

I shake my head. "I have no idea. I don't even know why we got this one." Both statements are of course, a total lie. I don't like lying to Astrid but if I tell her about Rich asking me to stay and then the deal I've done with Colin ... it would just complicate things. I have every intention of leaving after the next twenty-four hours is up, so I don't think it really matters.

Beside me, I hear a jingle as Astrid stretches her arms above her head and yawns. "I cannot tell you how good that feels," she says. "I have a full belly, a warm bed and an adorable companion." She looks down at Rex to clarify that it is the four-legged, wiry creature she covets, not me. "Oh, and some clean clothes. That guy that did the breakfast, what's his name?" She waves her hand around, accompanied by more jingling. I don't respond. "Anyway, it doesn't matter; I'll just ask him again." There is a smile forming at the corner of her mouth, and I see her eyes dilate a little. Wow. She likes him. She likes Coffee Man. "He said," she carries on, and I struggle to remember her initial point, "that we can have another set of clean clothes once we've showered. I have to tell you, baby girl, I can't remember the last time I wore two sets of clothes in two days. My body won't know what's hit. I might wash all my skin off in the shower!"

I laugh. I can't help it. Astrid is the person I would love to be. Funny, infectious, living life for the day, taking the good when it comes and dealing with the bad. It is impossible to be around her and remain glum.

"Aha," she says, pointing a finger at me, "finally. You're in there. I was beginning to wonder. What gives, baby girl?"

I know she is referring to my subdued mood and realise that I do at least owe her some form of explanation.

"I guess being here, surrounded by people who care ... it's made me realise how crap our lives are, and I wonder what the point of it all is. Why the fuck do we spend every day trying to survive just to continue that crap existence?"

"Okay," Astrid says as she drops a jingly arm around my shoulders, "that's way too deep for me, but just so you know, baby girl, we all carry on because one day we hope that things will change."

"But what if they don't? What if we end up like Denver?" Though Denver is the guy who introduced us to this place, it is more luck than anything else that it turned out to be a good tip-off. Denver spends most of his time talking to walls and inanimate objects, such is the destruction of his mind. He lived a life of luxury and excess, and when it all fell apart, so did his brain.

"Hey," Astrid says, "look at me."

I lift my eyes to hers, struck once again by her beauty. If she has set her sights on Colin, then I fear he will capitulate before he even realises what's happened.

"We won't end up like Denver because we're different. We're smart in ways that he never was, and we've survived so much crap. Being a woman on the streets is way harder than being a man, yet here we are. I've got your back, baby girl; I promise we'll be okay."

I don't know if it's true about the women on the streets thing - I have no metrics to back this up, and from what I've seen, this life is equally shitty for us all, but Astrid believes in the two of us and as I watch the sincerity in her eyes and remember what she has saved me from, I know that she is right. We will be okay.

Because we have each other.

TWO YEARS EARLIER

It has become apparent there is no obvious exit from wherever the hell it is I am. When I first explored I assumed there would be some access, but I cannot find anything other than mud and that small hole in the roof. I have used the facilities for what they are worth and splashed some water on my face, but now, as I lie on the mattress with no clue as to what is happening, I feel my chest tightening. I am scared now. I am frightened. I am terrified - perhaps more so than when Alex pointed a gun at me. At least then, I could see the enemy, but now there is nothing.

I wonder if I am finally about to depart this earth.

I breathe deeply from my tummy and count each breath slowly. It works to calm my heart rate, and the band around my chest eases. I am still trying to remember the sequence of events, but after sipping the bitter tea, everything is hazy. I have a vague recollection of being carried and then of voices, but I couldn't make sense of what was being said. I squeeze my eyes closed and try harder to access the files in my brain to see if I can discover anything that may help me now, but they remain stubbornly closed, and in the end, I admit defeat.

It has not escaped my notice that there is no food, and I wonder if I am supposed to suffer. Or maybe I am not to be kept here for long. Perhaps someone will release me soon, and I'll be back in my room on the top floor of Yarrick and Clarice's house. Watching the lights play through the coloured glass window.

I am lying on my side, curled up into a small ball when I feel something hit my back. I scream and leap from the mattress, expecting to see a huge spider, but it is nothing of the sort. It is a rope with a hand loop and it is dangling down through the hole in the roof. I look up but I cannot make out who is on the end of it - it is simply hanging there. I tug on it to determine if it is secure. It is. I don't know what it is connected to, but it wasn't there earlier, so I can only assume I am to grab hold of it. Do I attach myself to the rope or not? Is this my lifeline?

I realise that the rope could disappear as quickly as it has arrived, so I decide to take the risk. Whatever is waiting for me at the top cannot be worse than this.

I push my right hand through the loop and secure the knot around my wrist. For a moment, I am transported back to a time when I had a television and watched films—specifically those hero and heroine movies that always involved some kind of crazy rescue. I feel like I am being rescued, but am I a heroine? I very much doubt it.

The pull of the rope takes me by surprise as my arm stretches above me, higher and higher, until there is no more arm left, and my feet leave the ground. I am heading slowly towards the shaft of light in the roof, and though I could fall at any moment, I do not feel fear. I concentrate on breathing as a sharp pain in my right arm reminds me it is taking the entire weight of my body. Given a choice, I know my arm would not volunteer for such a role, for though I am reasonably fit and certainly spent enough time at the gym in my former life, I have never quite managed to achieve decent upper body strength.

The hole above gets larger as I approach. It is probably six metres above the ground on which I slept, and I can see that I have miscalculated the size of this bizarre form of exit. From below, it looked to be no more than a dinner plate. However, it is much larger, big enough for an entire person to be lowered horizontally to the bed beneath - which I guess answers the question as to how I got into the earth room in the first place.

Soft tones of female voices float through the hatch on beams of warm light that have begun to bathe my face. I cannot hear what they are saying, I merely recognise them as female, which I consider positive. Though I still don't understand what is going on and what has happened to me, my instincts tell me that if Yarrick is involved, so are other men, and that, I fear, will not lead to a pleasurable outcome.

I reach the top of the rope hoist and form myself into a ramrod-straight position. It will be easier to exit the hole without injury this way, even though my right arm is already in agony. A voice calls instructions to me, but I cannot understand. It is not a language with which I am familiar, and for the first time, I have a real sense of foreboding. I have only assumed myself to be somewhere close to Yarrick and Clarice's home due to the construction of this earth room, but I could conceivably be anywhere.

With a final pull, my head emerges into the bright sunlight, and I blink furiously as I try to focus. The rest of my body clears the hole moments later, and I feel like I have just been born. In the same way, I have watched childbirth on hospital television programmes, so I have been pulled from this hole - head first. Well, technically, arm first, but I'm sure I've experienced what a baby must. Will there be balloons waiting for me? Loving parents? Warm towels? Should I cry? I fear I have finally lost my mind - perhaps I am still drugged. My thoughts seem scattered and irrational.

Once my feet have cleared the gap, I am dropped, unceremoniously, onto the warm, hard ground. I have not been born, after all. Nothing but sand and dirt awaits my arrival as I land on my front and inhale both, deep into my nasal passages. No balloons. No smiling faces. I am reminded of my first day here on the island when I lay down in the sand and prayed to be reunited with my parents. Except I am not on a soft beach now; I am in the hills. This I know because the ground is scorched and cracked. Odd green tufts of what passes for grass and prickly foliage surround me. Every sharp needle of nature pressing painfully through the inadequate coverage of my lightweight nightgown.

The female voices are still chattering; some are close to my ear, their warm breath tickling the inside shell as they furiously communicate. It doesn't matter how close they get to my ears; I still don't understand them. After a moment, I feel a rough hand on my back, pulling at the thin material, which is my only nod to decency. With what must be a practised movement, the material is twisted, causing me to flip over onto my back. As my eyes adjust once more to the unfamiliar light, I get the first glimpse of my rescuers - if that is what they are. I recognise some, one in particular.

A shadow moves above me, blocking out the light. I open my mouth to speak but am halted by Clarice.

"Shhh," she says, placing her finger over my lips, "you must not speak."

I shake my head and frown.

"No," she says softly, "don't speak or struggle. Please. Trust me, Sandy. Trust me."

I look into her eyes, searching for the warmth of the Clarice I have come to love over the last months, but I see nothing. Her expression is vacant.

"Trust me," she repeats.

In my compromised position with no knowledge of where I am it is a pointless statement. I have no choice.

Satisfied that I will not speak, Clarice removes her finger and shifts to the side. Around me the rest of the women have formed a kind of circle, kneeling, almost as in worship. I don't know how to process this. The women are chanting; their eyes averted, focused on the hard ground. It feels creepy and surreal, and I wonder at Clarice's involvement. I wonder, too, if I am still drugged. Surely this cannot be normal.

I remain on my back, the nightdress bunched uncomfortably beneath me, though I am grateful for its meagre cover. Automatically, my eyes search out Clarice, seeking her comfort and reassurance, anything that will tell me what the hell is going on. None is forthcoming; she just continues to shake her head, and then slowly, her expression changes.

But it's not the warmth and reassurance I have been craving. It is pity.

There is a sudden shuffling as the women move aside, still on their knees. Three sets of male feet appear beside my head, one of which I recognise as Yarrick's. Odd to know someone simply from their feet, but this particular pair were the first thing I saw after making it to land. They are burned into my memory.

"Sit up." A command from Yarrick.

I do, taking the opportunity to adjust my clothing a little.

"This," he continues with a grand sweep of his arm, "is where you get to earn your passage."

I look around. The ground on which I sit extends no more than fifty metres in each direction, forming a perfect square. Around its perimeter is a tall metal fence. Immediately beside me is the ridiculous hole from whence I came, and in the far corner is a collection of wooden huts, much like those on the pier that I have painstakingly prepared for rich tourists, though much less luxurious. At first glance, I cannot see anything that explains how I would earn my passage here.

"You're probably wondering how," says Yarrick, reminding me of his uncanny ability to read my thoughts. "It's all about service. You will do what is asked of you, and in return, you will earn the right to leave."

I shake my head, even more convinced that I am still under the influence of whatever substance was in my tea. The way Yarrick is speaking, the two men flanking him on either side, the women who have remained on their knees with heads bowed - none of this is real. It can't be.

It's like some kind of dystopian world that exists only in movies and fantasy books.

"We are putting motions in place for you to leave. It can take a little while for us to obtain the correct permissions, but when the time is right, you will journey from here via cargo ship. The crossing will be arduous, but there will be ways to make it more palatable. In the meantime, you will stay here." Once again he demonstrates with a sweep of his arm.

"The earth cave," Yarrick indicates the hole beside me, "is where you will end up if you defy any of our requests. But, if you do as you are told, you will be given the luxury of those huts over there. We," he continues, "have complete power over what happens to you next, and believe me, there are those who will use it."

For a second, he pauses, and I allow myself to connect deeply with his gaze. I know he will see nothing but confusion and disdain on my face, for I have awoken in an alternate reality that makes absolutely no sense to me. Where has the Yarrick I have known and cared for gone?

Finally, I use my voice. "What do you mean?"

Yarrick shrugs. I am at a physical disadvantage, sat as I am on the hard earth, level with his knees at best, but I refuse to break eye contact. I need to find the Yarrick that I have come to love over the last months, because he has to be in there somewhere. But he isn't. It's like a switch has been flipped. All of the kindness, warmth and empathy I have come to know have evaporated. His gaze gives nothing away, and I am reminded of Alex. How when he left me on the sunbed on the top deck of the *Cassiopeia*, he was the man I believed was my future, and yet, when I saw him next, he had morphed into an evil killer. Just like that. Night and day. And it is because I have seen this before that I am able to accept it is happening again - with Yarrick. I have witnessed a mercurial change with no warning. I have felt the trust ripped from my soul and trampled into the ground. My only crime was to believe I could trust Yarrick in the first place.

The two men beside him grab my arms, one on either side and pull me to my feet. In a kind of odd six-legged walk, we make our way to the huts in the far corner, entering the first one. There are four in total. Inside, it is little more than a box room, but I can see that the basics have been considered. There is a bed, a sink and a screened-off area, which I presume has some kind of toilet facility. The only other item of furniture is a battered tallboy containing both hanging space and drawers. The hut is dark inside and musty, the floor bereft of anything save dust, and the only window which affords a view of the square is small and dirty. Above me, attached to the ceiling, is an ancient fan which whirs ineffectually. I don't see any provisions, food or a place to cook. There is nowhere to sit except for the bed, onto which I am now pushed. I perch on the edge, looking around me as the two men step back, making room for Yarrick.

"You will stay here," he says unnecessarily. It's not like I have options. "Food will be brought. And ..." he pauses, swallows, and for that split second, I see the old Yarrick, the one who purported to care. But it is fleeting. He raises his eyes back to mine. "And..." he continues, "you will be visited by members of our community. Each of them will have a request. These are the requests you must comply with in order to leave here."

I look at the two men hiding in Yarrick's shadow. They have remained mute, but they don't need to speak. The excitement in their eyes is barely disguised.

When Yarrick first mentioned 'requests' and 'services', I had no idea what he was referring to. Given the way this island works, I guess I figured I would be required to sew, garden … all the things I did anyway, but from a more restricted place. Somewhere that my output could be monitored. Somewhere that I would be isolated, a punishment for … well, what? Asking to leave?

Yet, as I watch these two men, see their features become increasingly animated and witness their lascivious smiles, the penny drops. But it doesn't simply drop; it plummets from a great height and settles in the pit of my stomach with a pain I have never before experienced.

Now I know what Yarrick meant. Now I understand what 'services' I will be required to perform, and any minute amount of remaining trust that I had for these people evaporates. I am to be a slave to the men. This I know. And I will be a slave to anything they want and need.

I look once more at Yarrick, my eyes pleading, begging him to tell me it's not real, that this is all some kind of sick entertainment and that I will return to the colourful room and my life on Añaposta Island - the one I had come to enjoy - almost - before I asked about leaving.

But I get no such reassurance. The warm face has gone, and in its place is a visage carved from granite. I close my eyes. Try to ward off the bile which is rising from my belly, but I cannot. I lean to the side and retch, emptying my stomach at Yarrick's feet.

He jumps to the side, an inelegant and clumsy movement and if I didn't feel so nauseous, so disgusted, so used, I would have laughed. But I don't. I remain where I am. Head bowed, looking at the dust on the floor, listening to the whir of the useless fan above my head, fighting against another wave of sickness, trying to process what is going on. I don't understand how it has come to this. How in such a short space of time - a matter of hours - I have been removed from all that I knew and placed here at the whim of whomever Yarrick decides. And more than processing the sudden change in my circumstances, I am struggling with a realisation. One that I believed I would never again need to face.

I have broken my promise to myself.

On that fateful night when everything I loved and held dear was wrenched from my heart, when I jumped into those swirling waters from the deck of the *Cassiopeia*, I promised myself that I would never trust another person again.

I broke that promise, and now it is coming back to haunt me. I believed in Yarrick, and he has shown me how misplaced that belief was. He became my substitute father, and as such, I afforded him that level of loyalty. I got complacent.

I am again, it would seem, expected to pay the price.

PRESENT DAY

Now that I have agreed to stay, I need to find out what this actually means. Though I try, I cannot help but remember those last few days on Añaposta Island, and I pray that Rich, however much I distrust him, does not have similar in mind.

Whilst I am very happy to remain invisible and, arguably, care little for myself, that does not mean I wish others to share that sentiment.

Some of my values have remained, and having had those challenged since Alex on numerous occasions, I am certain that I do not wish to have these breached again. In short, I want peace. I don't want to be accountable to anyone, and I sure as hell don't want to become a plaything.

Our strange little family, me, Astrid and Rex, have returned to our beds. Astrid is dozing, Rex too, but I am awake, staring at the vaulted ceiling above. It is huge. Cavernous almost, and for a moment, I entertain myself, allowing my imagination to picture what it would have been like when it was a warehouse bustling with life. And I wonder why they never installed a mezzanine floor. It would have made so much more sense, and there would certainly have been more than enough room. Perhaps mezzanine floors didn't exist when this was built, but no, of course, they did. It's not like an additional half floor is a modern invention.

I think I would like to have lived a hundred years ago. I know that women faced hardship, as did the men, and there were no modern comforts like washing machines, but hey, that's life on the streets right there. It often feels like those times were much simpler. Women did one thing, men another. No confusion. No judgement. In my old life, all I knew was judgement. Despite being rich beyond imagination, I lived a life of constant evaluation. Did I speak right? Was I wearing the right clothes? Did I mix in the right circles? Was I seen in the right places ... on and on it went. And yet, no one ever claimed to be the person who decided what 'right' was. How did anyone know what was 'right' when it was so subjective? I never understood who made those unwritten rules and why we all followed them like sheep. That's why I think living in a simpler time would have suited me better. Though I am sure I would still have had questions. Or would I? Who knows.

A movement to my right alerts me to the approaching Rich. He's left me alone for all of five minutes, I knew it was too good to be true. Wearily, I sit up and wait for him to arrive.

He looks at my face and immediately begins laughing.

"Ra," he says, "Ra Ra Ra Ra Ra...."

He's still laughing, and I have no idea why. What I do know is that he has very effectively reminded me of a dubious eighties fashion - the Ra-Ra skirt - and the never-ending debate (according to my mum) about whether it should comprise two or three layers. She never told me what the 'right' answer was, and, given I have never had cause to wear one, it's one of those nuggets I've buried. Until now.

"You look like you're on death row," he says, "like I'm about to ask what you'd like for your last meal."

"Burger and chips," I say smartly, "but make sure it's crucified."

He laughs again. "Like our Lord?"

I roll my eyes and ignore that comment. Maybe 'crucified' was the wrong word choice but back in the day, when I got to choose how I liked my meat cooked, 'crucified' worked. I usually got the desired result.

"Do you believe?" he asks, "In God?"

"Fuck no," I reply. "Look at where I am. If there was really someone looking out for me, do you think he'd have me living like this?"

Rich shrugs. "It depends. Just because you find yourself in less-than-ideal circumstances doesn't mean there isn't a God. Sometimes, we make our own luck."

I look at him, my stare withering. Has he really just said that? What planet does he live on? Certainly not the same one as me. I can absolutely confirm that I had nothing to do with the luck that sees me in my current situation. That happened at the hands of a man. A sick man.

Someone who was supposed to love me.

"Well, maybe that's true for you," I respond, "but in my experience, luck doesn't exist either."

He moves closer. I am still seated, he is standing, hovering over me. It makes me feel uncomfortable, and he knows it.

"Come with me," he says, "to the office."

I glance down at Rex. He is sound asleep. Snoring again. A few metres away, Astrid stirs, mutters something and then curls back up into a tight ball.

"Come on," he encourages, more softly this time, "let's leave them to rest."

I sigh and rise to my feet. Follow him the fifty-five steps from my bed to his office. I am beginning to hate this room and I sure as hell hate those bloody metal chairs.

"You need to get something better than these," I say.

Rich turns. He is ahead of me and assumes I will have followed him. "Better than what?" he asks as he sits in his oh-so-comfy faux leather swivel chair.

"These metal contraptions." I kick at the one in which I am about to place my derriere. "I may as well be on death row."

He smiles, showing two rows of perfect white teeth—teeth I noticed yesterday—teeth that confused me in their evenness. I didn't think Rich deserved to have even white teeth. Maybe they were fake. For some reason, the thought of him having false teeth because all of his own had rotted and departed his mouth is cheering.

"For someone who doesn't have many options, you have a truck load of opinions," he says mildly.

I look at him. The distance between us is the same as ever.

We are on either side of his desk. He has pulled his chair in close, and I have moved mine away. If I push it a tiny bit more, my chair will hit the wall and doorway, effectively blocking my escape or anyone else's entrance. I won't go that far.

"You wanted someone with an opinion yesterday," I reply. "Isn't that why I'm still here?"

Rich inclines his head, regarding me as if he doesn't quite know what to do with me.

"You're here because you can be of use," he responds, "but whether or not that gives you license to have an opinion ... we'll see."

I shake my head. "Whatever."

His eyes pierce into mine. "Why are you so difficult?" he asks. "I am giving you everything that many in your situation would literally kill to have."

"You don't have to. I never asked for this. If you've changed your mind I'm good with that. Rex and I will leave. I'd rather be alone than beholden to someone like you anyway." I stand. I know that my attitude stinks. Rich is right; he's giving me - and Rex - a lifeline for which I should be bloody grateful, yet for some reason, I can't get past the fact that he really gets under my skin. It's not that he makes my skin crawl, and it's not that he's repulsive - I am emotionally mature enough to admit he is attractive - but there is just something I can't get past.

I think maybe he frightens me. Perhaps he reminds me of two men whom I trusted in the past—the two reasons why I am where I am today. Perhaps it's because he is the first person in a very long time who might actually see me—not the surface me, not the outer shell, not the worn clothes, but me inside—the person who I truly am—or was. Aurora. Does Rich see Aurora? Is that my problem?

"Fuck's sake, Ra," Rich almost bellows as he too stands. "I am this close to doing precisely what you want me to and kicking you out there again. I thought we were getting somewhere, but you know what, fuck you. You're not that special. I don't know what the fuck I was thinking. I'm done." He throws his hands in the air, and I watch, transfixed.

In my previous life, no one ever challenged me; in my interim life (for that's how I compartmentalise Clarice and Yarrick), no one ever challenged me, and in my current life, it's set in stone that no one challenges me - because no one gives a damn. It's an odd feeling which develops into a curious reaction. Suddenly, I want to be special. I want to matter. I want to be important. I want to move beyond the mind-numbing existence I have courted for so long. I take a deep breath and look directly into his eyes. He has remained standing, hands braced on his desk, barely disguised anger cutting across his features.

"I'm sorry," I say, and Rich frowns.

"Fuck off."

"No, I mean it." I once more take a seat in that bloody metal chair. "I am sorry. I have no excuse except that I'm not used to people helping me."

Rich watches me for a moment as if trying to decide what to do, whether or not to believe me. I get it. I understand his hesitation. I don't even know if I believe me, so alien is the concept of allowing someone to help. Eventually he shakes his head and blows out a breath.

"You," he says, wagging his finger at me as if chastising a child, "are trouble."

I shrug as he sits back down.

"I don't mean to be," I offer, "it's just ... I don't know. Trust issues. Even though that's such a cliche. Apart from my family, I've trusted a total of two men in my life and look where I ended up."

Shit. I've just given the man more of my life story in those last two sentences than I have revealed to anyone since Alex. I dip my head, shaking it from side to side. Damn. Damn. Damn. I do not want this man to have any power over me, and yet, with little effort, he has me talking. How the fuck did that happen?

Predictably, Rich hasn't missed a thing. "Family? You have a family?"

Again, I shake my head in frustration. Though I have decided to be cordial and accept the help he is offering, I need to pull back here. I need to make sure nothing else gets through the net. I resort to sarcasm. Sarcasm I am safe with.

"Don't we all? I mean, no one has actually arrived on this Earth through immaculate conception. Well, apart from our Lord, of course."

Rich gives me a sideways glance. "And she's back," he says smartly. "Ra is back in the room."

I feign nonchalance.

"I knew it was too good to be true," he continues, "that you might - just might - open up to me."

"I don't open up to anyone," I say. "Ignore what I said. It's not important. You've made me an offer, and I am going to stay. For now. Let's start from there."

He nods. Slowly. His eyes are moving across my face,

connecting with every feature they can. Searching. What for? More clues.

"I'm not that interesting," I add hastily, as I feel the pressure of his intense gaze, "I'm like every single other person out there. I got dealt a shitty hand, and the streets are my home. End of."

Rich smiles, but it doesn't quite reach his eyes.

"No, you're not, Ra," he says, "you're different. And I don't care how long it takes to find out why."

I snap my head up in surprise.

"I mean it. I will find out who you are."

I take a deep breath. I have no idea whether that is a threat or a promise. A good thing or bad. He won't find Aurora. He can't. There are no traces left. Nothing to link me to her. Nothing left of my past life.

But what if there is? What if someone like Rich takes enough of an interest and starts digging? What then?

All I know is that I don't want to find out.

Aurora is dead and will remain so until I am ready.

Then, and only then, will she be unclothed.

Chapter Eight

PRESENT DAY

As much as I love Astrid, her incessant jingling is beginning to get on my last nerve. Since leaving Rich's office, my duties have been outlined by another one of his 'people', and Astrid has volunteered to help. To begin with, I have been assigned cleaning duties. In my previous life, I would not have been caught dead doing any form of manual work, but my time on Añaposta Island made me realise that not everyone lives such a pampered existence. Cleaning was a daily task there, helping Clarice - but I cannot think of Clarice. Not now.

At present, Astrid and I are on our knees in the showers, scrubbing out the drainage trays. The repetitive action is causing Astrid to jingle non-stop. I want to scream. I want to tell her to go away. I want to tell her that I need some mental peace. I need to think. To figure out what is going on with Rich and why he is so keen for me to stay. And I can't do that with a poor man's Santa next to me. But I say nothing to Astrid. She is the reason I have survived this long. I can't be cruel. Not to her.

"Do you think we'll get to stay longer?" she asks innocently. She has no idea how awful my thoughts were. "I mean, did Rich say we could if we do these jobs and stuff?"

I turn to the side. Her face is red with exertion, but her eyes are sparkling. She is happy. So fucking happy.

"I don't know, honestly. He didn't really say much."

"But why us?" she asks.

Technically, it was just me. To my knowledge, Astrid has not been invited to stay. She is here because I told Rich it was non-negotiable. She (and Rex) are part of the package. But I haven't told Astrid that. She doesn't need to know.

I shrug. "Maybe they don't get too many fit people here," I say. Astrid lets out a loud snort, and it is only then I realise there are two ways that comment could be interpreted. "Physically fit," I clarify, but that just causes her to laugh louder.

"Hey, what's going on in there, you two?" It's Colin, standing outside. I know this because I recognise his voice. Coffee Man. He has been one of the only people to talk nice to me since I became a street dweller.

"We're on our knees," calls Astrid and promptly laughs some more. This time, though, it is definitely dirty. I imagine Colin outside the door, red-faced. Or maybe not. Perhaps he's a bit of a go-er. I have no idea and even less comprehension of why my mind has gone in this particular direction.

"Okay," Colin responds. His voice sounds unnaturally high-pitched. Astrid and I exchange knowing glances. Clearly not a go-er. "Come and find me when you're done," he finishes. His light steps walk away, and it is not until I can no longer hear them that I risk another glance at Astrid. She has her hand stuffed into her mouth, trying to stifle any laughter that might unwittingly escape.

"You like him," I observe.

Astrid collects herself and then shrugs. "Maybe."

I smile.

We continue our cleaning in jingling, nerve-challenging silence.

"If I did like him," Astrid says after a moment, "It would be pointless. Right?"

I'm not sure what she wants me to say. It's not like I'm an expert.

"I don't know," I shrug. "Maybe. But then maybe not. He's a nice guy. He could be someone to build a life with. He could get you off the streets, you know."

Astrid has stopped scrubbing and is watching me closely. "I've kind of got used to this life, I never imagined there being an alternative. Do you really think there is? A different kind of life, I mean."

"Of course there is. It's just down to luck if we find it or not, I suppose. I've never really thought about it, but I guess finding a partner who could help you out ... yeah, it might work."

Astrid sighs and picks up the bleach. Neither of us knew what quantity of the offensive substance to use. Me, because on Añaposta Island we used only natural plant solutions, and Astrid because, well, bleach on the streets is not applied to dirty shower trays. I feel a stonking headache forming, which tells me we used too much.

"Have you finished?" I ask, and she nods.

We started cleaning one shower unit each but then realised it was quicker to do it together - one bleaching the tray, the other cleaning the floor - so we settled on screwing both of our bony asses into one of the cubicles at a time.

We've nearly finished. One more to go.

Collecting the various tools of our current trade, we make our way out of the last but one cubicle and enter the final unit. It's my turn to clean the shower tray, so Astrid hands me the bleach. My head is really pounding. The last thing I need is to inhale more of the disgusting stuff, but a gentle scratching followed by a soft whine outside the door reminds me I now have a dependant. I have to keep going and do whatever it is that Rich requires next. For Rex and Astrid. I have no choice. Not if we want to stay here for a while longer. I empty a dollop of the gloopy liquid into the tray and watch as it slowly descends towards the drain, assisted by the forces of gravity. A streaky white line is left in its wake, which shows how often this activity has been done before. Possibly never. Though the showers were clean and tidy - as per my heavenly experience last night - I can tell that it's been a long time since they were properly cleaned. The fact that Astrid had to break the seal on the bottle of bleach merely confirmed this.

"Do you think he likes me?" Astrid asks. It comes out of the blue, and I have to rewind my brain for a moment to get back on the same page.

"I have no idea," I reply. "I don't know him, so what he does and doesn't like is beyond me." I realise that sounds snarky. "I can't imagine he wouldn't, though," I add hastily - Astrid doesn't need to pay for my rotten headache and the demands of Rich - "he'd be a fool if he didn't."

Astrid laughs. It's a pretty sound. Light and delicate. It occurs to me that I've never heard her laugh in such a feminine way before. We have been here for less than twenty-four hours, yet I can see the change it has made to this beautiful woman already. It's like she's glowing. A lamp has been lit inside of her, and though some of that may have to do with Coffee Man, I'm sure it is mostly because she feels safe. She's relaxed. She's let her guard down. And that is something we just never do on the streets.

"I hope we never have to leave," she states with authority, and I laugh. She sounds like a petulant child. "What?" she frowns at me.

"You. You're like a kid at Christmas." What is it with me and Christmas right now? For heaven's sake.

"And what's wrong with that?" she sticks out her tongue in defiance. For a moment, I see her—baby Astrid, toddler Astrid, and teenager Astrid—and wonder, not for the first time, what her story is.

"How come you ended up on the streets?" I ask. In the back of my mind, I realise I've broken an unwritten rule, a code of the streets if you like. We don't ask. It's easier not to. Many of us have complicated stories, and some of us have no idea how our luck turned sour, so we don't ask. We greet each other the same. We have no pretence of class, wealth or standing. We are one class. One standing. A cohesive group. It's a place where you can both belong and be an outcast. It's a strange and frightening world. But I do still remember that time before *Cassiopeia*. My life was frightening then, too, though in a very different way.

Astrid has stilled. I can't tell if she is angry that I've asked or is considering her answer.

"My dad," she says at last, eyes downcast, "he left us, me and my mum. I was twelve. No idea where he went or what happened. Left the house to buy ciggies and never came back. Mum thought he was dead, but he never turned up anywhere, so we lost everything. Mum didn't have enough to support us, and at the time, we were over here illegally - she and Dad never married - so we couldn't claim anything.

She took an overdose, and the streets became my home."

"Shit," I say softly.

Astrid looks up. Unshed tears are glistening in her eyes. "I don't tell that story," she says, "because it's so bloody rubbish to realise I've spent half my life in this joke of a world on those god-awful streets out there. No parents. No way to prove I'm English, so I can't be anything different. This is it for me."

She sighs, and I am once more struck by her beauty.

"I shouldn't have asked. I'm sorry."

Astrid shakes her head. "I didn't have to tell you." But sorrow has settled over her, and I regret opening my mouth. It's like being in here, this 'safe house', messes with your head. Like you start to feel, well, safe, and so you drop your defences. That's what led me to open my mouth, and I'm certain that's why Astrid told her story. I don't know if being here is a good thing. I can't afford to let anyone know my story. Not yet. I have to keep my defences in place because I cannot trust. I made that promise a long time ago. Perhaps, one day, I will be able to, but before that, before I can even think about revealing the truth - even to Astrid - I have to know one thing.

I have to know if Alex is still alive.

TWO YEARS EARLIER

Despite its auspicious appearance, the bed in my new 'home' is remarkably comfortable, and I find myself resting well. There is little else to do. It has been a while since Yarrick and the two men left me here, followed by the women who filed behind them in one straight line, heads bowed, as if apologising for their existence. I still don't understand what this place is. It is bizarre, some kind of dystopia. It has to be. Clarice surprised me the most. I thought her to be strong, kind and loving, yet she appeared to bow easily to the men. I have never seen anything like it - apart from in movies. My mind searches its memory banks. Movies. Movies where I have watched something similar to this. Movies that portrayed an alternate world playing out alongside the true universe. Or perhaps there is more than one universe, each running parallel, their timelines in tandem.

I shake my head. The power Yarrick appears to yield is baffling, yet no one appears bothered. They go about their business every single day ... a sense of unease settles in my gut. I feel like I am missing something, but I can't reach its message. The only time I ever encountered a different 'world' was back in school when I was fifteen, and it is a time I will never forget.

For that was when I lost my best friend, Jayde.

Jayde was lovely. Willowy, tall for her age, stunning in a way that made boys stare - even at our private school. Though I had developed breasts early, they looked lumpy and out of place, yet Jayde's burgeoning assets were perfect. In proportion with the rest of her body. I don't mind admitting I became a little obsessed with Jayde the older we got to the point where I wondered if I might be gay. Not that it mattered, but it wasn't a conversation I relished having with my parents. They were closed-minded and 'old school' on a good day.

Jayde had this way about her, though, which made people stop. If we were together, then I would simply fade into the background, and I was okay with this. She exuded a kind of mystique that had everyone around her hooked, yet she chose me to be her friend - something I never really understood. The cynic in me decided it was because I was plain, dumpy, and nothing special, which made her light shine brighter, but the closer we became, the more I realised I was being unfair. Jayde loved me, and once I stopped questioning why, she became the most precious person in the world to me. The sister I didn't have. The beauty I could never be. The cool person who got invited to every single party. Jayde became my world.

Until one day, she simply disappeared.

The police were called. We were all questioned endlessly. Me more so than others, but I couldn't tell them anything. Jayde had never so much as hinted at a plan to leave, to run away from home - if that was what she had done. The night before she disappeared, we'd been out on the playing field, sitting in swings that were far too small for our teenage figures. We'd been laughing and making plans for our future. Where we would go to college, what we would do for university, what career we would have and who we would marry. There had been nothing at all to alert me to what was about to unfold.

At first, the police thought she had been abducted, and our town went into literal lockdown. The girls were told to stay at home until the authorities knew more. It was an odd kind of break from school. On the one hand, I enjoyed the lack of work, the freedom, and the fact I didn't need to get out of bed unless I absolutely had to, but the pain of missing Jayde tore at my heart. She was like the other half of me, and I knew I would never meet anyone as special as her again.

I was worried, scared, frightened, fearful of what had happened to her. With her phone switched off and no answers forthcoming, I felt myself spiral into a depression that I knew only Jayde could pull me out of. The police barely left me alone. Questioning me. Convinced I must know something. Her parents visited and implored me to give up her secret, but I could not. Because I simply didn't know. I was as much in the dark as anyone else. I prayed every minute of every day for news. Prayed that my beautiful friend was still alive.

The local schools came together to deliver an assembly, a reminder of 'stranger danger', cementing the fear that Jayde had fallen victim to foul play. This never happened in our quiet and wealthy suburb. We were not supposed to simply 'disappear'; it was beyond comprehension, and as the days without word dragged by, so my depression deepened.

It was six months of hell later when we finally heard the news. Jayde had been found. She was alive and well. I was barely able to contain my excitement, wanting so badly to be with my friend once more. To feel whole again. To finally climb out of the negativity.

But then we were given the full story.

Jayde had become a victim, but not of a murderer - of a manipulator. Someone who had preyed on her and promised a better life and higher purpose if she joined the others in his care. It was the first time I ever heard the word 'cult'. It was, we were told, a place where young girls like Jayde were persuaded to go with the promise of love, beauty and a meaningful existence. After tracking her down, efforts were made to retrieve her but Jayde had 'joined' of her own free will. Her parents intervened; she was, after all, only fifteen years old, but in a bewildering turn of events, they agreed she could stay. Her parents gave her actual permission to continue her chosen new life. She was fifteen years old! Who knows what the hell they want at fifteen?

I had many arguments with mum. I couldn't understand how any parent could choose to give up their child without a fight, but mum continued to reassure me that Jayde was fine. Her parents had met with her. She was doing well, flourishing, happy. And ultimately, mum said, that was all any parent ever wanted for their child—happiness.

I didn't know much, but what I did know was that it was all shades of screwed up. And I had lost my best friend in the world. My precious Jayde. I never heard from her again. One day, she was my everything, and the next, she was gone. It was as simple and complicated as that.

In later life I would think of Jayde. She had meant so much to me, and I knew I would always hold our memories close to my heart, realising I had been truly blessed to have been her 'person', even if only for the briefest of times. She was a beautiful soul. Her innocence taken by manipulators. As I grew into womanhood, I prayed for Jayde. I prayed that she had chosen well.

I prayed that she was happy.

I rise from the bed and look out into the large courtyard beyond. It reminds me of a prison - I suspect this is what it used to be. Either that or a military base, perhaps. The yard is covered in dust, and I watch as a breeze lifts some of it, re-distributing it, changing the basic layer and foundation. I don't know how long I have been in this room. When Yarrick and the others left, it was light, and the sun was high in the sky. Now, it is setting over the horizon, so I must have been here a good few hours. There is no light inside my new home, no electricity, so I find myself peering through the darkness.

Oddly, I am not afraid. Aurora would have been petrified. She hated the dark. She hated being alone, but Sandy is different. She is Aurora still, but another version.

Sandy is the fierceness within Aurora; she is the woman

who witnessed something no one ever should, and through this, Aurora's wimpish fears and worries have been replaced by a tougher version. Sandy. Sandy who has survived the worst life can throw at her.

I smile as I remember my innocence that night on the *Cassiopeia*. How stupid I had been to believe that my life then wasn't easy. In the months since, I have learned just how protected my life was. How unrealistic it was. How pretentious.

I have taken the lessons I was taught that awful night and have run with them, developed them, and grown into them in order to become Sandy. The yin to Aurora's yang. Sandy knows this world is full of fucked up people, that no one is who they appear to be. She understands we all have stories yet to tell.

I think back to that first night on the beach in the ridiculous pink towel and wonder again why I was spared. Why the hell did I live? I thought maybe God had spared me so that I could return to England and find Alex - if he was alive - and make him pay for what he did. But Sandy no longer believes there is a God. And neither Aurora nor Sandy have a clue why we lived.

The darkness closes in, and I hear voices in the yard. I brace myself. A light dances beneath the gap in the door. I hear a key being inserted, and then a torch illuminates my meagre quarters. It is Yarrick holding the torch. Behind him is another man—one of those who dragged me across the yard. Yarrick smiles at me in the same way he has always done, like a friend or a father, but I now know him to be neither.

They push through the door as the torchlight moves over every surface, every wall until eventually it shines directly into my face. I lift my arm to shield my eyes, which have become accustomed to the dark. This rude introduction of light hurts. Yarrick shoves the man behind him to the fore until he stands over me. I look up and note his features, though I don't bother to catalogue them. I can see no good reason to do so. He is already burned into my memory.

"This is Joseph," Yarrick says, and the man nods. The two share a secret smile and then regard me simultaneously. Studying me as if deciding something.

"Yes," says Joseph. It's the first time he has spoken. He has a drawl and an accent, but not one that is familiar. He is not a man I recognise.

Yarrick nods. "Very good," he says. He places the torch beside me on the bed so that Joseph is now illuminated. I remain still.

The men exchange one final look, and then Yarrick is gone, back through the door, the lock clicking into place behind him.

I raise my eyes. I have yet to move, to speak. Neither man addressed me directly, but I am certain that Joseph is here to collect my first payment.

I am alone in the all-encompassing dark with a man I do not know, but I understand precisely what is about to happen. Though I was well educated, it is not from education that I have drawn this knowledge. It is an instinct. One that has been present ever since I woke up in the earth room.

Bizarrely, I think of Jayde as Joseph approaches, removes his shirt and pushes me back onto the bed.

I lie still. I continue to think of Jayde, and I think of Aurora too. And Alex. I smile, but not in happiness. I am laughing at myself, at my stupidity back then. As Joseph's form causes the bed to dip, I laugh again at Aurora, the spoilt, innocent woman who genuinely believed Alex would be the next man inside her. What the fuck did she know?

Joseph's breath rakes over my cheek, and I turn my head away. I do not wish to look at him, and I do not wish to look at any man in this way again. From now on, I resolve to disconnect all feelings from my physical form. I will have no thoughts or emotions; I will simply exist.

I remain still and allow Joseph to take his payment.

PRESENT DAY

We have finished cleaning the showers and are taking a break in the kitchen. Rex sits predictably at Colin's feet, waiting. We've been given tea and a slice of slightly stale sponge cake. I am probably the only person who will notice it is stale. Most will just be grateful for food. I remind myself that so am I. The cliched days of champagne and caviar are gone. Actually, though caviar was readily available, I cannot say I ever became accustomed to it. Something about it just didn't feel right. I laugh inwardly. Over the last eighteen months, since I have been on the streets, I have ensured to retain only the most useful of memories from my life before. Despite my difficulties in quieting my mind as a teenager, I have become remarkably good at it now. I have discovered that by simply adding more boxes to that shelf inside my head, I have avoided the most painful and gut-wrenching of reminders. Why I have retained a reference to caviar is totally beyond me. Why the fuck am I thinking about caviar?

"How long have you had him?" Colin asks.

I look at my wiry friend. "No idea. A few weeks."

Colin nods. "Did he just attach himself to you?"

"Pretty much. And now he won't leave."

Rex turns his head towards me and lets out a whimper. If a dog could frown or throw shade, I think I just received it.

"Aw, it's okay, boy, she didn't mean it," coos Colin and I shake my head. What is it about babies and animals? As soon as adult humans encounter either, all logic and sensible conversation goes out of our heads, and the tone of our voices raise at least an octave.

"You don't know how lucky you are," says Astrid. It's the first time she's spoken in a while. I think she's been busy studying every plane of Colin's form, ignoring the mundane conversation we are making around her.

"Why's that?" I ask, reaching for another slice of the slightly stale sponge cake.

"At least you have someone." She pouts, which just makes her even more beautiful.

"Astrid," I sigh, "I have a dog that I didn't seek or ask for, and I'm going to be honest here; his conversation sucks almost as much as his breath."

Colin laughs loudly. "I think I know why Rex likes you," he says.

Really?

"You take no prisoners," Coffee Man continues. "You say what you mean, and I think he admires that about you. Maybe he thinks you're his pack leader."

"Or" I counter, "maybe you have taken leave of your senses. Since when did dogs decide which human they were going to attach themselves to based on their resemblance to a 'pack leader'? Their needs are simple. Something to eat. Somewhere to shit. Somewhere to sleep. Boom."

"Like us," Astrid says as she laughs along with Colin. They exchange a glance. In Astrid's face, I see barely concealed attraction, but Colin's face is closed. Interesting.

"What's next?" she asks, her question directed at Coffee Man.

He shakes his head. "I have no idea. Did Rich give you any more jobs?"

"No," I reply.

"I can help you here," Astrid offers as she moves a little closer to Colin, shimmying her luscious limbs along the side of the kitchen counter in his direction. We are still wearing the new clothes we were given yesterday. After our cleaning activities, mine are no longer clean, and I know that I smell. I could do with using one of those lovely sparkling showers right about now. Astrid, on the other hand, looks serene. She's one of those people I used to love to hate back when I could afford to have opinions. Every day, I've seen her at her worst, and yet she's always so ... put together. We are wearing little more than prison uniform, but she exudes beauty in the same way I exude sweat. We are the epitome of beauty and the beast.

"Sure," Colin says good-naturedly. He makes a show of getting Astrid an apron and a hair net - like the ones my grandmother used to wear - and she giggles prettily as they struggle to tame her mass of curls. I watch their interaction, surprised to feel a bolt of sadness settle in my belly. She is making no secret of her desire for Colin, and I am worried I may lose her. I've realised over the last twenty-four hours how important she is to me, and I want to keep her all to myself. Selfish. I know.

Interestingly though, Colin is being less obvious. His body language is distant, and I am not sure if that's because he doesn't feel the same attraction or because he's playing it cool. Living on the streets is definitely not the best environment for romance, so it is fair to say that both Astrid and I are rusty when it comes to the opposite sex. It's highly likely that I am reading the situation completely wrong. Why would he not be attracted to Astrid? I mean, if I swung the other way, then damn, I would be.

A repetitive click-clack alerts me to Rex moving in my direction. He sits at my feet, head tilted to one side as if asking a question. On the basis that he now has food, shelter, and somewhere to shit (there's a small garden outside Colin has taken him to), I have absolutely no idea what he could be asking for. Absently, I reach down and stroke his head. I wasn't being serious when I moaned about him not leaving. Not really. I've kind of got used to having him around now, and Astrid is right; at least I do have someone. Even if that someone is a canine with no grasp of the English language.

I look around the kitchen, wondering what is next. What should I be doing? Should I go and ask Rich?

I shudder. No. No fucking way. I'm not his slave, and if he wants me to do something, he's perfectly capable of finding me himself. This whole 'needing someone with an education still feels off, and yes, maybe a little suspicious. I get what this place is, and I get Rich's role here, but he doesn't need me especially. That is just Rich shaped crap.

I raise my head and connect once more with the duo that is Colin and Astrid. They have their backs to me as they fiddle with something at the stove, neither seemingly aware that I am still here. Rex whimpers once more, so I decide to take my leave. A rest in my lovely, comfy lavender-scented bed sounds good, and unless Rich appears to tell me differently, that's exactly what I'm going to do.

As I turn to leave, I feel the heat of someone's gaze watching me. I look up. It's Colin. Though I figured he and Astrid were in their own little bubble, I was wrong. She is chattering away, laughing, moving ever closer to his side, but Colin is frozen. Almost statue-like, and his gaze is boring deep into mine. I blink, then open my eyes once more. He is still watching me. We shared a moment earlier when he told me his story, when he opened up about his past and his parents, and I wonder if he thinks I owe him some kind of explanation of my own. Why else would he be looking at me so intently? I dip my eyebrows in a slight frown, which causes Coffee Man to smile. And it is then that I am able to interpret his unspoken message. I am seeing what I failed to see earlier when he was looking at Astrid. It's there in the glittery depths of his gaze and in the slight flush to his cheeks.

Colin is looking at me with desire.

Me.

What the actual fuck?

≈≈≈≈

"Ra?" Whatever was about to be said or communicated is immediately gone as the familiar and unwelcome voice of Rich drifts into the kitchen. Great. He has come to find me. That's just peachy.

I feel the atmosphere shift. When it had been just the three of us (well, four if you count Rex), we'd laughed, made conversation, everything light-hearted and jovial, yet as soon as Rich entered the kitchen, everything changed. I note with interest that Colin's face suddenly becomes closed, guarded and I wonder at its reason. Maybe I am not the only one with reservations about Saint Rich. A split second later it is gone, replaced with a warm smile which covers Colin's mouth as he greets the other man. The myriad of emotions that have chased across Coffee Man's face in the last few seconds tell me there is a hell of a lot more to Colin than coffee and skateboards.

"How did you get on with the showers?" Rich asks, his steps coming to rest two paces away from my side. Even though he is still just behind me, I know he is looking directly at me. It's not hard to fathom, for I instantly feel the discomfort that always seems to accompany Rich's presence.

"All done," I say.

I hear his steps moving around to the side, and then he's there, in front of me, blocking my view of Colin and Astrid.

"I have some other tasks," he says. "Shall we go to the office so that I can go over them with you?"

I shrug. "Whatever."

Rich sighs. "I thought we had an agreement," he says. "I thought you were going to be less prickly, more... obliging."

"I have no idea why you thought that" I respond with a smirk. I can't help it. I know I am risking mine and Astrid's place here, but this man just gets to me in a way I can't explain.

He moves closer. The toes of our feet are almost touching, and I smell minty breath as he speaks softly into the tiny gap between us. "It's not just about you," he says, inclining his head towards Astrid. I don't know why he feels the need to stand so close. Astrid is that wrapped up in Colin it would take a meteor to bring her back to Earth.

I raise my head, chin tilted in defiance. "I am well aware of that fact," I respond, my tone measured. "As you must also be aware, that is the only reason I am still here." I want to say, 'fuck you,' but I don't.

Rich closes what is left of the gap, invading my personal space in a way I have not allowed for a very long time. I want to step back. I want to break the contact. I want to get out of his orbit, but I know that is what he is looking for. The reaction he craves. He wants to make me uncomfortable. He wants to assert his authority. I will not let that happen. His dark eyes penetrate mine, and I match him stare for stare. Later, I will reflect on how bold a move he is making, being this close to me in full view of both Astrid and Colin, but for now, I am held by his gaze. Watching his eyes as they change. His pupils dilate. We remain in this kind of odd stand-off for what feels like hours, but in reality is only seconds. I don't know why we are doing this. I don't know why he is standing close enough for me to feel the warmth radiating off his body. I don't know what message his eyes are trying to communicate, and I don't know why I am allowing him to maintain his presence in my bodily sanctuary.

"You and I," he whispers, the words falling softly across my left cheek, "you and I will be friends."

It sounds like both a threat and a promise. With a final suspended gaze, he spins on his heel and walks away.

I watch. Counting every step he takes as he leaves the kitchen. I release the breath I had been holding in fear. But fear of what?

Because, though I hate to acknowledge it, I realise I am not frightened of Rich. Far from it.

Inexplicably, I am sexually aroused.

Chapter Nine

TWENTY-TWO MONTHS EARLIER

I have been in my weird prison-like cell for a total of sixty days. I know this because I have counted each and every miserable one. I would like to say that I have become accustomed to it, but I would be lying. I have not. I am in a place of tolerance because there is no other choice available.

My existence is that of an inmate. Every morning, one of the women arrives with a bowl of hot wash water and some foul-smelling soap. After 'freshening up', I am released from my confines into the heat of the dusty yard, where I am made to walk around in a circle for twenty minutes. I cannot deviate from this circle, and I must walk clockwise. I have no idea why. I tried something different once. It was a day when one of the younger women had come to my cell and I figured she'd be none the wiser if I changed it up a bit. So I walked the other way, even squaring the corners so it became a rectangle instead. She didn't say anything, and I congratulated myself on a small victory. I was not, though, a victor for long. That night I was visited by Yarrick - which was a rare occurrence. He spent no time on niceties, and as he left, he pointed at the yard, warning me not to break the rules again. Next time, he'd said with a definite hint of menace, would be a lot worse.

When I had made my first 'payment' to Joseph sixty days ago, I could not have conceived that I would still be here now. Initially, I was visited by three of the men, each a day apart. They seemed as uncomfortable as me and simply went about their business, doing what was necessary, before leaving as quietly as they arrived. None of them were rough. None of them spoke. They simply took what they came for without preamble. After that first week, the visits increased, such that I am now required to make a 'payment' every day. The only time I am allowed respite is during my monthly cycle - days which I have grown to love. It is odd how a routine bodily function that I had given scarce thought to before is such a beacon of hope and joy.

You may wonder why I am so emotionless. Why I seem okay with what is happening and to be honest, I have wondered that too. I wasn't at first. I screamed, kicked at the locked door, scratched at the window frame, shouted obscenities to the silent night sky, and called for Clarice ... but nothing happened. The routine continued every day in exactly the same way. It didn't matter what I tried; I remain locked in this room for twenty-three hours and forty minutes of every day. Meagre rations are delivered at the same time as the wash water and foul-smelling soap. I see no one then until it is time for the debt collector to arrive.

I asked the women questions to start with as they gently soaped my worn and ever-thinning frame. Who they were. Why I was here. What the hell was this place. But they never answered. Nor did they meet my gaze. In the same way as the men, they did what they had to do, and then they left. To date, Clarice has not been one of the women, and I wonder at her role in all of this. She warned me that I shouldn't have asked to go home, but she was the one who spiked my tea. Was she as demented as Yarrick? For that is how I think of him now. Demented.

It was halfway through the second week when Yarrick first returned. The momentary relief I experienced evaporated instantly when he came to sit beside me on the bed. For a split second, I'd allowed myself the hope of rescue, of freedom, but as soon as he began to speak, I was rapidly disabused of such thoughts. He explained patiently, as if to a small child, that if I wanted to leave Añaposta Island and return to England, I needed to stay here. No one was going to hurt me, he said, but they had to put several things in place, and the men who could do those things didn't work for free. He had talked so calmly and so rationally that in my sixty-days-in-captivity-semi-delirious state, I had almost considered him to be speaking sense. Currency, he'd said, comes in many forms.

He hadn't touched me that night. Not in the way the other men had. He'd hugged me close to him, but I had remained stiff and unwelcoming. How he could expect reciprocal warmth was beyond me. This was not the Yarrick I knew. Not the same man who had found me on the beach and given me a safe and loving home. This person was a stranger. Someone who held some kind of power over the women here. I prayed daily for Clarice, for her to come and help, to give me some answers, but she never came.

I can be so emotionless now simply because I have ceased to feel. I am just a vessel. A body that is used for the needs of others and from which my soul has become detached. I realise there is no escape, that there are no answers, so I must find a way to survive. Though why I am so determined to survive is a mystery. Since boarding the *Cassiopeia*, I have been hurt and betrayed by people I believed to care.

For a time, I allowed myself to open up a little. To let Yarrick and Clarice nurture me and show me there was good in the world.

I had even begun to think of them as family and the upside-down shack my home, with its rickety stairs and strange colourful patterns on the wall.

Yet here I am, deceived again. Fooled into thinking there could be a life after Alex.

And so, it is sixty days later. I am walking around the yard as a young woman watches. I am continuing the same torturous existence day after day. My mind has long since departed from sanity. I cannot remember the last time I spoke aloud. I am accompanied only by my own thoughts, which, as the days go by, are less and less.

Often, my mind is empty. Devoid of conscious deliberation. I have gone into hibernation, I think. Though I am still awake. It's strange what effect enforced incarceration has on a human. At first, it is frightening, deeply so. Every noise bred fear as I watched out of the small, grimy window. With no other option, I would sit huddled on the end of my bed, arms tight around my knees until my legs were forced open. Then, after a while, the fear disappeared, and I began to sing to myself. Softly. Quietly. Mostly nursery rhymes and lullabies, remembered from my childhood. Their words filled my brain and I began to live in those times rather than the real world.

The songs became my friends, and I took comfort in their refuge as they transported me back to another, happier time. Then finally came the acceptance and numbness. The realisation that I was not to be released or helped. And this is the stage at which I remain. I am a collection of cells connected by skin and bone, an inhalation of oxygen and an exhalation of carbon dioxide. I am a functioning human, but that is it. There is nothing behind my eyes anymore. I have no substance. It has been sixty long days.

And I am nothing.

PRESENT DAY

I have returned to my lavender-scented bunk and am currently feigning sleep. I know it is working because Astrid has also returned to her bed and made no effort to communicate with me. Occasionally, I let out a small sleepy sigh, just in case she realises I am actually wide awake. To be honest, I don't think I could sleep if you paid me. My interactions with both Colin and Rich are troubling and I wonder if, having spent a good couple of hours in a series of small cubicles inhaling a heady dose of bleach, I may have imagined them.

As I lie here, I am picturing Colin, standing stock still, staring at me with a depth of desire I don't believe I have ever before witnessed. I know it is me that he is looking at because Astrid is beside him, facing the opposite way, and there is no one else in the kitchen. I cannot describe how I feel. It has been so long since anyone desired me. Seeing that flicker in Colin's gaze is not something I can easily comprehend. I wonder, too, at my response. Granted, the moment was mere seconds in length, but I had no reciprocal feedback. My heart jumped a little, but that was all, and perhaps that was simply a visceral reaction to another human's unspoken message.

Since I have been living on the streets, I have enjoyed being invisible for the most part. I needed it when I returned to England. I was damaged, almost beyond repair, and though I still harboured hatred for Alex - for I believe him to be the catalyst in the shit show which has become my life - I could not function in normal society until I had healed from those last few months on Añaposta Island. Sometimes, I wonder if I imagined those too; so unbelievable was the depravity of my existence back then. But I only have to look at the ugly scar zig-zagging across my stomach to know it was real.

The thing that is bothering me more than Colin though, is my encounter with Rich. Up until that moment in the kitchen, he has never breached my personal space. Uncomfortable as it was to have him that close, I am struggling to understand my reaction. The last time I was complicit in any form of arousal was that final day on the yacht when Alex and I stood on the top deck and I watched the setting sun dance off his fine form. During my time with Yarrick and Clarice, that part of me died. At first, because I had no need of it, then latterly, well, I don't need to go there. Thus, my femininity had no need to breathe, and I was good with that. Am good with that. So why the hell did anything remotely physical in the way of a response happen with Rich just then? Jesus.

I have no answers and find I am tired of this status quo. I never seem to have any answers, aside from the need to constantly protect myself, and even that's wearing thin. I still have every intention of finding out what happened to Alex so that he, or someone he loves, pays for what he did, but can I reasonably expect to do that if I am constantly protecting myself? Guarded in every encounter? Reluctant to trust?

Yet again, I have no bloody clue.

≈≈≈≈

One thing I had forgotten to factor in whilst keeping up my pretence of sleeping was that Rex would have no qualms challenging my act. The moment his wet, sloppy tongue connected with my nose, it was game over. I meant what I said earlier, his breath stinks.

I sit up, pushing him to one side as I do so.

"Ugh, that's so gross."

Rex just looks at me with his head on one side, the way he always does, as if butter wouldn't melt.

"Hey, baby girl, you're awake."

"Yeah, no thanks to this lump." I indicate my beloved companion, who has now stretched himself prone across the entire width of the small bunk. On top of me. I can't believe he's still here. The room is full of homeless down and outs. He could have his pick of suckers. Why me? This train of thought brings me up short and reminds me that this innocent dog is not to blame for my reaction to Rich in the kitchen. Before those bizarre few minutes, I had been loving on Rex, thinking that I liked his company. No human, even one as annoying and perplexing as Rich, should change my opinion. I decide to try being nicer to the mutt.

"What you been up to?" I ask Astrid as I try to swing my legs from beneath my canine cocoon.

"Nothing much. Mostly helping Colin in the kitchen. He asked me to come find you but you were asleep so he told me to rest too. He's so kind. And thoughtful. You kept that man quiet, baby girl."

I smile. Astrid's beautiful face has reddened with a not-unattractive blush. If I can forget the look aimed in my direction from the object of her desire, then I can enjoy her happiness. I choose to do both.

"He wasn't really anything to 'keep quiet'," I reply. "It wasn't like we were friends."

"Well, whatever. I am going to give Denver a really nice gift at Christmas for getting us into this place."

I laugh. No one gives Christmas gifts on the streets.

"You know what," I say, "we could go and shop for it in Clifton Arcade, in one of those posh shops. Get it gift-wrapped and everything."

Astrid laughs even more. "Yeah," she responds, "and we could get our hair done too. Maybe buy a new outfit."

Simultaneously, we look down at our second-hand offerings, mine significantly more crumpled than hers, and dissolve into fits of giggles.

"Can you imagine?" I ask in-between gasping for breath. "Us, walking into those shops dressed like this? Even if we had money. It would be like Pretty Woman."

"Pretty Woman?" Astrid frowns, and too late, I remember where I am. Who I am. I am not surprised Astrid doesn't understand the reference, but neither should I. Damn.

"I mean, we'd be far from pretty," I say. Astrid watches my face. Closely. And for a second, I feel an uprising of panic. Has she seen through me? Has my unwitting reference, when my guard was down, led her to questions I have no wish to answer?

She frowns once more. "Don't say that" she comments softly. I risk a glance at her features, surprised to see an unshed tear glistening in her eye. "You *are* pretty. And we will shop like normal people one day. Don't let anyone tell you differently. You are the most beautiful woman I know."

I swallow hard. A lump has formed in my throat. Astrid was not studying my face for signs of duplicity; she was studying my face so that I would believe her when she told me I was beautiful. I feel myself welling up, so I shift to the edge of the bed and reach my hands across the divide between us. Astrid does the same, and our hands meet in the centre.

"Promise me, baby girl," she says softly, "whatever happens

in this screwed-up life, you won't ever let anyone tell you you're not beautiful and that you don't belong someplace. What we look like on the outside - that's just window dressing. It's what's in our hearts that makes us truly special, and I see you, baby girl. You're hurting like most of us out there," she inclines her head towards the window above my bed, "but you have a beautiful soul. don't let anyone take that away from you."

Her wrists jingle as she squeezes my hands, and I realise this is the first time anyone has bothered to care for me in this way. My parents loved me, of course they did, but they were also busy. They never sat with me like this. As an only child, I was forced to rely on the company of staff who were paid to do my every bidding. None of them were emotionally invested in me, and nor should they have been. I guess Clarice was the closest anyone ever came, but even she was never totally free with her emotions. I thought I didn't need this closeness from another human. I believed I was hardened to life. But it turns out I am not. For those few words and simple gestures from Astrid have turned my insides to mush. I do need this, after all. I need human company. I need human love. I need human connection.

Who knew?

I squeeze her hands in return and swallow past the lump in my throat once more. "Right back atcha," I say quietly, and we share a moment so pure, so real, so true that I know we will never lose each other. Not now. In some strange twist of fate, this exquisite being has been thrust into my life, and I finally understand why.

Since Jayde, I have allowed no other female into my emotional space. Once again, I was protecting myself. Or that's what I thought I was doing. In fact, I was doing the exact opposite. I was closing myself off to the good in this world - because there is some. I see that now. Sure, I have been dealt a shit hand, but as I look around this expanse of beds, who hasn't? It isn't about obsessing over the road I have been on; it's about looking for a road that is unchartered. One that may be difficult to navigate but worth every challenging mile.

Damn. I fucking love this woman.

"I love you," I say aloud, surprised that I have spoken my thoughts. But I had to. It felt like the right time, the right moment to share an emotion I have buried so deep for so long.

"I love you too, baby girl."

We squeeze our hands tighter, looking at each other across the short expanse of concrete floor and in that moment, we are both emotionally raw. A single tear drops from Astrid's eye and trickles down her cheek. I don't need to feel the sudden wetness on my face to know that I have wept in answer.

TWENTY MONTHS EARLIER

The days tick by. I am now at one hundred and twenty, though it is getting harder to keep count. Not, I don't think, because the curse of arithmomania is failing me, but more because with each passing minute, hour, and day, I close down further. I cease to exist. The one thing that was constant in its presence has deserted me recently. My body would perform its monthly function with precision timing, yet I have not experienced this for a few weeks.

I expect this to be from the conditions I find myself living in and the stress that is hiding where my heart used to be.

176

My routine remains unchanged. I have no idea how many times I have paid my unwelcome debt, but I am sure it is more than I could ever realistically owe. I am amazed at how calm I remain. It's not as if I have any reason to, and I know that my thoughts are not as seated in reality as they once were, but I have this kind of other-worldly feeling of serenity. Where once I sang nursery rhymes, now I chant prayers and snippets of inspirational quotes inside my head. I know an extreme number of these, courtesy of the hours I used to spend on various social media platforms. Though I would snort in derision every time I read someone's 'thought for the day', I clearly took them in and filed them somewhere in my memory banks. I have no idea if they are useful to remember, but I have little else to fill my days. The Serenity Prayer lingers more so than most. I don't know if I am chanting the exact version as it was originally written, but I continually reiterate that I only have the power to change circumstances within my control. At present, I do not feel there are any circumstances within my control, but it is cathartic to look beyond today and to believe that someday I may once more be free. This interminable nightmare will end - one way or another.

A sound at the door indicates someone arriving, yet it is not the right time for visitors. I tense. Am I to be visited more than once each day now? How much could it possibly cost to get papers in place for me to leave? Surely, I have more than paid my passage.

The key turns in the lock, and a form shuffles in. It is one I have not seen for one hundred and twenty days but one I would recognise anywhere. Clarice. It is all I can do to remain hunched on the bed. I want to throw myself at her, breathe in her squishy scent and beg her for answers, but I cannot. Though it pains me to believe that she is part of whatever the fuck this twisted place and community is, I have to remember she is the one who gave me the drugged tea. She saw to it that my consciousness was taken from me without my knowledge or consent, so I have to consider the very real possibility that she is as deep in this sick ritual as Yarrick.

She closes the door quietly behind her and advances towards the bed. As she stands over me in the gloom, picked out only by the meagre slant of light from the small grimy window, I get to see her up close and am shocked at her appearance. She is nothing of the Clarice I remember. Her hair is unkempt, her eyes deep-seated and ringed with tiredness, her face thin where once it was round and she has lost weight. I want to ask her what the hell happened, but I am careful to keep my surprise hidden. In the few moments when I have allowed myself to remember the good times in the upside-down shack, I have always pictured Clarice exactly as I last saw her: bustling, helping, smiling, laughing, loving. Something has changed in her world, too, since I have been kept prisoner here, and I wonder if she is ill. Perhaps she has fallen prey to some awful disease, which would explain her changed appearance and why I have not seen her until now.

"Hey, Sandy," she says softly.

"Hey."

Her hand reaches towards me and gently touches my hair. I know she means this to be comforting. "I am so sorry for everything," she continues in the same soft tone, "I did try to warn you."

I nod. I have so many questions, but I am not sure Clarice has the answers. Even if she does, I get the impression this is not to be a long visit so I don't want to waste time on conversation with no likely resolution.

"I hope..." she swallows and moves her hand from the top of my head to my cheek. Even though Clarice has changed, she still has the same warm hands, and I find myself nuzzling into her palm. "I hope you've been okay. I haven't stopped thinking about you since that day when I ..." She stops.

"Brought me the tea?" I offer.

"Yes. Since that day."

"Why have you not come before?" I ask.

Clarice shakes her head. "It's complicated. I've - let's just say I've not been well."

I incline my cheek away from her hand. I want to say I am sorry if she has suffered, but I hold back. I am still unsure of her role in this whole sick set-up.

"What is this place?" I ask instead. Clarice glances around.

"It used to be a home for the naughty children in our community," she says, "until it was outlawed. They destroyed most of the huts, but these few remained."

"Who are they?"

Clarice shrugs. "The men in charge. The ones who decide everything."

"Is Yarrick ...?"

"Sshh..." Clarice places a thin finger over my lips. Gently. "We don't have much time. Yarrick is part of this, yes. He is in charge of the men in our community."

"I don't understand," I say. "The people we used to meet with, your friends - and Yarrick's - they have never visited. I have not seen anyone I know. What is this community?"

Again, Clarice shakes her head. "I cannot tell you. There are things that go on behind closed doors of which we should never speak."

Now, it is my turn to shake my head. "That sounds like such a cop-out. I went from the relative comfort of your home to this." I use my arm to indicate the sparse surroundings. "And I am visited ..." I stop. Clarice knows about the visits. She must do. I don't need to draw a diagram of the acts I am forced to be a part of simply to leave this wretched island. "Why? Why did they do this to me?" I am becoming angry now. Some of the will and strength I thought departed has reappeared and is escaping through my voice. A voice that is hoarse from lack of use.

Clarice moves to sit beside me on the bed. "I don't know everything," she sighs, "only what I need to know, but it goes deeper than you. Much deeper. I wish it wasn't so. How I wish it wasn't so. I prayed to God and asked Yarrick to leave me here instead of you, but he wouldn't. He said it didn't work like that."

I feel a bony arm slip around my shoulders. "But why is Yarrick doing this? I thought he cared about me. I thought we had built a home, the three of us."

"We had, we had, and even though I have seen this side of him before, a long time ago, I thought it buried. I was wrong."

"What does he get out of keeping me here? Surely I have more than paid for my passage to England?"

Clarice drops her head on my shoulder. "Oh, Sandy. This isn't about your passage to England; it never has been."

I frown and panic fills my being. I am about to question her further when the door is once again opened. This time it is Yarrick who occupies its wooden frame. I feel Clarice tense.

"Have you done it yet?" he asks.

Clarice stands and goes over to him. "No, I was just about to. Sandy wasn't quite ready."

"Get on with it!" he commands, and I watch as Clarice reaches into her pocket for something. A box. A long, slim box. I recognise it immediately. I don't need to read the label. It is a pregnancy test. What the actual … ?

Clarice extends her hand towards me, encouraging me to stand and enter the alcove where my meagre facilities are. "Come on," she says quietly, "we just need to check."

I cannot form thought. Is it not bad enough that my body is used day in and day out? Now they want to check if I am carrying some bastard's child? If I am, I will kill it. I know I will. I don't know how, and I don't care if I die too. If one of these disgusting human beings has impregnated me, then it's game over. I will run. I will do whatever I need, and God may take me if he wishes.

I wanted to go back to England, and I was prepared to wait it out. I prayed every single day for Yarrick to come and tell me I could leave. For some inexplicable reason, I still believed there was good somewhere deep inside of him and that one day, my 'debt' would be repaid, and I would be able to go. I was certain that locking me up forever was inhumane and that Yarrick would eventually come to his senses.

It sounds crazy even as I allow that thought to migrate through my brain, but I suppose I switched off and clung to anything I could. The good times with Yarrick. The way he smiled and laughed with me. The way he taught me about the island and its heritage. I held onto those moments because they were all I had, and in my prayers, I asked for mercy, believing that God would save me somehow. Instead, he has sent me Clarice and a stick to pee on. I feel sick. I am numb. I didn't think it was possible for my pitiful existence to get worse, but it has. These fucking men should have protected themselves. I cannot comprehend how debased I have been and how actual human beings can inflict such pain on others for their own - what? Sick pleasure? Clarice said this was never about my passage to England, so what the hell was it about?

My head spins as I dutifully pee for the required time. Clarice puts the lid back on the stick, and we wait. Watching - before Clarice moves away. I have remained in the alcove. I don't want to see the result. I don't want to know if my life is about to be even more messed up, and I don't want to see Yarrick's face.

Silence. Then I hear steps, light steps, moving away. Clarice must be leaving. The door opens, and I remain precisely where I am. In the confines of an alcove that I use every day to perform the most basic of bodily functions.

Laboured breaths accompany Clarice's steps, and I hear more shuffling, heavier this time, and then a brief rush of air accompanies the sound of a lock being secured. They have left, and I am once more alone.

Or am I?

Maybe it isn't just me anymore.

Chapter Ten

PRESENT DAY

Watching from the sidelines is both entertaining and exciting. Especially when those you are observing have no idea they are being monitored.

I tap a few buttons on one of the many keyboards at my disposal, nodding as I watch cameras move and whir and change their angle. I love this. It's what gets me out of bed every morning and makes my dreams so sweet at night. I often think it a shame that one day I won't be watching anymore, but that is what must happen, and so I am resigned to my fate. That day, however, is not today, and so I sit back and sip the smooth, warm latte that has just arrived on my desk.

Maybe I'll move from here today, perhaps go outside when it is safe to do so. But maybe not. Words cannot convey how captivating it is sitting here hour after hour, silently, anonymously watching.

I stretch my arms above my head and hear a crack as my neck adjusts into position. That's the one thing that bothers me. Ever since the accident, my neck hasn't functioned properly, and the pain can, some days, be debilitating. Many a time I have slept the hours away, high on prescription painkillers, both loving and hating the experience. I love it for the beautiful, relaxed state in which I find myself with the pain no longer present. It is intoxicating. But I hate it because I miss hours of this. Though everything is recorded so that I can rewind, check, and loop it time and again, there is still nothing like seeing real lives unfold in real-time. There's no doubt that the injury I incurred interferes with my plans, but it's no matter. In the end, all will be well.

I get up from the luxury office chair in which I spend most of my waking hours and pace towards the comfortable bunk on the far side of this room. It's a strange kind of space, neither square nor rectangle; in fact, it's not a discernible shape at all, likely due to the multitude of uses it has enjoyed over the years. Each function would have warranted some change, I assume. A wall here, an alcove there, perhaps a staircase down to the main building, though that, if one ever existed, is no longer present. I can still gain access easily enough, though. A small fire door is nestled in the corner, which leads to the outside via some heavy steel stairs. When I first took over this place, the door was difficult to open; I had not visited it first, nor had the estate agent, both of us basing our knowledge on photos taken many years before. Thus, when presented with a door reluctant to open, the agent seemed genuinely baffled at how to overcome this dilemma. More used, I am sure, to modern properties with indistinct UPVC entrances. An angle grinder from the outside was most effective in our situation, though, and soon I was in. I would have figured out a way to get up from the main building, of course, but using these stairs is much more preferable, for I can come and go as I please, virtually undetected.

In reality, I rarely leave this room, for it serves me well. In addition to the bed, I have a large wardrobe and I have created a small kitchenette on the only really straight wall which has everything I need for eating and drinking. As fortune would have it, the previous occupant plumbed in a basic toilet, sink and shower behind a functional curtain, so essentially, I want for nothing. The room isn't large, perhaps ten metres square - although it isn't a square - but its size doesn't matter. I have food delivered every week; I have somewhere to sleep, somewhere to clean up, a skylight for fresh air and natural brightness and, of course, my desk of computers.

I remember a time, somewhere between puberty and adulthood, when I would spend hours at internet cafes, trying my hand at programming, connecting with others who hid their reality behind anonymous screens, and honing my craft. My parents had long since given up any pretence of caring, but they still felt qualified to afford me their opinions.

'You'll never amount to anything staring at a screen all day' was my father's favourite. Delivered at volume around various friends who would nod in agreement. I never responded though it was a herculean effort not to point out their flaws, to remind them of their pitiful existence and pointless contribution to society. In the end, it simply wasn't worth the energy, and I knew that my time spent drinking foul coffee and tapping away on a keyboard was not a waste. I was bigger than them and their world. I was destined for greater things. For Success and Power.

And now, in this tiny hovel of a room, I have the ultimate power.

How may not be apparent, and you might wish me to elaborate, but I won't. Not yet. You need to be patient and trust me.

Everything will become clear, and life will play out exactly as it should. All you need to do is sit back and enjoy the show.

I should, though, educate you as to why I am revealing these mundane details of my existence and I realise it would perhaps have been helpful to introduce myself sooner.

Apologies. I have forgotten my manners.

My name is Alex.

It's lovely to meet you.

Chapter Eleven

TWENTY MONTHS EARLIER

I rub my stomach idly as I watch the familiar light patterns on the wall of my room. I am back in the upside-down shack with Yarrick and Clarice, and it is as if those endless days of entrapment never happened. For them, anyway.

No one actually told me the result of the godforsaken pregnancy test, but I assumed it to be positive when, the following day, I was moved hastily from my prison-like cell and returned to the place I had once called home. Though I had been away from this room for two months, nothing had changed, and I have now been back here for a further two months, forced to endure a life of unspoken denial whilst my belly swells of its own accord.

I cannot think of these two, Yarrick and Clarice, without bile rising from my stomach and settling uncomfortably in my throat. The treatment I received at their hands was beyond monstrous, anything I could ever have imagined and worse. To them - well, to Yarrick at least - it appeared acceptable to treat me like a piece of meat, to be used by his 'friends' as a ruse for securing a passage to England. Clarice told me, on the night we did that bloody test, that my being held captive and unforgivably abused had nothing to do with my return to the land of my birth, yet no one has seen fit to tell me what the hell is going on. Where two months ago I was simply a vessel for the sexual satisfaction of Yarrick and his depraved male community, now I am the vessel expected to grow and nurture some bastard's child.

Though I am back in the relative comfort of this room, I am afforded no more freedom than when I was in that cell. I can move around the house, go downstairs, and make myself a drink or some food, but I am forbidden from going outside. The rules are made by Yarrick and we, Clarice and I, simply obey them in what I can only describe as a bizarre capitulation to a despot. I have tried to get Clarice alone on many occasions for I am sure she knows more than the little she has revealed, but she is barely without Yarrick at her side. They seem to have forgotten about the holiday huts as, apart from essential food trips, they don't go anywhere. And on the few occasions they do leave the house, I am locked in my room until they return.

Inside my head, I have catalogued all of the demeaning acts into which I have been forced and placed them into one of the boxes in my mind, ready to open later. I have stored them there so that I may recall them when I am in a position to seek revenge on the men of this screwed-up community, whenever or however that may be.

My list of those on whom I have an unwavering desire to seek revenge is growing. Of the many, there are two things which haunt me the most, and these I find especially sickening about my current situation. Firstly, I despise having this creature growing inside of me that I neither wanted nor desired. This 'thing' is the product of an evil act, and I am being forced, against my will, to nurture it. I feel nothing toward it save hatred. I know that the collection of cells which are burgeoning in my belly are not responsible for how they came to be, but that doesn't change anything. I don't even know which sick bastard put them there, and frankly, I don't care enough to ask. All I know is that the unspoken expectation that I will bear this child is twisted beyond belief.

The second is that Clarice and Yarrick act as if nothing has happened. With the exception of their changes to routine and habit, they are the same Clarice and Yarrick I met that first day on the beach, wearing nothing but a kid's pink towel. They are back to being friendly, warm and accommodating, just as if the last two months didn't happen. Though they may be able to forget, there is no way I ever will, especially with a physical reminder growing inside of me every single day.

I fantasise about ways to rid myself of it. I have no intention of carrying it for one minute longer than necessary, and I sure as hell am not going to birth it. Cruel? Perhaps. Maybe even harsh on this tiny innocent life, but you have not been through what I have. You don't know what it is to have men violate you night after night for no reason. To have every liberty and dignity removed so that all you have left is your shell of a body. I cannot ask you to understand, for this foetus is certainly blameless, but I can ask you not to judge.

I am no nearer to leaving this wretched place, it would seem, for there is no mention of cargo ships and papers anymore. Clarice and I cross paths a few times a day, and she smiles in her own squishy Clarice way, but it does not reach her eyes. She is looking better than she did two months ago. Filling out more, looking less drawn and pale. I assume that is because I am back here in the house, but I don't know that for certain. She looks at me sadly on occasion, too, and sometimes I see a tear glistening in her eye, but she says nothing. We exchange the most basic of greetings and continue on in our separate and lonely existences. I asked her a few days ago if she knew what the plan was, given I have been back for two months, and this nine-month energy-sucking companion continues to thrive. When she replied, it was with that ever-present sadness.

"Oh, Sandy," she'd said softly, "I don't know any more than you. The only thing I do know is that you are back here now, and I can keep a better eye on you."

"But why am I back here?" I'd asked, though I suspected I already knew the answer. I suspected it had less to do with me and was more about the 'being' nestling ever deeper into my womb.

"For the baby," she'd stated reasonably as if it were the most normal thing in the world. "It's not just about you now and Yarrick ... well, he's always wanted a child, and we weren't blessed so..."

It had taken a moment for her words to sink in. "You and Yarrick want this child?" I'd asked. "You want to bring it up? As your own?"

Clarice had shrugged. "That's what he says. But no more of that; we need to make sure you are both well."

As she had gone on, pressing her hands gently over my stomach, poking and prodding without permission, I instinctively knew that these few moments, this handful of comments - they would be the only time I would get any insight from Clarice.

Yarrick and his sick and twisted cronies had these women under their control. I couldn't believe I had never seen how much power Yarrick yielded.

But why would I?

I wasn't looking. At least, not back then. Now, though, I am on high alert and above all else, two questions remain that I need answers to.

One: Why was I put through those months of hell? And two: Would I ever get to go home?

I resolve that I will go to any lengths to find out.

PRESENT DAY

Colin has found me and we are once again seated in the second office with the half-moon-shaped arrangement of chairs. Rex has followed, so Colin pauses on the threshold whilst my four-legged friend clears the doorway before closing the solid hunk of wood neatly into its frame. I sit at one end, and Colin is at the other. A carbon copy of our previous visit with the exception that Rex stretches out in the centre this time. Give that dog a few rashers of bacon and some baby talk, and his loyalties are clearly compromised.

I wait as Colin twirls a large silver ring around his finger. He is leaning forward, elbows braced on his knees. One leg is jumping slightly as if he is nervous.

"I think we need to clear the air," he says at last, and I frown. That wasn't the opening line I had been expecting.

I look across at him, twisting my neck to the right. "There isn't any air to clear," I say. Yes, there was that moment, that glance in the kitchen, but I don't feel it warranted another trip to this office.

"There is," Colin says as he swivels his torso to the left. We are now practically facing each other across half a dozen seats. "I know you saw how I looked at you in the kitchen … I'm so sorry. I … you were never supposed to see that; it was just in that moment when Rich came in and got right in your face - I don't know, it just made me angry, I guess. And what you saw, well, that's the reason why I got angry."

I blink slowly then shake my head in confusion. Coffee Man has gone to places of which I have no concept.

"Sorry, what?"

Colin sighs and looks down at his knees. "In the kitchen ..." he begins.

I cut him off. "Yes, I heard you, but I think we're on two very different pages, hell we're not even in the same book. Until yesterday, you were simply Coffee Man, someone who was nice to me now and again and ..."

"Coffee Man?" Colin questions. I nod, and he laughs. "Coffee Man," he repeats, "I like it."

I shrug. "It's kind of my thing. All the regulars I see on the streets, I give them names - for my amusement as much as anything. Usually, they begin with 'R', but in your case, well, you're 'Coffee Man.'"

"Who else have you given names to?" he asks, and I watch as his shoulders drop in a release of tension. I sense he is grateful for the subject change.

"Mainly those that go into Clifton Arcade, you know, where the posh shops are?"

He nods and smiles. "They're not that posh."

"When you're on the streets, every shop is posh," I reply, and Colin inclines his head. "Go on."

"There's Roland," I say. "He's a business guy in a nice suit, always talking on his phone. He never speaks but drops money by my usual bench. Astrid and I often share it for lunch. And then there's Roseanna. She's a bit of an enigma. She looks like she'd be homely and kind, but she barely glances my way. She smells of strawberries."

"And this is how you define people?"

"I guess. You know, there's not really a lot to do from day to day, and when you see regulars, it's nice, I think, to pretend. I pretend that life is different and that I know who they are and that maybe I have a place in their world." Rex moves from his central spot and rubs against my legs. I reach down and scratch his head. "And you do as well," I say to my dog as he looks up lovingly. For the millionth time I wonder why he is so enamoured with me.

"And I became Coffee Man," Colin states.

I shrug. "You did."

He watches me. "I am sorry," he says after a moment, "for what happened in the kitchen. I can understand how it looks and that it probably makes no sense to you, but...I don't know. It's like you make sense to me."

"But you barely know me," I counter.

Colin shakes his head. "That's true, but I've admired you from the first day I found you sleeping in the coffee shop doorway. I guess I sensed you were different, that you were not where you were supposed to be. It's in the way you talk, the way you carry yourself, and I don't know, I just got this feeling that we were supposed to meet. Your incredible strength, that's what I felt that first day and every time since."

"But I'm a mess," I say, "how can anyone admire this?" I gesture at my albeit improved clothing and appearance.

"It's not about that," Colin smiles, "you know my story. You know that I understand your life to a point, which means I see beyond the exterior. My parents were so worried about fitting in, about being seen in the right places, about having a son they could be proud of - it sickens me to remember that superficial world. They missed out on so much with their prejudices and misguided beliefs, yet it still kicks me in the gut when I remember they're no longer in my life, even if it was by choice." Colin inhales a lungful of air. "Truth is, I'd much rather be here, in this world where I am free to be myself, as are others. That's what I recognised in you. I just knew in my gut that you should have been living a different life and," he shrugs, "seeing you deal with the crap of the streets day in, day out, I admired that. I still do."

I swallow, knowing how right he is. I am not living the life I was supposed to, but I am surprised to realise that I am not afraid of him seeing this in me. I know it is only recognition of a kindred spirit, not because he has somehow stumbled across my real story.

"Let me ask you something," he says. "When was the last time you let someone take care of you?"

I snort. I know it's not remotely feminine, but I can't help it. Of all the ridiculous questions …

"No, seriously," he says, "I mean it. When was the last time someone took care of you?"

I close my eyes and take a deep breath. Automatically I go back to that night on the yacht because there is nothing in the years since which remotely qualifies as being cared for. I watch the world unfold before me and rewind, go back through my teenage years and my younger years, and search for that time, that moment when I felt totally cared for. I come up blank.

"You've never had someone truly look out for you, have you?" he asks softly, and slowly I shake my head. "No." And that is the absolute shitty truth. I had everything I could ever have wanted, but the one thing that my parents never gave me was a sense of emotional safety. They knew I would be physically safe because they had staff to look after me. They knew I would go to school because they had drivers and nannies to take me. And they knew I would go to the places I was supposed to because they accepted every invitation on my behalf. Yet now, in the cold light of this pittance of a life, I realise that they never cared for me in the way I needed. I know that they loved me, but they just didn't - or maybe couldn't - give me that heart-warming hammock I didn't even realise I craved. The words of the famous religious story come to me, where God is walking alongside until his footsteps disappear.

"It was then that I carried you," I whisper, shocked when I realise I have spoken aloud.

I look up, unsurprised to connect my gaze instantly with Colin's. He nods. Slowly.

"Let me carry you, Ra," he says. "Let me carry you."

I swallow again, and I think about it. I really do. I imagine what it would be like to have someone like Colin in my life who could help shoulder some of the crap. Someone I could tell my deepest secrets to, someone who would be there when I needed a hug. Someone to laugh with, share moments with, make memories with, someone who could be my lover and my friend. Someone to snuggle up with on cold nights. It is tempting, so tempting. It would be so easy to melt into what he is offering as he regards me with those arresting green eyes. Even though I don't fully understand what it is that he is offering, it would be effortless to curl up in his world for a while and allow him into mine, to go forward as two rather than one. I know this, and I realise how lucky I am to have this chance, in the same way I am lucky to have Astrid. We are solid, and we will always look after each other on the streets - and beyond. Colin is offering me the chance for a different life, a better life, a street dweller's dream if you like, but in that split second it takes for the hundreds of thoughts to swirl around my head, I realise it can never be. It doesn't matter how kind he is. It doesn't matter how thoughtful. It doesn't matter how much he may or may not care. It doesn't matter what he can offer, and it doesn't matter that there would be a glimpse of happiness. Though I am being foolish and recognise this, I know I must turn him down. With Astrid, it's different. We are in the same world, regardless of whether or not either of us fit. But Colin is suggesting I walk into a world whose boards I trod in another life, and I am not ready for that. Not yet.

I cannot, in all conscience, allow myself to trust that deeply again.

Slowly and sadly, I shake my head. "I can't," I whisper, and I watch as hurt and confusion chases across his face. "I just can't."

With the back of my hand, I swipe at the tears already forming and rise from my seat in the half-moon-shaped array. Rex stands, too, and together, we walk to the door. I open and close it quietly before making my way to the toilets, Rex in tow, and enter the small space, heading straight for the grimy mirror into which I had refused to look earlier. This time, though, I do look; I make myself look because I have to. I need to see who I am deep down inside. I need to find what Colin recognises, but more importantly, I need to find myself.

Round eyes stare back at me, moist with emotion. I blink carefully, experimentally, examining myself ever deeper each time I regain focus. I try to see hope, the future, excitement, and joy, but I do not. I see exactly what I expected to see.

I see nothing. Absolutely nothing.

NINETEEN MONTHS EARLIER

Another four weeks have passed. I am reassured that at least my arithmomania is still functioning, for I am counting everything. Literally, everything, not least of which is the number of days I have been 'blessed' with the care of another being. Despite my eternal prayer that I may somehow rid myself of this thing, it is still there, growing, pushing my belly ever further outwards. It's not that I'm big yet, for I am barely at five months, but my body is changing in ways that I am not remotely comfortable with, and I hate it. It's bad enough knowing what has happened, but to feel the tenderness in my breasts and the tightening of my stomach is too much to bear. It is a cruel dichotomy, this situation in which I find myself. As it has been several weeks since I was forced to do anything against my will, I am feeling a little more comfortable here, and I really do understand that this creature I am nourishing is wholly innocent. Yet I cannot entertain ever wanting it or loving it. I will always be reminded of how it came to be. The two sides of this argument are exhausting.

When I spoke to Clarice, she implied that she and Yarrick would bring up this baby, which immediately brought bile to my throat. If they were intending for me to keep it, to give birth to it, then that was even more shades of screwed up, and it hardened my resolve that this foetus would never be allowed to live. I know now that I have been returned to this house for the very purpose of producing this baby, which is sick. So fucking sick. Everything about what has happened to me is sick. I thought that Alex had dealt me the ultimate betrayal on the yacht that night, but on reflection, what Yarrick has forced me into is equal. He took me into his home and made me feel safe and cared for. He fooled me into thinking that my time here would be temporary and that once I felt able, I would return to England. He taught me about community life and spent time helping me to acclimatise so that I might get used to the heat and the diet, which was so far removed from what I had been familiar with back home. We would spend many an evening, he, Clarice and I, talking, playing a game of cards, or just simply sitting contentedly in each other's company. Not once did I conceive of the evil that lay within Yarrick. There were no red flags, nothing to alert me to anything. I saw a warm and welcoming couple, stalwarts of their homeland, who simply wanted to help others. I guess I saw only what they wanted me to see.

I remember vividly the time when I woke up in the Earth Room with no idea as to what had happened. In my mind, all I had done was ask for a way back home, something which I genuinely believed both Yarrick and Clarice would have expected. But the twisted reality that I was then dragged into is something from which I know I will never recover. The community Yarrick values so much abused me with his blessing. As if I was Yarrick's property, and he was allowing them to use me as they saw fit. It is like something from the Dark Ages. A time that has long since been outlawed in every civilised society, yet there seem to be no laws here, not now. Perhaps Yarrick has that much power, or perhaps people are too scared to speak the truth. If the younger women are treated as I have been, then I understand how they would be fearful of bringing attention to the fucked-up happenings in this corner of Añaposta Island.

It was only a few days into my cell-time when I resigned myself to never being released, but still, I wanted to know why. Nothing made sense to me. I begged every 'visitor' to tell me, but despite my pleas, to a man, they remained silent. They simply turned up, did what they needed to do and left. I quickly learned to switch off the physical sensations and disconnect my soul from reality, but I could never quieten my mind when it came to understanding why. The 'why' almost became an obsession. Why was I here, and why was I being treated this way? And with no other credible explanation, I arrived at the conclusion that, at best, this was a sick man's entertainment and, at worst, a death sentence. A prison where I am the fugitive, held in accordance with one man's whims.

If you had told me when I was sitting on the top deck of the *Cassiopeia* that this would be my life, I would have laughed. I could never have imagined what fate had planned once Alex showed his true colours. I remember congratulating myself, once I had become accustomed to my new world, on making my way to the shore so that I could have a chance at life. Because if I was alive, I could still find Alex. I celebrated the fortune of being found by Yarrick and Clarice and of them welcoming me wholly into their lives. I was so innocent back then. I could never have comprehended what was about to unfold.

I wonder, sometimes, what would have happened if I hadn't asked Yarrick about returning to England. Would my life here still be going on as it had been? Would I be cleaning the huts with Clarice, and picking the fruits, and sewing the clothes? It's a pointless thought process, though, for here I am, locked in purgatory under the eye of a man I realise I never knew. If I have learned anything, it is that I can only live in the present and take each day one at a time. I cannot look back, and I cannot look forward. I can only deal with the here and now.

I think often of dying and realise I am okay with that. I don't believe there is any pain left to hurt, so I fantasise about how that could happen. Perhaps I would bleed out should something happen to this thing that continues to grow in my womb. The thought excites me, which is a stark reflection of how messed up I am. I would get to be with my parents again, and although it would mean leaving my plans for Alex behind (you can be bloody sure I'll be waiting for him on the other side), it would be a blessed relief. My head aches daily as I try to understand what I have done to deserve this. What did I ever do to cause my life to journey down such an abhorrent path? For I firmly believe I am at fault - how could I not be? I am the one who brought Alex into my parents' world, and I am the one who trusted him. If I had not done so, then he would never have been on the yacht that night, and my parents and I would have sailed alone. We would have been together, and we would all have been alive.

They say that life is planned for us, that somewhere, someone has this map that we are all following. I say that is crap. I say that we are fucked over by life every single day. By people we have loved and trusted. When I reflect on my short life thus far, I cannot really remember many happy times. Truly happy times. Jayde - when she was my friend, then I was happy, but she left me. Finding true friends when you are rich is almost impossible because everyone has an agenda. That is something I was reminded of time and again by my nannies and companions. They drilled into me how flawed humans are and that I must choose my friends carefully, for many will want to be in your world simply because you are rich. I know there are some in my previous circle who were okay with that. They didn't mind living a surface existence where their money effectively paid for their friendships, but I have never been okay with that. The perils, I think, of being a Gemini. And enjoying my education and learning. Settling without substance never appealed, and so I have spent much of my life alone, often by choice. There were the odd few who I let in, but after

Jayde, no one ever captured my heart in the same way. Until Alex. When Alex and I met, I thought I had found a kindred spirit. Someone who understood my world because it was his world, too. Someone who would love me for who I was, who I really was, because money didn't matter.

My judgement, despite all those years of advice, was clearly off.

So here I am, living, breathing, existing and for what? To produce this heir to Yarrick's perverted world?

The colourful lights fade as the sun dips below the horizon, and I am reminded of the first time I came into this room. The first time Yarrick showed me the wardrobe full of clothes. How he normalised something which I instinctively knew to be strange. I knew, deep down, that having women's clothes readily available was abnormal and to have brand new underwear plain weird - yet I believed what he told me because I was so damaged, so numb with grief, that it was easier not to question. And Yarrick knew I wouldn't have the wherewithal to ask. I am sure of that now. He knew exactly what to say and how to conduct every single aria. He knew to give me all the corrupt details when I was at my most vulnerable so that I wouldn't even notice. He had been clever. I see that now. I see so much now. I have had endless hours to reflect over the last few months, and I realise there were clues and signs everywhere, but I simply did not see them. I have been focused solely on my purpose.

To live so that I may find a way back to England and Alex.

And that focus has been so laser-sharp that I have ignored warnings I should have heeded a long time ago. The morning cup of tea ritual, which I thought caring and tender, was, in fact, nothing but a control mechanism. Clarice would bring the tea at the same time every day, and Yarrick would follow behind, telling me what the plans for the day were. Never was I allowed to think for myself, and it didn't occur to me to mind. I was grateful for their kindness and hospitality, but now that my eyes have been opened, I can see how manufactured every part of my time here has been.

I was never left alone. And though I became a part of the community and spent time with others, I was always with Clarice, too. A chaperone. I think, perhaps that describes her role best. I was encouraged to ask questions only of Yarrick because the others in our society would not have the answers. They were not educated enough, he would say. And I believed him. I knew nothing of the community and its people, so I had no reason to doubt his assertions.

I should have taken pause when I first came to this house, this upside-down shack. A place so cold and dark downstairs yet so warm and welcoming upstairs. The contrast between my room and the rest is stark, morosely so, yet it didn't occur to me to question why. Why was I given such a cheerful space to recover? Why would they lovingly furnish only one room of the house? Who lives like this? Who lives in virtual poverty but creates one room of luxury?

The signs were all there. I just didn't look. Now, I see it, the scarlet flag waving from high on the hill, the one that I should have taken note of all those months ago.

The light fades completely, and I roll onto my side, curling up in the foetal position, hugging my knees, waiting for sleep to claim me. I close my eyes and allow my breathing to settle into a relaxed pattern. I am tired of these endless, unanswerable questions. I am tired of having no voice. I am, simply, just tired.

And that's when it happens. Something I prayed I would never experience, yet something so magical, so unbelievable, that it takes my breath away.

From inside my swollen stomach, a butterfly flutters. So gentle. Like the tiniest of tickles.

Shit.

I am in wonder. I am in denial.

This creature, this foetus...

Fuck.

...it just became a baby.

Chapter Twelve

NINETEEN MONTHS AGO

To say that I am freaked out is an understatement. In the back of my mind, I knew that eventually, the 'baby' would start to move and that I would feel it, but I didn't expect to care. Let me rephrase. I didn't expect to ever think of this thing inside of me as real, and now that it is making its presence known by the lightest of flutters, I am forced to acknowledge that I am genuinely growing another human being. All along, I have been mindful of its innocence, that it did nothing to deserve the thoughts I have directed towards it. When it was just a line on a stick, though, it was easy to ignore. Now, I can no longer ignore it, and that regular tickling reminder is messing with my head. I hate that I can feel it. I hate that it is there. I hate that it is growing. I hate how it came to be. I hate that it was created out of an act which was neither consensual nor wanted. I hate the sick and twisted games that made me become more than one person, and I despise Yarrick and his fucked-up world. I don't want to give him the gift of this baby if, indeed, that is the plan.

But ... and it's a big but ...

Inside of me, there is another life. A human life. A tiny being who didn't ask to be created, but now that it has, it is thriving and reaching out to me, telling me it is okay. Reluctantly, I am forced to acknowledge that this foetus is a part of me, too. However it came to be, it is a part of my body, a part of my essence, half of my DNA, a direct descendent of me, Aurora, a person who will be helpless without me, a body that will need me more than anyone has ever done in my life so far ...

However messed up and sick this whole scenario is, those thoughts - they are pretty bloody powerful.

It has been a few days since I first felt those unmistakable movements, and I have told neither Clarice nor Yarrick of its happening. Eventually, they will ask, I am sure. Eventually, they will be able to see me growing bigger and the baby inside of me shifting, but for now they are unaware, and I plan to keep it that way. For some reason, it feels right that it is just me and it for now. No one else in our screwed-up bubble of existence. I wonder about my future. I cannot conceive of a time beyond this, but I suppose if this baby and I make it to the actual birthing moment, then I will be surplus once I have done the necessary. Though no one has said in so many words, I get the feeling that Yarrick's plans to raise this being do not include me, save perhaps for the maternal functions I will need to perform initially.

When Clarice told me that they would be bringing up the baby as their own, it sickened me to my core. Not because I felt - or do feel - any love for it or because I want to keep it, for I am still hoping that one day it will miraculously disappear. Yes, judge me all you like, but you cannot begin to comprehend how it feels and what I have been through. Despite those tender thoughts I shared moments ago, this new life is a constant reminder of the two months of twisted hell that Yarrick and his like forced upon me - simply because I asked to go home. But no, I am sickened by the idea of bringing an innocent being into a place which I now know lacks any kind of moral compass. Who, given what I have experienced, would willingly bring a new life into this world? Sure, as Yarrick's child, perhaps it will have certain privileges but even still... and why the fuck should I trust half of my DNA to such a warped individual?

What I have discovered over the last two months plays on my mind endlessly. Though I witnessed it with my own eyes and body, I still struggle to connect the love that Yarrick and Clarice showed me initially, to the world that they have created beneath that facade. From the earth room to the cell to the bizarre rituals, the two entities could not be further apart.

In some respects, I get the whole 'cult' thing, especially after what we were told when Jayde left. I understand how easy it can be to fall under the spell of others, of people who promise to provide parts of your life that are missing, who promise to hold you up no matter what, to ensure you will never be without warmth, love or hope. It's formidable stuff. Those who bring unsuspecting followers into their world are perceived to have power and a wealth of knowledge - all of which excites the naive. They want to be touched by that power. They want to feel a deeper purpose. They want to reach the end of their search for belonging and find a home where everyone is equal. I get it; I really do. As I said, it's heady stuff, and for a while in my cell, when my mind was barely this side of sane, I almost wanted to capitulate. To ask how I could become one of the women rather than a slave, a mannequin to cater to the men's needs.

Thankfully, I retained just enough of myself to remain mute. I did not know for certain that this was a cult and regardless, I recognised that if I were to capitulate, to become one of the sheep, then I would lose my chance to find Alex, however small that chance remains.

Don't get me wrong. Though I have rationalised all of this—more so since my return to the upside-down shack—I still don't understand. Why did the men have to use me? Was it about sexual gratification, power, control - or all three? Clearly, there was never any plan to provide me with papers and an identity, so why was I held captive?

And then it hits me. It is so bloody obvious I can't believe it's taken me this long to figure it out.

Yarrick wanted me to become pregnant. That was his plan all along.

Shit.

Clarice let slip that she and Yarrick hadn't been 'blessed', so he must have seen me as the solution. A young, healthy woman with no ties to anyone. I have been a gift to them both, a way of getting what they want without repercussion. But why would Yarrick have all the men visit me? Surely an heir, if that was indeed his motivation, is only a true heir if the blood of its father runs through it? This thing could be the product of any one of those bastards.

Unless ...

Unless Yarrick is the problem. Perhaps he is concerned he may be infertile, so is playing the odds. Clearly, he wouldn't want other men to impregnate Clarice, yet he has no such qualms with me. That way, there is no way of knowing whose illegitimate child I am carrying, and it could well be Yarrick's. With everyone firmly in his control, no man will deny him the right to this thing inside of me, and Yarrick goes forth as a virile male - regardless of its DNA.

Is he really that calculating? My gut tells me he is. That the man I met on the beach that day was nothing but a sham.

But what of the women? Why did they continue to visit day

in and day out, say nothing, perform the duties as required and then leave? What were they frightened of?

Yarrick, I assume, is the only one with the answers, and I have little hope of him offering any.

This 'thing' and I must, therefore, remain as we are, in the dark.

Praying for a solution.

PRESENT DAY

Someone is watching me. I can feel their gaze piercing into my back as I lie prone on my lavender-scented bed. I am certain it is Rich, so ignore the irresistible urge to roll over and find out.

The heat on my back increases. Clearly, whoever it is, is still focusing the weight of their eyes on the centre of my spine. I shift a little, thinking that it may alert whoever is watching to the fact that I know they are there. And then they will feel embarrassed and look away. No such luck. It doesn't matter how much I move, the heat burns as if it were a real flame.

Once upon a time, when I had the luxury of learning, I remember a psychology professor talking about this exact thing. When you know that someone is watching you, even though you can't see them. It's called 'gaze detection' apparently and is a complex phenomenon related to several areas of our brain and its neural network. I remember thinking it was fascinating, especially when it caused paranoia amongst the boys in our class when they got caught staring at a girl they liked. For context, no one ever stared at me.

My neural network, though, is definitely functioning today; in fact, it's in overdrive right now, so I give up and submit to the primary human force, allowing myself to roll over and sit up. When I am upright, I scan the room. The first thing I notice is that Astrid is not in her bed. I had returned here after my slightly awkward exchange with Colin, and she was chilling with Rex then, so she must have gone somewhere since. I don't think I dozed, but it's entirely possible. Rex is not around either, so perhaps the two of them have gone outside to the small square of grass.

As it is mid-morning, many of my fellow occupants are resting on their beds. Some I see are playing board games quietly in one corner of the vast space, a sight which makes me smile. There is a gentle hum as light chatter reverberates. There are also several empty beds; in total, I count twelve remaining 'residents', including those engaged in the 'games room' corner. I still don't see Astrid, but what I do locate is the source of the unwanted heat which has been burning into my back. I stand and walk fifteen paces to a bunk in the next row over, upon which sits a young woman, bedraggled, moth-eaten and, to all intents and purposes, half dead.

"Is it you?" she asks.

I shake my head. It's not unusual to see people in this state on the streets. Sadly. When I do, it reminds me of how lucky I was to find Astrid and survive to the extent that I have. It is impossible to tell how old she is, but I am guessing she has only just arrived, for her clothes are filthy and stick limply to what there is of her body. She has not received her clean garments yet.

"I don't know what you're talking about," I say. "It's rude to stare."

She shrinks back at my admonishment, becoming even smaller. I notice her eyes are too large for her face, though they are nonetheless striking in their aquamarine hue. Her hair is matted and plastered to her head. After a moment, she nods fervently.

"It *is* you."

Once more, I shake my head. Partly in sadness, for this girl of a woman has clearly lost some of her sanity.

"I don't know you," I repeat, "and you sure as hell don't know me. You just think that you do, and that's okay, but believe me, you don't." I wonder what has happened to this woman for her to have lost such a grip on reality so young.

The woman frowns. "Your hair," she says, "I would recognise it anywhere."

Instinctively my hand lifts to my wavy mass of blonde. Haircuts don't generally happen once you become a street dweller, so though it has retained its colour, it certainly has no style to speak of. To me, my hair looks no different to anyone else's.

With a sigh, I walk four paces to the right and sit on the bunk opposite hers. "Look," I begin gently, "I am sorry for whatever happened to cause you to end up here. You don't deserve it, none of us do, but you are clearly troubled, and that's okay, but it's also not okay because you need help." I look around as if expecting a psychiatrist to appear at any moment.

The woman smiles, and it is a movement which lights up her face. Beneath the dirt and grime and confusion, I notice how incredibly beautiful she is.

"I am okay," she replies, her voice quieter now. "There is nothing wrong with me. Well, apart from this." She gestures to her threadbare clothes and thin frame.

"You've come to the right place for that," I say. "They're pretty good at finding clothes, and the showers are decent. Plus, you'll get a couple of meals as well. Believe me, you'll think you're in heaven."

She laughs. "Heaven," she says, almost to herself. "Once, I believed there was a God and heaven."

For some reason, it strikes me as odd that God, the great man himself, has turned up in both of my most recent conversations. I have no strong views either way, as I explained to Colin earlier, but what I have come to realise is that God - or a version thereof - is prevalent on the streets because these people - we - have nothing left. No one else to help, so we kind of hold onto this higher being in the hope and belief that one day, our lives will change.

"When did you get here?" I ask. I haven't been monitoring the door by any means, but I haven't noticed her before. I was unaware of her presence - until I felt her gaze on my back.

"Not long ago," she responds, "it's so nice here."

I nod. I'm about to speak, though I am not sure what I am going to say when the hairs on the back of my neck rise, and I know that Rich is about to enter my personal space.

"Ah, I see you've met Ra," he says as he stands to one side of me and regards the young woman. "She's one of our helpers here. I hope you're making our newcomer feel welcome." This last part is directed at me. I shrug. I wouldn't say I've been making this woman feel welcome; if anything, I've been more frosty than warm, but this is so insignificant an issue that I choose not to respond. What is significant is how easily Rich has transitioned me into one of his 'helpers'. I don't remember ever agreeing to that.

"Ra," the woman says softly. "Ra. What an unusual name."

"Well," says Rich as he sits just a fraction too close to me on the bed, "you'll soon discover that there is nothing 'usual' about our Ra."

I cringe. Yuck. He really actually said that.

"I don't think that any of us fit a mould," I respond as I shift away from Saint Rich and smile at the waif of a woman. Though she is seated, I can see that her limbs are long, so I imagine her to be tall. Similar in build to Astrid, in fact. I squint, and through the tiny gap of light, I give myself permission to picture this woman cleaned up, dressed in better clothes and with a bit of meat on her frame. I was right in my first observation; she is incredibly beautiful. I feel that it is criminal for all of us who end up here and on the streets, but I feel it more so for someone like this woman and Astrid. I am saddened that their allure is lost amongst those with whom they live.

"Maybe Ra can show you around," Rich says as he throws his arm around in a wide arc. I am so tempted to laugh. No one needs a guided tour of this place. It is basically one huge warehouse with beds, a kitchen, toilets and a couple of office-type rooms. One thing I have yet to find, though, is where Rich sleeps. He said he lived on-site, but I have never seen him anywhere other than in his office. He must have a separate room somewhere though I have absolutely no intention of asking. That would indicate a marginal interest, which is something that I most definitely do not have.

"Sure," I say, "I can show you where everything is. And I'm guessing you'll be arranging some clothes?" I ask, turning to Rich.

"Spencer's on it," he replies. "It's kind of his thing."

I stand from the bed and hold out my hand, indicating for the woman to come with me. She rises too, and I realise I am right about her height. She steps closer to my side.

"Ra," she says again, and I frown. It is awful to see someone so young with so little grasp on reality. And then I stop that train of thought. She is standing right next to me now, and for the first time, I experience a sense of recognition. A shiver runs down my spine as I try to place the feeling. I wonder if I have been wrong all along; maybe we have met before. Perhaps she isn't as lost as I feared.

I turn to face her, our gazes now inches apart.

"I knew it," she says softly, "you recognise me too, don't you?"

I peer into her features, trying to put a name to her face, trying to sort through the depths of my memory banks for who she is and why I, too, am experiencing a moment of recollection. And then it hits me. I have finally paged far enough back in the search history of my mind to place her, though the last time I saw her feels like a lifetime ago. We have both changed significantly since then.

For a second, I feel a rush of pure joy, knowing that at last, here is someone who knew me before Alex, at a time when the world was unencumbered by the harsh realities I now face, and instinctively I move forward as if to embrace her, to capture this moment. But then she speaks. And too late, I realise that Rich is still standing next to me, watching, waiting, listening and hearing every word.

"Ra?" she says again, "have you changed your name? When we were at school, you were Aurora."

Fuck.

"You two know each other?" Rich pounces. I see his frown

mingled with confusion which is aimed squarely at me. I am without speech. I have no idea what to say. I want the concrete floor beneath me to open up so that I can escape. For now, something I have lived in fear of for so long has come to pass. And it has happened in the most surreal of coincidences that I could in no way have prepared myself for.

"Yes," she replies to Rich, oblivious to the panic which is chasing through my every nerve. "We were best friends at school. You remember, don't you, Aurora? It's me. Jayde."

NINETEEN MONTHS AGO

Something is amiss. Not with me, but in the house. Clarice has not been in with my morning tea, and I cannot hear her usual chatter as she bustles about her chores. Yarrick visited me in my room last night, enquiring about my health, making sure I was eating enough and getting enough rest - like he actually cares. We both know the only reason I am being treated to any kind of humane life is because I am carrying a baby, a child that he believes will be his. I was tempted to ask him.

After formulating my thoughts during the day and realising that Yarrick was the only one who had all of the answers, I was really tempted to find out why. Why I had been treated the way that I had and why things have changed so significantly since I became pregnant - though that I believe is more obvious.

I am also partly curious as to the man who impregnated me. Not because I want to know who it may have been necessarily, but I wonder if he, the man, knows. I wonder if Yarrick has imparted that nugget of information to whomever of his 'friends' did the eventual deed. I suppose it doesn't matter either way, but I cannot deny a morbid interest in exactly whose DNA has had a party with mine.

But I didn't ask. To be honest, I wasn't ready to rock the boat. I am still getting used to having something moving inside of me and knowing that I am responsible for the creation of a beautiful new life - which then contrasts with the moments of crippling hatred of it, of the man who did this to me, of Yarrick, of Alex ... and it is exhausting. It's an endless rollercoaster of emotional peaks, and I am so, so tired of it all. I wonder if I should give in, admit defeat and just go along with whatever corrupt plans await. Would that rid me of this endless internal turmoil? I don't know, and I have yet to arrive at any considered decision, hence Yarrick came and went last night, and I said nothing. I asked nothing. I gave nothing.

You might find it strange that I can stomach being in the same room as Yarrick, and believe me, it's hard. It would have been difficult enough before but following that night in the cell when he visited after I had broken the rules by walking the other way around the exercise circuit, I have struggled to hide the revolt I feel in his presence. Keeping the bile at bay takes all of my willpower, and though I would love nothing more than to empty my stomach contents at his feet, I know it would do me no good. I would feel like shit, and he would undoubtedly check on me with increased frequency.

I know how unbelievable all of this sounds. The path that my life has taken in the last eighteen months, along with the things I have both witnessed and experienced, are barely conceivable, but I promise that this is a faithful narrative. I am (barely) living proof of an existence which is beyond comprehension to most, and I say that as a fact. I attach no emotion to this statement.

At last, I hear a noise outside the door, and though it is much later than usual, I am relieved Clarice will finally be arriving with my tea. It's amazing how much I have gotten used to this routine, and with only water to drink otherwise, the morning cup of hot tea has become the highlight of my day. Though I interact with Clarice, my relationship with her has changed, too; there was no way it could not have done, and she is wise to that. She has withdrawn into her own world more, but I can still feel her warmth. I genuinely believe she wishes things were different, and I often wonder what kind of hold Yarrick has over her and the other women. How they have come to live this 'outer' life of normality and routine and yet bend to a much darker world that is created, crafted and corrupted by their men. Again, I could ask, but I am not entirely sure that I want to know.

The door opens, and Clarice walks in. I notice instantly that she is not carrying anything. No mug of tea, no water for my wash, nothing. I look at her in askance, and it is then I note what she is wearing. Gone are the flowery, bright dresses in which she is usually clothed, replaced by a pair of lightweight dark trousers and a simple t-shirt. It is the first time I have seen her wear anything like this, and though I have no apparent reason to feel it, I am instantly alarmed.

"Are you okay?" I ask.

Clarice shakes her head and puts her forefinger to her lips. I frown.

"What?" I ask.

"Come with me." She extends her hand, fingers pointing outwards, wiggling as if encouraging a child. Again, I frown.

"Come." She repeats. "Hurry."

I reach down and grab the plimsolls that I keep under the

bed for the odd occasion I am allowed outside.

"Hurry," Clarice says again, and I hear the urgency in her voice. I have no idea what is happening, but I am alert to the strangeness of this day.

After slipping my feet into the soft shoes, I grab Clarice's hand and allow her to lead me out of the room. We virtually race along the landing towards the rickety stairs, Clarice keeping a firm hold of me. She doesn't even release her grip when we awkwardly navigate the uneven descent, our feet landing on the ground floor in virtual synchronicity. I pull back a little, wanting to slow her, to find out what is going on, but she turns towards me and with a single look, I know now is not the time.

We exit the house and go out into the morning sun. I squint as my eyes become accustomed to the sudden light. Clarice looks furtively around before pulling me onwards, towards the large hill that crests the back of the house.

"Quickly," she says, and instantly I know I am to up the pace.

By now, we are at a run, skirting the base of the hill and turning to the right, heading along one of the many dust roads that lead to the village. And the beach. All the while, Clarice is glancing around behind her, checking and then checking again, and I realise she is fearful of us being followed. Whatever is going on, I assume that this is not something of which Yarrick would approve, for I cannot imagine who else she would be afraid of.

We reach the village. It has taken barely a few minutes, and at last, Clarice slows our pace a little. Here we can blend into the crowd, for it is market day which means there are many people milling around the small square. Some are locals, some are tourists, and it is to a small group of the latter that Clarice attaches us, following along behind, hiding our presence as best she can. Once more, I want to ask her what she is doing, but despite her advancing years and the run we have just endured, she remains strong and determined in her mission, pulling me behind her like I am nothing more than a small suitcase. One of those on wheels. Like I used to have, way back when.

Feet flying, I keep pace, ducking in and out of stalls and along behind groups of happy, chattering foreigners. I envy them. They are seeing Añaposta Island as it should be seen, a beautiful island with a vibrant energy. They have no idea of the depravity hidden within the underbelly of one small community here. Inside of me, the baby kicks, almost as if in protest at such a bumpy ride. Perhaps it was asleep, and now it has been rudely awakened. Whatever. I cannot do anything except keep going, so it's going to have to suck it up right now.

We have reached the dock, but a different part of the dock. Not the one where the luxury huts are, but another area, larger, more industrial. This is not somewhere I have visited before. It is, I presume, where the cargo ships dock. We round another bend, and rearing up in front of me, at the end of a long wooden pier, is a huge goods vessel, vibrating loudly as its not inconsiderable bulk rests barely restrained in the sea beyond. I was right. This is where the important stuff happens.

Clarice pulls me until we are at the foot of the pier.

"We're leaving," she states, her breath coming in short, sharp gasps. "I have managed to arrange it. You don't need to know how, but this is our way out." She indicates the large ship docked several metres away.

I swallow. I am both excited and scared. I am also unsure if I should trust her.

"What do you mean?" I ask.

"Come on," she pulls me onto the first of the wooden strips of decking, "I'll explain everything when we're on board."

Together we move along the walkway, the ship getting larger the closer we get. Clarice is mumbling something, but I can barely hear over the roar of the sea and the growl of the cargo ship's engine.

"Hurry!" It's a shout from the boat. Someone is standing on the side nearest to us, waving frantically. I see two men on the dock, next to the ropes, waiting to cast off the lines so that the vessel can set sail. They are waiting for us. I still cannot decide if that is a good thing.

We are almost there; a few more steps, and we will reach the ramp that leads from the dock to the huge hulk of metal. Clarice is still in front, but her foot catches momentarily, and I find myself dodging around her to avoid falling. I reach the ramp first, and now our positions are reversed. It is me pulling Clarice.

Except I am not.

A loud shout comes from the shoreline, causing me to turn.

Yarrick is running towards us. Yelling at the top of his voice.

An arm reaches out from the ship and yanks me aboard. Clarice steps onto the ramp, barely a metre behind me. I look back towards Yarrick, and it is then that I see a sight I had hoped never to see again.

A man's arm, outstretched, pointing a gun.

"Clarice!" I scream as the strong arm around my middle forces me to stay where I am on board the ship. I am struggling against the restraints though, trying to get to Clarice, trying to warn her of Yarrick's obvious intent. I need to help her; she still hasn't made it to the deck, but I am bereft of voice. All around, there is noise, confusion, and men shouting. My arms are outstretched, willing Clarice to take the last couple of steps, willing her to grab my hands so that she too may be free because finally, I realise that she is a prisoner too. She may have had more freedom, but she has been Yarrick's captive in every other way that matters and now, in an act of bravery and defiance, she has risked everything to free us both.

Our gazes meet, and time slows to nothing as I watch Clarice open her mouth and her lips form words. I fight against the strength of an unfamiliar man, all the while begging him to help Clarice, and finally, he shoves me away, deeper onto the deck, further from Clarice. I watch his feet move, covering the final steps between the ship and the woman to whom I am certain I owe my life. Large male hands reach towards Clarice, closing the distance, fingers almost touching, everything unfolding in slow motion.

Behind her, the formidable figure of Yarrick looms closer. Arm raised, metal weapon of death glinting in the sun. I scream.

"Clarice!"

She turns to look behind her, and in that split second, it happens.

Again.

A shot rings out.

Reverberating loud in the sudden silence.

I watch in horror as Clarice crumples to the ground, inches from the cargo ship.

"Clarice!" I scream, but there is no sound.

Her squishy form comes to rest, blood pooling around her stricken body.

"Clarice!"

Gravity settles her in the most basic of positions: flat on her back, head dropping slowly to the side—toward the cargo ship, toward me.

"No....!" I shout. "No!"

Clarice's eyes are open, their warmth extinguished, and I realise it is too late. She has been liberated. Finally, she too is free, but unlike me, she cannot be rescued. My saviour has paid the ultimate price.

Around me, there is chaos as men rush to release the boat from its dock, and in seconds, we are moving—slowly but surely—out to sea and away from a man I once loved and a life I once cherished.

I look back at the carnage we have left behind, and all I can see is Yarrick standing over the warm and squishy life of the woman I believed he worshipped. A woman strong of heart who bore more decency in her smallest fingernail than in the entire being of the monster now watching on.

The sunlight catches once more on the barrel of the gun, flashing across the sea like a beacon. To the uninitiated it could be a signal, a glimpse of safety from a lighthouse, a port in a storm, somewhere to rest - but I know it for what it is. An evil weapon in the hands of a devil. It is too much.

Bile rises in my stomach as tears stream down my face. Fingers of fear thread through my veins. I cannot believe what I have just witnessed - but yet, disturbingly, I can. It's as if my life during the last eighteen months has completed its cycle, one that began with a madman, a gun and needless death and now ends with a madman, a gun and needless death. The difference in the beginning and end of this lifecycle is marked only by the incomparable sumptuousness of their locations. A luxury yacht. A cargo ship. Beyond that, my arrival and departure from this island have been heralded with exactly the same massacred fanfare.

I pinch myself to check I am not in the realm of a nightmare and feel the expected pain as redness bursts my skin.

I am awake.

I am alive.

I have just witnessed my second murder.

Fuck.

I lean over the side of the ship and vomit.

Chapter Thirteen

PRESENT DAY

I am beginning to wonder if I should have my name engraved on one of these chairs in Saint Rich's office because I find myself here yet again. Usually, though, the plaques you see on wooden benches are placed there by loved ones, for loved ones, and represent a place which their departed had enjoyed, perhaps revered. I cannot say the same for these chairs, and, looking across at Rich, I cannot claim there to be a great view either. Perhaps, then, I shall not progress this idea, though the thought of it makes me smirk. Imagine. A chair in Rich's office with my name permanently engraved on it. I doubt he could get it to the bonfire fast enough.

"What's so funny?" he asks as he takes his customary seat in his oh-so-comfy faux leather chair.

I shrug. "Nothing." There is no point in explaining. His mouth has been set in a grim line ever since Jayde - who I still can't believe is here; how the hell did that happen? - let slip that my real name is not Ra. My emotions toward the other woman are decidedly mixed, yet I have not had time to process these to any great extent. As soon as Rich realised Jayde and I had history, he dragged me back into his box of a den, presumably to demand answers.

"So, you two know each other," he states unnecessarily.

"We do." There is no point in denying it. I don't have enough brain power to weave a convincing story of mistaken identity, and even if I did, Jayde would tear it down in a heartbeat.

"And you weren't going to tell me?"

"For fuck's sake," I explode, "firstly, I didn't realise who she was until literally a few seconds ago; secondly, I haven't seen her for god knows how long and finally, it is none of your fucking business."

Rich sits back, hands steepled on his desk as he exudes an air of forced calm. "Your language…" he says and shrugs. I am instantly transported back to that moment on the top deck of *Cassiopeia* when Alex took issue with my language. Then, I believe the word I used was a lot less offensive than the language which is now part of my daily repertoire. Alex would die if he could hear me. Hopefully.

"And?" I counter. "I live on the streets. What the hell do you want? The Queen's English?"

Rich shakes his head. "It's the King's English now."

What the actual? I know that our former beloved monarch is no longer with us, but the 'Queen's English' is a turn of phrase. What does it matter which gender of monarch prefaces it?

"Semantics," I say. I don't need to look to know that Rich is smiling. He is about to remind me that only I, with my education, would use a word such as 'semantics'. I know he is. It's the kind of comment that he thinks gives him some kind of edge like he knows me. But, of course, he has no fucking clue.

"don't," I say, holding up my right hand, palm towards him. This time, I do look up, and he is, as predicted, smiling.

"How do you two know each other?" he asks instead.

"From school."

He nods. "Strange coincidence, you both ending up here."

I remain mute. I don't disagree, but right now, I haven't the wherewithal to ruminate on the law of coincidences. Or whatever the hell it is.

"So, you were friends?" Rich prods.

"Yep."

"Are you going to give me any more than that?"

"Nope." I shake my head. "I refer to my previous comment. It is none of your fucking business."

He releases a sigh. "Oh, Ra," he says softly, "when are you going to stop fighting me?"

"I'm not fighting you," I respond, "but you know nothing about me, and you have no claim to know anything either. I owe you nothing."

"Well, apart from the bed and the food and the warmth and the shelter and the ..."

"Yeah, yeah," I interrupt. "But if you remember, I was ready to leave. It was you who forced me to stay."

"Forced?" He laughs. "I did not force you. I made you an offer, and you accepted."

"Is that what you call it?"

Rich watches me. "Yes. That's what I call it."

"Whatever."

The table moves as Rich leans back in his chair. "I really thought you were going to be less prickly," he states.

I smirk. "It's a gift; what can I say?"

He closes his eyes and takes a deep breath. "Fuck me," he mutters in a low tone that I don't think I was supposed to hear, but I did. I want to give a smart retort, something like - 'no, thanks' - but there is a resignation in his tone and posture. Like he's given up. I say nothing. Eventually, he reopens his eyes, his dark gaze seeking mine immediately. He takes another deep breath.

"I don't know what to do," he says quietly. "You are an ... enigma. You frustrate the hell out of me with all your secrets and smart-ass comments, but I have this insane feeling that I need to protect you, and yet you block me at every turn."

I widen my eyes. What?

"What?" I cough and swallow at the same time. It's not attractive. "What do you mean?"

"What I said. I feel the need to protect you. Shocked?" he asks. I nod and then shake my head.

"Not really. You're supposed to protect everyone here, isn't that in the job description?"

Rich smiles. "It is, to a point, but with you - it's different. I can't put my finger on it. Why do I feel so drawn to you?" I feel like it's a rhetorical question, but he appears to be waiting for an answer.

"Because I don't roll over and let you tickle my tummy?" I'll admit it's a lame response, but I am still reeling from his being 'drawn to me' confession.

He laughs. "No. I can assure you there are several women of my acquaintance who do not fall at my feet."

"Really?" I can't help the sarcasm that attaches to the single word. "I find that hard to believe."

"You do? Why?"

"Because you're so … confident, full of yourself. You know how to get exactly what you want. Look at me. I stayed here against my better judgement. All I wanted to do was get away, but somehow, you managed to persuade me not to leave. I would have thought that was an attractive trait to most women."

"But not you?"

I frown. "Where is all this coming from? I have been here less than forty-eight hours. You don't know me; you know nothing about my past or why I am here, and there are at least two women who are way more beautiful out there. Women who would, I am sure, welcome your need to protect them."

"I don't want to protect them," he says softly, "not in the same way that I want to protect you."

Up until this moment and that minor lapse of judgement in the kitchen, my reaction to Rich has been negative and hostile, and when those words first leave his lips, I want to puke. I mean, I literally want to vomit. It's right up there on the list of top ten cheesy lines, but then I take a second and allow myself to return his unwavering gaze. And his gaze is unwavering. His dark eyes do not flicker nor move from my face. A bead of sweat breaks out on his brow and chases down his forehead. There is no duplicity in his body language, no hint of arrogance, no sign of game-playing or narcissism. In fact, it is the opposite. The more I look, the more open he becomes, and finally, I see what I have been missing all along. Rich is not dangerous, at least not in the way I feared. I have tarred him with my Alex brush because he's easy on the eye and is outwardly confident, just like that bastard was. I decided within moments of meeting this man that he was someone I had no interest in spending time with simply because I had typecast him and put him in my Alex box. But maybe I was wrong. Maybe I have misjudged him. Since Añaposta Island it has been impossible for me to trust any man, and luckily, on the streets, there is little call for this. As a rule, we trust no one, so when I met Rich and saw his confidence, I perceived it to be arrogance. When I watched Astrid fawn over him, I believed him to love only himself.

But here he is, sitting in front of me, sweating, nervous, eyes glittering with emotion, and it hits me square in the stomach. He is telling me the truth. He is drawn to me in a way that he doesn't understand, and he is allowing me to see that whilst laying his vulnerability at my feet. We may have only met a couple of days ago, but in this heightened moment, it feels like I have known him forever. That age-old cliche.

My gut is reaching out to him. Responding, reacting, urging me to communicate my understanding, to tell him that I feel this same crazy connection and that I am just as confused. But my head is telling me to get the fuck out of here. I cannot afford to react to anyone. I cannot afford to care about anyone. And I sure as hell cannot afford for someone to care about me.

I am broken. I am lost. I am tainted, and I am a prisoner in my world. A world from which I won't escape until justice is done. Justice that may come at a high price and perhaps even cost me my own life.

I don't want this. I don't want someone to be nice to me. I don't deserve it.

And Rich, for all his gestures and grandiose mannerisms, doesn't deserve any part in my screwed-up world. He needs to stay who he is, where he is, without the clutter of a fucked up ex-wealthy kid turned-woman, with a killer's agenda.

I close my eyes, blocking the directness of his gaze from my brain.

And then, with a long, deep breath, I stand, pull open the door, and walk slowly back to my bunk.

≈≈≈≈

I hear Jayde call out to me as I leave Rich's office, but I ignore her. Whatever she wants to say can wait. It's not like either of us are going anywhere. Instead, I keep walking until I have reached one hundred and four steps and arrived at the metal-lined door leading to the square of grass outside. I have only been out here once with Rex. Every other time he's had a call of nature, someone - usually Colin - has been more than willing to take him, so apart from being aware of this space outside, I know little else about it.

The door is unlocked, and I push it outwards, shoving against it with all of my weight. It's heavy in deference to the metal lining affixed to both sides, which, given the age of the building, is definitely not lightweight aluminium. As soon as my feet hit the soft grass, I squint, the bright morning light playing havoc with my eyes.

"Hey, baby girl." I was right; Astrid is out here.

I blink furiously before letting the door swing closed behind me. In a matter of seconds, I feel a wet nose rub against my feet. Automatically, I reach down and rub the ears of my canine friend.

"Hey," I respond. My vision has now adjusted, and I can see that this area is larger than I originally thought. Last time, I just opened the door and let Rex out to do his 'thing', so it's the first time I have stood out here. I take a moment and breathe in the cool, sweet air. Overhead, a seagull dives and calls, and the faint tang of salty sea floats on the breeze. I take another breath. Deeper, slower, enjoying the moment. It is unbelievably quiet out here. I cannot hear any traffic or street noise, just the quiet hum of nature as earth's creatures go about their daily toil.

Astrid is sitting on a large swinging seat to the right, so I make my way over, Rex at my heels. I sit beside her, and together we move our feet as one, allowing the swing to go forwards and backwards at a gentle speed. I drop my head back onto the soft padded cushion and close my eyes once more. It is the most relaxed I have been in a very long time.

"You okay?" Astrid asks.

I open my eyes and turn towards her. "Yeah. You?"

She nods. "You were asleep, so we thought we'd come out here, didn't we, boy?"

Rex inclines his head at Astrid before jumping clumsily onto the seat between us, making the chair swing wildly for a moment. Both Astrid and I laugh. It feels good.

I look up at the sky. Light blue is dotted with white clouds which are being chased by larger ones tinged with grey. It looks like rain. I wrap my arms around myself and rub my hands up and down in a bid to ward off the chill. It is beautiful out here, a true place of serenity, and though I know it will rain soon, I don't want to go back in, not yet.

I feel safe out here.

Untouchable.

And I am with my two favourite people in the world.

For a moment, life seems perfect.

And very, very simple.

NINETEEN MONTHS AGO

The Atlantic Ocean is as unforgiving as it is stark. I can feel the swell of the current as the cargo ship bravely ploughs through wave after wave. We are on our way to England, exactly as Clarice promised, and we will be docking in Bristol. That is all I know, and to be honest, all I care to know.

Jim, the man who pulled me aboard the vessel, has barely left my side. He is one of several deckhands and has taken it upon himself to make sure I am okay. This is our second day of bleak sailing into nothingness, and Jim has asked me precisely twelve questions in that time, none of which I answered. After we left Añaposta Island, he took me to a small cabin and gave me the chance to rest. I did not. I lay on the tiny, hard, cold bunk but did not sleep. I was in shock. I am in shock. I know this because I have once more shut down like I did that day when I swam from the *Cassiopeia* to Añaposta Island. This time, though, I am not alone. I am not on a beach with only a small pink towel for company. I am on a cargo ship that is both noisy and smelly. Metal is everywhere I look, and my nose is full from the permanent stench of oil. Jim has told me we are on our return journey. They offloaded at several of the other islands before picking me up at Añaposta. Now, we are an empty ship, plundering the seas towards home. Wherever the hell that is.

I haven't eaten. I have sipped some hot tea, but that is all.

I have so many questions. So many things I need to know and understand, but I cannot vocalise any of them. All I can see is Clarice dragging me through the village, the market, and up the dock towards freedom. I hear her urging me on, telling me we will be okay - until suddenly we are not. Her beautiful face, frozen in shock, is imprinted on my mind as the bullet from Yarrick's gun tears through her body. Squishy, warm, loving, kind-hearted, Clarice. How I wish I had known that she was as much a prisoner as me. How I wish I could have saved her. How I wish Yarrick had taken me instead.

I am leaning over the rails, watching the swell of the ocean as it peaks, showering white foam over the hull of the boat. Jim stands next to me. I know that I am pressing my stomach up against the barrier, and I am aware that I am putting more pressure and weight through my swollen belly than I perhaps should. But I don't care.

"How did you know her?" I ask finally. Jim lets out a sigh. He doesn't need clarification. He knows exactly who I am talking about.

"We all knew her," he says, turning his worn, ruddy face towards me. I think he is probably in his mid-forties, though it is hard to tell. His skin reveals the effect of years of sun and salt water, and his light brown hair is long and matted. I don't see any grey at his temples, nor in the shaggy beard that is in desperate need of a trim - hence my assumption of his age - but, at the end of the day, I couldn't give a monkeys how old this man is. I catch my thoughts before they drift into a pointless pondering of follicle colour and age. It is insignificant and irrelevant. What isn't, is Clarice.

"She used to meet us at the dock," he says, "always smiling and happy. Sometimes, if we had a lot to unload, she'd chat with us awhile and bring us fruit. I think most of us were half in love with her." Jim's voice has a soft lilt, which seems at odds with his work-roughened exterior. I find myself enjoying its tone.

I nod. "Sounds like Clarice."

"I don't know," he continues as he stares off into the distance, "there was just something about her. Then, one day, it all changed." Jim's breath wobbles as his voice breaks, and suddenly, a burst of realisation hits my brain.

Shit. This man - and several of the crew, no doubt - have also witnessed what I did, and for them it means the loss of a friend too, someone close, someone they were half in love with. This is not all about me, far from it. These men are hurting, and I am shocked that it has taken me forty-eight hours to understand this reality and access any kind of empathy. The urge to give and seek comfort is overwhelming, so tentatively, I reach to my right and place my palm gently on the sleeve of his fleece shirt. He looks down at the small gesture and allows the slightest of smiles to touch his lips.

"We'd been coming here a few years," he continues, emotions momentarily in check, "and every time she would be there at the dock, waiting. Then, one day, she wasn't anymore, and no one seemed to know why."

Jim briefly closes his eyes before taking in a deep, cleansing breath. "It felt strange not seeing her, and I guess we all thought there was something off. It was probably another six months before we saw her again. She was with Yarrick this time, and they were both waiting for us. We'd got several boxes of women's clothing, and as soon as we docked, Yarrick was there, trying to get his hands on them. Directing us to where he wanted them unloaded."

"Clothes?" I ask, my voice small. Shit. I am immediately

transported back to the room at the top of the upside-down shack and its wardrobe filled with garments. I am not okay with where my recollections are headed.

"Yeah, women's stuff. Usually, we don't know what's in a consignment, but one of these boxes was damaged. Some of the men found the underwear and ... you know ..." he coughs in discomfort, and despite his already rosy features, I notice the hint of a blush. I nod. I don't know, but I can imagine.

"The men were penalised for messing about with the cargo; that's why I've never forgotten that trip. There was real unrest on board, and several crew left when we returned to England. Said they didn't want to work on a ship where they couldn't have a laugh. We're at sea for months at a time," Jim shrugs, "so I kind of see their point."

I say nothing. I have no wish to hear any more stories of these men playing with women's underwear, no wish to be reminded of their sexual needs. I have a permanent reminder growing in my belly every single day. Since my time in the cell, every atom of my being has fought to erase those memories. I realised, soon after returning to the upside-down shack, that if I continued to re-live the atrocities to which I was subjected, it would do nothing save give those memories and experiences more power. Worse still, they would be warped by the effects of time, their re-telling would become less accurate, and I was afraid I would begin to blame myself.

So, I chose not to think or remember. I chose to live as if I had no past - despite the uncomfortable proof of its existence pressing relentlessly on my bladder - and after a while, I simply stopped remembering. This is why I have no intention of listening to a story that, to the men on board, would have been a joke. Yet, I cannot forgive even the most innocent of objectification toward my fellow women right now. My relationship with men has been abused beyond comprehension, and I don't even know if I have the ability or desire to rebuild it. I suspect men and their needs are what got me here in the first place, and I am almost certain it is why Clarice was killed. When it comes down to it, humans are really only driven by two motivators: money and sexual gratification. Everything else … it's all just fluff.

Of course, you can argue that there are many who are driven by the desire for change, and you wouldn't be wrong; it's just my opinion that without money or sexual gratification at the end of the rainbow, human desire would be more metered and less intense. If those men who visited me night after night did not seek physical release they would have had no interest in turning up, for it wasn't as if we made sparkling conversation or played board games. Like I said, just my opinion.

As ever, my thoughts have drifted, so I drag them back to Jim. He is continuing his tale of Yarrick and the clothing, telling me that the cargo should have been destined for the market, but Yarrick insisted on several of the boxes being loaded into his truck. I frown as he speaks. Something about what he is saying feels wrong. And then I realise. I had no idea Yarrick had a truck. I never saw or heard of one; I don't remember anyone in the immediate community using anything other than their legs for transport.

"His truck?" I ask.

Jim looks down at me, confusion on his face. "Yes. We loaded the boxes into the bed of Yarrick's truck. Why?"

I shake my head, returning my gaze to the darkness of the ocean for a moment. Does it matter that I didn't know about a truck? Is it important?

But then I remember something else.

Añaposta Island is small; this I know from the time Yarrick spent teaching me about the island and its inhabitants. Initially, I believed everyone knew everyone, such was the minimal number of official residents; however, I once asked Yarrick if he could name everyone on the island, and he said no. He could not. He then went on to explain how the community in which we lived was just a tiny part of Añaposta Island. We were, he said, separate from the main residents, with our own rules and colony. Though the distance from one end of the island to the other wasn't great, Yarrick always told me that he never ventured outside of our 'territory'. No one in the community did.

I'd asked about supplies, where they came from, did they travel to other areas to collect these, and Yarrick had laughed. They relied on themselves for supplies, he'd said, because they had no means of transport to carry goods from anywhere else. What they had either came in on a cargo ship and was moved by hand or was grown and cultivated here in the colony. The community did not possess any vehicles, which was also why exploration of the whole island was not possible (I had expressed an interest in this in the early days but was told it would be out of the question). Though we lived 'alongside' the larger population, he said our community generally preferred to remain on their own side of the fence, primarily because the island was way too small for any form of civil unrest, so everyone kept to themselves, and peace prevailed.

At the time, I didn't think much of it, though it always struck me as odd that our community never integrated with the rest of the island, and I failed to see how doing so would result in civil unrest. Now, of course, I understand it better than anyone. Yarrick's success relies on control, and to integrate with a larger society, one with laws and humane values, would undoubtedly strip him of that control. He would risk exposure from those unwilling to bend to his wishes, and if he was prepared to shoot the woman with whom he had shared his life dead in cold blood, then he wouldn't hesitate to attack anyone who dared question his authority.

I knew nothing of this, though. In my mind, I had likened our colony to the travelling community back in England. I believed us to be similar: a group of like-minded families living our own way with our own traditions but respecting the harmony of wider society. I believed what I had been told, took everything at face value and regarded Yarrick as a genuinely kind and caring person who wanted nothing more than to give me another chance at life. I should have been less accepting. I am reminded of an observation made by the author, Arthur Conan Doyle, the mastermind behind Sherlock Holmes. He was once heard to say, "It is easy to be wise after the event."

Yeah, too fucking right.

In the cold light of day, with no one to mould my interpretation, it's as if another piece of the puzzle has slotted into place. I now know why I was subjected to two months of sickening hell and why no one did anything about it - because there was no one to do anything about it.

The community into which I had been brought was a place to call home, to respect and be respected in, somewhere to enjoy a life of idyllic proportions where those on the outside could only dream of belonging. And in return for all it gave, the community expected loyalty. But it was so much darker, too. Those in charge were their own rulers, culpable to no one other than themselves. It was a place of secrets and lies, hidden truths and underground caves. People didn't leave, weren't allowed to leave, maybe because they knew its secrets or perhaps simply because to leave would wound the community and show its weakness. And that could not be allowed. The community was bigger than any one individual, and, as its leader, Yarrick was the community.

When I asked to leave and return to England, I had unknowingly shown a level of disrespect that was not to be tolerated. My departure to somewhere outside of Yarrick's control would mean questions being asked and he couldn't risk that, so I was brought back into line. What I still don't completely understand is why Yarrick is so afraid. What secrets is he hiding that warranted the death of a beautiful woman? I have no insider knowledge, know no secrets, yet Yarrick would have turned the gun on me too. Without a shadow of a doubt. I can only conclude that whatever he's hiding is big. Big enough to instil fear deep inside that man's cold heart.

I close my eyes and breathe in the salty air as I empty my mind and allow it a moment of relief. The sounds of nature gently soothe my aching heart. I am aware of Jim beside me, and I know that I have not answered his question, but the truth is - I cannot. I don't know why it matters about the truck; I just know that it does. The wardrobe of clothes which bothered me eighteen months ago, bothers me even more now that I know how it came to be. Yarrick's explanation was innocent enough, but there are just too many parts that don't make sense. The whole picture is a lot bigger than the one created by the ever-changing colours on the bedroom wall of the upside-down shack. It has to be otherwise, nothing that has happened since the day I swam into the clutches of the world from which I am now running makes any kind of sense.

In the same way that I resolved to find Alex, I resolve to bring Yarrick to justice.

For me.

For Clarice.

And, in the same way I know this to be true of my quest for Alex ...

... I know that once more, I am the only one who can do so.

Chapter Fourteen

PRESENT DAY

I've always hated chess. It's one of those games, as a boy, you're expected to be good at, but I never was. I think it's because I am impatient. I was always one move ahead of my opponent - in the way of the greatest Chess Masters - yet my moves were not calculated. I didn't care whether my Pawn ended up at Queen Three; all I wanted to do was get the game over as fast as possible. My parents, though, believed that learning the ultimate tactical game was a necessary developmental skill, and I ended up at the school Chess Club on more occasions than I care to remember. It sickens me to this day that if a parent decides their child must do something, then that child toes the line regardless of their own feelings.

Propaganda will have us believe we now live in a progressive society but I disagree. Wherever you look, we are all following rules made by someone else, and it has been this way since the beginning of time. Since Adam was created from dust and Eve from his ribs before both were banished from the Garden of Eden after eating 'forbidden fruit'. Perhaps that is why I am where I am today.

On the outside of the world. I am a non-conformist.

Chess Club did have its perks, though. Once I'd played the allotted number of games at my usual breakneck pace (I literally didn't give a shit whether I won), I was free to leave, and leaving meant the chance to catch some action at the skate park whilst waiting to be picked up by whichever 'family friend' was assigned the task that day. My preference for this role was 'Uncle Joe'. No matter how many times he was sent on the errand, he always got lost and always arrived late. Often, I'd get a decent hour of skateboard viewing before 'Uncle Joe' found his way to the club. And let me tell you, skateboarding was a pastime that I did enjoy.

On reflection, the only pleasure I ever gained from playing chess was hitting the clock after each move. Watching the table shake as I thumped the button just a bit harder than necessary was immensely satisfying. I struck it so hard during one match that my opponent's King toppled, which signalled the end of the game. It wasn't a planned strategy, but seeing the disgust on that other boy's face when he realised what had happened was priceless. Of course, he hadn't actually surrendered the game, but no one witnessed my unintentional part in his demise, so when the referee was alerted to a fallen monarch and declared me the winner, I decided it would be wrong to reveal the actual truth. I was enjoying that stupid little boy's misery too much. Now that was an epic fucking game of chess.

You might wonder why I am talking about chess, something for which I have already revealed my dislike, but it is because of its similarities to my current activity. It turns out that watching and manipulating real lives is immensely rewarding and reminds me of a rather large game of chess - without the clock.

Although I am a little embarrassed to admit this, I have also found my ongoing occupation hugely arousing. It's an unexpected but extremely pleasurable bonus. Some men -

of which I will admit to being one in the past - rely on porn and all its fake-ness to get their kicks, but now I simply power up my computer, watch the screens flicker into life and enjoy the very real show. Even just thinking about what I do on a daily basis causes a most enjoyable tightening in my groin.

It hasn't all been euphoric, though. You cannot spend six months living in a single room without getting a touch of cabin fever, so I have been forced to take the odd risk, which has led to unnecessary angst. The most concerning of which was the day that I chose to walk brazenly into the main building. I thought I had calculated my entrance and associated peril to the last detail, especially as none of the major players were present, but my appearance was somewhat out of place due in no small part to the high-end jeans and sweater in which I was clothed. A schoolboy error I have since realised; thus, after becoming the recipient of more than one questioning glance, I swiftly departed. It was a reminder of how high the stakes are in this particular game.

It also taught me I could never afford such complacency again. One word in the wrong ear, one innocent question from a down and out, and my cover would have been blown. The last three years would have been nothing more than an exhausting, if salacious, waste of time.

I am, therefore, resigned to no more clandestine outings and have remained well hidden ever since. There is no way anyone can find me or trace my activities now. I am an expert stalker, a peeping Tom if you like, but with added gravitas ...

... for I have twenty-four-hour, one hundred per cent access to those I wish to observe - without any of the jeopardy. It is a heady and powerful mind fuck.

I rub my swollen member as it tightens beneath the constraint of my jeans, enjoying the resulting bolt of pleasure. The ambient light from the monitors flickers and bounces off the walls - the product of ever-changing black-and-white images switching from one camera to another and then another. I feel invincible. In this moment, I am invincible.

There is a knock at the fire door - one, two, three, pause, one, two, three, pause, one. The coded knock. The one which tells me my latte has arrived.

I stretch and push my chair away from the desk, standing, then wincing slightly as my neck groans. It is annoying that this injury still affects me, the one I received in that unfortunate dinghy accident - although, in some ways, I am grateful for it happening. Though that night unfolded in a way I was not anticipating, I was still adequately prepared and left nothing behind, something of which I am immensely proud. There was no discernible evidence of my existence - except for the small dinghy, but they were ten a penny, so it was of no consequence. That I was able to pull off such a stunt gave me immense confidence as I moved onto the next part of my plan.

It was, of course, a little unfortunate that a dead body accompanied the dinghy on its final voyage, washing up on the shore safely ensconced inside the small craft - but nothing is perfect.

The one regret I have, for I do have one, is the extent of collateral damage. I have reflected at length and wondered if it was necessary to end so many innocent lives, but the truth is I panicked and got sloppy. I did experience the smallest amount of sympathy for the loved ones who were left behind, but that didn't last for long. What's done is done - and when I revisit these events, I choose to congratulate myself instead on the 'piece de resistance'. The master-stroke. A bomb so cleverly disguised, so ingeniously engineered, that it ended the sailing days of the *Cassiopeia* with a swift finality. I have never been more excited than when I watched her considerable hull slowly sinking, far from land, far from civilisation, taking the evidence of my crimes to the depths of the ocean bed. I picture her now lying in the abyss, a place never to be reached as it rests alongside some of the most sacred of secrets. It was like a film that only I got to watch. Mind-blowing on another level.

I have to be honest; for a while, I was convinced someone would join the dots, but it's been three years, and the only person left who has any knowledge is now firmly in my sights. At last. It's been a long three years. My patience and resources have been stretched to their absolute limits, but I am finally reaping the long-overdue benefits. I am not quite done, though. I have one final, carefully laid plan to execute, and then, once everything has been concluded to my satisfaction, I will sit back and count the spoils. I cannot wait. The anticipation of this last move is such a head rush. I will be toppling another matriarch, just like that poor fallen King all those years ago. I can almost feel the rush of intense pleasure.

I open the door to the outside world and find Colin standing at the top of the metal stairs, waiting patiently for me to take my coffee in the same way he does every single day. It's been fun playing with Colin. He recognised me instantly, and I him. Though there had been a few years of absence, there are some you never forget, and the times we'd previously shared were profound for us both. Colin was a fucking genius back then, one talented skateboarder looking for his big break, and I was happy to be his wingman. Everyone loved him, and by extension, they loved me too. But then he had to go and fuck it all up with his injury and the fallout with his parents. I had been so close to living his life, so close to moving in with his family and enjoying all the trappings their wealth had to offer...

Colin and I go way back. We are - albeit somewhat loosely - friends. I probably should have mentioned that earlier. The barista and I know each other intimately. More intimately, I am sure, than Colin would ever wish those of his current acquaintance to know. Especially his latest object of desire.

I have to commend Colin. He's always had impeccable taste in lovers - I count myself amongst his finest - so it isn't surprising to find him fawning over Aurora. If I look at her objectively, I can acknowledge her physical charms. She is enough to turn any red-blooded man into a whimpering boy and, if you allow her name to roll slowly off your tongue, it tingles awareness in places you didn't know existed.

Aurora.

I expect you're more than a little confused. Right?

You're probably wondering why, if I am aware of her beauty, I refused her advances on the yacht that night - especially when *everything* was so blatantly on offer.

Well, the answer is actually staring you in the face. It's blindingly simple.

I don't like women, not in that way. I can admire the female form, but beyond that, they do nothing in the arousal stakes. I've dabbled, of course, I think it would have been rude not to, but the pink side of the fence is really not for me.

I almost choked when Aurora straight out asked me if I was gay. She had no idea how right she was. Of course, I lied to her. I had to. I didn't want her to think of me as anything other than her perfect man, and the pretence was easy to maintain. I'd had years of practise.

Colin, on the other hand, does float my boat and what a god he has become. But he is blind to me. All he sees are two long-lost friends, grown men reminiscing. Our intimate times I know he has brushed off as teenage curiosity, but it was always more than curiosity for me. I believed, no, I know, that I was in love with him for a bloody long time.

When I think about where I am today and what has happened in my recent past, I cannot help but be amazed at the sheer number of coincidences that have aligned. In the back of my mind, I had always planned to find Colin, but to have him almost fall into my lap at the same time as that bitch, Aurora - well, you couldn't make it up.

And yes, I know I've just called Aurora a bitch when a few seconds ago, I was commenting on her magnetism, but you'll have to trust me. I have my reasons.

The only thing that worries me is Colin and how he will fit into my world once all is said and done. Make no mistake, I want him back in my life and bed - the feelings I had back then have merely lain dormant - but so much has changed. I need to remind him of the fun we used to have and allow our closeness to develop organically, though I cannot dedicate any time to this right now, which means he may form a false opinion of me. He may only see me in a negative light and so I must tread carefully. For now, we must keep our exchanges to lattes, and I must restrain myself.

I bet you're recoiling at the idea of Colin becoming a part of my life aren't you? Thinking he is way too good for me. You're right, he is, but I care even less about what you think than I do about Aurora.

I hope, actually, that you fear for Colin, for what might become of him because you have no idea, yet, what I am capable of.

And Colin. Oh, Colin. He thinks he knows me, too. He genuinely believes our friendship has survived unscathed and celebrates the serendipity that made our paths cross once more. He is so naive. He believes that I have also moved on from our teenage fumbles. He has a lot to learn. But I love his naivety. I love that though everything else in my life has changed beyond recognition, Colin is still Colin - just a tiny bit more alluring in adult form.

I did consider bringing him into my world and showing him what I was doing. My ego is desperate to impress and share every sordid detail. I want to see the excitement on his face when he realises how much power I wield and how perfect his life could be - but I can't share it with him. Not right now. The risk is too great. The stupid sap has fallen for Aurora. I can see it in his eyes, his face and, as much as it pains me to watch, I have to let him believe they will have a future. Because I know the reality. I know that one day, he will wake up alone and realise she does not feel the same.

Then I will be here - waiting to pick up the pieces.

Until that day, I shall observe from the sidelines and slowly sip every single cup of steaming hot latte that Colin lovingly makes.

The screens in front of me change once more, and I smile.

What a day to be alive.

Chapter Fifteen

NINETEEN MONTHS AGO

I cannot decide if the scene I am witnessing is morbid or beautiful. The engines on the cargo ship are idling, the craft drifting slowly along with the waves which have gentled in their force. The entire crew have made their way to the bow of the ship, twenty-one of them in total, and are forming a semi-circle facing over the bow and out to sea. In front of them stands the captain, a man I have seen only briefly during my two days on board. He, like everyone else, has his head bowed, and I am close enough to see the beginnings of a bald patch in his salt-and-pepper hair. He is talking quietly, slowly, like a vicar or reverend, reciting passages from the bible where good overcomes evil. Then they are praying. Clasping their hands together as one unit, nodding solemnly as they listen to the captain's words before each murmuring their acceptance of the prayer. As I watch, I observe more than one tear dripping from the eye of a rugged crewman and land on the cold metal deck below.

They are remembering Clarice. Spending a few moments, now that we are a good distance from Añaposta Island, praying for her and sending their love to carry her safely to the next stage of her journey. Though Jim told me that most of the men were half in love with Clarice, it is not until I see the bare emotions present on every single face that I actually believe him. Her loss was brutal and wholly undeserved, and it is only now I realise how lucky I was to spend even the smallest amount of time in her world. I vow, as I watch the men hug each other before dispersing, to one day be like Clarice. If I can be even half the person she was, bring half the love and joy that she did, then I will almost feel like her death had not been for nothing. Almost.

Jim materialises at my side and hands me a large sou'wester jacket. It is yellow with a hood, and though it will swamp me, I know that it will provide plenty of warmth and protection from the worst of the sea. We will be sailing again soon, so I take the jacket gratefully and shrug into it. For some reason, I am reminded of Paddington, the fictional bear who always wore a similar jacket. Though I don't think he was ever a passenger on a remote cargo ship sailing the waters of the Atlantic Ocean.

"She was really important to you," I say to no one in particular, although I know that Jim is still beside me. I feel rather than see him nod.

"She was."

There is so much more I want to know and understand. We have not resumed our earlier conversation about Yarrick and the truck and the clothes, but I know that I must if I am ever to unravel the mystery of the community I have just left behind. Now, though, doesn't feel like the right time.

"Are you doing okay?" Jim asks.

"Yes," I reply quietly, "that was beautiful."

He shrugs. "Just felt right. We all knew that Clarice wanted to get away from there," he hikes his thumb back towards the islands we left, "I just wish we could have helped. She deserved so much more." His words drift out on the wind as he stares wistfully at the yawning ocean. We have picked up speed, and the waves are now cresting the bow, their worst damage held at bay by the solid bulwark that fringes the hull.

"I wish I'd realised how special she was," I say.

Jim sighs. "She loved you; you know."

I turn my face towards him. "She told you that?"

He nods. "All the time. She was so proud of the woman you had become."

I frown. It seems odd that this perfect stranger knows so much of my existence. "Do you know how I came to live with them?" I ask.

"Yes," he replies. "We were in the dock a day or so after they found you. There was some commotion over a dinghy that had been washed ashore, and that's when Clarice told us about you. Said you had come from the dinghy."

I smile, and for some reason, I find myself compelled to reveal a part of my past. "I wasn't really on that dinghy," I say.

Jim returns my smile. "I know," he says. "Clarice knew, too."

"Wait, what? Clarice knew?"

He nods again. "Yes. If we ever saw you, we were sworn to secrecy, but we all knew; I think the rest of them did too - on the island, I mean - and ... well, I guess now it doesn't matter."

I reach behind me, searching for a safe place to sit. I cannot process the idea that everyone I had believed to be family knew that my story wasn't true.

But Jim has no reason to lie—not anymore.

My legs are shaking. A metal box rests six paces away; it is cold and hard, but I sink gratefully into its support. Jim watches me, hesitant and unsure, and then I see his face change as he makes a decision. His comforting form joins me, close enough but not touching. He waits, silent and still, as we watch the lifeblood of the Atlantic Ocean swell and dip, form and de-construct.

It is a full five minutes before I find my voice. "Where did they think I came from?" I ask. There are so many questions, but I think I need to start at the beginning. I have to know how much they knew - so that I can also know how much they were keeping from me.

Jim sighs. "It's not that simple. Yarrick ... he has a lot of secrets, but he also has a lot of friends. That community, it's all about him."

I shake my head and wrap my arms around my body. I am shivering, though I am not sure if it is entirely due to the cold. It occurs to me that the baby has been silent for a while. I would have expected it to protest at my ever-changing emotions and shift when I tightened my arms around my belly, but it hasn't moved. At least one of us is blissfully resting.

"I ... I don't know what to say, what to ask first. I just ... I ..."

Jim reaches an arm around me cautiously. Instinctively, I freeze, but I do not feel threatened, so after a moment, I relax.

"Let's get you inside," he says, "you're cold and wet. It's not good for you or the baby."

I close my eyes and take a deep breath, watching the last

few moments of Clarice's life on repeat. My brain empties of all conscious thought. I know that I should be pushing for answers, asking Jim to explain what he means. What exactly is the story of my life - according to those in that screwed-up community on Añaposta Island? And why the hell is a humble deckhand on a cargo ship aware of it? Who else knows that I didn't arrive on that dinghy? The one I didn't even know existed. And actually, does it matter?

It is too much. I know that I am letting myself down, for my troubled mind craves the answers, but I just cannot. I have no reserves to pick any of it apart and put it back together. Not right now.

Jim is right. I am cold and wet and it is no good for me or the baby.

I nod and then rise to my feet, allowing him to lead me into the bowels of the ship and the crew mess. He seats me on one of the benches beside the table, and I watch as he ladles sugar and tea into a mug. Sweet tea. The irony of this is not lost on me.

I look around at my bare surroundings and listen to the hum of the powerful ship's engines as it takes me ever closer to home. Once more I close my eyes as I try to block out reality. I am where I wanted to be, I am on my way back to England and I am safe, but those few words from Jim have made me realise just how little I knew about my existence on Añaposta Island.

Clarice was my port in the storm, my reference point, and I have lost her. I am reminded of her fear on the day I asked to find a way back home and how everything changed after that. I don't understand any of it, but what I have started to realise is that my situation, the life that I had with Yarrick and Clarice was false. All of it. Every single moment. Now I have to do everything I can to uncover the true depths of

Yarrick's depravity. For me, for the baby and ultimately for Clarice.

Despite everything that I have been through since that fateful night on the *Cassiopeia*, I know with gut-wrenching certainty that I have never been more scared than I am right now.

PRESENT DAY

We have been in the garden for a while, gently swaying on the comfy swing and listening to Rex snuffle and snore. We have spoken very little, but I feel a level of comfort in Astrid's company that I don't with anyone else. There is no need to speak.

I wonder how long we will be left in peace until someone - most likely Rich - comes to find us. I have yet to tell Astrid about Jayde, and I realise that I must. Rich will no doubt take immense delight in filling in the gaps for anyone prepared to listen, and if Astrid is going to discover my true name, then I want her to hear it from me.

"There's a new girl, in there," I indicate the metal-lined door which leads to the warehouse.

Astrid nods. "I'm sure new girls come and go all the time."

I laugh. Not because her words are particularly funny but because I have the most entertaining vision of girls coming and going from Rich's office and every single one of them telling him to go to hell.

"What's so funny?" Astrid asks, and I shake my head.

"Nothing. Nothing." I take a breath. "This girl," I start again, "she's someone I used to know."

"What the fuck, baby girl? That's awesome. Right?"

I shrug. I have yet to decide.

"It's not good that she's here?" Astrid picks up on my hesitation.

I swivel sideways and reach my hand across Rex's wiry back to hold onto Astrid's.

"I don't know," I say quietly, "I honestly don't know."

"Okay, baby girl. Okay." Astrid squeezes my fingers, and I know that if I were to say nothing more, she would be fine with that because that's just who Astrid is. She never wants more than I am prepared to give, and I guess I'm the same with her. We have each other because we want to have each other, and we know what we know. The rest ... well, time will take care of that.

"I need to tell you about her, though," I say after a further sixty seconds have elapsed, "because she recognised me too. We were at school together a very long time ago."

"Were you friends?" I feel Astrid turn her gaze towards me.

"Yes," I say, "we were best friends for a long time. She was ... is, like you. Tall, beautiful, the cool girl, the one everyone wants to hang out with."

Astrid smiles. "That ain't me, baby girl."

I shake my head in response. "It is, you just don't see it."

We share a smile. "I've not seen her since we were fifteen, and then today, she shows up here."

"Wait, she's like us? Not a helper or anything?"

"No, no ... she's like us."

"Fuck me. That's one hell of a coincidence."

"Yep." I incline my head. "Tell me about it. She recognised me straight away, but I didn't until she stood close and that's when I realised. Bloody Rich was there, too. He heard us talking and dragged me into his office demanding answers."

"What the hell is it to do with him?"

"Precisely. He said ..." I pause, wondering if I should reveal what happened in his office. Tell Astrid what he declared. I decide I have to. I need to confide in someone, and there is no one I trust more. "He told me that he feels the need to protect me. But like, really protect me, not just because he has to."

Astrid lets out a low whistle. "Shit. As in ... you know ...?"

I shake my head. "I don't know. He seemed genuine, not creepy, but who the hell knows with him."

"It's only you who thinks he's creepy, baby girl. I personally think he's bloody hot. Maybe Rich isn't the only one with a crush." She winks at me.

I throw her a look of disgust. "I absolutely, one hundred per cent, do not have a crush on Rich, thank you very much."

Astrid smiles, her beautiful face lit by the morning light. "I think you are protesting too much ..."

I growl. "Fuck off."

She laughs and starts tickling Rex under his chin. "We know, don't we, boy?" she says.

"Really, Astrid. Fuck off."

She laughs louder, and despite myself, I smile. It's impossible to be angry with Astrid. I disagree with her theory; she is way off the mark - though there was that moment, the way he looked at me right before I got up and walked out - did I feel something? I shake my head. I need to clear this train of thought. I dislike Rich. I have disliked him from the second I met him. There is no reason to change the status quo. Determinedly, I push my de facto protector to the depths of my thoughts.

"Don't you think it's strange," I ask, changing the subject, "that she turns up here at the exact same time as me?"

"Ah," says Astrid, "we're back to your old friend." She smirks, acknowledging that I have deliberately moved away from Rich. "Sure, baby girl, it is, but that's okay, right? I mean, there must be loads of us who know each other."

"Yes," I agree, "but not like this. We mix with the same people out there, on the streets, but most of us don't get our pasts revisiting us."

Astrid studies me for a moment. "Are you okay?" she asks.

I close my eyes for a second. "I think so. It's just ... she knows stuff about me. About who I was, and I don't know if I'm ready to face that. I can't help wondering - you'll think I'm crazy - but it's, like you said, such a big fucking coincidence. I mean, think of how many things had to fall in place - literally - for the two of us to end up here at the exact same time."

"What are you saying?" Astrid asks.

I rub my eyes with the hand that isn't holding hers. "I don't know what I'm saying. Maybe it's nothing. Maybe I'm just paranoid, tired, overwhelmed..." I drop my head back against the soft cushion and sigh. Astrid shifts a little closer, squashing the snoring Rex in between us.

"Whatever you're feeling, it's okay," she says softly. "You know life is shit, and yeah, it's a mindfuck - I mean, if someone I'd known as a kid showed up here, I think it would freak me the hell out too - but maybe it is just a coincidence, yeah? Try not to make this into something bigger than it is."

"Yeah," I say, "you're probably right." I breathe in the cleansing salty air, enjoying the cold as it fills my nose. It feels good. Clean air. No fumes. "There is one thing I need to tell you, though."

"Sure. Anything."

"This girl - woman - her name is Jayde. She left school by choice, but not in the way anyone expected. She joined a cult."

"Shit," Astrid responds. "That's heavy."

I nod. "It was crazy for a while - she disappeared. Everyone thought I was covering for her, but I wasn't. I had no idea where she'd gone either. When I found out, it messed with my head for a while. To think that one person could have that much power over another, so much so that they will literally give up their life." Though I have since experienced a similar world, I didn't choose that world, so I'm not sure I understand it any better now than I did back then.

"Sometimes," Astrid says softly, "we just need somewhere to belong. Maybe that's what she found."

"Yeah," I reply, "maybe. It's not like I've got life sorted anyway." I take a moment to consider Astrid's words. In the months and years after Jayde left, I never really thought about why she did what she did. I was too busy being angry with her for leaving, and I was certain she was being naive. Not that I was any more worldly-wise, but after I'd researched where she had gone, I believed I was right and that Jayde hadn't known what she was doing. It had never occurred to me until now that she may have had her reasons and that perhaps, despite outward appearances, she had simply been looking for somewhere to belong.

"What happened?" Astrid jingles as she rubs her hand over Rex's snoring back, "Did she quit the cult? Is that why she's here?"

"I don't know, we barely spoke." I shake my head. "Rich took me into his office the second he realised we knew each other. She looks rough, though, Ast, like she's been doing it hard. I have no clue how she ended up on the streets and in this place."

Astrid laughs lightly. "I don't think any of us know how we ended up on the streets; it just kind of happens. Right, baby girl?"

"Yeah. I guess so."

I still have to tell Astrid my real name, but I pause for a second, reflecting on what I have revealed thus far. Astrid has asked no questions beyond the simple and obvious, and I appreciate her for that, but she must realise that Jayde holds the key to at least some of my past. Rich did.

I clear my throat. I need to be honest with her, but it is a huge risk. The more people who learn I am Aurora, the harder it will be to remain hidden, but I love Astrid, and I cannot leave her in the dark.

"My real name - it's not Ra," I say quietly, "it's Aurora."

"Aurora," she rolls it around on her tongue. "Cute. I like it. How come you don't use it?"

This is the question I have been dreading. Ever since Jayde arrived and my true moniker was revealed, it was only a matter of time before one of them asked.

"I kind of do," I respond, "I mean, I use part of it." I am stalling.

"Fair enough," Astrid shrugs, and I know she will leave it there. But I don't want to leave it there. I feel the need to confide a little about my past, like she did with me. Astrid shared her story, and now it is my turn to do the same. Suddenly, it seems really important that someone understands who I am and where I came from, just in case.

Just in case - what?

But now that the time has come to open up and let someone in, I find I have no idea where to start. I take a deep breath. "It's an unusual name," I say, "and ... it would be easy for people in my past to find me - if they knew I was alive. And I don't want to be found. Not yet."

"Wait, what?" Astrid shakes her head. "Back up a bit. If they knew you were alive?"

"Yes." I give her a moment to take that in. It doesn't take long for her to arrive at the obvious conclusion.

"Someone wants you dead? Shit, baby girl."

I shrug. "I'm not sure, but there are people out there who wouldn't want their secrets revealed, and I know too much. I can't risk being found. Not yet."

"Fuck ..." Astrid lets out a long exhale. "And I thought my life was messed up."

I smile. "It's not a competition."

She laughs. "Shit, though. So, you're what, on the run?"

"No, no." I hold up my hand, "nothing like that. I promise."

Astrid nods. "Why are you telling me this now? Is it because of that Jayde chick?"

I pause. "Partly. It won't take long for my name to become common knowledge, and I didn't want you to hear it from anyone else."

"Are you famous or something?" she asks, and I laugh.

"No."

"Good," she says, "can't stand those fuckers, all up their own arses."

I laugh more. "Oh, Astrid…"

"What?" she holds her hands up innocently.

I can't believe I am laughing. For the first time in three years, I am sharing my story - or a small part of it - and the world hasn't ended. Yet.

In some ways, I am relieved. Though I have told Astrid very little, it feels good to have a confidant. I know there is so much I have yet to process, so much I have put on those little shelves in my mind to deal with later, and as a result, there are days when the pressure of the secrecy and the hiding is overwhelming.

I have stuck to my mantra - that I would never trust another human being for as long as I lived - but I also remember there was a caveat - until it was time to do so. I think, sitting here in this calm oasis in the midst of a fucked-up world, I may just have found that moment, the time when it is okay to trust.

I only hope that I don't live to regret it.

NINETEEN MONTHS AGO

I am feeling warmer and a little better. Since we returned to the relative comfort of the crew mess, Jim has said nothing. He has given me hot tea and a slice of buttered toast, and then he has simply sat, waiting.

"Thank you," I say as I push the plate away and wipe the few crumbs from my mouth.

"No bother," he replies. "Feeling better?"

I nod. "A little."

"Good."

The baby, though, has still not moved. I am surprised that this concerns me. I have never wanted this child, nor have I necessarily done anything to look after it, but once it started moving within me, I felt an undeniable connection, and oddly, its presence makes me feel less alone. I rub my swollen belly.

"When are you due?" Jim asks as he watches my hand.

I shrug. "I'm not sure. I think I'm about six months along."

He inclines his head but says nothing.

"You must think I'm a terrible person," I say hurriedly, surprised that those are the words I formed. My intention was to ask him about Yarrick.

"Of course not; why would you say that?"

"Because of Clarice. She died ..." my voice breaks as I blink away tears. "She died because of me."

"No," Jim shakes his head. "She died because that bastard killed her. He would have killed you, too. You know that, right?"

I frown. "I don't know, the baby ..." I stop. I've always thought Yarrick valued the baby above anyone else - he intended to bring it up as his own, so perhaps naively, I had believed myself protected from the worst of Yarrick whilst the baby was part of me. "I had no idea Yarrick was capable of killing anyone," I say quietly. "And he wanted this baby. I didn't even know he had a gun. Or a truck." There is no logical order to what I am saying, but my brain is literally full. I have no space left for logic or reason.

"It's his?" Jim asks.

"What?"

"The baby," he glances at my stomach, "it's Yarrick's?"

"Hell, no." The thought of carrying anything remotely related to Yarrick fills me with disgust. I have tried hard to block out the one occasion on which he crossed the line - as part of my punishment. Bile, though, still rises in my throat as I fight to make sense of the last forty-eight hours. "No fucking way," I repeat as an uncontrollable shiver convulses through me.

Jim says nothing. He just watches me. Waiting.

"What do you know about him?" I ask at length. "Yarrick." Even saying his name makes me want to gag.

On the other side of the table, Jim takes a deep breath. "Enough," he replies. "Enough."

I lean my head against the back of the bench and briefly close my eyes. "I thought I knew him," I say quietly, "I thought he was a good man."

"You wouldn't be the first to make that mistake," Jim responds, equally as quietly.

"What do you mean?" I open my eyes. The other man is looking over my shoulder, gaze distant as if caught in a memory, a moment of time.

"We go way back," he says. "I don't just know him from the docks and the island; I knew him before, and that's why ..." Jim pauses, and I see moisture glittering on his eyelashes. "I could have saved her," he finishes at last. "I should have saved her."

"No," I say as I reach my hand across the table towards his arm. "You told me just a moment ago that I wasn't responsible for what he did. You can't blame yourself for not saving Clarice. No one could have known what he was capable of."

"Oh, Sandy," Jim says, "if only that were true."

I frown. "isn't it?"

"No. I knew what Yarrick was capable of," Jim sighs. "I knew how manipulative he could be. I knew everything, yet I left her there because I was too scared to bring her home."

I shake my head. I know that my brain isn't functioning at its best but even still, what Jim is saying makes no sense at all. I don't know if he's gone into another world, thinking aloud, deluding himself that he could've changed the course of fate. Maybe he did know Yarrick better than I realised, but none of us can ever be responsible for the actions of another. I don't know what he meant about saving Clarice and bringing her home; I feel he will tell me in time. But what is important now is for us to comfort each other. Acknowledge our feelings of guilt and put them to one side because ultimately, the only person responsible for what happened to Clarice was the man holding the gun. "You couldn't have known," I repeat as I squeeze his arm gently.

He looks up at me, dark eyes connecting with mine, and there is a moment when I feel our collective guilt merge. Just as I am about to voice this and have us reassure each other, an agonising, tearing pain rips through my stomach.

I clutch at my swollen middle. Agony, like nothing I have ever before experienced, knocks me to the ground, where I curl instinctively into the foetal position. Groaning. Swearing. Cursing.

I am scared. I am frightened. I don't know what is going on.

But then, it ceases to matter, for warm liquid gushes forcefully from between my legs, and I don't need to look to know it is red.

The baby.

I feel rather than see Jim scooping me up. I hear him calling for the ship's doctor. I sense being carried to a bright white room and placed on a hard leather bunk, and then, because there seems little else to do, I close my eyes slowly and drop my lids, feeling every eyelash connect with its counterpart.

Then, finally, I hear nothing more. There is silence.

All that's left is blackness, filling the void that I know is my now-empty womb.

Chapter Sixteen

PRESENT DAY

Coincidence.

According to the most trusted of dictionaries - the Oxford English, of course - the definition of coincidence is thus:

Coincidence (noun)

1. *a remarkable concurrence of events or circumstances without apparent causal connection: it was a coincidence that she was wearing a jersey like Laura's | [mass noun] : they met by coincidence.*

2. *[mass noun] the fact of corresponding in nature or in time of occurrence: the coincidence of interest between the mining companies and certain politicians.*

3. *Physics the presence of ionising particles or other objects in two or more detectors simultaneously, or of two or more signals simultaneously in a circuit.*

I am not convinced that we need to ponder the merits of ionising particles, but I think that 'circumstances without causal connection' and 'corresponding time of occurrence' describe the current situation perfectly. There are so many delicious coincidences playing out in this sordid little tale of mine that even I am beginning to wonder if someone else - as well as me - is pulling the strings.

Coincidences. Do you believe in coincidences?

My parents were big believers in all that nonsense. The power of the universe. The law of attraction. Divine intervention ... yada yada. I don't think it was their lifetime belief per se, but when they won the lottery (yes, the story of my creation is true), they started buying into that otherworldly shit. Of course, when I was first born, I did not know this, but as the years went by and I grew older and developed a mind of my own, I found it incomprehensible that they were prepared to allow so much of their daily lives to be dictated to by a 'higher being'. Some 'thing' that couldn't even be seen or quantified.

I, for the record, am very black-and-white. I need evidence. I need to see an event happen or a situation come into being to genuinely believe its occurrence - so perhaps I do subscribe to the 'ionising particles' after all.

The problem with my parents was they had no forethought. Money was never an issue, so they spent it like it was never an issue. They were, at the time of winning, the recipients of the largest ever lottery payout, which, when given to an uneducated dock worker and flighty barmaid, was always going to be a recipe for disaster. No offence to dock workers or barmaids.

I only had to ask, and my every desire was bought. The latest toys, electronics, gadgets, clothes - well, until I was eight. Things changed for a few years after that, but then I met Colin. He was a skateboarder, and I would spend hours watching on the sidelines. Not because I gave a shit about skateboarding, you understand, but because I wanted into Colin's world.

We hit it off and hung out, two buddies doing what any sane late-teen boy does.

We partied, and we made out.

With each other.

I spent time at Colin's house listening to his every word, watching him, loving him, pleasing him ... but then he changed. Overnight. One minute we were fooling about, and the next - he didn't want to do those things with me anymore; he preferred girls. My heart broke into a million pieces.

A few days later, he disappeared. He argued with his parents and walked out. There was no note, no message, just endless silence.

I hated him for a while, but it didn't take long to re-focus, especially when I discovered some particularly juicy intel. I switched my obsession to my true purpose instead, and though I never forgot Colin, he resided only in the deepest depths of my memory.

Until, that was, the day when he literally walked onto my computer screens alongside Rich. I still cannot conceive it happened. Kismet? Or some such shit? Anyway, it happened, and as I watched him that first day, every feeling came flooding back, and my balls felt fit to burst. I no longer gave a fuck that he walked out of my life without so much as a goodbye. Colin was back. More than a decade later, and this time, he won't be able to leave. He won't want to. He will realise what I have always known - that we are each other's destiny. Once I've tied up these bothersome loose ends.

Thinking about it, Colin will be easy - I don't need to worry. I'll manipulate him to my way, just as I've been manipulating everything and everyone for the last three years. Because I can. I am a master who learned from the best. My parents. The most manipulative people I have ever met - especially my witch of a mother, though I am grateful to her for this skill. It never ceases to amaze me how easy the average person is to manipulate - and they have no fucking clue it's happening. That's how I got onto the *Cassiopeia* with Aurora that night. I manipulated the situation; in fact, I manipulated our whole relationship, and the stupid bitch had no idea. Until the end, which was, I admit, unfortunate, but no matter, I will rectify my mistake in due course and then move on. I won't shed even one tear for her, which is callous, I know, but in my world, only two people exist - and the other one is Colin.

Surprised at my depth of feeling for the skateboarding barista?

I suppose, if I'm honest, I am, too. I was totally obsessed with him back in the day, but when life took us down two very different paths, I decided not to think about him and instead slept my way through my parents' world with little care or thought for anyone. That is until my universe collided with Aurora's, and the plan for her and her stuck-up family formed. She thinks we met by chance, but that could not be further from the truth. Once I was party to the results of a certain routine genetic test, I orchestrated every single meeting. Planned and plotted it all, right down to the last detail.

See what I mean about manipulation?

And I manipulated her so well that she fell completely in love with me - though I have to admit that was a little uncomfortable. Re-buffing her advances without letting on that I had no sexual interest in her was challenging, but beyond that, she fell for every little morsel I fed her. It was delicious.

I only wish I could have told her to her face that she was never going to rock my world, that her charms and talents were wasted - but maybe I can now. Though it is inevitable for her life to end, there is no reason why I can't share that final choice piece of information with her beforehand.

Hmmm. What a thought.

I am instantly and completely aroused.

The cameras whirr and I watch her in the garden, sitting on the swing with Astrid. They are deep in conversation. Talking about Jayde? I hope so. Bringing her here was a masterstroke, even if I do say so myself. It's a pity I have been unable to install microphones with the cameras, then I would know for sure, but it's not important. Aurora won't be going anywhere. I have all the time in the world to play this game with her.

I reflect on what is just one more beautiful coincidence and the reason why I know she won't be leaving.

That stupid sap Rich has fallen for her, too.

I twist my neck from side to side to ease the ever-present ache. They are holding hands, Aurora and Astrid; it must be getting deep. I wish I knew Astrid. I think I would like her. She is beautiful, though that is immaterial, but she has this serenity, a way of holding herself that puts two fingers up to the world. She intrigues me, and I do regret that when we eventually meet face to face it will be in unfavourable circumstances. In another life, I feel Astrid could be an asset to me, but it is what it is.

I shrug and switch to the camera in Rich's office. He hasn't moved since Aurora walked out. He sits in the same position he adopted when she closed the door - elbows on his desk, head in his hands.

I feel sorry for Rich, but it's only a fleeting thought. I guess it's because I owe him a debt of gratitude. He has already made my life so much easier by keeping Aurora here. He won't let her leave now - not whilst she's in his head - and that is a huge fucking bonus. One less thing for me to arrange. I am a little sad that he will be caught in the final crossfire, not least because he is exceptionally easy on the eye. When he and Colin are in the office together, and I have them both on one high-definition screen, it is all I can do to keep my cock from exploding.

I smile as I watch Rich shake his head. Again. He is lost. Confused. Lonely.

Oh well. I sigh, lean back and settle in for another day of viewing.

Maybe I should have played more chess as a kid, after all.

Chapter Seventeen

EIGHTEEN MONTHS AGO

In less than twenty-four hours, I will be back home on English soil. The ship has continued to slice across the sea, pushing forward through the waves, battling the elements to bring her crew safely home. We will be one less when we arrive, though, for the baby made its own choice. She decided not to live - it was a girl - and quietly slipped away inside of me as I mourned the loss of Clarice.

That was two weeks ago, and I am almost recovered. Physically. I have a wound across my abdomen, held together with staples and gauze, which gets less sore by the day. Though she had already passed on, the medical supplies on board are basic, and there was no way to force her to be born naturally, so they cut her out. I have made it sound more brutal than it was. The medics were excellent, I cannot fault the care I have received, especially since we were in the middle of an inhospitable ocean.

There was talk of getting me to a hospital - a helicopter could be sent, and I winched aboard - but I refused. I know the crew wanted what was best for me, but I could not go through the inevitable interrogation that such a circumstance would create. I still have no passport, but that wasn't the main reason I refused. Here, on this ship, they know me - or as little of me as I want them to - and more importantly, they knew Clarice. Though Jim remains the only one who talks to me about what happened, they all understand. I know that they do, and I need their support around me. Even if it is all going to end soon.

I have spent a great deal of time trying to determine my feelings towards the baby. The crew christened her Clara - in memory of Clarice - when I refused to be drawn on identifying her. They are together now, Clara and Clarice. Perhaps that is how it was always meant to be.

But for me, considering I spent six months generally detesting the thing that was growing inside of me, the loss I feel at my unexpected emptiness has caught me off guard. Is it because a part of me had grown to love her? Or simply because her death was yet another loss in a time when everything has been ripped from me? I cannot decide.

Part of me thinks her fate cruel. She was wholly innocent, created out of some misplaced narcissistic demonstration of power, none of which was her fault. She deserved a chance. Yet then, I reflect on my life. Her mother. What kind of world would she have been born into? What opportunities could I have given her? Would I have even loved her, or would she have been a constant reminder of the sick and twisted world in which she was conceived? I have no knowledge of how I will take care of myself. I have no idea what awaits me in England, so to bring another person with me, someone completely dependent on me - that would have been too much.

On reflection, I am glad she made her choice. Yes, I feel guilt, for I know I didn't always give her the best chance, but I cannot blame myself for that. She was forced inside of me in an act of the most heinous depravity at a time when I was simply a vessel of entertainment for Yarrick and his perverted community. If there is anyone out there who would have felt differently and would have welcomed the presence of a growing reminder, then they are a better person than me. By that barometer, I am prepared to take the consequences of how I treated her.

I wish fate had allowed me to go with her, but life, it seems, is not done with me. Here I am, heading towards home, a land that once held everything yet will no longer resemble the world I left behind.

They gave her a burial at sea. The crew. I didn't attend. I didn't even see her. They told me she was perfect. Beautiful. But I shut down my feelings towards her. I cannot grieve. I cannot allow myself to feel.

Clara. Her existence - now sits in another box on the shelf inside my head. Maybe one day I will revisit her, but maybe I won't.

She is gone.

Clarice is gone.

And I am once more totally and utterly alone.

≈≈≈≈

The hull of the ship creaks and groans as it rides the waves to shore. I am sitting on the hard cold box on deck, watching the crew as they go about their daily tasks. I have been given clothes to wear, oversized trousers and jumpers which smell of fish, and I have barely removed the bright yellow sou'wester. Everything is big, huge in comparison to the *Cassiopeia*. I know they have vastly different functions, but the contrast could not be more stark. Where the deck of the yacht was smooth, shiny wood, on this colossus of the sea it is metal pitted with holes and random extrusions. I have lost count of the times I have stubbed my toes or tripped, which is odd for someone who counts everything. Where the yacht was beautiful, a white angel rising from deep blue waters, the cargo ship is a hulk of ugliness, a collection of greys and muddy browns that more resemble a monster from the deep. It has been an education, though, this time aboard, and I know I will always be grateful to its crew for taking me in and caring for me. They didn't have to; they owe me nothing.

But it has never been mentioned. I have never felt an unwanted burden to these men. Food, warmth, comfort and solace have been given freely, along with necessary medical attention. I don't know how I will ever be able to repay their kindness, especially knowing the risks they will be taking to get me safely ashore. Though I am a British citizen, my lack of identification means I will need to hide my presence and sneak ashore like a fugitive. I could front up to the customs officers, of course, but I know that I won't. I need to get my bearings to understand what has happened since I've been gone, and I cannot do that from the depths of an interrogation room. I am also not emotionally prepared to answer their questions. I have too much baggage. So, I must take my chances and let the universe decide how this next phase of my miserable life will play out.

A sound from my right announces the arrival of Jim and a steaming mug of tea. He hands it to me wordlessly before sitting. We both watch the uncomplicated lives of several deckhands as we sit in silent contemplation.

"How are you feeling?" Jim asks after a moment.

I nod. "Better, thank you. Every day."

We lapse once more into silence.

"Thank you for the tea," I say as I sip delicately at the rim of the mug.

"You're welcome."

Again, silence descends, though it isn't awkward. Jim and I have been through too much this past month for there to be anything awkward between us.

"Almost home," he says, turning his head towards me.

"Yes."

"Another couple of days."

"Yes," I repeat. I don't know what else to say.

"Are you going to be alright?" he asks. "When we get there?"

I let out a breath. "I have absolutely no idea."

"Look, the guys and I were talking. We can put you up for a while, you know, until you get on your feet."

I turn to face him and see the sincerity in his ruddy features. A single tear drips from my eye.

"I can't," I say slowly, "I just can't."

"Okay." He remains silent, resuming his examination of the ocean and its stark treasures.

"I'm sorry, that sounds ungrateful."

"Yeah," Jim smiles at me, "but I kind of get it. You've been to hell and back."

"It's not even that," I say, as suddenly I am certain that I do not want to be identified when we finally dock. "I left home eighteen months ago with my parents and boyfriend. It was supposed to be the trip of a lifetime, a dream holiday, yet I am returning alone. I need to understand why that is. I have to know what happened."

Jim clears his throat, and for the first time since I met him,

I sense a feeling of unease.

"What?" I frown. "What is it?"

He shakes his head. "I feel so responsible for you. And Clarice."

"Why?"

He shifts a little so that his torso is angled towards me. "I knew Yarrick," he says. "Before all this."

I nod. "You mentioned that before."

"Yes," he says, "but I haven't told you the full story. It was something I swore never to tell, but now..." he rakes his hand through his hair, "...I think you have a right to know."

I take a moment and swallow. "I don't know if I want to know. He's a sick and twisted bastard who has some kind of control over that community. He lied to me, and he killed Clarice to stop her from getting away. In cold blood, Jim. Right in front of all of us. Why?" I breathe deeply as I try to erase the last few moments of Clarice's life and remember her as warm, squishy Clarice. "I know that he needs to pay," I say into the silence, "but there are others who need to pay, too. I've lost everyone. I don't know if I can cope with knowing anything more than I already do."

I stand and take eight paces to the crane which is used to haul cargo on and off the ship. "Before I lost the ... baby ..." I have my back to Jim, but I know he can hear me. "I swore to get even with Yarrick. I promised myself that he wouldn't get away with what he did to me, what he did to Clarice and what he is probably doing to others, too. But" I swing around. Jim is watching me intently. "I don't think I have the capacity anymore. Even though I detested every moment of her being inside me, she was still mine, you know? I didn't realise how much it meant having her with me until she wasn't anymore. It's too much." I rub my hands across my face, which is damp from both the salty air and ever-present tears. "I'm not strong," I say quietly as I move back towards the hard, cold box. "I'm just a stuck-up rich kid with no bloody clue how to be an adult."

Jim stands and meets me halfway, enveloping me in his big, warm embrace, and that's it. That's all it takes for the floodgates to open. I crumple onto the deck, Jim supporting me, and cry every last ounce of sorrow into the silence of the Atlantic.

I cry for Clara.

I cry for Clarice.

I cry for my parents.

I cry for the innocence I have lost.

I cry for those left behind.

And I cry for the future. Because somehow, I have to get through this. I have to make good on those promises. Alex and Yarrick have to pay. They have to.

But right now, I need to allow myself to be weak. I need to allow someone else to support me, just for a while. Then I will find out all I can about the fucked-up world I have left and the one I am about to re-enter.

And I will slowly but surely, make a plan.

PRESENT DAY

The cold has finally reached our bones. Astrid and I have been out here, talking and relaxing, for what feels like hours, but it is time to acknowledge the need to move. We do it simultaneously, almost choreographed, both of us standing from the comfort of the swing at the same time. The motion sends the seat backwards, then surging forwards, dumping a startled Rex from its cushions. He shakes his body as he lands unceremoniously on his feet.

"C'mon, boy," I laugh, "let's go find something to eat."

Astrid and I link arms as we make our way towards the door.

"This was nice," she says as she rests her head on my shoulder.

I turn into her embrace and drop a kiss on her cheek. Something has changed since we've been outside. The fact that I have opened up a little has deepened our friendship, and I feel that now, more than ever, we will always have each other's backs. Whatever happens.

"It was," I agree. Rex trots ahead, reaching the door before us, only to jump back as it is pushed open from the other side. Colin's face appears.

"Sorry, boy," he says as he realises he has inadvertently frightened my four-legged interloper. Rex is a better being than me, though - he doles out forgiveness like it is going out of fashion - so it is mere seconds before man and beast are once again enjoying their bizarre bonding ritual.

"Colin!" Astrid's eyes light up, and she rushes towards him, arms outstretched. I love Astrid so much. She says and does whatever the fuck she wants, whenever she wants. I can't imagine having that sense of freedom within myself.

Colin just about manages to pull himself from canine bonding to standing before he is engulfed in Astrid, jumping into his arms and locking her legs around his middle. He laughs as he catches her before spinning her around.

"Well, that doesn't often happen," he comments with a smile as he deposits her safely back on her feet.

"Yeah, right," she says. I watch as she twirls a tendril of hair between her fingers and looks up at him through hooded eyes. "Bet women throw themselves at you all the time."

Colin's Adam's apple bobs and a slight flush begins to creep from his neck to his face. "Not really," he replies, and I note his discomfort. Is he finally beginning to see that Astrid is perfect for him? God, I hope so. If nothing else, they'd make beautiful babies.

"There's plenty of food," he says as he indicates the entrance door, "make sure you get some. But, Ra, can I borrow you for a second?"

The flush on his face intensifies as he drags his eyes from Astrid to me.

"Boring," Astrid says with a shrug. "More jobs from the boss?"

"Something like that," Colin replies. His eyes, though, remain focused on my face. I allow my gaze to meet his, and for a moment, everything stills. In the background I hear Astrid taking Rex inside, chatting happily to him about bacon and useless owners. Then the door closes, and there is just me and Colin.

"What's up?" I ask. I move away, taking six paces. We are standing right next to the warehouse wall, and I am conscious that prying eyes and eagle ears could infiltrate whatever it is that Colin is about to say. For I very much doubt he is bringing further instructions from Rich. Boss-man would do that himself.

He takes my elbow and guides me to the far corner of the garden, opposite the swing where Astrid and I have spent most of the morning. As we walk, he glances around as if expecting someone to jump out of the bushes at any moment, to the point where I find myself looking behind to check we are still alone. I have no idea why.

Eventually, we come to a standstill at an archway formed out of crumbling stone from its supporting wall. Beneath the archway is an old bench - wooden and rotting but stable enough. We sit as one. This outside space continues to surprise me as the wall adjacent to the bench, the one that is crumbling from lack of care, meets the waterfront - a location I thought to be a considerable distance from the warehouse.

Perhaps I have lost my bearings, which is entirely possible, but I know without doubt that we are right next to the docks, for the gaps in the sandy cement afford glimpses of the outside world. It also smells more like the sea here, and the volume of gulls crying has increased. A shiver runs through me, and I instinctively shake as I am reminded there is a reason that Astrid and I were going back into the warehouse. To warm up. Colin notices immediately.

"Cold?" he asks.

"A little. That's why we were going inside."

He nods and, in one swift movement, removes his oversized jumper, placing it over my shoulders. Beneath, he is wearing only a single long-sleeved top, and my eyes are immediately drawn to his nipples as they pucker against the unwelcome chill.

"You're cold too," I say, "I'm fine. Keep your jumper."

Colin shakes his head. "No."

We sit for a few seconds, our breath condensing into the cold air as we inhale and exhale without thought. The most basic of human functions; oxygen in, carbon dioxide out. And repeat.

"Are you okay?" Colin asks. I watch as his breath changes shape around his words. It is no longer a steady stream of air - now it forms short curly puffs.

"Sure."

He nods. "I heard about Jayde."

"Of course you did," I reply. "I knew Rich wouldn't be able to keep that juicy piece of information to himself."

"It wasn't Rich who told me. I haven't seen him this morning."

"Oh," I frown, "how ...?"

"She told me. Jayde. I have to warn you. She's telling anyone who will listen that you and she used to be friends."

"For fuck's sake," I shake my head. "Why? I'm not that interesting." I try to quell the panic rising from my stomach towards my throat. Though this was expected, I am still not ready with any answers. I need to deflect somehow. All it takes is one wrong word in one wrong ear, and the last three years will come crashing down around me. I cannot allow that to happen. Not whilst Alex and Yarrick are still out there. I choose bravado as my weapon of choice.

"Who cares if the two of us were at school together? Haven't they got better things to talk about?" It's frightening how much has changed in such a short space of time - simply because one person has walked back into my life. I hate that I am now gossip fodder - not because I care what people think but because my real name has been revealed. I am going to have to think fast, but first, I need to figure out how the hell such an inconvenient coincidence has happened. What's that line from the movies? "Of all the gin joints in all the towns in all the world, she walks into mine." Thank you, Humphrey Bogart, couldn't have put it better myself.

"Apparently not," Colin smiles as I quickly rewind my brain from the depths of Casablanca. "I think the novelty of someone having their past walk through the door has created unexpected entertainment."

"Jesus. It was bad enough when only Rich was making it into a big thing. can't they all just go back to their board games and leave me the fuck alone?"

Colin laughs. "Damn. I think I prefer you pissed off."

I thump his arm with my right fist. "C'mon," he says, "nothing ever happens here; you've got to give them a bit of slack."

"Erm, no. I think you'll find I don't."

Colin shakes his head, and we sit in silence for a moment.

"You wanted something ...?"

"It's a pretty big coincidence ..."

We both speak at the same time and then smile at each other in that 'you go', 'no you go' way that we endlessly polite Brits have. "I was just saying it's strange how she ended up here."

"Yes," I respond, "I know. But anyway, you wanted something?" I am keen to move the subject on. We could easily debate the arrival of Jayde for hours and still reach no useful conclusion.

"I did." Colin shifts beside me, and I feel his thigh press

against mine. My instinct is to move out of the way, recoil, and put as big a distance as I can between us, but instead, I allow it to remain. It is warm, and it feels nice to have a solid human touch. "I wanted to talk about earlier," he is saying, "and regardless of what you do or don't feel towards me, I will be here for you. Always. Aurora."

I flip my head to his rapidly. "You heard my name then," I state unnecessarily.

"Yes," he says, "I like it."

"Yeah. You and Rich both."

"We have taste," he says and then laughs. It is an awkward laugh, a nervous laugh, and I hate that I make Coffee Man feel this way. He takes a deep breath. I watch as he blows it out into the crisp, cold air. "Why won't you let me in?" he asks softly. "I won't hurt you. Ever."

I shake my head. "We barely know each other. Before this place," I indicate our surroundings with my left arm, "we spoke a few words every now and again, and that was all. I can't suddenly give you my life story; it doesn't work that way."

Colin shifts a little, stretching his legs out in front. "I know, and I understand that. I guess I'm seeing things from a different perspective."

"There is only one perspective."

"No," he says as he reaches across with his left hand and lifts the cold fingers of my right into his palm, "there isn't."

"There is," I reiterate. The warmth of his hold on my hand feels nice, and I close my eyes briefly. It would be so easy to capitulate; believe me, I've given myself to men that I've spent way less time with than Coffee Man, but all of that was in my previous world. "There are things that you don't know, and I have to keep it that way, especially now that my name is out there." I open my eyes and turn slightly to face him.

His green orbs bore into mine. "How can I get you to trust me?" he asks softly. In truth, I have no answer, so I remain silent. "We're all fucked up; you know that right?" His fingers are now massaging my palm, and a warm tingle floods from my wrist all the way up my arm.

"Yeah," I laugh, "I know. But there are degrees of fucked up. Why me?"

Colin lets out a sigh. "I told you. Since I first met you in that awful doorway, I've felt something. Like I know you. I can't explain it."

"But until yesterday, you treated me like every other person. There was no indication of anything other than your pity. How am I supposed to accept that you feel differently in the space of two days?"

"Oh, Ra," he runs his right hand through his long, wavy locks. "You make quite an impression. You have no idea."

I frown. "What the hell is that supposed to mean?"

"Nothing. don't worry about it."

"You can't say something like that and then back off," I reply, my tone raised in frustration.

Colin moves away from me a little, and I feel the loss of his thigh pressing against mine.

He drops his head back and looks up at the sky as if for inspiration. White woolly clouds have been replaced by a varying palette of greys and blacks, great big pillows of rain waiting for the right time to empty themselves;

I'm not sure how inspiring a view this makes.

"I told you about my family," he says, "and how I left home and spent some time on the streets."

I nod.

"It was the worst time of my life. Even though my parents were embarrassed to have me as their son, when I didn't have that luxury to fall back on, I realised how easy they had made my life, but pride wouldn't ever let me go back. I wanted to prove that because they no longer believed in me, that was the exact reason why I had to believe in myself. So, I got a job in the coffee shop, found a place to stay and am slowly rebuilding my life. But, and this is the key, I'm rebuilding it in the way that I want to." He pauses, and emotions chase across his face. Like he is trying to figure out what to say next. I wait. This is his story. His time. I owe him the space to speak it.

"I didn't tell you this part," he hesitates, "but my dad came into the coffee shop one day - like your Jayde coincidence - and it was nice. We sat and chatted for a while, and he took the time to explain why they reacted the way that they did - my mum and dad. It all came from being outsiders way back when - two 'geeks' is how he described them - who did good for themselves and were subsequently hated for their success. It hardened them, so they chose to fight back by getting more and more successful. More money. Bigger houses. All material stuff. They were clever, building a business at the height of the dot.com boom, and then I came along. When I was skating at my peak, it fitted with their plan, but when I wasn't ... they couldn't get past it because they had conditioned themselves to abhor failure for so long."

"Shit," I say.

Colin shrugs. "It's okay, and actually, understanding them has helped me to understand me better. Dad wanted me to visit Mum again, but I refused. I think they have to figure out their shit first, and so do I. Money isn't important to me; it never was, and the only time I wished for it was when I was on the streets. I spent weeks - months - hating them for allowing me to live that life, but finally, I got out of my own way, and that's when I realised I had a choice. I had chosen to walk away from the luxury that my life offered, so I had to make a choice to return. But not to that life as such - my version of it."

He turns to me, face earnest.

"It wasn't easy, showing up for job after job, knowing how I looked and what they must think, but I guess I inherited some of my parent's desire to succeed because I was determined to prove there could be a life beyond hopelessness. And now I am beginning to build that - and you can, too. None of us belong on the streets, and if I could save everyone, I would, but I can't. I am only one person. But I can save you, Ra. And despite what you think of yourself and whatever shit you've endured to end up here, you deserve to be somewhere else. You deserve to be cared for and loved because I feel you deep down inside, and I know that this exterior isn't who you are. You've been conditioned by life in the same way that my parents were, which is why I get you. I see you. I want to be there for you, I want to know that you are safe and in my life."

"Why?" I ask, shaking my head, "Why me? Why not Astrid or Jayde or anyone else for that matter?"

Colin inclines his head, and the ghost of a smile hovers around his lips. "Because it's you that I want," he says simply, and I realise, for the first time since Alex raised a gun, that actually it can be that simple. As humans, we overcomplicate everything. We think too much, worry too much, and live in fear of our true selves being 'outed' - all of which make our lives ever harder - yet there is an alternative. To live simply in accordance with our values; our real values, not those imposed by others - and build our world around those.

I am tempted. The way he is looking at me, the patterns his fingertips are drawing on my palm, and his knee pressing against my leg are all sending warm tingles from my stomach to my heart. I could let Coffee Man in. I could let him take care of me. I could lay the past to rest as he did and focus only on the future.

I could do all of that. I really could. But the kicker is ... I actually can't.

The promise I made to myself three years ago has not been fulfilled, and though that came from a different life, a different time, it was my true value then, and it must remain so now. Too many people died. Too many bad things happened. I have to at least try to make those right - honour my parents and the crew of the *Cassiopeia*. Honour Clarice and Clara.

Sadly, I shake my head. "I'm sorry," I say quietly, "I'm not done with this life yet."

Colin nods, and even though I have told him nothing, I feel instinctively that he understands. "Come back to me," he says, "when you *are* done with this life. I mean it, Ra."

I let out a breath as Colin releases my hand, transferring his palm to the side of my face. I close my eyes and allow him to support my head for a moment.

I hear him moving closer and feel the warmth from his body as he pulls me into his embrace. We hug. Tightly. Heads resting on each other's shoulders, heartbeats pounding together as we share warmth and something else. Hope?

He pulls back and looks deep into my eyes. We are millimetres apart, and I watch as his gaze alters, becoming more intense. "I'm sorry," he whispers, "but I have to do this."

And then his lips are on mine. Tentatively at first, then harder, exploring, their warmth encouraging me to let him in, so I do. We take from each other what we need as the kiss deepens, our bodies merging almost into one. Our breathing becomes heavy as arousal takes over our actions. We are acting on instinct, no longer in control, and right here, right now, it feels so damn good.

Colin kisses in the same way that he lives life. Generously, warmly, with just the right hint of sensuality, and it takes bare minutes for me to lose myself in him completely. I allow my hands to wander up and down his back, nails lightly grazing his body beneath his top. We move even closer as time stands still. For the first time ever, I forget to count.

Colin slips his hands from my back around to my front, allowing them to wander from my waist upwards. And that's when it happens. His palms gently caress my breasts - over my clothes - but it is enough to make me stiffen in fear. It may have been months ago, and I may have filed the heinous crimes done to my body in a box in my mind, but Colin's hands, moving oh so gently over me, have revealed that box is yet to be sealed.

Without warning, I am transported back to the cell. Back to the time when every night would bring a man wanting something they believed they were owed. And though it was the most disgusting experience, that was the last time my breasts were touched by another human. Another man, Colin, now doing the same, triggers everything I had long

since blotted out. I cannot be here. I cannot do this. Using the palms of both hands, I push him away. Abruptly.

"Don't, " I say as I stand and walk five paces from the bench. "Don't."

I recognise the inadequacy of my words. I understand that this wonderful man deserves an explanation, and I see the hurt in his eyes as he tries to work out what the hell is happening. He thinks it is him, but it is not. Yet, I cannot tell him that because I don't have the words. I am struck dumb. Overwhelmed by feelings and memories I thought I had buried.

I wish I could allow Colin in. I wish I could let him carry me. But I can't. I am too broken.

And so, with a sob of pure pain and heartache, I turn and half run back in the direction of the steel-lined metal door and the relative safety of the warehouse. The safe house - for that is what I believe it represents.

I glance back once. Colin has not moved. I have left the most incredible person on that bench alone, wondering what the hell he did wrong.

God, I am such a bitch.

Chapter Eighteen

EIGHTEEN MONTHS AGO

Jim and Yarrick grew up together. They were the sons of fishermen and spent most of their lives at sea. From babies to grown men, the oceans ran deep in their blood. Coming from a small community in South Devon, they relied on each other for friendship and company, with their bond being the envy of many. Jim tells me this story as we sit again in the crew mess, nursing yet another cup of hot sweet tea. I feel as if I have spent the last month doing nothing except drink tea.

"We were always on the fishing boats," Jim says, "it was the life of the whole village; everyone got involved with the haul - and making the pots." He smiles, and I can tell he is remembering times so different to where we are today. "We'd weave pots until our fingers were raw some days. Willow it was, grown, dried and twisted into shape." Jim laughs. "Were never enough bloody pots. It's all frames and netting now, but back in the day, if you couldn't weave a pot, you weren't worth knowing."

I smile. I cannot imagine being able to weave anything, though thanks to Clarice, I can at least now sew a mean smock.

"It's still fishing, but mostly crabs. Occasionally lobsters and scallops, but you got to dive to get those and much as I love the water, you ain't getting me down there." He gestures below our feet to indicate the depths of the ocean. "Nah, I'm happy doing this now. Keeps me busy."

I wait. I want to ask about Yarrick. I want to understand how the two men who began life in the same place ended up so far removed from each other, but I remain patient - Jim will tell me in his own time.

Forty seconds later, Jim is continuing his story. "Dad had a big boat, so we could pretty much fish all year, but Yarrick's folks, theirs was much smaller. If the tide was messed up, then they couldn't go out. Made him real blue the days he was left behind. He always was a competitive bugger."

Jim shakes his head. "His family - well, what there was of it - were descended from the pirates, you see, so he always had that need to hunt for the next shiny thing. When we were kids, it was stones and shells, then metals and fish. If I got a big crab, well, his was bigger." Jim glances across at me. "Bet you didn't know about the pirates?"

"No." I shake my head. I don't know anything, it would seem.

"The pirates - Barbary pirates they were," he continues, "sailed over to Europe from Africa to attack ships and coastal settlements. They were wanting to steal whatever they could get their hands on and capture anyone they could."

"Why?" I ask.

"They took 'em back to the slave market in North Africa," Jim says. "Men, women, kids - didn't matter. They weren't fussy. People were currency, simple as that, which made it hard for the early coastal settlements. According to legend, it wasn't until the mid-eighteenth century that things changed; laws around slavery and such like. Then the fishing villages took hold, but there were still pirate boats mind, descendants who sailed across to our shores, trying their luck now and again. It even happens today in some waters. Boats being attacked. Sorry," Jim shakes his head, "getting carried away."

"Not at all," I press my palm on the table between us, imploring Jim to keep talking. I intend to use anything I learn about Yarrick to bring about his downfall.

"Yarrick's great-grandfather," Jim continues, "was one of them pirates, descended from Africa, but he was cast out when he fell in love with an English woman. They pillaged her family home; she was supposed to be taken as well - a young, fertile woman," Jim coughs awkwardly, "well, you know." I nod. "She would've been used," he says, then immediately turns bright red. "Sorry ..." he swipes his hand in front of me as if to erase the words. "He saved her."

I swallow the bile rising at the back of my throat. "Ironic," I mumble to myself, but Jim hears.

"I know," he says kindly. "Given what you've told me and what I know about Yarrick, it seems he doesn't follow his great-grandfather's morals."

"No," I agree quietly. "It would appear he did to me what his great-grandfather prevented from happening to his great-grandmother. Definitely not cut from the same cloth."

Jim watches me for a moment. "You okay?"

"Yeah." I close my eyes and inhale deeply. "I'm okay. I need to know this stuff."

"We can take a break, have another cuppa."

"No," I reach my hand across to touch his weathered fingers, "the sooner I know, the sooner I can decide what to do when I get back."

Jim nods. "There's no jurisdiction over there, mind," he says, "on that island. It has its own laws. Ain't nothing you can do about that."

"I know." I sigh. Crossing the Atlantic has given me time to ask questions of the crew. I have discovered that though Añaposta Island is an overseas British territory, it makes its own laws - not that I was planning to walk straight into a police station when we reach port and demand Yarrick's arrest anyway - but I wanted to know if the fact that Yarrick held me hostage and killed Clarice in cold blood could be legally punishable. His crimes undoubtedly are, but I cannot reach him from the UK, at least not straight away, so I have resigned myself to focusing on Alex first. They are both killers, and they each ended the lives of people I loved, so in the scheme of things it matters not where I start. They will both get what is coming to them, law or no law.

Jim and I fall into silence, and I watch as the expressions change on the weathered face of the man sitting opposite. It is like he is fighting some kind of internal battle: what to say, how much to reveal. I understand his struggle. If, as he says, Yarrick was his friend, then this can't be easy.

"There was hatred when they married," he continues finally, "his great-grandfather and great-grandmother, but they were in love, so they stuck it out and made their home on the south coast in that tiny little village. They had one son, Yarrick's grandfather, and he had one son - Yarrick's father. When Yarrick was born and became the only boy again, it was like some kind of weird pattern. The only difference with Yarrick was no one knew who his mother was. She dumped him on his father's doorstep as a baby in the middle of the night with a note. His father had an eye for the ladies, you see, so it could have been any one of a number, but whoever she was, she never came back. Yarrick ended up being raised by his father alone - 'cept he preferred drink and women to looking after his boy."

Jim pauses for a moment, allowing his words to sink in. Yarrick's role models were questionable, and without any female influence, he may have missed out on some valuable life lessons - like respect and morality, for example - but none of what Jim has revealed gives me any reason to change how I feel. The man is despicable, and regardless of where he came from, he's been an adult for long enough to know the difference between right and wrong. Between manipulation and persuasion. Between being imprisoned and being free. Between ending and nurturing a life.

"He was always the wild kid," Jim continues, "never had any rules or curfews, always in trouble, but what he did ... even I couldn't believe."

"What he did?" I ask.

Jim nods and extends his arm towards me, angled at my stomach. "Yeah."

I frown. "You mean what he did to me?"

Jim shifts uncomfortably. "Yeah," he repeats, "but not just you."

"You're saying there are others?" The words whisper from my lips as I force them out. I want to know, but I don't want to know. I need to know, but I don't know if I can handle it.

He nods and raises his head from studying the table to look directly into my eyes. "Clarice," he says quietly and without him finishing the sentence, I know what he is about to say.

Cold fingers of dread run up and down my spine. Goosebumps form on my skin.

"Clarice was the first," he says. I close my eyes. I don't want to believe him. "She was a victim too," he says quietly, "and I knew what he was doing to her. I should've saved her."

It is too much. I cannot form thought. All I can see is the earth room, the cell, Yarrick's laughing face, the men - all the men, and Clarice on the day she brought me the pregnancy test. She went through this, too? Was she abused in the same way? Imprisoned in a room and used by men for their own sick gains? My head is pounding. I don't know how I feel. Do I pity Clarice for experiencing the same abuse as me, or do I detest her for allowing this to happen? If she knew, couldn't she have prevented that loathsome creature from taking another victim? Was she the first, and was I the second? Or were we just one of a number? Who knows.

A noise alerts me to Jim, and I turn my head, watching as a grown man, a strong man, a man of the seas, begins to crumble before my eyes. Huge sobs wrench from his gut as big fat tears land on the cheap plastic table, bouncing and splashing before merging into an ever-expanding puddle.

"I loved her," he says brokenly, eyes wild and unfocused. "And I let her die."

In the depths of my mind, I know that Jim is not responsible for what happened to Clarice, but I am unable to offer him any platitudes or solace. I am filled with fear and disgust - Jim knew what kind of man Yarrick was, others likely did too, and yet they did nothing. They stayed silent, ensconced in the safety of shadows, fellow men and cargo ships.

I can understand that Jim is a victim, too. I cannot hold him responsible for the actions of a monster, yet he knew. I don't know how he knew; I don't know how much he knew, but he knew, and right now, I cannot stomach breathing the same air as him.

Despite what he and the men on board this ship have done for me, I cannot reach out. There is no room in my heart for forgiveness, even though rationally I appreciate Jim may in some way have been as helpless as I. But until I know everything, I will not allow his pain to be mine. There is more to his story, yet I am not ready to hear it. My stomach clenches in a reminder of what I have lost. Clara. Clarice. My life.

I stand and carefully place my empty mug into the tiny dishwasher beside the sink. I hear his sobs, but I am not Jim's solution. I barely have enough within my heart to be my own.

The dishwasher is full. I add a wash tablet, close the door and press the single button on its front.

As the mechanism whirs into life drawing water into the machine to cleanse its contents, I turn my back on the bench, the table and its sole occupant.

And, with measured steps, I walk slowly and purposefully away

≈≈≈≈

Perhaps I should be judged for my emotionless response to Jim, for leaving him when he was clearly distraught, but I need time to think. My brain is tired and overwhelmed. The days ahead will not be easy - I have no idea what awaits me in England, and I need to find the strength to face it. I am aware that many of the crew think me cold simply because I have held my emotions in check and given that I have lost both Clarice and Clara as well as my parents, I concede they may have a point. Am I cold, or have I, as I suspect is more likely, switched off those parts of me that would grieve in order to function? It's not that I don't feel because I do, but my emotions are complicated. I don't think it's as simple as grief. There is anger, frustration, hatred, disgust, and fear, to name a few, all of which I am facing alone.

I could fall apart - perhaps I should - maybe then I would start to feel again, but I can't. I am numb, and even my basic human desire to care for others disappeared when Jim told me the bones of his story. Does that make me a bitch? Does that make me as mercenary as Yarrick? Does it make me selfish? Does it matter?

I spend the rest of the day on my small hard bunk, letting the events of the last eighteen months play over and over again, before finally my brain seizes on something. The fact I am still alive. It could be nothing, but in the natural order of events I should have joined my parents a long time ago.

I should have drowned - but I did not.

I should have died with Clarice - yet she died alone.

I should not have survived such a traumatic childbirth with only basic medical supplies - yet I did.

I don't know what it means, if it means anything at all, but I remain safe. I came from a world of luxury which required little conscious thought. I knew nothing beyond money, parties, and who was sleeping with whom. The brain I had so belligerently exercised in an after-school business club lay dormant for years whilst I allowed my increasingly fake reality to take over. He had been right, the professor. He may have been an ignorant pig, but he had been right.

If Alex had turned out to be the man I'd believed him to be, I would have got married and had babies with no further thought of my own life and career. Alex would have succeeded as the head of my father's company, and I would simply have birthed Alex's children. Shit. Shit. Shit. Shit. Shit.

Until that awful night on the *Cassiopeia*, I had done everything my twelve-year-old self vowed not to do. I had subscribed to the narrative. I had moulded myself to the stereotype, lost in the abyss of fortune. Whilst I had recognised its sham and indulged in occasional feelings of misery, I had done nothing to divert my journey from its pre-ordained, Louboutin-shod path.

Though it had been in the most heinous way imaginable, I realise now that Alex has awakened that girl, reminded her there was a world beyond her obscene existence. Yarrick's repulsive actions then nurtured her, perpetuating the anger she had felt all those years ago when she'd wanted nothing more than to take on the world. To rail against society and its expectations.

Inexplicably, I am forced to recognise that the men who crippled me have also given me my freedom. They have reminded me of my purpose. Of who I am and what I believe.

That. That is why I have survived.

It is time to prove that ignorant pig wrong and show him that women can be so much more than their biology—yet the stakes are higher now. That twelve-year-old girl is a grown woman with a world of pain in her heart, a woman who will accept nothing less than the lives of Alex and Yarrick.

The past no longer serves me. I cannot change it, but I can reject its attempts to colour my future.

I roll onto my back and stare into the nothingness as daylight fades. I believed, before the earth room and the cell, that I was living in a warm and loving community on

Añaposta Island, a place where the outside world didn't exist and its intrusion wasn't allowed. There was no means of communication with anyone beyond our little circle, and in many ways, I welcomed that. Not being bombarded with daily news and insignificant celebrity gossip gave me the space I needed to heal, to ready myself for a return to reality, to confront Alex and make him pay. It was a peaceful existence and I was more than content - until I wasn't.

Until I asked to return to England.

Yarrick's reaction was so far removed from the man who had welcomed me into his home. Understanding this is the key. Jim told me I wasn't the first, that Clarice too had been a victim of Yarrick's ways and, though I don't know if I am ready to hear it, I now realise that I have to. He has the answers. My brain is fried and can no longer be relied upon to determine what is real and what I have contrived or exaggerated. My gut is an unreliable witness so I have no choice but to place my trust in Jim.

I turn onto my side and shake my head. I genuinely feel as if I am losing my mind. Nothing makes sense, and the more I search for answers, the more confusing life becomes. I direct my thoughts from Yarrick to Alex and consider how I will find the murderer. I focus on the anger and revenge that tears me apart - the image of my parents lying dead on the deck is as vivid today as it was on that awful night - and that is what will keep me moving on.

I breathe deeply, counting in and out slowly, methodically.

Counting.

I am good at counting.

I live to count, and now I must live to find Alex. I must allow my emotions and feelings to become nothing more than sensations, elements of myself that I can discard and keep in check until it is time. It is crucial to my survival in the days and weeks ahead; this I know. If I can keep any reactive, nurturing or human feelings contained and allow only anger to surface, then I will continue to survive, and I will deliver Alex to the gates of hell.

As I allow my eyes to close, a grim smile of determination forms on my slack lips. This detachment from reality is my secret weapon, and I have to channel it now. I need to be that cold, uncaring bitch whom others have observed because that is my advantage. Once I start to feel, it is almost certainly an advantage I will lose.

I cannot make sense of these last eighteen months, but I don't need to, not right now. All I have to focus on when my feet touch the earth of my homeland is being ready. Ready to run, fight or hide - whatever is needed.

Clarice and Clara will not have died for nothing. My parents' lives will not have been culled in vain. Whoever or whatever I am fighting, I am ready.

I will get to the truth. I will find Alex. I will topple Yarrick, and I will do it without a single care or backward glance.

It is time.

No one else will pay for the evil actions of these two men.

Not whilst I have a single breath left in my body.

≈≈≈≈

It is morning. I am awoken by the familiar sounds of the crew going about their daily business. Fingers of light push their way through the air vent above my head, and I can hear the squawk of sea birds as they hover and dive. I am dressed. I must have fallen asleep in my clothes. My mouth is dry, and every bone in my body aches. I turn over, wincing slightly at the pain in my abdomen, where a scar is beginning to form. Every day, it becomes more manageable. Every day, it hurts less physically, but I fear the psychological scars will not heal so easily. Those, I believe, are yet to fully form. Their pain is waiting in the wings, standing to one side, watching the main play until their cue is called.

There is a light knock on the door, followed by Jim's head peering cautiously through the tiniest of gaps. His weathered face is comforting and welcoming, and I see no trace of the man I left last night. This morning, he is back to being Jim, the kind, thoughtful companion and saviour. In a way I am grateful for the lack of awkwardness, but I cannot ignore the things I have learned or the pieces of his story I am still to be told.

"Morning," he speaks quietly, "hope you slept okay. Can I come in?"

I nod and swing my legs to the left which allows me to sit up on the bunk. I place my feet firmly on the floor.

"Are you okay?" I ask.

"Me? Always," he replies with a cheeky smile.

Again, I nod.

"Here," he hands me a steaming mug. "Tea." Another mug of tea. I wonder if it's possible to overdose on tea.

"Thanks." I reach for the receptacle and take a sip. I must have consumed hundreds of cups of this steaming beverage since the one Clarice laced, but every time I take that first sip, I am transported straight back to the earth room. I wonder if that memory will ever fade.

"I wanted to check in," Jim says, moving closer into the tiny cabin, "I don't know if I did the right thing, telling ya. About me and Clarice and Yarrick."

I sigh. "I don't know either," I say, "and I can't pretend it didn't mess with my head. I feel like there is still so much I don't know. I watched that man kill Clarice in cold blood, Jim. I endured his men punishing me day after day for having the audacity to seek a way back home, and then, the second I became pregnant, everything changed. I went back to their house, to that room at the top with its mocking rainbows of light, and it was as if nothing had happened. Except this time, I had no freedom. I may have been living in comfort and luxury, and I may have escaped the clutches of sick and perverted men, but beyond that, I was still a prisoner. And then they told me - Yarrick and Clarice - that they wanted me to have the baby so that they could bring it up themselves. Do you have any idea what that feels like?" My voice raises as emotion threatens to overwhelm me once more. "It was like they planned it. They planned for me to get pregnant so that I could give them the child they never had, but why? And how the fuck am I supposed to deal with knowing that I was simply a human incubator? You may have loved Clarice, and God knows, I loved her too, but she went along with it..."

"Stop." Jim lifts his hand, palm towards me. "Stop." His voice is loud and reverberates around the metal of the cabin.

I widen my eyes. I have never heard Jim raise his voice, not even to his men. I was right. There must be something I don't know.

"What are you not telling me?"

"You..." he begins, then stops, drawing in a deep breath. "I won't hear a bad word said about that woman, do you hear? She did everything she could to save you. You were a prisoner, but so was she," Jim asserts. "She was as powerless against Yarrick as you. Every single day she played a game, trying her hardest to bring happiness, giving to those Yarrick had wronged. Those children…" Jim shakes his head and presses his index fingers into the sides of his temple. "Never mind. You don't need to know. It doesn't matter now." He turns on his heel and begins to walk away.

"What children?" I ask. "What don't I need to know? Dammit, Jim. Whatever it is, I have to know the truth. You didn't come in here to walk away again."

His shoulders slump as I wait for him to decide what to do. Slowly, he turns around to face me and, at the look in his eyes, a sense of fear and foreboding chases through my body. I don't know why, but suddenly, I feel that whatever Jim says next will change the course of my life forever. Angry red blotches have formed on his cheeks, and his jaw is rigid, the planes of his bones drawn as he battles whatever demons are haunting him. He wants to tell me; I know that he does, but at the same time, I sense he is just as scared as me.

I wonder at the power of Yarrick, and the influence of this man who is thousands of miles away yet exerts an invisible control. Over us both. Jim fears Yarrick; that is blatantly obvious, but what I don't understand is why. What happened to make their childhood friendship end this way?

"The children in the community. I don't know the exact number, but well over fifty per cent of them are his." Jim's hands are clenched at his sides, the words forced out with disgust.

"What the hell?" My mouth falls open in shock as thoughts race around my head. Yarrick said they didn't have children, which is why they wanted me to carry Clara. I rub my eyes, trying to erase the confusion. "Yarrick can't have children," I say, "you must be wrong."

Jim looks at me sadly. "I wish I was, but think, Sandy. What did Yarrick actually say?"

"I can't. I don't ... " I search my brain for the distant memory. "He said they had not been blessed. Shit." Coldness seeps outwards from my heart. "He lied." I say softly as I wonder if there is anything about which he has been truthful.

"He did."

I shake my head and release a deep breath. Goosebumps chase over my arms.

"He fathered them?" I ask, though I don't need to see Jim nod to know the answer.

"Some," Jim shrugs. "Like I said, I don't know how many."

Jesus. I close my eyes and inhale. The web of deceit has grown, its tangles reaching further than even my worst nightmare could have conjured. Yarrick no more needed my baby than I did. It was a ruse. He was not bereft of children - though maybe Clarice was.

That man deliberately engineered my fertilisation to keep me there, to keep me a prisoner in his world. But why? Clearly, he hadn't needed me to incubate his offspring. Nothing makes sense, and my world has once more rocked on its axis. I cannot process anything. All I can feel is pressure building inside my head, inside my body, inside my heart.

With shaking hands, I raise the forgotten mug to my lips. The liquid is lukewarm, though I barely notice. I smile as a thought passes swiftly through the fog, putting the kettle on, making a cup of tea. So British in times of crisis. Yet I don't know if I have a kitchen anymore, let alone a kettle.

The brief diversion is welcome, and I think about my home for a moment and what may await. Do I even have a home?

I'm sure the bricks and mortar remain but anything could have happened to it in the time I've been gone. It could have been sold, unclaimed as it was when none of us returned from the *Cassiopeia*.

Jim stands silently by, watching as I process. Now more than ever, I need to hear the rest of his story. He is the only person who can help me make sense of this. I take one more deep breath as Jim shifts his stance, leaning back against the tiny corner table whose function is unclear. It is barely large enough to hold a book or mug, yet it is solid and, thus far, doing an adequate job of supporting Jim's bulk.

"You have to tell me," I say at last. "You have to tell me everything you know."

Jim sighs. "I don't know much, but what I can do is tell you about Clarice." A smile lights his features at the mention of her name and then immediately disappears. The shadows are back. He has remembered she is no longer alive.

I nod. "Sounds like a good place to start." I pat the bed next to me, indicating for Jim to sit (I am - in amongst all of this craziness and desolation - concerned about the corner table). "I used to think I had my life sorted, all planned out, but now I have no idea where the hell I am heading." For the briefest of moments, I consider telling Jim about Alex, about the murderer who infiltrated my family and about where this really all began, but I hold back. I am exhausted.

The truth of that night on the *Cassiopeia* remains sealed in that box on the shelf inside of my head. I have told no one what really happened. Yarrick and Clarice thought I had lost my friends in a dinghy accident, and no one else asked.

Yet, I want to trust. I want to open my life. I have been alone for so long.

On Añaposta Island there was always someone around, yet loneliness prevailed. I think it was because I lacked that one person who was there just for me. Perhaps, in wishing for this, I was selfish. Everyone who has crossed my path in the last eighteen months has let me down, leading me ever further into more secrets and more lies. So many that I feel as if I am drowning.

I want to, but I don't think I can trust Jim - not yet. He and Yarrick go way back. Jim and I do not. It's that simple.

"Hello?" Jim leans forward and angles his face towards me. "You in there?"

"Sorry," I say, "miles away."

Jim nods. "So you were. But you want to know everything, right?"

"Yes."

"I'll tell you about Clarice," he continues, "because she is everything. Was everything," he amends.

He shifts a little next to me. "It all began when we visited the islands," he says, "me and Yarrick. We were eighteen and restless. Our community was small, and the elders didn't readily accept outsiders; everyone knew everyone. Life was dull. Only good part was getting out on the seas, but even that wore thin after a while."

I can understand how he felt. The life of luxury, with its heavenly appearance, was at times incredibly claustrophobic - for almost the same reasons Jim is giving now. The number of people we truly knew in that world could be counted on one hand. The rest were hangers-on with an agenda and a begging bowl.

"That was when we figured we'd go on an adventure. Neither

of us had any ties to speak of, so we spruced up an old sailing rig and set off. Two teenage boys full of hormones and no common sense." I watch Jim's face, emotions chasing the ghost of a smile. "Good times, they were - at least to start with. That first trip we stayed on Añaposta Island for a few months and then came home, but Yarrick, he never settled. Said he wanted to go back there to live - but he had no money. In the end, he twisted my arm, and we went again a few years later. That's when we met Clarice." He shakes his head. "She was so beautiful."

"Well," Jim sighs, "she only had eyes for Yarrick, and before I knew it, they were in love, and I was sailing home alone. I don't know how he did it, but he managed to stay, and that was that."

I frown. So far, there's nothing sinister in Yarrick's story. He fell in love and stayed on Añaposta Island. That doesn't explain anything. Jim glances at me. "I know," he says, "that don't explain anything, just giving you the background."

"Okay," I reply. There's not really much else I can say.

"A few years in, I got wind of him being into some dodgy stuff. By that time, I was on the ships, cargo ships, and word gets around. Seemed he'd been dealing - drugs, you know - and that was how he got money."

I inhale a shocked breath. "Drugs?"

"Yeah. There was never any proof, mind, but the people I heard it from ... let's just say I had no reason to doubt what they were saying. I started worrying about Clarice. I'd always been sweet on her and thought if Yarrick was getting in with the wrong sort, well, something could happen. So, I went back to see for myself, and they'd set up a right community by then. Those huts for the tourists, Yarrick built every single one, and he told me that's where the money was from - how they afforded to live. Clarice said the same, but something didn't ring true. I don't know, a gut feeling maybe, but they couldn't look me in the eye. You know?"

I nod.

"Then I realised I was never on my own with Clarice; it was like Yarrick was her shadow. If he wasn't with her, then someone else was, so I tried to get her alone, but every time … that's when I really started worrying. I knew something was off, and knowing what I'd heard, well, it didn't take long to put two and two together."

"One night," Jim continues, "we were at one of them parties, you know, with all the others?"

"Yes," I reply, though Jim's eyes are fixed on the wall ahead, and I am not convinced he is listening.

"Yarrick had gone off, and I finally had a second, like a quick moment with Clarice, so I asked her if she was alright, and she told me she was, but her eyes … well, they said something very different. I tried to ask more, but she shook her head, like a warning, and that's when I knew. That look in her eyes told me all I needed to know. He was messing about with the other women. It was right there in front of me."

I shake my head. "Shit. I had no idea."

Jim nods. "Thing about Yarrick, he's a master at making others believe what he wants them to. That's how we got out of so many scrapes as kids. I'm pretty sure Clarice thought she was the only one at first," he takes in a shaky breath, "but by the time I'd figured it out, she had too, probably a long while before. I could tell she was hurting, but she was so scared. It killed me to see what he'd done to her. She'd lost who she was, so I asked her to leave with me. I told her I'd sort it, but he came back at the wrong moment and overheard."

"Shit." I close my eyes. I know what it's like to be on the wrong side of Yarrick.

"But he didn't scare me, so I asked him right out. What he was doing with those other women, and he laughed. Right in my face. Told me there and then how many kids he'd had, how they all did everything he asked, like they were his slaves. And the men were too frightened to change it. He'd brainwashed them, see. Even Clarice. Made them all think he was some kind of God, and the women were grateful when he spent time with them. If he fathered their children, then they were forever in his debt. That's what he said. Them exact words. Made me sick to my stomach. I'd known he was a ruffian; I'd known that since we were boys, but this … it disgusted me. All I knew was that I needed to get Clarice out of there. Then I figured we'd work out how to save everyone else."

Jim pauses and swipes at his eyes. "I could've saved her. All of them…"

"No," I say, "no. This is on Yarrick, not you." Though I am shocked by what Jim has revealed, I am not surprised. "Maybe they weren't ready to be saved," I add. He shrugs.

"When I was in the cell, and the women and men all did his bidding, I often wondered why. Why they all did whatever he asked without question, but after a while I accepted it as my normality, too."

"You know why, don't you?" Jim asks, and I frown.

"Why what?"

"Why he was never questioned. Why he could get away with it. Why she didn't think she could leave."

I shake my head. "No ... I ..."

Then, suddenly, it hits me. A vague memory from a time long passed. A documentary half-heartedly watched in a life where money ruled. A narrative about men - for it was mostly men - who gain ultimate power and control. I remember callously laughing at the naivety of the women - for it was mostly women - who worshipped every word. Congratulating myself from the luxury of my gilded sphere, knowing that I, Aurora, would never be so gullible.

"Shit," I say as the missing puzzle piece drops brazenly into place. Mocking me for not seeing it sooner when it had been hiding in plain sight. "Fuck."

Jim nods. "Yes."

"How ...?" I begin to ask, and then I shake my head. I know how. It was there in that documentary. It formed part of my every breath on Añaposta Island. It happened so subtly, had been so cleverly concealed that none of us stood a chance. Least of all, Clarice.

I can barely form the words, but I must. I know I am right, yet there is a tiny part of me still denying my stupidity. Denying what I witnessed. Normalising behaviour that was anything but.

I swallow. "It's a cult, isn't it, Jim?" My voice is scratchy. Barely more than a whisper.

Jim nods. He doesn't speak, he doesn't need to. The moisture pooling in his eyes says it all.

Shit.

Clarice didn't leave with Jim, not because she didn't want to, but because she couldn't. She was scared, terrified even, and being the closest to Yarrick, she must have been one of the only people to glimpse the true depths of his depravity.

In their power, Yarrick's messages were teachings that wound around the hearts of every member, infiltrating their lives until they could see nothing but him. Nothing but what he wanted them to see. Their own identities were forgotten; they were simply an extension of a sick narcissist whose addiction to power rendered him incapable of human emotion.

I was a gift to Yarrick, washed up on the shore with no past and no future and no one to care. Through his attentiveness, Yarrick helped me to trust and believe again, made me think that there could be a life beyond Alex and what I had witnessed that night on the *Cassiopeia*. And I fell for every single word, right up until the earth room, and now I understand. People didn't leave Yarrick. They revered him, worshipped him, cared for his offspring, catered to his foibles, serviced his desires, all without question. They did not leave.

And I, by asking for the chance to be free, had threatened his empire. He couldn't risk me getting away; I see that now, and my heart bleeds to know that I, by making such a demand, sealed Clarice's fate. It should have been me who died from the bullet of Yarrick's gun - but it was not, I survived. And, by surviving, I have guaranteed one more thing when my feet touch English soil.

"Fuck," I repeat quietly as the last scales of confusion fall from my eyes.

I have not escaped; I have not made a bid for freedom; if anything, I have imprisoned myself in a room with no walls, a pawn in a game for which only one man knows the rules.

I have a price on my head now, and until Yarrick can be brought down, I will remain his captive.

This is the life I am guaranteed.

≈≈≈≈

It's been an hour since Jim and I talked. He got called away almost as soon as the full story unfolded, and now I am waiting in the crew mess for him to return. I am shaken. The more I reflect on my time with Yarrick and the community, the more I am in disbelief. How could I not see what was right there in plain sight?

I am reminded of Jayde, my former best friend. Though details were scarce when she left, I did try to understand what had driven her to make the choice and devoured what little information I could. The messages were compelling, offering a different way of living, promising love, care and compassion. A community united, a place to belong and I remember romanticising the idea myself. I had been lost without Jayde, the thought of being able to go to a place full of everything I was missing was overwhelming. Like running away with the circus or the fair. Meeting the guy who spun the cars around on the Waltzer ride, catching his eye, his cheeky smile, admiring his freedom and looks, believing his life to be so much better than anything I could ever experience stuck in an ice palace with servants. Yet something held me back. Something deep inside - intuition maybe - a rationality of it all being too good to be true. If it sounded too good to be true, then it probably was.

Back then, I had no way of knowing just how right my fifteen-year-old-self had been.

Men ran these communities mainly. They were charming, kind, thoughtful, caring, considerate, empathetic ... and incredibly skilled at hiding their true selves. They were master manipulators who believed their own propaganda. Propaganda that was far too easy for the lost and vulnerable to buy into. The promise of heaven. The reality of hell.

I am sure Jayde believed it to be heaven. And maybe it was. Her parents ultimately left her there, and after the first year, her name was rarely spoken. It was as if she'd never existed, but I knew she had. She was in my heart.

I cannot believe I didn't see who Yarrick was. I, who prided myself on being so clever, so knowledgeable, astute enough to run my father's business in time, had missed every blindingly obvious hint or suggestion of truth about where I had ended up.

Every single thing that Yarrick did, every word he said, I now see as coming from the mouth of a puppet master - and with apparent ease. He moved every single member into the exact place he wanted them. Those caught in his spell were powerless, and he made sure to give them just enough time and attention so that they never realised. And if they did, then I'm guessing they were too scared to speak up because they knew what happened to anyone who dared ask questions or, worse, ask to leave.

Shit. I literally lived in one of the most fucked up of worlds and Yarrick played me. He knew I was grieving. He knew I was alone. He knew I had nothing. He must've thought it was pay-day when they found me on the beach. What a disgusting bastard. And how much did Clarice know? I need Jim to finish his story because I refuse to believe that everything Clarice and I shared was a lie. Jim told me that she was a prisoner, too, and if that were the case, she would have been as powerless as everyone else. Yarrick abhorred traitors. I witnessed that with my own eyes as he delivered Clarice's punishment for helping me, for trying to help herself. I saw the bullet rip through her heart. I escaped with my life - barely - though Clarice did not. Nor did Clara. Will I be next?

I am exhausted by the never-ending merry-go-round

of thoughts. Whatever I choose to do when I get back to England, I realise now that I have to do it calmly and quietly because not only do I need to find Alex, but I also have to make sure my identity is hidden. I have to protect the woman whose heart beats inside my chest. I am Aurora. I am Sandy. But I cannot be either now. If I am to make both men pay for their crimes, I have to be smarter than I have ever been before, and I have to do whatever it takes to make that happen - even if it means playing the long game.

It's ironic. Eighteen months ago, I believed my life to be dull and boring. Eighteen months ago, I saw the good in everyone. Eighteen months ago, Aurora Foster died.

I just didn't realise it until now.

≈≈≈≈

"I asked him, I did. I asked him right out what was going on and if it were true about the drugs, and he laughed. Right in my face. Laughed." Jim has returned and is carrying on where we left off. At the party with Yarrick and Clarice.

"Then he did something I'll never forget," Jim shudders, "he grabbed me by the shoulders, pulled me all the way into his face and spat at me. Spat in me face. Said if I ever so much as looked at Clarice again and if he heard I'd been spreading rumours, he'd do more than spit at me. Then he dragged me to the dock, punched me in the head and pushed me into the sea. Didn't care if I drowned, just left me to my fate."

Jim shakes his head. "Even now, I can't believe it. We'd been so close for so long ... anyhow, I made it to an old sea vessel and got patched up. That was a few years ago now, and every time we docked since, I've avoided Clarice. Until one day, she walked right up to me, brazen as anything, smiling in her way." His eyes mist in memory. "Joking with the other lads as if she didn't have a care in the world. Came as close

319

as any woman ever has, and in that second I saw her. The smile didn't reach her eyes. The deadness behind them. She never said a word. Just looked at me, then lifted my hand and pressed something into my palm before walking away. Back to the old Clarice as if nothing had changed - but it had."

I wait. Jim is clearly reliving every moment, opening up old wounds and, though I am desperate to know more, I exercise as much patience as I can. I begin counting slowly backwards from a hundred, breathing deeply as I watch the expressions on the face of this man of the sea. I have reached twenty-seven when my patience is rewarded.

"It was a letter," he says at last. "She gave me a letter."

What the ...? I want to scream, ask him why it's taken him this long to share this with me. But I do neither. I re-commence my counting. Twenty-six, twenty-five, twenty-four, twenty-three, twenty-two ...

"I still have it. I've kept it with me every day since." Jim's eyes connect with mine. There is uncertainty in his gaze. He doesn't know if he can trust me. Not so much on a basic level but on a visceral level. This is his secret, his part of Clarice, and I suspect I am the only person he has ever allowed this close. He is being cautious with his heart and emotions, and almost as quickly as it came, my frustration evaporates.

Of course he didn't tell me before. Jim needed to keep a part of her all to himself. The depth of love this man had for my beautiful, squishy Clarice is breathtaking. His pain is raw. I can feel it. I can smell it. I understand it.

Slowly, Jim fumbles in the top pocket of his thick body warmer vest and produces a crumpled piece of paper. I recognise it immediately. There was no paper in the upside-down shack, no writing tools, so Clarice had to be creative, and what she gave to Jim all those months ago was a page torn from a book. From a bible. Yarrick's bible. I would know it anywhere. The worn and faded ink, the slight curl to the corners, the light brown hue - all so familiar. In my mind's eye, I see Yarrick's large paw-like hands turning the pages night after night. Thanking the Lord. Making me believe he was a good person.

I take the folded sheet from Jim, afraid to open it, fingers suddenly incapable of movement. I fumble and drop the paper, terrified to see which page Clarice had chosen.

"It's okay," Jim says as he lays a comforting hand on my shoulder. "It'll all be okay, I promise."

I reach down and retrieve the item, this time managing to unfold the creases before spreading it carefully on my lap. The small cursive type is so achingly familiar, and through eyes blurred in disbelief it takes a moment for the words to come into focus. When they do, I see that Clarice added nothing to the page except for a single word scraped into the top left corner using the burned end of a match. It's a technique she showed me in the early days—a way for the children to write using materials they could easily get their hands on. Nothing was to be wasted, she'd said, not even a spent match.

Beneath the single, scratched word is a verse I know well. Psalm 86. A prayer of David. I scan through it, recognising the message and cadence of delivery before focusing on three lines, each of which has the faintest mark at their first word. A dash from a used match.

> *'You are forgiving and good, O Lord, abounding in love to all who call to you.'*

'Hear my prayer, O LORD; listen to my cry for mercy.'

'In the day of my trouble, I will call to you, for you will answer me.'

The Psalm continues, but I do not read on. These are the lines Clarice highlighted using the only resources she could.

This is the message she was sending to Jim.

I am distraught. In literal black and white, she was reaching out.

"I failed her," Jim says, but I do not respond. My fingers are tracing the four letters scratched into the top of the page. How could I have been so blind? How did I not see that Clarice was a prisoner, too?

The letters jump out at me mockingly, and I close my eyes against the barrage of guilt.

"I should have known," I whisper as my lifeless fingers drop the offending page once more. "I lived in the same house; I should have known."

I hear Jim shuffling beside me, retrieving the paper from where it lands before I am pulled tightly into his side.

"No," he says quietly, "no."

Maybe we are both culpable; perhaps we both missed opportunities to save her, but I know, had I not made it to the ship, Yarrick would have ended my life.

In a moment of clarity, I realise there is nothing to be gained by Jim and I blaming ourselves, though. We may be the only two people right now who know the danger Clarice was in and her bravery in getting me aboard this ship, but we won't be for long. I will make sure that every single person in that community knows what kind of a man Yarrick is, and beyond that, I will tell whoever I need to make sure that bastard is forced to live the rest of his days in a cell no bigger than the one he afforded to me. I might not have been able to save Clarice when she was alive, but I will not let her down in her death.

The power of the Psalm, the three highlighted lines and the word she wrote on the top of the page are burned into my brain, jostling with the story Jim has told and my need to find Alex.

That word Clarice wrote will haunt me until my last dying breath because it is those four letters that will give me the strength I need to make Yarrick and Alex pay. I am forced into a situation which I neither wanted nor desired, but if Clarice had faith in the Lord, then I must have faith in her.

She saved me for a reason. She pushed me in front of her when she could have left me on that dock to die at Yarrick's hands. Clarice believed in me, and now I must repay her. I must believe in myself.

And the four letters she wrote on the top of the scrunched-up page? The letters that will forever be burned into my deepest memory?

H E L P

Help.

Chapter Nineteen

PRESENT DAY

Unlike that poor wench, Aurora, my journey back to England was fast and substantially more comfortable. I made the trip in a little over forty-eight hours, which means I have had almost the entire three years before Aurora re-entered my orbit to put the finishing touches to my - even if I do say so myself - ingenious plan. God, I love how that sounds.

You're probably confused. How, you may wonder, do I know what happened to Aurora?

Well, it's really very simple. From the moment we set sail on the *Cassiopeia* three years ago, I was in control. Every tiny detail was planned and executed, and, sadly for Aurora, she was simply a pawn in my grown-up chess game. That's not to say I'm not fond of her, for I am - we are, after all, related - but as I have previously mentioned, there are only two people in my world, and the other one is Colin.

Oh, wait. Have I let slip that Aurora and I are related? That's the trouble sometimes with having so many balls to juggle; I don't always remember which ones I have dropped.

In case you haven't already figured it out, let me enlighten you. Otherwise, none of what is about to transpire will make sense. You see, the truth is that I, Alex, am the key to this whole story. Nothing, I repeat, nothing, has happened that I have not planned or orchestrated, and let me tell you, the power has been heady. For all of those times I was mocked as a child for being different, not only because I veered in an alternative direction sexually, but also for the life my parents chose to live. This power has been the perfect antidote, the balm that has soothed the deepest of wounds. Those who thought me beneath them or who barely acknowledged my existence have been made to notice now. And the best is yet to come.

I feel like a playwright or perhaps a screenwriter, creating and nurturing characters, bending them to my will, making them behave in a way which suits my purpose, and then seeing them perform. It fills me with so much pride. This, I imagine, is how it must feel to be a parent watching your child in the school nativity play. I never had a part in the nativity play. I was always in the chorus at the back, shoved to the far extremes of the stage where it didn't matter whether I sang or not. Sometimes I joined in; sometimes I didn't. It was fun to tease Rory (who was almost as unpopular as me) by singing the wrong words loudly in his ear. I was always placed behind him, so his back was the only view I ever had.

We were arranged in alphabetical order according to Ms Dundie-bum. (Not her real name, but no one could pronounce the rest of it, and her bum wobbled when she walked, so …). But that was bullshit. Rory and I were never alphabetically related; we were just the least popular kids. Simple. I think that was the moment when I realised that *everyone* lies.

Every kid, every adult. Every person lies.

Some - which I find rather amusing - try to dress it up as a 'white' lie, one that has been told to protect feelings, but that's bullshit, too. A lie is a lie, and our entire existence is open to interpretation. The only truth in which I believe is that we're all making it up as we go along. Or, to put it more bluntly - no one has a fucking clue.

Take Rory, complaining to the teacher that I was shouting in his ear. Poor kid thought Ms Dundie-bum cared. Nope. The reality was that Dundie-bum didn't care. She simply reminded him that we were all in the chorus, so it didn't matter how loudly we sang because it would be out of tune anyway. I laughed. I couldn't help it. It would have been rude not to.

Rory's face and neck went beet red as an entire class of pretentious sprogs gaped at him - most of them, I'm sure, having no clue who the heck he was. I did start to feel a bit sorry for him after that. I may have slightly deafened him with my screeching, and now he was on everyone's radar as the kid who made rehearsal go on even longer. Ah, well. No matter.

I made sure to sing especially loudly next time. After all, Christmas is a time for giving.

I digress. Unlike Rory and I, Aurora and I are actually related, and it's more than just a flimsy bullshit alphabet connection. Way more.

You see, though I have confirmed the story of my creation to be accurate - I *was* the product of my parents' champagne-fuelled celebration party - I may have been a little creative with the details. I failed to confirm who I was the 'product' of, and you, being the good little believers I'm sure you are, presumed it was my parents. I can't fault you for that. It's a logical assumption, and to be fair, you're half right.

My mother is my real mother, but my father, well, he's not.

According to local gossip, before the big lottery win, my mother was a barmaid at our local pub and was well-known for interpreting her wedding vows somewhat loosely.

Until that was, she found real love ...

... with someone other than the man she married.

This 'love' frequented the pub every Friday evening, arriving at seven pm on the dot, staying for precisely two pints of whatever the current ale was, and then leaving at exactly eight thirty pm. He always paid the exact amount in cash (plus enough for mother dearest to have a soda water). He, according to legend, was handsome, dashing and filthy rich.

Their affair (he was also married) began several months before the big lottery win, and I am led to believe that those stolen hours spent with my sperm donor were the happiest of her life. (Note to reader: If you're going to conduct an illicit affair, don't do it in the local pub. Even the minutest of details will be common knowledge before last orders. Once I knew my biological history, all it cost was the price of one pint of the pub's finest ale to discover every sordid detail of my mother's life.)

My filthy rich sperm donor turned out to be a local businessman and pillar of the community no less, so it was only natural that he be invited to the *big lottery win party*. Despite his marital status, my DNA provider attended the now infamous *big lottery win party* alone, leaving him and my mother to enjoy their champagne a little too much. Protection obviously went out of the window and nine months later, a bouncing baby boy arrived. Tugs at your heartstrings, doesn't it?

In a twist, which illustrates how wet and weak daddy-by-default was at the time, I was welcomed into the world as his son and passed off as being wholly legitimate for the first several years of my life. I don't know who was trying to protect whom, but the end result was the same. Everyone lied and the ill-conceived tiny human became the bow attached to the gift wrap of a neatly packaged lottery win. Thus my parents began a whole new life as a family of three - except now they had money.

≈≈≈≈

For those of you yet to work it out, the real colour of the blood running through my veins, is that of a man sadly taken before his time, though I fully intend to honour his legacy and memory. He may have a daughter, but it is the man who rules, and I cannot wait to see the face of one Aurora Foster when I finally reveal my true identity.

Because my real father, the man with whom my mother was very much in love, was none other than Andrew Foster. Father of Aurora.

And yet, still, you have questions. I know, I know. How did I find out? Why do I hate my sibling so much? And, of course, why did I kill my father?

I understand your curiosity and even perhaps your desire to know everything, but patience is a virtue and I don't want to spoil your enjoyment of this sordid tale by revealing all. Not yet.

In the meantime, I turn my attention back to the screens and, as expected, become a little aroused when I see Colin's handsome face. He is there, front and centre, in the garden, talking to Aurora. They have walked to the far end of the grassy area (which is most inconsiderate as I am forced to zoom the camera to its full capacity) and are seated on a rotten old bench. I hadn't realised it was there. Perhaps, when I can, I will go out and add another camera closer. Especially if Colin is going to use it.

He's so innocent. He has no idea how much I covet him. He simply delivers my coffee every morning at the same time and in the same way and thinks nothing of it, yet once I let him in on my secret, he will be impressed. I know he will. I can't wait to have him all to myself.

He and Aurora are involved in an animated discussion which involves much gesticulation, and as I watch, they turn to look at each other. I can only see Aurora's face, for Colin has his back to me, but I can tell their conversation is uncomfortable. For my (half) sister, at least.

But then something changes. He leans in and pulls her close. I hold my breath. The two of them are becoming more intimate than I am comfortable with, but wait, she draws away. It's nothing more than a simple hug between friends. I exhale in relief. A hug between friends is of no concern.

Until.

Until it does become my concern. Colin has moved towards Aurora again, even closer this time, and is now cupping her face. I don't want to look. I sense where this is heading, and I cannot watch. Yet I must. In the same way we rubberneck at the scene of an accident, I cannot avert my eyes.

He kisses her. The seconds still, and I am consumed with nothing except the view on the screen.

The man I love, the man with whom I fully intend to spend the rest of my life, is making out with my nemesis. This is too much, even for me.

I race to the toilet and vomit before returning slowly to my bed.

I knew he liked her, but this ... this was so not in the plan.

Chapter Twenty

PRESENT DAY

Returning to the warehouse, I am immediately accosted by Rich, who appears from nowhere.

"What the hell?" I place my hand over my heart as it threatens to beat out of my chest.

"Sorry … sorry …" he says, "I've been looking for you."

"And that's a good enough reason to scare the shit out of me?" We have entered the main sleeping area, and I stride ahead towards my bunk. There is a buzz of noise and chatter, which accompanies the warmth emanating from old-style radiators lining the walls. There are forty-four of these, equally spaced and distributed from front to back of the large unit. As we approach my bed, I am surprised to see another plastic bag on top.

"More clothes," Rich says, indicating the bag.

I nod. "What did you want?" I realise I am exhausted. Emotionally drained. I need time to think.

"I was concerned after you left the office. I don't know," he exhales deeply, and I turn to face him. He looks like crap, a far cry from the polished features of the Rich who met us at the door just over a day ago. His hair is a mess, sticking out at odd angles, and as I watch he runs his hand through it, tugging absently at its length. There is a wildness in his eyes, their darkness more intense as he shifts from foot to foot. Nervous energy radiates, and a tiny part of me responds, wanting to reach out. He is clearly distressed and I am surprised to find this has triggered the emotions of my old self, the original Aurora, who hated to see others suffering. I am shocked to witness this uneasiness from Rich, yet perhaps he is not as strong as he would have the world believe. I sit at the top end of my bunk and move the bag of clothes to one side, indicating a space for Rich.

I am instantly reminded of a very different time, eighteen months ago, when I sat beside another man on a similar bunk. It was the time when I finally understood the depths of depravity some men would go to in order to satisfy their desires. It was the time when I fully realised that I could not simply walk back onto English soil as if I had never left. It was one week before invisibility became my permanent friend. It was the last time anyone spoke to Sandy.

I guess I have compartmentalised the last three years into blocks, or rather, I have split my life into three parts:

There are my early years - in fact, everything that came before that night on the *Cassiopeia*. Jayde falls into this part, despite her recent return.

Then there is the time I spent on Añaposta Island after witnessing a madman murder my parents. For a while this time felt happy and beautiful; I believed I was loved and maybe even settled. Until the earth room and the cell and the pregnancy and Clarice's death. That's when I discovered who Yarrick really was.

Finally, there is my life on the streets. A time when Aurora and Sandy were consigned to the depths of memory whilst

Ra fought to pull through, her destination unsure, her cause clear. A woman without history or future. A survivor, existing on her wits. As Ra I have nothing, yet oddly, the months of invisibility brought a much-needed level of peace.

It is fitting, I reflect, to have lived under a different name during each of these 'lives'. Though it may not have been by design - simply driven by my subconscious need to survive - it works. Allowing myself to be three different women has given me a glimpse into the many facets of my being. Each one favours alternative versions of the original. It would be impossible for any of them to complete what is required of us alone. I am proud to be the sum today of each of those lives - Aurora, Sandy and Ra - yet I am terrified. It was only a matter of time before the three of us needed to become one, but I am unnerved by this man sitting beside me. Somehow, I have dropped my guard, and he has reached inside us all in one way or another. Aurora wants to comfort him, Sandy wants to confide in him, and Ra is experiencing a level of arousal and attraction that both Aurora and Sandy considered dead.

When Astrid and I walked through that heavy oak door, I couldn't possibly have known what was behind it, yet for some reason, I am being forced to confront my past and present simultaneously. It's like I have entered my very own reality check.

This old relic of a building, which in itself has changed use and identity through the years, is unravelling parts of me that I am not ready for others to inspect. I don't have my plans in place yet.

I didn't realise just how hard it would be to survive out there, and there were days when I was so worn down I questioned my desire to 'even the score' with the two men I had come to hate. These questions, though, were merely moments of weakness, fuelled by the good days on the street when I allowed myself to let go a little, safe in the knowledge that no one knew who I was. The days when people like Roland pitied me and those like Roseanna passed me by. It was so much easier to be Ra, that shadow of a woman avoided by the good and preyed on by the bad whose past remained in the past. But then I would remember my parents, the crew of the *Cassiopeia*, and Clarice and Clara, and I would know that I had to do what I promised myself I would.

I had to make Alex and Yarrick pay and the 'how' was simply a puzzle to be solved - eventually.

Life on the streets is all-consuming and drifting from day to day becomes - oddly - an easy habit. I was waiting during those long cold days and even longer colder nights - but I didn't know for what.

'Serendipity, my girl,' my father would say. *'Wait for serendipity.'* It was one of his favourite life lessons.

'Horace Walpole,' Dad was fond of recounting, *'conceived the notion of serendipity when he was inspired by a fairytale. The heroes - who came from Serendip - made happy discoveries that were neither planned nor desired but gave a favourable outcome. Thus, serendipity. Be master of your own serendipity, Aurora.'*

This never struck me as a useful life lesson. If serendipity is unplanned, then how can I be a master of it? I also had no idea who the hell Horace Walpole was (still don't) and where the fuck Serendip is, if it even exists.

But I guess the point of this lesson is that 'things' align, and maybe this place, this supposed safe house full of ghosts and skeletons, is my serendipity.

Perhaps my father had a point.

Shit. I have no clue.

A gentle cough reminds me of Rich's presence.

"Penny for them?" he asks, and I offer a weak smile. I could respond with a trite cliché - 'they're not worth it,' or 'how long have you got?' But I don't. They are clichés for a reason: they add precious little value to a conversation.

"Sorry," I drag my mind back to the present. "You were saying?"

"I wasn't saying anything, other than I'd been looking for you."

"I was outside."

Rich gives me a sideways glance. He knows I was outside because he pounced on me the second I came back in. "With Astrid and Colin," I add. His lips lift at the corners in a half smile that barely reaches the rest of his mouth.

"I see." He nods and then turns away from me, placing his forearms on his knees and leaning his upper body onto them, his gaze fixed to the floor. This version of Rich is unsettling. I have never seen this side of him before and I am floundering. I don't understand why he was looking for me. I don't understand why he is being so weird, and I sure as hell don't understand what the heck is so interesting about a grey concrete floor.

In that strange habit we humans have, I find myself mirroring him, adopting exactly the same pose - though I amuse myself by taking my gaze a little to the left so that I can at least look at the thin brightly patterned rug which I instinctively know was dirt cheap. It's a nice thought, though. It breaks up the monotony of grey and was welcome on my bare feet when I stepped out of bed this morning.

Beside me, Rich exhales but remains mute. The silence extends.

In my experience, there are two kinds of silence: comfortable and uncomfortable, but I am rapidly discovering a third. A 'Rich' silence for which there is no suitable adjective. It is neither comfortable nor uncomfortable; it just is, and I have no idea how to deal with it.

I want to get up and leave, hide somewhere so that I don't have to find out why he was looking for me, yet I want to stay because I actually do want to know why he was looking for me. Whether I am ready to admit it to myself or not, this man intrigues me and having accepted (after our earlier encounter in the kitchen) that there is a certain sexual frisson between us, I am curious. I thought Rich was shallow. A man in love with himself who searched only for people and circumstances that would benefit him. But this person sitting beside me is not that man, and I am beginning to wonder if I was wrong.

Perhaps there are layers and facets which are hidden and perhaps it is those which intrigue. If you'd asked me less than twelve hours ago, I would have had no problem describing Rich as arrogant, full of himself, a little narcissistic even, and definitely lacking in any kind of human emotion - for that is the persona he showed Astrid and I the second we walked through that door. Yet, during our last couple of encounters I have seen a different side to him. He has shown several human emotions, including anger and sensitivity and now, given the way he is sitting, vulnerability. His stillness and almost prayer-like pose do not scream arrogance; they indicate a man unsure, a man troubled, a man unreachable.

"You were with Colin," he says suddenly, breaking the silence. It is neither a question nor a statement, merely a comment left hanging in the vaulted interior.

I shrug. "I already told you I was."

Silence returns. Rich has yet to look at me; his attention remains captured by the floor.

"And Astrid," I add.

He nods. Again, nothing.

I sigh. "Have you seen Rex?" I assume Rich will eventually tell me what's on his mind, but in the meantime I realise I am missing my adopted mutt.

"In the kitchen," he replies.

"Great. Thanks."

When I was six-years-old, I decided to climb the apple tree in our garden. I was fearless, as many six-year-olds are, and convinced that I would be able to reach the top without any difficulty. I couldn't. Before I knew what was happening, I had landed in a heap on the ground, sobbing uncontrollably. On closer inspection my left ankle was twice its usual size, so I was carted off to the hospital, where the doctor asked me to tell him how much it hurt from one to ten with ten being the highest. Of course, I told him ten. I was six-years-old and thought that a sprained ankle was the worst pain I could ever experience.

How wrong I was. This non-conversation with Rich is easily a twelve.

I rub my palms on my knees and make to stand up. This is pointless. I know we've only been seated for a few minutes, but it feels like forever, and unless there is a reason for this unbelievable discomfort, then I see no need to be its audience any longer. I manage four strides in the direction of the kitchen before I feel Rich at my side. Grabbing my arm, he pulls me towards the office at the far end of the unit, the one where Colin and I sat before, in our weird little half-moon arrangement. I am caught off guard and end up sitting on one of the chairs with the door closed and locked before I have a chance to realise what is happening.

"What the hell?" I breathe deeply.

Rich has locked the door, and though he has no way of knowing it, a small room with a locked door is a major trigger. I try not to panic, reminding myself that this is a safe place, a safe house, and there are people just outside the door.

I breathe again and count slowly in and out. Rich has either not heard my question or is ignoring me; either way, he pays me scant attention as he strides to the furthest corner from where I am sitting. A limp-looking bonsai stands in an oversized pot; the tree and tub are at odds, with neither appearing to match the needs of the other.

Rich reaches the tree, and it is then that my gaze snags on the wheeled screen which I noticed last time I was in the room. Then it must have been in front of the pot, hiding it from view, but now it is drawn back against the wall, and as Rich gives the screen a less than gentle push, it slides further and reveals that the bonsai tree was not the only thing it was obscuring. There is another door.

As I watch, Rich places his fingertip on a small pad adjacent to the door and seconds later, a large metal hulk swings open. It is thick, maybe ten inches in depth, and the inside frame has holes into which corresponding bolts from within the door slot, to secure it closed. It is the entrance to a safe or strongroom. I know this because we had one at home. When we had money. When my parents were alive.

"Come on," Rich turns and beckons, but I remain rooted to my chair. I don't know what is behind that piece of cold grey steel, and I am not sure that I want to know either.

"No," I say as I shake my head. My legs have turned to jelly, and my stomach is in knots. I cannot be held captive again; I can't. I try to stand, using my hands as leverage, and pray that my legs will respond. "No," I say again. "No."

Willing my unsteady limbs to comply, I head towards the exit, but I am too slow. Rich has inserted himself between me and the door that leads to freedom.

"Get out of my way," I say, voice dangerously low. "I am not being locked up in that hell hole or whatever the hell it is. No fucking way. If you want a plaything, then you've come to the wrong place."

Confusion crosses Rich's handsome features. "I don't want to lock you up," he says calmly.

"No? Well, I don't believe you, so why don't you go out there and find someone who'll be more than happy to do whatever your sick and twisted mind desires? I am never allowing myself to be used again. Never. Understand? Either get out of my way or so help me, God, I will end you."

Rich shakes his head and holds his hands up as if in surrender. "I said I don't want to lock you up, Ra, I want to talk to you, and the only way I could think to do that without being interrupted was to bring you here. Why the hell would you think I want to lock you up?"

I study his eyes and face for signs that he is lying and find none. His breath remains even, his eyes sincere, and his cheeks aren't flushed. Not even a stray bead of sweat peeps from beneath his hairline. I inhale a calming breath and remind myself that Rich knows nothing of who I am or was and cannot possibly know about Yarrick and the cell. It's possible that I've overreacted, although, in my defence,

Jayde has shown up here and started telling anyone who'll listen about our past, so I feel justified to be on my guard.

"Sorry," I say. "It's just ... Jayde ... " I shake my head. I have no clue what else to say. Her arrival has shaken me more than I first thought, and I am feeling pressure to get my shit together. I have to deal with Yarrick and Alex before others besides Jayde begin to ask questions.

"Jayde locked you up?"

"What? Oh ... no. There's stuff in my past. Her being here is a reminder."

"Thank fuck for that," Rich says with a smile. "I've never actually evicted anyone from here, but I guess there's always a first time."

"You'd evict Jayde?" I manage a shaky laugh.

"Of course. I am responsible for everyone's safety - which includes yours whether you like it or not - and if we are invaded by miscreants with a penchant for locking others up, then eviction would not be my only course of action." The dimple in his left cheek has deepened, and the lines around his eyes crinkle.

"You're joking," I say, and Rich nods, his smile broadening.

"Though the thought of Jayde manhandling you has a certain appeal." His smile turns into a leer.

"You're sick," I say, "in here." I tap my temple, and Rich laughs.

We share a moment of pause. Smiling easily.

"I like teasing you," he says, eyes boring into mine, "it's nice. Feels like we might actually get on."

I snort. "You are also deluded. In here."

I tap my temple again.

"C'mon," Rich laughs, indicating the door behind the screen. "Let's go."

I eye him warily. "Why? What's back there?"

"My room. Where I live." Rich points to the large metal door. "It's a converted strong room and the only place I am guaranteed not to be disturbed. The two people who know it exists also know better than to intrude on me here - unless the building is literally on fire."

"Okay," I feel my voice waver a little and clear my throat. "You're not helping matters by telling me that only two people know about this place and that you won't be disturbed. I know nothing about you, Rich. You could literally be the proverbial axe murderer."

"I could," he nods, "but I'm not. Far too messy."

I shake my head. "Not funny. Why can't we just talk out here?"

"Because" Rich shrugs. "Look, can we just go inside? Please? I promise not to lock you up, murder you, or entertain impure thoughts about you and Jayde; I really do just want to talk. The second you've had enough, you're gone. Okay?"

The way he is looking at me, almost pleading, I am reminded of the man who sat on my bed mere moments ago, the one who showed vulnerability far removed from the first Rich I met. I don't know if I can trust him, and I sure as hell can't trust my instincts - look what happened with Alex - but one thing that life on the streets has taught me is that you have to let people in sometimes. It's the key to survival, and I've never regretted letting Astrid in. It's also been three years since I trusted Alex and Yarrick; I am a very different person now. Perhaps it's time to take another risk.

"Okay," I incline my head, "but be warned. If you so much as leave me alone in there, even for a second, then I will scream at the top of my lungs."

Rich smiles as he retraces his steps to the corner. "It's a strongroom, Aurora. No one will hear you."

"Fuck you."

His back is to me, heading towards the entrance to his living space, but I can tell he is smiling. "Fuck you, too," he replies.

As he reaches the door, he turns back towards me and indicates for me to go ahead.

"You want to know what Jayde knows, right?"

"No," he shakes his head. "I don't."

I frown in confusion. I can't imagine what else he wants to talk about, but my train of thought is abruptly derailed when I make my way into the space Rich calls home.

"Wow. This is something."

"Isn't it?" Rich says. Behind me, I hear the door close, yet what has opened up in front is so far removed from any kind of cell or prison that I forget to be scared. This place is huge. Much larger than I could have imagined.

The former secure room has been converted into a spacious living area and kitchen, decorated in shades of blues and greys with a modern feel. Two dark blue sofas occupy most of the lounge section and are dotted with several brightly coloured cushions.

The kitchen is at the back of the unit and, from what I can tell, contains everything a modern kitchen should.

As I walk further inside, I notice a wooden screen to my right stretching from floor to ceiling, beyond which I can just about make out a bed.

"The bathroom's through the bedroom," Rich says, indicating with his hand. "There's another screen, although that one has a door." He laughs. I don't respond. I am trying to take in every detail of the place this man calls home.

I look upwards. Daylight is pouring in through several glazed roof-lights.

"Since when do strongrooms have holes in the roof?" I ask. "Doesn't that defeat their purpose?"

I feel Rich beside me. "That's the first thing you're going to say?"

I shrug. "Yeah. I guess so. Although technically, the first thing I said was 'this is something'."

The soft smile that I have recently become accustomed to touches his lips. "I have no idea. This was all done before I took over the warehouse. I'm guessing a previous owner lived here. I didn't know about it at first. I used to just sleep out there in the main area," he swipes his hand in the direction from which we have come.

"And then you found it?"

"Not exactly. It was hidden behind those screens and the entire world's supply of tables and chairs." Rich smiles. "I'd had no need to move them, so the office just became a place to dump things - and then, out of the blue, I got this weird email. Telling me where to look."

"Email?" I echo.

"Yeah," he shrugs. "No idea who it was from or how they knew the room was there, but I assumed it was forwarded from the agent after we'd taken over this place. Although the sign-off was strange. Something about swans mating for life." Rich shrugs. "I figured it was part of another message or something. Anyway, I moved all the crap and voila!"

"Swans mating for life?" I ask.

"Yeah. Really odd, but I'm definitely guilty of copying and pasting emails without always checking, so it's easy done. I was actually kind of relieved that it's not just me who sends the wrong messages to the wrong people." Rich smiles self-deprecatingly. It is a smile that I mirror.

Emails. A technology and means of communication from a lifetime ago. Not something I've had to worry about for the last three years.

I take a few more paces.

"This is crazy," I say as I look around. "Out there, it's nowhere near luxury, and yet in here ..."

He nods, his dark blonde hair swinging across his face.

"I know. To be honest, I feel bad knowing this is here, so I don't spend much time in it."

I continue on towards the kitchen at the back. As I thought, the surfaces are littered with every modern appliance. A washing machine and fridge are tucked beneath the worktop.

"Shit," I say, "I haven't seen this much luxury since ..." Suddenly, I realise what I am about to say and immediately stop.

Since the *Cassiopeia*.

But Rich doesn't know about my previous life, and he definitely has no clue that I once called a luxury yacht home. I want to keep it that way.

"Since?" he questions.

"Nothing." I walk back towards the sofas and sit down. The seat moulds to my shape, and I sink gratefully into its comfort. Shit. This feels otherworldly. I can't remember the last time I sat on something that wasn't hard and cold. Not for the first time in three years, I miss my old life.

"This is nice," I say as I spread my hands across the seats, revelling in the softness of the warm blue velveteen. Nice doesn't really cover it and sounds way too uptight. What I really want to say is, 'This is fucking awesome!'.

"Scratch that," I say as I watch Rich settle in the matching sofa directly opposite. "This is fucking awesome!"

He laughs. "A step up from the office chairs."

"Only for some of us," I reply. "You get your comfort hit out there, too. Don't think I haven't noticed your faux leather executive seat."

"Oh, Ra, what am I going to do with you?"

I take it to be a rhetorical question, so say nothing.

"If I was in any doubt as to your," he pauses, "intelligence, then I'm not anymore."

"Intelligence? Don't be so patronising. Just because we live on the streets doesn't mean we can't tell a good chair when we see one."

"I don't doubt it. What I do doubt is how many of your counterparts would know it was faux leather."

"Wow," I say. "That's even more patronising. You know how fucked up this is, right? There are literally hundreds of people outside this place who live on the streets with nothing. And you have all this. You don't get to be a patronising bastard as well."

"Did you not hear me when I said I feel guilty about it?" Rich points out.

"Yeah," I respond, "but it's easy to feel guilty when you have this at your disposal. Less so if you actually have to live that life."

I should know.

Rich smiles. "And she's back."

"What the hell are you talking about?" I ask. I am still feeling affronted on behalf of all street dwellers. Especially when this man is supposed to be all about saving us.

"The argumentative Ra. The one I met on day one."

"Wait." I hold up my hand. "You said those things just to rile me?"

He nods and places his palm over his heart. "Guilty as charged."

"You bastard." I throw one of the brightly coloured cushions at him, and he ducks.

"My intentions were good," he laughs. "You've been off-kilter since Jayde arrived, and I missed our spats."

"You're a lunatic," I say, and Rich shrugs.

"Let me ask you something," I continue, "why me?"

"Why you what?"

"Why am I here? Why are you sharing this with me? Why not the others? I don't get why you keep singling me out. Getting me to stay, giving me jobs, then showing me this. We've literally just met. Is this what you usually do? Single out someone in need for fuck knows what?"

Rich closes his eyes and exhales. Slowly. "No." He says, "I don't 'usually' do anything."

"Then why am I not back on the streets like everyone else once their bellies are full?"

"Astrid isn't either," he points out, and I shake my head.

"Semantics."

"That is exactly why," he replies, "semantics. We've had this conversation, Ra. The language you use and the way you carry yourself. I told you, you're different. You're not meant to be here and ..." he shifts in his seat before capturing my eyes with his, "... I feel like I need to know why. I want to know who you are. It's like ..." he shrugs, "... I don't know. You intrigue me."

For a moment I fight a wave of panic. He wants to know who I am. Does he have suspicions that I am not being entirely honest? Has Jayde already told him I'm far from poor? Well, I *was* far from poor. Now, I have no idea.

"Why?" I ask. I'm stalling. I need time to think.

Rich sighs and shifts forward in his seat. "You're like one of those annoying kids," he smiles, "when all they do is ask why."

"Thanks." I can't avoid the sarcasm which drips from the single word.

"Hey," he reaches his right arm towards my left knee and taps it lightly. "It was a joke."

"Yeah?" I move my knee, watching as his hand falls limp.

"Things like this don't happen," I say. "Not out there. We don't get a decent bed and food, and we sure as hell don't get it for more than one night. And this ..." I gesture around the luxurious space, "... it's more than most out there will see in their entire lifetime. So maybe I do ask '*why*', but if you were in my shoes, I'm pretty sure you'd want to understand what the hell was happening too."

"Jesus, Ra," Rich pushes back into the depths of the sofa and runs his hand through his hair. "Why the hell won't you give me a break?"

"I'm sorry, what?"

"You." He stands abruptly and moves towards the kitchen area before spinning on his heel to face me. Oddly, I feel a sense of loss at the increased distance between us. "You're always so bloody pious when all I'm trying to do is be nice. It's like you're so far up your own backside that you can't see what's right in front of you."

"You have no right," I hiss out. Anger rises and I stalk towards him, heavy steps echoing the beat of my ire.

"You have no idea what my life is like, and you have no right to make a judgement. I didn't ask to come in here. I didn't ask to stay another night. I didn't ask for your help." I have arrived in front of Rich, my finger pointed menacingly at his chest.

"If you remember, I asked to leave, yet you made me stay. Persuaded me that you needed me, yet all I've done is clean a few bloody showers. You don't need me any more than you need Colin or the rest of the minions who do your bidding. You're just a stuck-up bastard who can't function unless he's some kind of hero, so that, what? You can bask in the glory?"

My voice rises in both tone and volume. "You say I'm pious? You need to take a long hard look in the mirror because from where I'm standing, you're the one with their head up their arse, not me. Now, let me the hell out of here so I can get my dog and go back to a place where I can at least live without judgement."

I turn on my heel and stomp angrily towards the door. I can't believe I was softening toward him, and I can't believe I was almost taken in. Who does this man think he is?

I hear his steps behind me.

"Ra, wait."

"Fuck you."

His hand on my arm is less of a surprise than it should have been. I knew that someone as entitled as Rich wouldn't let me just walk out. His ego would never recover.

"Let me go." I have stopped a metre from the door, facing its soulless steel veneer.

"No." His voice is soft. He is directly behind me. I can feel his breath blowing through my hair and onto the tender skin of my neck. "No," he says more firmly. "I won't."

"Let. Me. Go." My voice wavers. His proximity is affecting parts of me that haven't been awakened since Alex. Or maybe even before then. Perhaps ever. "Please."

"No."

He doesn't move. His grip neither tightens nor releases. He just stays exactly where he is, right behind me, our bodies almost touching. I feel my heart quicken. "Please," I repeat, "please."

My tone is bordering on begging, and I am angry that I'm letting this man affect me. I tell myself that I need to leave because he is insufferable, that he is a sanctimonious bastard who represents everything I hated about my life as

Aurora. I tell myself he's a player and that his words, what he says about wanting to get to know me, are meaningless. I tell myself he only ever acts in a way that serves Rich almighty. I tell myself I detest him. That he sickens me. That I cannot bear to be around him.

I tell myself all of these things and whilst I believe them to be true, it is time for me to finally accept that *none* of these are the real reason I am running.

I am not running *because of Rich.*

I am running *because of me.*

I don't trust myself around this man and whether I am Ra the independent, or Sandy the trusting, or Aurora the naive, I vowed never again show vulnerability to anyone, least of all a man. That is non-negotiable.

"Ra, look at me." His voice is barely more than a whisper.

I shake my head. "No. Let me go, Rich. Please."

His hand relaxes on my arm, and I miss its warmth.

"Okay." The breath that had been tickling my neck increases in force as he exhales a sigh of defeat.

Silently Rich moves ahead of me and takes the last few steps to the door. He reaches into his pocket and retrieves the key. I watch his back, the movement of his arm as he inserts it into the lock whilst at the same time offering his forefinger to the detector on the wall. I hear a click when the mechanism releases followed by a tiny creak as Rich's hand presses down on the large steel handle.

The door opens a crack, the crescent of light increasing as he does exactly what I have asked.

I step towards him. Towards the door. Towards safety.

I reach his side, my left shoulder inches from his right arm. We could just have easily been separated by metres as we face the door in silence. I pause for a split-second. I don't know why.

"For the record," he says quietly, "all of this," he nods his head in the direction of the luxury I am about to leave, "I would give it up in a second. In a heartbeat. Fuck, I would live on the streets, too, if it meant I could spend time with you. I want you, Ra."

My breath hitches. I say nothing. I do not move. Nor does Rich. We maintain our places side by side, both staring at the steel passage to freedom.

"I know it makes no sense," he continues, "and that it's probably all kinds of messed up. Hell, I barely know you."

Rich runs his right hand through his hair. I wait. For some reason my feet are rooted to the floor. The air between us crackles. He exhales before turning sharply, a quarter of a turn to his right, facing my frozen form in profile.

"The second we met, everything changed for me. You arrived, all fire and anger, pissed at the world, pissed at me and ..."

I feel his gaze burning the left side of my head. I know that if I turn towards him, even a fraction, our eyes will meet and lock.

"I want you," Rich repeats with quiet finality, "and right now, nothing else matters".

The hairs on my arms prickle. My breathing quickens, and warmth pools in a place it hasn't pooled for a very long time.

He's right. There is something connecting us which is why

I was running. I cannot define it any more than he can; all I know is that I am scared. More scared than I have ever been on the streets. More scared than in the earth room and the cell. More scared than the day I watched Clarice die. More scared than the emptiness I feel deep inside in the place I nurtured Clara.

Because this is not physical; this strange pull towards Rich goes so much deeper than that. This is something that threatens my emotional safety and that is not a part of me I am willing to play fast and loose with.

Yet, here is the kicker. I cannot walk away, because finally I understand why I react so strongly to this man.

I want him too.

It's a reason as old as time, with one devastating twist.

Rich has the power to break me. This I instinctively know. If I allow him in, if I trust him with even the smallest part of my soul, he will have a power I cannot relinquish.

I raise my eyes, letting him see that I get it. That I feel it too, but though we might just be one man and one woman engaging in desires over which we have no logical control, we cannot do this. Our shared vulnerability is too raw, too close to the surface. Neither of us would survive.

We cannot do this. We just can't.

Slowly I shake my head.

"Don't do this," I whisper. "Please. Don't push this." I feel the dampness of tears as they drop onto my cheeks.

"I'm sorry, Ra," his eyes bore deeply into mine. "I can't stop."

The glistening of his tears mirror my own and, as time is held suspended, I realise he understands. He gets it. He gets my fear and vulnerability, he gets his own uncertainties - but his need, his desire for this, for us, is more powerful. Despite everything screaming at us to stop, he cannot.

And neither can I.

Fuck.

It is time to roll the dice.

"Shit, Ra," Rich pushes on the door, and I hear it close heavily. I am still inside.

His head descends towards mine. His eyes darken. His hair flops onto his forehead, and there is that inevitable moment of pause. The final chance to back away.

In that final moment I think of Colin, innocently kissing me, telling me things I wasn't ready to hear. I think of Alex, and what I still have to do. I think of Yarrick and how much hatred I harbour for him. I think of Clarice, Clara, and Jim, of the journey I have been on and the path I still have to travel. I think of my parents. I think of the *Cassiopeia*.

And, in that briefest of moments before Rich's warm lips gently touch mine, I am thinking of Aurora, Sandy and Ra. The three identities I have been forced to create; the one woman I have been forced to become.

His lips are soft. His kiss warm and passionate. Rich is kissing me as if I am the only woman on earth. Kissing me as if I deserve this time of happiness. Kissing me as if the world will end tomorrow. Kissing me like I have never been kissed before.

Kissing me with care, tenderness and meaning. Just kissing me.

And then I am thinking no more.

≈≈≈≈

The bed is comfortable. The sheets are soft and fresh. The body beside me is warm, and I stretch luxuriously, forgetting where I am for a moment. Forgetting who I am.

Muscles that haven't been used in forever tingle with soreness, which is neither pleasurable nor painful. I have no idea what time it is.

I roll onto my back and stare at the ceiling. I am naked, covered only by the light blue comforter that Rich pulled over us. I don't care that I am naked. It wouldn't matter if I was covered or not. Any hang-ups about my body disappeared in the cell when it became nothing more than a vessel of pleasure for Yarrick and his men. I wonder how I feel. I have occasionally thought about being intimate with another man, but it hasn't been high on my list of priorities. I didn't know if I would feel anything or if I would even be able to allow another man near me. I didn't know if everything that had been taken away in that cell would ever return.

And I no more have the answers now than I did before I slept with Rich.

He was thoughtful yet passionate, gentle yet firm, and though I believe I enjoyed our moment, I still feel disconnected. I have denied all feeling in my body for so long that I don't know how to allow it to return or if I even want it to return.

I wanted to sleep with Rich. When I realised I was attracted to him and that I had been lying to myself, I wanted to end up here. I wanted to have the comfort he so willingly gave. I wanted to feel the warmth of another person simply holding me. I wanted to not be alone for a while. I wanted to forget. I wanted to pretend I didn't have such a fucked-up existence. I wanted to see how it felt.

And now I have.

I watch the light playing through the roof light, slanting across the wall and highlighting the modern art canvas painted in shades of yellow and blue. I wonder at its cost. I wonder if it is valuable or something picked from a charity shop. Not that it matters.

I squint, and the light refracts. Beside me, Rich stirs. A warm hand snakes across my abdomen, brushing my scar.

The light becomes a rainbow, dancing in the room - and suddenly, I am back there. Back in the cell, back in the room at the top of Yarrick's house, my belly stretched to accommodate my daughter. Clara. I thought I was ready for this, but maybe I am not. Rich's fingers play across the dip of the wound as if he can read my thoughts. He noticed the scar as soon as we undressed but he didn't ask. I saw his eyes drift to it and then glance at me in askance. I ignored the silent question, and he didn't push.

Now, though, his fingers are caressing it, caressing the place where my dead daughter was removed from my body. The baby I detested because of how she was conceived. The baby who secured my freedom from the cell. The baby who made Clarice take one too many risks, and the baby who ultimately gave me this second chance. And what have I done with it?

I've spent it on the streets feeling sorry for myself. I haven't fought. I haven't done anything except survive. I've made excuses for not returning to my home. I could have proved my identity; I could have claimed my birthright - or whatever remained of it - and I could have used the resources left behind by my parents to find Alex. Yet I haven't. I am and have been a coward. The realisation hits me like a crushing weight, suffocating me. I have been playing the victim all this time. I haven't done anything I promised I would.

I have in no way compensated for the sacrifice Clarice made or the innocent baby that was Clara. I have let everyone down. And ultimately, I have let myself down. It took this moment with Rich; this time when another person began to ask intimate questions, for me to realise.

The rainbow moves to the left, and the light becomes one again.

"You okay?" Rich's voice is low.

I want to tell him that I am not. I want to tell him that he has just fucked a woman with three different identities and two screwed-up lives. I want to ask if he enjoyed breaking my drought. I want to ask him what he felt. I want to crawl deeper into his bed and never leave. I want to ask him to protect me forever. But I also want out of here. Regret pierces my stomach and mingles with the nausea that has been increasing ever since Rich put his fingers softly on my scar.

This is wrong. I cannot be here. I won't be here. I don't deserve to be here.

"I have to go," I say as I scoot from underneath the cover.

"What?" he asks, and I shake my head.

My clothes, for what they are worth, are scattered around the room, and it takes a few minutes for me to locate them all.

"Where are you going?" Rich asks as he watches me dress. "Stay. You don't have to go. We need to talk."

"Talk?" I throw at him. I am angry. Not at Rich but at myself. Yet I cannot shout at myself.

"You needing to talk is how I ended up fucking you in the first place."

I see him flinch. I watch as his expression changes. The warmth disappears, and any residual desire is neutralised.

He shakes his head. "You're nothing but a head fuck," he says, "a prick tease."

I'm not. He knows I am not, but he is lashing out. I understand. I've lied to him since the day we met. In the same way I have lied to everybody. Colin, Astrid ... everyone.

I pull the dark navy hoodie over my head and bend down to tie the laces on my borrowed trainers. I feel his eyes burning into me. I complete my task and walk towards the gap in the screen and then to the obnoxious steel door. It opens as I approach, and I frown. Rich is not with me. He hasn't pressed any buttons or put his finger on the pad.

I turn and see him standing beside the screen, holding something that looks like a remote control. As the door clears its hinges and opens enough for me to exit, I step forward but cannot resist one final look back.

I hear rather than see his anguish as he launches his fist directly into the light wooden screen, his roar of anger echoing through the quiet of the room. I hear the sound of wood splintering, and I force myself to leave.

"Ra!" he shouts. "Ra!"

I keep walking. Looking straight ahead as I pass through the office and towards the warehouse. Behind me, the large door swings closed, and I hear the locking mechanism click into place. A single tear runs down my cheek, and I swipe it away, preparing to enter the reality of my life.It is official. I am no longer going to hide. I am going to own my shit and let the chips fall where they may.

And I am going to acknowledge that I am a selfish fucking bitch.

Chapter Twenty-One

PRESENT DAY

The only way to win at chess - or any other strategy game, for that matter - is to be one step ahead of your opponent. For the last three years I have enjoyed that privilege, yet now I must acknowledge a misstep. A slip-up, a blunder, a miscalculation. Call it what you will. I have fucked up.

I say that like I am okay with it, like I am calm despite this observation, yet let me be clear; I am far from either. Inside I am seething with anger. It has taken every ounce of my small grip on sanity to prevent my fist from ending the lives of the myriad computer screens I watch every single day. I have tortured myself for countless minutes, jabbing at every button and adjusting every setting on every bloody camera, yet I seem to have lost Aurora and Rich. I cannot see them. They have disappeared into thin air and been MIA for the past forty-five minutes. Shit. And despite this, life in the warehouse has continued on as normal, its occupants going about their pitiful lives. It would appear I am the only person who has noticed Rich's absence.

I hit all the buttons again and refresh every camera, but still, there's no sign. I can't have lost them. They will not have left. I have all the exits covered, which means there must be a blind spot, and I have no clue where the hell it is.

I am not in control - a state that does not work for me.

Reflexively I squeeze the arms of my sumptuously ergonomic computer chair, lean back, and close my eyes. I am going to take some deep breaths. I find it very helpful in times of severe trauma.

Perhaps you would like to join me? In for a count of four, out for a count of seven, in for a count of four, out for a count of seven… and relax. Deliberately I peel my hands from their death grip on my chair. A wave of warmth begins to flow through my body, and I open my eyes, looking around the small room I have called home for the last couple of years.

What I love most about this place is its solidity. The whole warehouse was built way back when things were constructed to last. Such a contrast to the modern rent-a-kit units which are popping up everywhere with alarming speed. My humble abode is directly above what would have been the delivery bay, which means I have a concrete floor, walls and roof, perfect for the discretion I require. It is virtually impossible to hear anything from below, and those milling about beneath my feet are unlikely to hear anything from above. Win-win. I can do whatever I like up here, and no one down there hears even the slightest squeak. It is genius. Apart from the fact I have a fucking blind spot, and I have lost Rich and Aurora.

I need to breathe.

This, though, will not be a catastrophe. They haven't left, so according to the laws of physics, they must reappear, at which point my plan will continue. I just need to breathe and be patient.

I let my eyes become heavy and allow myself a moment of fantastical dreaming of the future. How, when all of this is done, I will live the rest of my life with Colin by my side.

He returned from the garden dragging his feet, head hung low. It was painful to watch. It's clear that his embrace with Aurora did not end well, and whilst my heart dances in celebration, it also goes out to him. He deserves so much better than that entitled bitch, and I can't wait until the day I am able to reveal my true self.

You have more questions, I'm sure. Things you don't understand, and that's to be expected. I have indulged the bare minimum of fact. One thing you do need to know, though, is that I am not a terrible person. Far from it, in fact. I pride myself on taking actions that are neither good nor bad; I simply endeavour to do what needs to be done so that the wrongs of others can be righted. I make the world a better place. If you will, I am a superhero, an ambassador for the greater good.

An ambassador for the greater good. I like that.

I think, when Colin and I are finally together, I will buy us matching robes to befit my status as an 'ambassador'. Black, with our names embroidered in tacky gold lettering. Like those in a cheap hotel with ideas above its station. They will be a tasteless branding of our unity. A kitsch symbol of the tawdry life we are going to leave behind. Because, believe me, we will be leaving this life behind. Soon. Very soon.

I return my attention to the matter at hand. As engaging as it is to think of my life with Colin beyond this place and to educate you, I have to focus. Nothing will be achieved until everything is in place, and right now, I still can't see Aurora and Rich. It has been forty-nine minutes.

Deafening silence. Fuck.

Okay. I lied about being calm. I am not calm. Anger is roiling just below the surface. I am incandescent. I want to know how the hell they have disappeared. One moment they are on her bed, and I am enjoying a leisurely wank as I watch Colin's perfect form moving around the kitchen; the next they get up, and that's it. In one painful moment I lost my King and Queen whilst simultaneously being deprived of my state of arousal. That alone - as any half-decent red-blooded man will confirm - is nothing short of an anger-inducing head-fuck.

Images continue to flicker before me. Colin is crouching down feeding that mutt some shit. Bacon probably. I hope he isn't too attached to that four-legged fleabag. Once there is no one left except Colin and I, the mutt will have nowhere to go which works for me. I am not an animal lover, and I will not have anything taking Colin's attention away. The mutt will have to go it alone.

With another deep breath, I force myself to stand, closing my eyes and fists at the same time. My nails dig into the softness of my palms, but the pain is good. It is a reminder that I am here, and I am alive, and I cannot lose it now. I am so close to the end.

In the last three years I have found reserves of patience that I did not know existed. And I found them because I knew the day of reckoning would come. Her day of reckoning. Aurora. That entitled bitch. She had everything which rightfully belonged to me, and just when I was about to take it all, she fucked it up. And, as if that wasn't bad enough, it took her eighteen months loitering about on the streets before she finally ended up here. The trap was expertly laid, yet I've had to bide my time for eighteen months and watch that pillock, Rich, parading about.

Don't get me wrong; Rich is tolerable; he's exactly the type I asked the overly fragrant stupid recruitment woman to find; easy on the eyes, light on the smarts - but Rich genuinely believes this place is born out of charity, and it sucks watching my money being wasted on others. I am, for clarification, that charity, and even though my pockets are deep, I hadn't expected Aurora to take quite so long to get her sorry ass back into my game. And yes, before you make any further judgements, I realise how many employment laws I am breaking, but do you honestly think I care? All I care about is that we are nearly at the end of this game because, apart from when I made that prick in school cry, I really fucking hate chess.

I should also offer reassurance that Colin wasn't part of my initial plan; I don't want you to think he is in any way associated with the inevitable conclusion of this game. He was an unexpected bonus. I couldn't believe my luck when he arrived with Rich. The two of them friends. A serendipitous happening. The universe blessing my plan.

It was more than a little awkward that first coffee delivery. I recognised him, but it was obvious there was no such recollection for Colin. I wanted to tell him everything right there and then, so overwhelmed was I by having him in my orbit again - but I resisted. I couldn't risk my feelings - which are apparently just as strong as ever - affecting the plan. With Colin, I need to bide my time.

You might be thinking our arrangement strange. Why I am living above a crumbling warehouse, for example, and if Rich knows of my existence. The latter is the easiest to answer. Rich is well-aware of me, though he has no clue who I am. He believes me to be a slightly eccentric dropout who makes his living data mining and hacking computers. It was the easiest way to explain the extensive equipment when Rich came to introduce himself.

I weaved a tale of a loner's life, of anxiety around people, a man who has retreated to become little more than a hermit. I was to be viewed as a tenant, nothing more, all of which contributed to a story plausible enough for Rich to swallow - and then I saw Colin.

If Rich considered my sudden need for a daily coffee strange he never let on. Nor did he comment when I asked for it to be prepared and delivered by Colin (though I didn't refer to Colin by name). He just accepted my reasoning that he, Rich, would be far too busy in his daily work to be running coffee up here at my whim. It was almost embarrassing how easy it was to get Rich to believe every word I said, though it did prove one thing: on the recruitment front, fragrant woman had more than delivered.

I allow myself a moment to remember her. She did a good job; it really is a great shame she went and ruined it by asking for more than I was willing to pay. Her assets were unquestionably glorious, but they were never going to float my boat. Unfortunately, she misunderstood my arousal at watching the penny drop from her brain all the way to her fragrant core, which left me with no choice but to add her to my growing inventory of collateral damage. It's a shame, as I said, and I sometimes wonder if anyone misses her.

Still nothing. Shit. Fifty-three minutes.

There is a well-meaning lie that all parents tell their kids. You know the one I mean. It rips the heart out of your innocence, scratches the shine from your world and evaporates any belief in magic. I cried solidly for two days when I uncovered the lie. I was ten years old and far too young to understand why. Just because the global economy booms every December does not make it right. As far as I can tell, it's one huge marketing con that plays on the vulnerability of even the poorest parent, who then causes untold hurt to their offspring a few years later. That's not beautiful. All it does is open young eyes to a shit reality.

It's also a lie that is rarely spoken about once uncovered. The world stands by and watches it in perpetuity, generation after generation believing, before having the rug cruelly pulled from beneath oversized red stockings. It was, as you can probably sense, a defining moment for me. Whilst friends around me all sucked it up, I chose to weaponise it, using its deceit as a constant reminder that the world is false and people are not to be trusted. I have thus, from the age of ten, dealt only in known quantities - what can and cannot be proven. Which is why I know it's impossible for Aurora and Rich to have simply disappeared, yet my brain is seriously messing with my head right now. I planned every inch of this place, pored over plans and blueprints like a man possessed, and installed enough cameras to launch a reality show - yet I am facing what would appear to be my fallibility. They are gone. And it has now been fifty-five minutes.

I pace to the bed, the far wall, the kitchenette, the door, the curtain shielding the basic facilities, then back to the desk, fingers clenching into my palms.

I need something to occupy my mind. I guess I could share a few more secrets while we wait.

Perhaps you will indulge me if I reveal a little about my mother, who was widely known to be the promiscuous type. She didn't even have the decency to brand me with her husband's genetics, though on reflection, that was a smart choice. Daddy-by-default turned out to be a major disappointment. He sat me down, man to man, at the age of eight and told me the truth about my biology, or rather, where the bits that made me came from. Despite this, he still loved me, he said. To be honest, I was beyond caring. He was so fucking wet it was unreal. I mean, why the hell would you happily bring up another man's child? Says it all.

The only thing he didn't tell me was whose seed had engineered my life, which didn't bother me at first. It could easily have been any one of several 'uncles' who came in and out of my early life. For the record, both my mother and daddy-by-default didn't have any siblings, so it didn't take much to figure out that these 'uncles' weren't real. I can only assume that 'entertaining' all these uncles drained the lottery money, but I can't be sure. All I know is that by the time I was eight, there was nothing left.

Not that daddy-by-default was honest. At the same time that he sat me down to reveal his lack of biological input, he also gave me some bullshit about leaving our life of luxury to become 'more enriched', claiming that he and my mother had 'seen the light'. I'm not sure what 'light' they'd seen but it clearly didn't involve money or my wellbeing.

I mean, think about it. What the hell is an eight-year-old kid supposed to do when their world is turned upside down?

In reality, though, it worked out just fine. I began to realise that I was infinitely smarter than both my parents put together - especially when they continued their ridiculous assertion that community living would be the idyll for which we were searching. I saw through it. *We* had no money. *They* had no choice.

I often wonder if things would have turned out differently if my parents had just been honest and told me there was no money left and we were going to have to live somewhere that didn't cost a lot. Instead of which, they moved us into the kaftan-wearing commune, promising quality time with others who 'shared our ideals and beliefs'. This life, they said, would serve us all better than the one of excess we were leaving behind. It would be a world of wonder, harmony, reverence and nurture. We would live off the land and practise gratitude for all that the Lord bestowed. In short, we would enjoy a life of infinite happiness without the scourge of outside influence.

At the age of eight, I called bullshit.

At the age of fifteen, I still called bullshit. We'd been living in this weird colony for seven years, and all anyone seemed to do was chant all day and float around in their knock-off kaftans.

Our home was a glorified hut, and schooling came courtesy of an old woman who could barely walk. Some of the men fashioned her a kind of chair, like the old bath chairs, and in her later years, she was carried everywhere. Like some fucking Queen.

That old woman, it turned out, was the person we were all supposed to revere. She was the One. The wisest of us all.

Yep. Still bullshit.

The freedom was good, though. I could explore my interests without anyone noticing. With all the good little disciples busy caring for each other, no one actually took any responsibility so, when I realised my preferences tended towards those with a couple of Y chromosomes, no one cared. All daddy-by-default said when he caught me messing around with Travis from the fairground was that I should find a more 'manly' pastime. Hence skateboarding. Little did daddy-by-default know how spectacularly that genius plan would backfire.

Skateboarding led me to Colin, and meeting Colin showed me another life. Colin's world back then knew nothing of kaftans and peace chanting. His life was edgy, risky, and heady, and I loved every minute. I'd spend time watching Colin, thinking about Colin and wanking over Colin whilst plotting the downfall of all those good little disciples. Their downfall, I believed, was imperative if I was to spare the rest of the world unimaginable pain. Maybe, on reflection, I took things a bit too far, but the rush of adrenalin you feel when witnessing genuine fear in someone else's eyes is a 'high' beyond compare. And it's a high to which I became addicted.

Most of them had no idea they were being manipulated. I messed with their heads and pleasured my way through them all, loving the sheer terror written all over their peace-loving faces as I stripped them of their decency. It was such a fucking power trip. I knew, by the time I was fifteen, that I was invincible. I am invincible. I can make anyone do anything I ask of them, and they will thank me for it. There really is nothing quite like the wielding of omnipresent authority.

The screen to my left flickers to life, and I sit bolt upright. Aurora - finally. I consult my watch. Sixty-seven minutes. Where the hell has she been for sixty-seven minutes?

I scour the other cameras. Still no sign of Rich, but no matter. He's a minor player. This woman is the important one. She is the one who shares my genes, and she is the key to everything. But I'm not going to give you any more now. No. I've revealed enough for this little session, but I will just let you into one more secret. You're going to be impressed.

Back in the commune, the wise One eventually got wind of my activities and decreed I was to be 'relocated' to a 'place where I could learn'. A place of 'improvement', a kind of finishing school if you like.

To be honest, I was happy to go. I was ready to move on to bigger and better things so before I knew it, I was on a plane to God knows where.

I'd like to say I looked back - but I didn't.

What makes me smile, even today, is knowing how much they would have congratulated themselves - my parents included - as they wafted around in their kaftans, believing they had eradicated the poison. They would have chanted and sung and given thanks for a job well done, yet they couldn't possibly have known where their actions that day would lead.

Now they do - but that's a story for another day. Their miscalculation was, however, monumental.

Why?

Because that plane they sent me on, the ferry I boarded afterwards and that secret 'finishing school' to which I was sent to be cured of my ills, was on an island. A small overseas British territory.

It goes by the name of Añaposta Island.

You might have heard of it.

Chapter Twenty-Two

PRESENT DAY

I need Rex. In amongst all of this craziness, he feels like my anchor. Which is strange considering how inauspicious our beginnings were. I find him in the kitchen - predictably - lolling about on the floor and making gooey eyes at Colin. I see him before he sees me, and for a moment, I experience a pang of jealousy. Rex and Colin look good together, and Coffee Man feeds the mutt, so what's to say he'll want to come back to me? All mammals are inherently driven by the basic need for food, which I'm not that hot on providing.

"Hey," I say, watching as two pairs of eyes turn towards me. The expressions in each could not be more different. The canine pair light up, and within seconds my faithful shadow has clickety-clacked to my side, tail wagging in welcome. I breathe an inaudible sigh of relief. The human eyes, however, do not show any sign of warmth. I understand. I did a shitty thing to Colin back in the garden, and I have nothing to defend myself with except for the fact that I am seriously screwed up.

"Hey, yourself." Colin levers himself from the floor and walks towards the gleaming stainless steel work surface seventeen paces away. I am reminded of the seventeen paces Colin took the last time I counted his entry to the coffee shop. How much our lives have changed since then.

"Everything okay?" I ask.

His back remains towards me, but I see his neck dip forward. "Yep."

"Great." I shuffle my weight from one foot to the other, trying to dislodge Rex, who is enthusiastically slobbering all over my feet. It is at this point I realise I am not wearing any shoes which means I must have left them behind. With Rich. Shit.

A loud crash makes me jump, and I raise my eyes to see Colin slamming a frying pan onto the large gas burner.

"Why the fuck are you still here?" he asks. "You've got your dog. Now get the hell out of my kitchen."

I swallow, aware that my breath is coming in rapid gasps. Tremors course through my body, and the room begins to swim. I know what is happening. I have been here before. The events of the last couple of hours have nudged me towards overwhelm and panic. I am distraught that I have hurt Coffee Man, I am disgusted that I have slept with Rich, and I am appalled at the coward within who has yet to take action against Alex. The world starts to close in around me and I feel more trapped now than I ever did in Yarrick's cell. Every event of the last three years has finally come together in one perfect storm. All I need now is …

"Aurora, there you are!"

Jayde. I was not ready for her when she first arrived, and I am sure as hell not ready for her now. I grab hold of the metal plate trolley next to me for support and begin to turn towards the kitchen's exit. She stands there, all waif and stray and big soulful eyes.

"Oh, and you have your doggie with you." Her voice drops to a cooey baby level.

I say nothing. Partly because I am being rude and I don't give a shit and partly because I can't think of a single word to say. I also need my bed. Now. If I don't get safely horizontal soon, then I will be enjoying the pleasures of gravity in a rapid and most unfavourable way.

I push past Jayde and hear the reassuring sound of Rex following behind. Though I barely touched her, I am still horrified at how little of my former best friend remains. She was always tall and thin, but now she's at risk of blowing over in the slightest puff of wind.

"Sorry," I say, "later."

"No problem, Aurora. We have plenty of time."

She hasn't followed me. I know this because her voice has become more distant. My bunk comes into view, and I aim myself towards it, uncaring of anything other than landing on it, closing my eyes and pretending that the last two hours never happened. I literally fall face forward into the soft lavender-scented pillow and breathe in its calming scent.

My throat is constricted, my knees are shaking, and every sense is urging me to run, but I cannot move. Rex's warm body settles beside me, and I reach gratefully for his comfort as I slow down my breathing.

In my mind I picture a hill covered in lush green pasture, leading to a field burgeoning with daisies. I feel the heat of the sun as it warms my face and I watch the dance of fluffy white clouds as they drift across the clear blue sky. Birds sing happily, talking to each other, echoing calls, male to female, in age-old mating rituals. A butterfly flutters past my nose, and I giggle as I watch its colourful wings elegantly and rhythmically carrying it onwards. The smell of freshly cut grass permeates the air, and as my breaths deepen and the beating heart of my adopted mutt drums tattoos on my legs, I allow the weightlessness to overcome me. And it is in this exact position that I fall into the most peaceful of sleep. In fact, when I wake, I will remember it as being the first decent rest I have enjoyed since that fatal night on the *Cassiopeia*.

≈≈≈≈

For some reason I am dreaming of swans. I am lying in a field surrounded by wild grasses, the sun pushing through cotton wool clouds as a group of swans fly overhead, their muted gaggle unmistakable. I can hear the beat of their heavy wings as they swoop almost low enough to touch and absently I count them. Eight. An even number. Of course. Because swans mate for life.

Shit. I sit bolt upright and rub at my eyes, suddenly wide awake. My dream became too real and that is why I have awoken. I know exactly why I was dreaming about swans. It was because Rich mentioned them earlier when he was telling me about the email, which informed him there was a strong room. The place he now lives. The place where Rich and I fucked.

Bloody hell. A few days ago, I was sitting on my bench watching Roland and Roseanna going about their business, angry at the world. Today, I am in a place of relative luxury, yet I am incensed. Beyond angry. Ever since Astrid and I walked through that great big plinth of a door, my life has spiralled to depths even I could not have predicted. Nothing makes sense.

Being given the chance to stay here, Colin arriving, discovering that Rich does actually have a heart and then Jayde. Bloody Jayde. I shake my head. I am trying to sort through the muddle of time, yet all I can think about is swans. Bloody swans.

The feeling of panic and claustrophobia returns, and automatically, I search out Astrid. She is my one constant, and I know that we must leave. Whatever sick and twisted plan the universe has for me now, I'm not playing. I have one goal: to find Alex, and the only way I can do that is by getting the hell out of this mindfuck of a place.

My eyes land on Astrid, and I breathe a sigh of relief. She is heading towards our bunks yet my relief turns to alarm when I see she is not alone. In another place and another time, I would be watching two supermodels casually strutting down the catwalk wearing the latest line of clothes, yet I am not. Instead, I am watching two beautiful homeless women walking arm in arm, focusing on their destination, smiles wreathed across their gorgeous features. I realise my luck in avoiding Jayde has finally run out. I am going to have to talk to her whether I'm ready or not.

"Ra. Hey baby girl, you were dead to the world." Astrid jingles in that achingly familiar way as she plops down on the bunk next to mine. "We were catching up," she says, indicating the thin figure of my former best friend. "How lucky are you two, meeting up again like this?"

I glance at Astrid. Am I lucky? Somehow, it doesn't feel that way.

"Are you going to join us?" Astrid ignores my silence and pats the space beside her for Jayde. The other woman hovers in uncertainty.

"For fuck's sake," I say, "just sit down."

"Ra!" Astrid reproaches me. "Seriously? Drop the attitude, okay?"

I sigh. "Fine." Beside me, Rex groans and rolls over. His legs hang over the side of the bed, baring his tummy - and everything else - to the three of us.

"How long have you had him?" Jayde asks.

Astrid eyeballs me, imploring me to play nice. She's right, of course. Every instinct is clamouring to explode in rage at Jayde. She turns up in my life when I'm literally up shit creek, having abandoned me when we were fifteen. I don't owe her anything, but I do owe Astrid. Everything.

I swallow my anger. I may have fucked up my friendship with Colin, and I may have literally fucked Rich, but the one person I will always need in my life is Astrid. We made our bond right here in the garden. I will play nice. For her.

"Not really sure. He attached himself to me, and now we're kind of a team." I manage a neutral tone, which is the best Jayde's going to get.

"He's great," Jayde responds as her eyes graze over my dog's warm wiry body. "I bet it helps out there, not to be alone."

"Yeah. Maybe." This is painful. Small talk when we both know there is a chasm of missing years. One of us is going to have to make the first move.

With a sigh, I raise my eyes. "How long have you been out there?" I ask.

"I don't really know," she replies. "A while."

I nod. I get that. Time means nothing on the streets. You simply live from moment to moment.

"You've lost weight," I observe.

Jayde's smile is weak. "Haven't we all?"

"Yeah. I guess. Even me." I incline my head with a wry smile.

"I never understood why you were so hard on yourself," Jayde says. "You were - are - beautiful."

I shake my head. "Compared to you, I was fat and dumpy. You had all the guys. I carried your coat."

Jayde laughs. It is a light sound. Musical, and for the first time since she arrived I see a glimpse of the girl I once knew. "That was your problem," she replies, "you always thought it was about boys, but it wasn't. It was never about boys. You should have believed what you saw when you looked in the mirror. Anyone who made you feel less than beautiful didn't know the real you."

"Amen to that," Astrid murmurs and I slant her a sideways glance.

"Whose side are you on?" I ask and she shrugs, wrists jangling.

"I've always told you you're beautiful, baby girl; you just never believed me."

"It doesn't matter what any of us look like," Jayde continues.

"Of course it does," I snort. "We may have been through the suffragette movement and basked in women's rights, but we are still judged by one thing only. Our bodies."

"Oh, Aurora. You are so wrong."

I run my hands through my hair. It's all well and good for these two stunning beings to disagree with me, but they have never been on my side of the fence. Neither of them knows what it is to be just that little bit too short or that little bit too curvy. Any self-respect I finally managed to build was destroyed slowly by Alex every time he refused my advances. Then, in Yarrick's cell, my body became little more than a vessel. I had no choice, and neither Astrid nor Jayde could possibly conceive what that was like. To have their body refused by the person they loved. To have their body abused by the people they trusted. They are too beautiful for that.

"To truly understand another person," I say, "you have to walk a mile in their shoes."

"What the hell is that supposed to mean?" Jayde asks.

"Exactly what I said. Neither of you knows what it's like to be me."

Jayde stares at me, mouth agape. "Are you suggesting I didn't understand you? That all the time we were friends, you were the only one with problems?"

"Of course that's what I'm suggesting," I respond. "Look at you both," I swish my arm between the two of them, "you can never know what it is to detest the person you wake up looking at every single day."

Astrid sits forward. "Ra," she says, "really? You're really going there?" She shakes her head, clear green eyes boring into mine. "You know how fucked up my life is, and I've been out there a shit ton longer than you. Who gives a toss what anyone looks like? Don't play that game, Ra. Seriously. Wake up and get the hell out of your own self-pitying way. You," she points directly at me, "are not a victim."

I frown at Astrid. "What the …? Of course I'm a victim, we all are. Well, apart from Jayde, who chose her own fate." I hear the sarcasm dripping from my words, belatedly realising I have stopped playing nice. But perhaps that's part of the problem. Perhaps I need to give that anger a home because I am So. Bloody. Angry.

I am angry at Alex and Yarrick for their sick manipulation. I am angry with Rich and Colin for making me go places

I am not ready to go. I am angry at my parents for dying and Clarice for leaving me, too. I am angry at Clara for not being strong enough, and, most of all, I realise with blinding clarity I am angry with Jayde. Because she abandoned me without a second thought.

Ever since she walked through that huge oak door, the scars of her actions have been reopened. It is only now that I can see how what she did has affected my entire life since. When she decided to leave me behind with not so much as an explanation, that hurt in a way so painful I have been seeking to escape that pain ever since. I have lurched from one crisis to another, confused, lost, angry, grieving for my friend yet hating what she did. When I knew she was safe and she had left our world voluntarily, the pain seared even deeper. Those who knew how close we were aimed their blame at me. They wouldn't believe I knew nothing. For months I was a pariah, hated by her family for allowing Jayde to throw away her life. No one listened; all they did was blame.

I had no choice but to turn inward. I had no one to blame. No one to help me make sense of what happened. I was fifteen years old with hormones running riot, parents who believed money was the answer to everything and a best friend who excluded me from her future.

Perhaps, if Jayde hadn't left, I would have been able to get through those awkward teenage years, the cruel taunts from boys who relentlessly mocked my figure. The pressure of being in the spotlight, on display for those who my parents wished to impress. The endless parties I was expected to attend simply because it was 'good to be seen'. The lectures I received on what I should look for in the perfect husband. The dates that made me physically sick. The hours of crying as I tried to squeeze into dresses that everyone else wore effortlessly. The lack of warmth and comfort from parents too busy to realise I was anything other than a prop. The barely concealed assumption that I would carry the next generation well due to my 'child-bearing hips'.

I had everything, yet I was nothing more than a puppet. A robot programmed to move in certain directions, perform certain duties and reliably keep the Foster name alive.

Perhaps, with Jayde by my side, I could have endured all of that. Instead, I lurched blindly from day to day believing I was happy because that was what I was programmed to believe. I steadfastly refused to acknowledge the glaring signs of emotional neglect from parents too busy to care and threw myself into relationships with abandon. Until Alex. I genuinely thought Alex was the one. My soul-mate, my rescuer, my future. And now look at me. Sitting on a rigid bunk in a large draughty warehouse wearing someone else's clothes, faced with two beautiful women who represent my past and my future. I am the glue in the middle. I am the one who connects them.

I close my eyes, allowing the bitterness to settle. The fog is clearing. I have spent every day since I was fifteen subconsciously blaming Jayde for the shit-show that has become my life, but now that I am faced by her once again in a different time and place, reality comes crashing in. It was so easy to lay the blame at someone else's door instead of taking accountability for the decisions I made. I could have opened my eyes years earlier and seen my life for what it was, yet I didn't because I was too busy feeling sorry for myself. Too busy blaming Jayde for abandoning me. Too busy believing that I wasn't enough for her to stay.

"No," Jayde shakes her head, "you're wrong."

"Why? Why am I wrong?" I whisper. Though I almost think I know, I have to be sure. "You had everything. We had everything, and then, one day, you just disappeared. What the hell was I supposed to do with that? I wasn't enough for you to stay."

"Shit, Aurora, no. I'm so sorry. But no. You're wrong."

I drop my head to look at the rug beneath my feet. The same rug I was looking at less than two hours ago when Rich and I sat in this exact spot. I pinch the bridge of my nose. Tears form, and though I blink furiously, it is not enough to prevent them from falling. I watch as they land amongst the jagged patterns.

"There's so much you don't understand," Jayde says softly, "so much you don't know."

I raise my eyes to hers, aware of Astrid and Rex silently watching on.

"Then tell me," I say, "tell me how you disappearing had nothing to do with me."

I hear her sharp intake of breath. "You really believe it was about you?"

Did I?

"I ..." I shake my head. "I don't know. All I know is that you left, and I became a target. Everyone was convinced I was lying and that I knew where you'd gone. The police questioned me for hours, even asked my parents to convince me to tell the truth. No one listened, Jay. No one believed you'd just gone."

Jayde looks at me for a long time. Everyone is still. The only sound comes from Rex snoring lightly. Even Astrid has stopped jingling. I watch Jayde's face, her expression, waiting for a glimpse of my old friend. Time is suspended - and then it happens.

The smile of understanding between two teenage girls.

The sadness of missed chances between two grown women.

Our connection is still there. I feel it, and I know she does, too.

≈≈≈≈

The years fall away and I am back at school, Jayde by my side. We're walking through the corridors, bags slung over our shoulders, carrying what feels like our body weight in books. Other kids stare as we walk past - not at me, but at my beautiful friend - yet she acknowledges no one. The story she is telling continues without pause as we make our way up the stairs at the end of the corridor.

We climb one flight, then two, reaching the small landing that opens onto the top floor passageway where our maths classroom is. The queue of our classmates waiting for the room to be unlocked snakes towards where Jayde and I stand at the window on the small landing, which looks down on the car park below. It is full. Vehicles are parked in neat rows, teacher's cars mostly. We are all too young to drive.

I turn and lean my back against the window, enjoying its cool, solid presence. For a moment I wonder what would happen if the window broke or simply gave way. I would end up on the rough tarmac, broken, I am sure. It is an odd train of thought, one loaded with a gloom that has appeared out of nowhere, so I turn my attention back to my friend, listening to her idle chatter. She is telling me about the latest poster she has bought for her bedroom. Some pop star she's been in love with forever. I don't share her taste, but her eyes dance so beautifully whenever she talks about him, so I love him too, simply because Jayde does. She has that effect on people - an aura that draws you in and makes you want to be her everything. I smile to myself. I am her everything. I got lucky.

Suddenly, Jayde stops speaking, and I glance up at her, wondering if she's expecting me to answer. My thoughts have wandered, and I worry I have missed her question, but she isn't looking at me; her attention is elsewhere. Smiling at someone out of the window.

I follow her gaze and see an older boy waving. He is too far away for me to make out his features, but I know he is older. He is standing by a car, the door open on the driver's side, as if he is in the process of stepping in or out of the vehicle. He is also not in school uniform. Lucky him. We have maths class any second now; he clearly does not.

Jayde blows a kiss towards the stranger, and a cute blush creeps over her cheeks.

"Jay?" I question, "Do you know him?"

She shrugs her shoulders in a way that only Jayde can. The way that tells you everything and nothing, all at the same time.

"Maybe," she says with a wink.

"Jay!" I admonish. "He's like - ancient. Seriously?"

She turns away from the window and grabs my arm, pulling me into the corner furthest away from our queuing classmates.

"Ssshh," she says, her voice low. "I met him a couple of days ago. He's at the college." Jayde giggles. The college is next door to our school; however, there are strict rules about mixing with college students, especially for girls. In the same way there are rules about girls taking business classes.

"What do you mean you met him?" I can't work out how she would have done. Jayde and I are inseparable.

She laughs. "When you decided to walk home the other day,

and I hung around waiting for our lift."

I remember now. I'd been in the girl's loo when I heard some of the girls bitching about us 'privileged' kids - specifically me and Jayde - and how we had it so easy. It got me really angry - not because I disagree - we are privileged - but because they are so wrong about our lives being easy.

The pressure is intense. The expectations on us to succeed, achieve the highest marks, and mix with the right friends - it's suffocating.

Usually, I ignore the comments, yet for some reason, I lashed out. Due in part to my dismal 89% score in English Lit. My parent's expectation was 95% minimum which meant trouble when I got home. And some kind of explanation, of course. I told you my life isn't easy.

Having managed to relieve one of the girls of her hair extensions - in my defence, she pulled my hair first - I ended up in the Head's office and got sent home early. I walked, to give me time to think and perfect my 89% story, which is why Jayde was on her own in the car park waiting for the driver. (We are transported by private drivers whilst most of our year have to bundle onto the community bus. I never said there wasn't merit to their derision of our 'privileged' status).

"He's cool," Jayde is saying, "nice. Not like the other college guys."

"Yeah, right. Like you know any other college guys."

Jayde touches the tip of her nose with her finger. "Maybe I do, maybe I don't."

I roll my eyes. "Please tell me you didn't get in his car."

She executes that mysterious shrug again.

"Jay! You didn't?"

"He was nice," she repeats, "the perfect gentleman."

"Jesus. You could get in serious trouble. Seriously, Jay, do not go there again. Promise me."

Jayde smiles and takes my arm, steering us both back towards the classroom. "You know I love you, Aurora, and you know I hang off your every word," she throws her left arm wide in a mock bow, "but sometimes you can be a real buzz kill."

I shake my head. "You're so not funny and I'm serious. We're not supposed to talk to the college kids. You know that. Anyway, they're old!"

We have reached the door to our maths class, and Jayde bursts out laughing. "Sometimes," she says, "I have no idea why we're friends."

I poke her in the ribs playfully.

"C'mon," she says, pulling us through to door, "let's go slay some algebra."

For the record, Jayde is not the only one wondering why we're friends. Who the hell 'slays algebra'? Her obsession with television from over the pond is clearly having a detrimental effect.

"As long as you're not slaying a college kid," I whisper, loving the mix of shock and admiration that crosses Jayde's face.

"You, Aurora Foster, will keep."

The bell rings, and we take our seats—at different desks. Maths is all about order, apparently, so the teacher seats us alphabetically. A and J don't even get us on the same row.

Sixty minutes later, my brain is cooked, and I've squared

enough x's to last a lifetime. It's only then I realise that I didn't even ask Jayde what the college guy's name was. I make a mental note to do so, but we go in different directions after maths, and when we reconnect, Jayde reverts to pop stars, posters, fashion, school discos, and grades, and I forget all about the college guy standing in the car park waving.

So does she. For she never mentions him again.

≈≈≈≈

It was me all along. Astrid has seen right through me and been brave enough to call me out. Sure, my life has been crap, but I only need to look around this room to realise I am not alone. Everyone has their story; everyone has their challenges - the only difference with me is that I have spent the last eight years of my life blaming a young girl, now a woman, who wasn't around to defend herself.

At fifteen, I didn't have the emotional maturity or awareness to see that self-pity was my friend. I believed that Jayde took Aurora with her the day that she left, but I was wrong. I could still be Aurora without Jayde. I could become who I wanted to be and be proud. I didn't understand that then, but now I do.

Jayde was the catalyst for the path my life took, but she was not to blame.

I was one hundred per cent to blame. I allowed myself to become the victim, and by doing so, I allowed Alex and Yarrick to manipulate me. Their actions were unforgivable, and I still intend to make them both pay, but I realise now that they could only have that power over me because I let them.

It was up to me to be proud of myself and to value my life - not others. I only wish I had known that three years ago.

Chapter Twenty-Three

PRESENT DAY

As much as I have enjoyed believing Rich to be a fool, I must now concede he may be smarter than I gave him credit for. He reappeared thirteen minutes after Aurora, which gave me thirteen minutes to scour every plan of this place and figure out where the hell he and Aurora went, which is why I have to be gracious and concede Rich has outsmarted me.

You may wonder, knowing of my need to control, why I am apparently comfortable in this concession. To put it simply, I am content to allow him this small victory because I know for a fact that he has no idea what he's done. He doesn't even know he's in a game of chess, let alone that he has no control of his pieces. Therefore, the impact on my self-esteem is negligible.

One cannot realistically celebrate an achievement of which one is not aware - so I shall ignore his and Aurora's minor discretion and focus on the important: the fact that there is a strongroom.

A fucking strongroom!

Until a few minutes ago, I knew nothing of its existence. Now, courtesy of a previously ignored footnote on the original blueprint, I am informed there is a *'draft C'* which, according to the aforementioned footnote, includes construction metrics for the strongroom. I don't even remotely care what construction metrics are, but I do bloody care that there is (a) an entire space of which I was unaware and (b) no fucking *draft C* - anywhere.

I grind my teeth and hiss angry air out from between them.

Someone somewhere has really screwed up. I explicitly requested every single plan from the day the first brick was laid, and yet here I am with no *draft C*. Those idiot estate agents. To think I paid them. Even gave them a bonus. Two smarmy Gen Z upstarts trading on their looks.

Not that I was immune, mind. I happily enjoyed a little trouser action, watching their young backsides striding purposefully ahead in this empty shell of a space. A little clandestine trouser action was all I allowed, though. They were far too up their own arses to entertain anyone else. All sharp suits, cufflinks and cheap cologne. You know the sort.

I glance once more at the thin paper file, which contains one original blueprint, various contracts, a memorandum of sale and definitely no *DRAFT C*! I feel the rage building, starting in the pit of my stomach and arriving rapidly at my clenched fists. I need to breathe again.

In for four, out for seven.

In for four, out for seven.

The whole point of this elaborate scheme was to have eyes on Aurora 24/7. *Draft C* - or lack thereof - was definitely not part of the plan.

In for four. Out for seven.

Okay, I need to think. In the scheme of my greater gain, does this really matter?

In chess, those who are successful play a strategic game comprising several standard or complex moves. These moves, or sequences, have been created by masters over time and, used well, will almost always result in a win. The key to the win - as I have stated before - is to be one step ahead of your opponent. Though I cannot deny I am pissed at my recent discovery, I am still one step ahead of Aurora, and I always will be - because I am invisible, and that is the ultimate in strategy and power play.

In for four. Out for seven.

In for four. Out for seven.

I am back in control.

I move one of the cameras to a slightly different angle. The one in the kitchen where Colin remains. He has been there ever since Aurora and Jayde left, giving the appearance of cooking, yet no food has touched his hands. What I would give to touch his hands now. And any other part he cared to let me. I cannot comprehend why he is so knotted up about that bitch, Aurora. Whenever I spent time with her, to be honest, I found her boring, which made everything I had to do so much easier. If I'd enjoyed her company, then constantly having to rebuff her advances might have pulled on a few of my heartstrings, which would have been most inconvenient.

It was an interesting education in the laws of attraction, though. Not the laws of attraction that my kaftan-wearing family claimed to manifest, but the levels of attraction we feel physically based on another person's appearance.

What I discovered is that attraction merely begins with that initial shiny layer; however, its true depth is only attained once you have looked directly into another person's soul. If you don't have both these elements of attraction, you'll get bored. It's kind of a two-for-one deal and has absolutely nothing to do with kaftans and manifestation.

Colin is still crashing around in the kitchen. Aurora, Astrid and Jayde are seated in a huddle on their bunks. Jayde's introduction was a genius move. She is yet another piece of the greater puzzle and, to be honest is the only person I trust - other than Colin. Jayde and I are kind of in this together, you see. No, scratch that. We are one hundred per cent in this together.

Surprised to hear that Jayde and I are acquainted?

Hmm. I feel you should have been expecting it or something similar because even I couldn't orchestrate and deliver the entirety of my plan alone. Jayde has become the most delicious right-hand woman. Indispensable to the point of sacrifice, and I could not be prouder. She has delivered everything I have asked of her - and more. Her entrance to this place, looking all gaunt and dishevelled, has been true brilliance. The finest of performances.

Because all of this is a performance. Jayde is no more a street-dweller than I, but she couldn't arrive well-fed and smelling divine. Even Rich would have smelled a rat. Poor girl has been starving herself and has resolutely refused to shower. Method acting. I think that's what it's called.

Thankfully, we haven't met in person for a while. I fear her newly acquired stench would be a little too much. Though her sacrifice to this greater cause has me feeling all warm inside, I know my disgust at her odour - should I be close enough to experience it - would be hard to disguise.

It was Jayde who decided it was time to enter the warehouse, and it is she who is calling the shots on the inside. I've shared my recordings and observations with her, but now that she is inside, my control of her actions is little to none, which, if I'm honest, has kept me awake at night. I trust her implicitly - she has more than proved herself - but having someone else execute the most important part of my plan is not easy to watch. I have been forced to trust in my training of Jayde, which hasn't been comfortable at times, particularly given that I have waited so long for this moment. I cannot afford even the tiniest of errors. So far, though, she has excelled, and I congratulate myself on the completeness of my manipulation and power over another human being.

Put simply, Jayde is as close to an Alex-clone as I can create.

You're probably wondering how we are connected. As far as you're concerned, she left Aurora's life at the age of fifteen - but, what you don't yet know, is that I have controlled her whereabouts every single minute since that glorious day.

The college guy in the car park?

That was me. Except I didn't actually attend the college, but convincing Jayde I did took very little effort. She was wide-eyed, innocent and naive as fuck. Ripe for the taking. Ready to believe in adventure, excitement and love.

In some respects, I was disappointed at how easy it had been to make her fall in love with me. I thought she might have put up at least a little resistance, which would have made the necessary physical contact a little more palatable.

Her capitulation and eagerness did, on occasion, disgust me, and I was plagued with worry on many sleepless nights, wondering if she had the backbone I required. But, as it turned out, I need not have been concerned.

Jayde is one of those women who fall in love completely and irrevocably and will do whatever it takes to retain the love and affection of their chosen partner. A few weeks away from her old life, and Jayde metamorphosed into perfect clone material and the rest, as they say, is history.

Even without her undying love, I know I would have found it easy to remove her from the life she knew. She was the perfect age and eager to be moulded, desperate to be part of something worthwhile. So that was the dream I sold: a life with meaning and purpose, a life of freedom, a community. It was embarrassing at times, witnessing Jayde and the others hanging onto my every word as they followed me blindly, but I metered my frustration. I needed these followers like Jesus needed disciples. Thus, any discomfort experienced I viewed as a small sacrifice.

The pinnacle of those heady days still excites me. Delivering every single one of those fools to Yarrick and watching as the great man secured their surrender to his control - one by one and piece by piece - it took my arousal beyond the stratosphere. I am grateful to Yarrick for that, at least. Without him, I would never have known the possibilities or the nirvana that could be reached. The part you have yet to understand, you see, is that when I arrived on Añaposta Island at the tender age of fifteen, it was to study under Yarrick's tutelage, tucked firmly beneath his wing.

The community, at that time, was relatively small, although his reputation was rapidly spreading. Yarrick was the one who could 'straighten out' even the most challenging of members, and he 'specialised' in those who were navigating their awkward teen years. Hence, my parents sent me directly to the 'oracle'. I wonder if they would have been so keen had they known the outcome of their master plan, but no matter. What's done is done.

Communities - in my experience - operate ostensibly alone, yet key members can be fluid, leaving one and joining another or even starting their own, like Yarrick. His work was so influential that before long there were many factions besieged with Yarrick copycats, which, I came to learn, pleased and angered him in equal measure.

At first, I was in awe of the man; it was hard not to be, and I could scarcely believe my luck when he offered me a place to stay. The beauty of those rays of light on the bedroom ceiling remains one of my happiest memories, though it wasn't long before I realised I was so much better than Yarrick in every sense. Don't get me wrong, I told him what he wanted to hear, but behind the scenes, I was slowly and meticulously working to overthrow him.

I am obsessed with power - you may have noticed - and Yarrick wielded the ultimate power. It was all going so well, particularly once I left Añaposta. Recruitment for the cause is my speciality, and it is only a matter of time before I usurp the great man. I have already taken spoils from his business - how else would I have built my fortune? Now, it's simply a matter of dispensing with Aurora, and then I can live the life I deserve.

With Colin.

The masterstroke, I think, was when Yarrick told me of Aurora's wish to return to England. Of course, he had no way of knowing just how intrinsically mine and Aurora's lives were entwined, which meant he listened when I advised him against letting her go and, further, that he should punish her.

In truth I hadn't quite aligned everything I needed here, so suggesting Yarrick use the earth room and cell was ideal. It gave him even more power over everyone in his community, kept Aurora where she needed to be for my needs, and gave the men their kicks. My plan was genius. Until she went and got knocked up. Then the whole fucking plan went tits up.

But I have jumped ahead. There are still so many gaps in your knowledge and understanding. I think it's important, at this point, for you to know precisely how Jayde fits into all of this.

When I was at school, I remember some businessman giving a talk. I was seven years old, and it was just before I entered commune life with my parents. We were a class of young kids, wide-eyed and malleable, and this guy asked what we'd like to be when we grew up. Several hands shot up in the air, eager to reveal their fantasy role, but not mine. The problem I had with such an asinine question was that I knew, even at the tender age of seven, I would never be able to follow the rules made by others. I remember thinking it strange that so many of my classmates wished to be put into a box of restrictions, roles and expectations for the rest of their lives.

Whatever.

Each one of my classmates revealed the role they wanted to fill that day, but as far as I could tell, these roles rendered them little more than puppets who would be dancing to the tune of someone else's song. And in that moment I realised I was so much better than everyone in that room, even the guy giving the lecture. At just seven years of age, I realised that I had options; well, two. One, to join the puppet circus with all the other good children, or two, to become the puppet master. I don't think I need to tell you which I chose. Let's just say Punch and Judy needed to move over. By the time I met Yarrick, I had already mastered the art of manipulation, but his skill was next level, and I was eager to emulate him.

The thing about manipulation is that it only works if the person you are manipulating has no idea they are being manipulated. I would watch Yarrick as he moved the followers around his colony and made them do his bidding whilst simultaneously creating a community of people who believed they were living their best lives. They had no idea they were little more than props.

Yarrick would fuck whoever he liked whenever he liked, and no one said a word. In fact, the gratitude he received from his 'chosen' women was sickening - and I absolutely loved it. It was like watching a chess Grand Master at work; so smooth was his attack that his followers became even more indebted to the cause when given the tiniest morsel of attention.

It was heady, liberating, and so many shades of messed up I was beyond impressed. Grown women swooned over a smile thrown their way and fawned over the endless babies they birthed. Behind the scenes, they would compare their ugly offspring, competing to see who had produced the son closest to Yarrick's likeness - for he would undoubtedly be the chosen one in years to come - and the men watched it all play out in front of them. None of them had even a hint of a backbone as they fetched and carried for Yarrick and their bitch wives.

It amuses me even now, imagining how those men must have felt being told they were to use contraceptive protection at all times, only to see their beloved wives growing large with another man's child. It was madness. Brainwashing on another level. Control and submission beyond my wildest dreams.

When Yarrick suggested I return to England to 'recruit', I grasped the opportunity. Not only to engineer a more significant cut of the profits from Yarrick's offshore business deals but to kickstart the plan for creating my own legacy. By now, I was seventeen years of age and ready to use whomever I needed in whatever capacity I wished.

I began by returning to the wonderful colony my parents had forced me to leave two years earlier. Little had changed in my absence. They still wore kaftans and not much else. They still chanted about peace, and they still had no fucking clue about anything ...

... which is why I was able to pick them off one by one.

I did, for a moment, think about recruiting some of them; they would have been easy targets, but it was a risk with them knowing me so well, and I couldn't afford a wrong word to be spoken in the wrong ear. Not when it came to impressing Yarrick. So, I ended them. After all, no one likes loose ends. One bullet here, a sharp knife there ... until eventually, there were just the three of us left.

Me and my ever-loving parents.

Daddy-by-default tried to be brave. He stood in front of my whore of a mother when I pointed the gun in their direction, but I already knew him as a weakling. A few choice words of persuasion, and he was on his knees, making the job of executing him military style so arousingly easy. There was an odd satisfaction to seeing my mother sob uncontrollably as she watched him breathe his last whilst begging for mercy.

Bizarrely, she asked to know why. What she had done to deserve this, and to be perfectly honest, I couldn't give her a good answer. Except that this is what I had been born to do.

There are times now, when I still ponder that question, but genuinely, I don't understand why I did what I did or why I continue to do so. All I know is that without the power this lifestyle affords me, I am nothing. I am not the puppet master. Punch and Judy are still top of the pile and I will not allow myself to be at the bottom.

At that moment, my mother's time of reckoning, it was like an out-of-body experience, one without conscious control. The same driving force Yarrick describes, and it is so bloody addictive. One down, two down … it was never enough. Is, never enough. Yes, I am sick. But do you think I give a shit?

I really did think about letting her live - my mother - after all, she was the one who gave me life, but then it occurred to me that I would still have one relative left, even after she was gone. The man who formed fifty per cent of my gene pool, the father that daddy-by-default had tried so hard to be. He, who knew nothing of me, would be a sitting duck. And, given she was doing the horizontal samba with him back when we had money, it occurred to me, as I stood there watching her sob and beg for life, that maybe he had money, too. After all, money only mixed with money back then.

I decided, in that moment, when she literally had nothing to lose, to ask her who my gene-daddy was. I even inflected some tenderness into my tone, for I am not a complete monster. Without her, I would not exist, and she needed some reward for that. Her tears, though, were ugly as she spoke through them, and it didn't take long for my fleeting moment of compassion and warmth to disappear.

It took less than two minutes to break her. Less than two minutes to hear the woman who birthed me say one name. One name that changed the course of my life forever.

Andrew Foster.

The father of one Aurora Foster.

Damn, the irony of my genetics is genius. I couldn't have engineered it better myself. And don't worry, you can be damn sure I wasted no time getting that DNA test done. When it was confirmed, all I had to do was get Aurora eating out of the palm of my hand. Of course, if you're keeping up, you'll have realised that my mother's revelation makes the delectable Aurora my half-sister, which, I'm not going to lie, made the whole romance thing tricky on occasion. Though pretending to the be 'man of her dreams' was the best way to get close and infiltrate her life, there were awkward moments when she got a bit too close. Batting for the other team definitely helped, but there was the odd moment when I felt a tiny segment of my heart melting towards her - which is why I always carried the results of that DNA test with me. Today, it reminds me why this plan is so important and why Aurora means so little and, back then, it provided (in a most uncompromising black font) a reality-check of exactly who Aurora is to me - my half-sister - and, no matter what you may think, even *I* am not that sick.

I lean back in my chair and move my neck slowly from side to side. As much as I love watching the lives of those below, my back is starting to give me serious grief. I can't afford Jayde much more time. She knows what she has to do, and I need to get out of here.

I sigh and stand, walking towards the small kitchenette. Time for another coffee, sadly not by the hand of Colin. I have no doubt that Rich is soft enough to send more than one a day up, but if I see Colin more frequently than I already do, I cannot promise to behave. And that could derail everything.

When this is all over, and I can finally emulate Yarrick, I know that my work and legacy will be revered on the level of Einstein. I am one of the greats. A thinker, a once-in-a-generation icon whose construct of the perfect world will move the entire population forward. Those living within my boundaries will want for nothing. I will show them how it is to be completely fulfilled, and in return, they will spread my word.

I am a modern-day *improved* disciple of Yarrick, and I will nurture many disciples of my own. I will create a race of obedience, where my teachings will become the law, and every single member will be grateful. It will be a world of beauty and colour and vibrancy - as long as you are on the inside. If you are outside, if you are unwise enough to flee from the wonders of this universe, or if you dare to question the narrative or, worse, develop your own opinion, then you will know nothing other than dark depression.

Captivity.

Everything you hold dear will be extinguished because that is the only way we will achieve one cohesive society. We are too divided as a world. My race, my people, will be as one. There will be no divisions. Hierarchy will be born of status, decided upon only once it has been earned. You will all be humans of the same value, following the same rules to achieve the same goals. Damn. It makes me hard just imagining it.

You can see how it's all coming together now, can't you?

And you must agree that my future is not only meticulously plotted, but that my plan is one only a true mastermind could conceive.

I know you still have questions - not least concerning the small issue of a drifting dinghy and a dead man - but I can't reveal all my secrets at once. I don't know how much longer I shall be forced to communicate with you in this way, so I want to save some excitement. For you and for me. One thing at a time. The last thing either of us needs is to be overwhelmed.

At this point, balance is key. Revealing enough to satisfy your curiosity whilst hiding enough to keep you engaged.

When I think about those below in the warehouse milling about, I like to compare them to an orchestra of which I am the conductor. Every movement they make is choreographed by me and their music begins and ends on my say so.

As you listen to the orchestra, I want you to be on the edge of your seats, knowing that the crescendo is near but unsure when it will hit. Right now you can hear the music getting louder and are watching the players become increasingly animated, so it is a given that we will collectively reach the finale soon. I am just not going to tell you when.

What I will do is outline my expectations because, when this is all over, I expect every single one of you to give me, the master conductor, a standing ovation. One that I so richly deserve.

Then, when you are comfortable in your seats once more, I want you to remember what happens at the end of every concert and brace yourselves. Because it is at this point I will be able to smell your fear.

Why?

Well, it's really very simple.

Any orchestra worth its salt, *always* plays an encore.

Chapter Twenty-Four

PRESENT DAY

Aurora

It's strange, that moment of clarity when finally, it hits. It's a feeling wrapped up in every conceivable emotion. Guilt, fear, excitement. Out of nowhere, there is this knowledge, this power that you can change your life and its outcomes; you don't have to leave it to others. In fact, you should never leave it to others because it is only you who can truly know your desires and needs.

My body aches at the tears it has shed, but I have not been alone. Jayde and Astrid have shared in this most precious of discoveries, each of us understanding, in our own way, that we can be masters of our destinies.

For Astrid, the hours of hushed conversation have given her courage. She will follow a different path when we leave here, one that involves knocking on model agency doors until someone gives her a break. I don't doubt she will succeed, but even if she does not, the bond that she and I share will not be broken, and together, we will carve out an alternative route.

For Jayde and I, it has been the most cathartic experience. We have filled in as many gaps as we can since the day she left, and through her calm presence, I have begun to understand what motivated her to leave.

At school, we were the rich kids, the ones who had it all, the ones that no one wanted to become friends with simply because we had money. Jayde and I weren't alone in this - we lived in an affluent time and area - but we were singled out often. Jayde because she was the one every boy desired, and I because I was her faithful and less-attractive friend.

When Jayde, oblivious to the attention, swatted her suitors away like flies, they would declare her to be frigid and lay the blame firmly at my feet. Apparently I was the 'loser' friend who couldn't be on her own. Though on one level I knew that to be untrue, it didn't stop me from questioning my friendship and dependency on Jayde. I often wondered if I was holding her back, preventing her from enjoying the spoils of our world because I was uncomfortable in my own skin. Now, in the ever-dimming light of this safe house, this place where broken souls come to be fed and cared for - if only for one night - I am learning how wrong I was. Jayde hated it every bit as much as I did, she just hid it well.

Jayde is explaining, as we sit amongst peers who couldn't be further from our roots, that she only ever wanted to protect me. She saw the emotional distance between my parents and I and realised how vulnerable I was. All she wanted, she says, was for me to be happy.

It had never occurred to her that she would meet someone and fall so deeply in love that she would leave everything and everyone behind, but, he had promised a better world and she had believed him. Her life, he had said, would be without judgement or censure, a place where she could truly be free and, in time, I would be able to join her.

Jayde never for one minute considered it could all be a lie - in many ways she was just as vulnerable as I was back then. When she finally realised the depths of what she had got into, it was too late. They wouldn't let her leave because she knew too much, so her only option had been to escape in the dead of night and hide in the shadows of the streets, where she hoped to recover and one day rebuild. I shudder as I remember my time with Yarrick and the parallels that I clearly now see between mine and Jayde's lives, even though we were miles apart.

It's at this point in her story we break for a while. We are tired, wrung out and, to be honest, I don't know how much more I really want to know. She has skated over the details of the commune and the life she lived, and I, in turn, have revealed nothing of my experiences with Alex and Yarrick. Though our bond is still there, and in many ways it feels like we are still fifteen, we both know that we are not and that there are some memories and some situations that are too painful to re-live. Not forever, maybe, but for now. We have to rebuild our own trust, our own relationship, and that isn't going to happen in one afternoon.

Eventually I become aware of the aroma of food and the sound of weary feet shuffling towards the kitchen. It is evening. The hours have disappeared as they fell one by one into our pasts, and I realise I haven't seen Rich since I left him this morning. He might still be there, but it's doubtful. I suspect he has retreated to his office, perhaps relieved to see me engaged in conversation with Astrid and Jayde thereby making it easy for him to avoid me. For a while at least.

I don't know what I'm going to do about Rich, or Colin, or Alex come to that, yet I feel an overwhelming serenity, a peace within which I know will guide me onward. I have shed the shackles of self-pity and opened my eyes to a new reality, one where I am in control and confident of my value and self-worth, because I have found the key to unlock my future.

No longer will I play the victim. No longer will I allow myself to be manipulated by others because I feel unworthy. No longer will I be the loser.

From today I shall take the words of the *Serenity Prayer* deep into my heart and, with the support of these two beautiful women, I know that I will have the '*serenity to accept the things I cannot change, the courage to change the things I can and the wisdom to know the difference*'.

Alex

I am on edge, watching, waiting, peering unblinkingly at the monitors. I move the cameras a little, keeping Jayde in view. She's been with Aurora and Astrid all afternoon, huddled together, hugging, crying … to be honest, the emotion is sickening, but Jayde is only doing what I've asked of her. Whatever it takes to get my bitch of a half-sister to lower her guard.

I have deliberately kept the details vague. Jayde knows 'just' enough with the promise of a decent payday when all this is over. Of course, I've promised her nothing close to the value of dough that will land in my lap as the sole, grieving heir of Andrew fucking Foster. I've done my research. Followed one of those genealogy sites to make sure there is no one else in my way and of course, I've tracked the most recent valuation of assets. It's a bit of a faff to claim his estate, application forms, proof of relationship and other shit, but

I have all I need. Well, apart from one thing. His deceased daughter.

Orchestrating the yacht to explode was genius - even if I do say so myself. By the time anyone could get near, the beautiful *Cassiopeia* was nothing but a few air bubbles on the surface, consigned to her watery grave. I, very helpfully, gave information as to the identity of the yacht. I had been cruising in a dinghy nearby, tourist-like if you will, and just so happened to have a photograph of the *Cassiopeia* bobbing majestically in the jewelled waters - part of a landscape image I'd captured purely by accident, you understand. At least, that's what the authorities believed. They were only too happy to be able to identify the stricken vessel without the expense of a diving expedition. I had watched the explosion from the shore, I said, and didn't believe it was at all possible for anyone to have survived. No one was picked up by rescuers in the days immediately after and so, as I had meticulously planned, the *Cassiopeia* ended her days at the bottom of the ocean taking her morbid secrets with her.

Until that was, Aurora turned up, like the proverbial bad penny. Though she had escaped me on the yacht, I knew she wasn't the strongest of swimmers and, given her reluctance to do any kind of exercise, I seriously doubted she would have the stamina to survive.

I have to admit to a little disappointment when her body failed to wash up on the shore, but in the end, it worked out perfectly. I simply alerted Yarrick to be on the lookout and when he was able to contact me a few days later, I was rewarded with the information that she was safely ensconced in the room at the top. The rainbow room.

It piques my arousal even now, thinking about that moment. In many ways, the plan was better this way. I got to vicariously enjoy Aurora's torture at the hands of my former master with the bonus of time to secure everything else I needed. That way I could be fully prepared to take her down and claim what is rightfully mine.

I stretch my neck; the pain ever present. There are days when it hurts like a bitch and I bemoan having to sit here hour after hour cooped up with nothing but screens for company. But then I remember what is at stake. Why I am doing this, and I picture that beautiful house, changed, altered to be a prison of my design. For those wishing to find peace and harmony who are naively unaware of the controlled trap they are about to enter. I have many ready and waiting, eager to find their purpose and live amongst similar souls. It's all crap. I hate all that fluffy chanting stuff, but it's a means to an end. And I don't intend to get involved. I'll have people to do that. I shall just count the pennies as they roll in courtesy of the members income which they will, unknowingly, have signed over to me.

Damn. I am getting a little too excited. My cock is pushing painfully at my jeans, but I can't help thinking of the end game for I know we are so close now. I can tell. Jayde is animated as I watch her, she has engaged Aurora, reeled her in and I can see my stupid sister lapping up every word. God, I love the power Jayde exudes, even as a skinny freakish looking thing. I'll fatten her up of course, when this is done, but I haven't yet decided what I shall do with her next. I shall have to keep her close, or ensure she is permanently silenced because she knows too much.

Jayde, you see, is how I escaped the *Cassiopeia* that night. She orchestrated everything with Yarrick - he'd always had a soft spot for Jayde, if you know what I mean. It was all done under the guise of a drug run. I was bringing drugs to Yarrick via the *Cassiopeia* and as far as he was concerned, Jayde was the go-between. The one he would pay once the drugs reached his grubby little hands. This wasn't a new thing. We'd done many deals in the past, drugs of varying identities and quantities running to and from our shores, and due to Yarrick's extensive network, I'd never been caught. Not even a sniff of a drugs bust which is exactly what I needed after my wonderful mother and daddy-by-default managed to relieve me of my inheritance. For my plan to work I needed money – lots of it - and Yarrick was only too happy to have another outlet for his sales operation. He wanted to expand into mainland Europe, he'd said, so me working in England was perfect. And, of course, we had history. He trusted me implicitly.

Stupid man.

His loss, though, is most definitely my gain. I feel the air in this tiny room buzzing, humming, ramping up in intensity as Jayde continues my work. The power, the fucking power, is insane.

Yarrick sent one of his men to collect the drugs from the *Cassiopeia* that night, and though the man wasn't expecting to transport anything other than illegal packets, when I explained how seasick I had been, he was more than happy to let me jump aboard the dinghy too.

His instruction was to take the contraband directly to Yarrick and, to be fair, I was tempted to go along with this plan. I hadn't seen the great man for a while, and with everyone on board now dead, I had a bit of time on my hands. But, as we sped towards shore, I realised I couldn't break cover until I knew Aurora's fate. I couldn't risk her seeing me, should she have miraculously survived, so instead, I diverted the henchman to a small stretch of shoreline alongside those bloody huts.

It was simple: all he needed to do was dock the dinghy and take the packets, leaving me to make my unseen departure, however, sadly for the henchman, he insisted on checking the stash meticulously which I assured him was unnecessary. It was then that things got a little heated and he beached the dinghy, causing me to fall and injure my neck.

I couldn't fault his loyalty to Yarrick and dedication to his duties, but what he hadn't bargained for was my possession of a 9mm protector, which I assured him I would use if he continued to check every single packet.

(Spoiler: the packets didn't quite contain the entire amount Yarrick had paid for. I'd needed to use some recreationally during my time on the *Cassiopeia*, just to make the pretence of being sick a little easier. I'd also pocketed some for insurance purposes, in case I needed to buy a few favours – so I wasn't thrilled that my indiscretion would be discovered. Especially since I had no intention of repaying Yarrick).

The henchman, though, was loyal to a fault and despite the threat of a bullet being lodged firmly between his ears, he continued to diligently search the packets. Big mistake.

Moments later he secured his unfortunate and wholly unnecessary demise.

I'm not a total monster, though. I did float his body back to Añaposta in the empty dinghy, just in case someone was missing him.

It also provided the cleanest solution to an unplanned hiccup; any unanswered questions from Yarrick could be explained away by the evil of the sea.

No drugs - presumed lost at sea.

No Alex - presumed lost at sea.

Dead henchman ... who cares.

All that was left for me to do was meet Jayde on the motorboat she had so thoughtfully arranged, and we were on our way back to England. Job done.

My one concern in recruiting Jayde - that she would be unable to execute the plan due to lingering feelings for her former best friend and family - had proved unfounded. Jayde was indifferent and appeared as excited by evil as I. She got off on inflicting misery and, in a revelation that can only be described as kismet, wished to also achieve omnipresent power. It was as if we had been separated at birth.

Evil, I soon realised, is Jayde's drug of choice which even I find a turn on. She's become such an asset and I don't mind admitting I've fallen in love with her twisted mind. She is the yin to my yang; not to mention her hold over Yarrick which is such a mouthwatering bonus. What she can't get that man to do is not worth mentioning.

I watch her again, the camera focusing on her back. She is too thin now; I hope she plans to gain a few pounds once she can drop her poor little homeless act. Not that I care what she looks like particularly, but Yarrick does and after this, he's the final loose end. I will need Jayde at her alluring best to carry out what I have planned for him.

A sudden movement catches my eye and I reach for the keyboard to my right. Jayde shuffles closer to Aurora. The press of a few buttons reveals the three women in profile. Zooming closer, my eyes seek out Jayde's left hand. As I watch, she lifts it from her lap placing it deliberately on the left side of her face, palm to cheek. My excitement mounts.

Astrid leans closer to the pair, her expression warm and open as she laughs at something Aurora says. The dog raises its head briefly before resuming its nap and I hold my breath.

Is this it? Is now the moment to execute my plan? The culmination of three years hard work? Fuck.

Jayde's hand remains on the side of her face and then slowly, agonisingly slowly, she spreads her fingers apart and slides her thumb below her chin.

Shit. I am about to explode. I can barely believe it. Is she really about to give me the signal?

My eyes are on stalks as I press closer to the screen. My right hand reaches beneath the chair, feeling for the cold metal object secluded within its base. I locate it without difficulty and withdraw it from its hiding place. The gun is loaded. It is ready.

I am ready.

Jayde's fingers lift from her face one at a time, little finger to index finger in a kind of fan movement and then ... then it happens.

She extends her middle finger whilst closing the rest of her fingers into a fist, leaving just that one digit visible.

The middle finger. The sign. It's time.

Game on.

In less than five minutes I will have toppled the Queen.

Check fucking mate.

Chapter Twenty-Five

PRESENT DAY

Have you ever seen the movie, *The Bodyguard*?

For some reason, as an alarm sounds within the safe house and most of its occupants rush to the huge oak door, I am thinking about *The Bodyguard*.

Perhaps it is because we are running, too. Astrid, Jayde, Rex and I, being swept up in the melee of bodies trying to exit the building.

It is chaos.

There is a smell; smoke, something burning. Deafening noise. Shouting. More people than I can ever remember seeing in this place running, pushing, screaming.

Maybe that's why I am thinking of *The Bodyguard*. I am reminded of the moment when the world-famous singer is mobbed on stage then rushed through the crowd to safety.

Except we are not nearing safety.

Acrid smoke is thickening the air and I choke. I am holding onto Astrid's hand, reaching down to find Rex, grabbing his wiry fur - yet we are not moving forward. The crowd is surging onwards, but we are going nowhere.

Smoke burns my eyes and I am struggling to focus. Someone is pulling at my clothes from behind.

In our odd little chain, our group is being forced backwards, deeper into the warehouse and away from safety. We are falling over each other and I hear Rex squeal as I tread on his paw. Astrid spins away from me, clutching at her neck, dropping to the ground. Desperately I rub at my eyes. We need to escape.

I turn around, seeking the owner of the hand insistent on pulling me in. I am disorientated. I can't see Astrid anymore. Nor can I see Jayde. I flail my arms to the side, screaming, the sound muffled by the noxious substance that is cloying at my lungs.

A figure looms in front of me and I reach forward gratefully, realising I am about to be rescued.

"My dog," I say, though my voice is barely more than a whisper. "Please find my dog."

I want to say more, I want to tell them to find Astrid and Jayde too, but I am exhausted. I will have to rely on the other women to make their own noise, but Rex cannot fend for himself. He will be frightened and I want nothing more than to comfort him.

"Rex!" I shout ineffectually.

The figure comes ever closer. It is male, I can tell by its build and frame. My first thought is Rich or Colin but no, it is neither. This man walks differently.

"Help," I whisper. "Help me."

He is almost upon me. Just as I am about to reach my hands forwards to touch him, to ensure he has seen me, a swirling sound hisses from overhead and is accompanied almost instantly by freezing cold water falling from the ceiling. Sprinklers. Thank God.

The smoke begins to clear as the fog lifts. The water is doing its job. I rub at my eyes, trying to flush away the stinging smoke with my soaking hands. It takes a moment and then finally, finally I can focus.

I look towards the man who was reaching for me, hoping that I will see Rex safely ensconced in his arms. My rescuer is holding something out to me, but it is not my dog.

It is a gun, pointing directly at my chest.

"Hello, Aurora. Remember me?"

Any warmth that remained in my body drains to the floor. I blink, convinced I am hallucinating. This cannot be real.

I open my eyes. I am not hallucinating. My heart beats out of my chest as my brain tries to catch up.

"Alex?"

Fuck.

"In the flesh," he replies, "and I appear to be pointing a gun at you. Again."

Gallons of water continue to rain down, freezing my skin; yet that is not what paralyses me. It is fear that keeps me frozen in time. I am struck dumb. Sick to my stomach. Shaking. I cannot form thought.

"Why?" I manage eventually. Alex smirks.

The sprinklers finally stop their deluge and I get a good look at his face. Alex. The face of the man I once thought my soul mate. Alex. He looks the same as he did three years ago. Alex. Right down to the gun. Alex. Pointing at my heart. Alex.

"Why?" I repeat.

He cocks his head to one side as if considering what to say, yet I know he will have every word rehearsed. You don't engineer whatever sick plot this is without knowing every minute detail.

"You know what, Aurora, I've waited three fucking years for this moment, though now that it's here, I can't decide whether to kill you straight out or tell you what you want to know. Make no mistake, you are going to die whatever option I choose, but I'm wondering if I should allow a little suspense. For old times' sake. After all, I've been waiting a long time to put a bullet in your chest."

He smiles. "What do you think I should do?"

I look at Alex. I am helpless. I am defenceless. He's really giving me a choice?

But then I realise his question is not aimed at me. Someone moves from behind him and paces a couple of steps forwards to stand on Alex's right.

The second person is also holding a gun. Which is also pointing directly at my chest.

What the hell?

"Jayde?"

I must be dreaming. I cannot possibly be standing in this supposed safe house with Alex and Jayde *both* pointing a deadly weapon at me.

"What the hell?" I vocalise my thought.

Jayde shrugs, her eyes not meeting mine.

"Loyalty," Alex says. "That's what."

414

I have so many questions but I realise I stand absolutely no chance of survival. Questions seem pointless. All of this time I have wasted, putting off searching for Alex, telling myself I was making a plan - but he has played a masterstroke and inexplicably he is here. Ready to finish the job he started three years ago. In a matter of moments, I will be dead. Answers will serve no purpose.

I shake my head. I don't know what else to do.

"Confused?" Jayde asks. "The boy in the car park ..." she nods her head towards Alex.

"The college kid?" I whisper. "When we were at school?"

"Got it in one," she smiles. The gun jiggles slightly as she moves. "I knew you'd like him."

Wait. What? This makes no sense.

"You knew I'd like Alex?" I cannot join the dots.

"Yes," she responds. "You were in love with him, too. Right?"

I fumble around the periphery of my brain, knowing there is a connection somewhere but it eludes me.

"You know each other." I state unnecessarily.

Both Alex and Jayde laugh.

"Intimately," Alex replies.

I flex my fingers hoping some movement remains. Though I still have two guns pointed at me. I can't see how any movement will save me.

"You're sick in the head," I spit out.

Alex laughs again. "Nope," he says. "Nothing wrong in my head. Yours on the other hand ... well, they'll be at least one lovely bullet right between your eyes soon. *You* will most definitely be sick in the head when that happens."

I flinch at his words. Hating the sound of his voice. Wondering what I ever saw in him.

Oddly my fear has subsided and I feel an overwhelming sense of calm. Perhaps I am experiencing the moment of near death that many who have survived such trauma reflect upon. Maybe these are my last few moments on earth.

Alex was the man Jayde ran off with. Alex was the man who took her to the place she told me mere moments ago that she detested. That she had no choice but to live on the streets to escape from.

Alex took her to that place. Alex was ... fuck.

The calm in my body has finally reached my brain as the scales of confusion fall from my eyes. Dots which had not even appeared on the same page, suddenly join in a line of twisted cruelty.

"Yarrick," I say. It's a statement. An admission of defeat.

"Damn," Alex says, "you're brighter than I gave you credit for. I thought it would take a lot longer for you to get there."

"Always was the clever one," Jayde responds. "That's partly why I hated her."

Alex laughs.

"You hated me?"

I haven't forgotten that my life is hanging in the balance, but for some reason it seems imperative I understand. "You really hated me?" I whisper.

My throat is clogged and I swallow pointlessly. How? Why? I am bereft of understanding. Jayde was my best friend. At least, that's what I thought. Has my entire existence been one elaborate lie? Told by deranged humans for their own twisted gains? Even if that were true, I cannot comprehend what either Jayde or Alex have to gain from this charade.

"Oh, yes," she replies. "Hated". Jayde draws the word out, elongating it for effect. I shiver.

"Look at you," says Alex, "all down and out. No Astrid, no Rich, no Colin."

"No parents," adds Jayde.

"Of course, how could I forget."

"No ocean to jump into either," Alex observes as he puts his head on one side. "I'd say, my darling Aurora, you are out of options."

"You are deranged. Both of you." I twist my head to encompass both my former love and my former best friend.

"What the hell kind of sick game is this?"

Alex shrugs. "Since you ask … it's chess."

"What?" I ask as I frantically wiggle my toes to restore circulation. If I am given an opportunity then I will run. "What the hell is that supposed to mean?"

My mouth might be functioning, but fear remains fixed in my core. I am confused. I am cold. And I am more frightened than I have ever been. Even more than that god-awful night on the *Cassiopeia*.

"Chess," repeats Jayde. "Cool."

I stare at the girl I thought I knew; the woman I was beginning to understand. I pin my eyes to her face, willing her to raise hers and meet my gaze. I cannot fathom any of this. If she would just look at me, connect with me, perhaps

I could reach her, perhaps everything would fall into place. But she keeps her eyes averted. She has no intention of giving me anything.

I brace myself and close my eyes. Somehow I sense that the time for explanations is over. Though I have tried, I cannot comprehend the scene with which I am faced so maybe it's better to give in. The whys and wherefores will not matter in the afterlife - should there be one. All that will matter is being reunited with my parents and when I am, perhaps between us, we can unpick the hell of the last three years. I do not have enough left in me to do this on my own anymore. Though this is not how I expected to meet my end, I am resigned. There is no point in fighting the inevitable. I drop my shoulders and exhale.

"Aw," Alex says, "she's getting all ready for us, closing her eyes in her final act of defiant protection. I always did admire your courage, Aurora."

I block out his words and close down my senses one by one. A shuffling of feet indicates he is moving closer. I brace myself knowing that in a matter of seconds, I will have the cold hard tip of a gun placed against my forehead and a bullet will be lodged between my eyes, just as he promised moments ago.

I take another deep breath, not knowing if it will be my last.

I hear Alex breathing, then feel the warmth of his exhale spilling over my face. I am sickened. To think I once kissed that mouth with passion and love. That I coveted his lips as my own.

The cold bite of metal makes me jump a little as it is placed firmly against my head. I squeeze my eyes closed as tight as I can, whilst at the same time offering up a prayer that Rex and Astrid will be safe.

The chamber clicks. The gun is cocked and ready for firing. My time on this earth is done.

Unexpectedly, I feel a hand reach into the pocket of my jogging trousers. I jump a little, startled by a touch I wasn't anticipating. What the hell is Alex playing at?

"What are you doing?" asks Alex.

Not Alex's hand then. Jayde's.

"Just checking she has no sharp objects, nothing to defend herself." My former friend's voice comes from beside my right ear.

"Good idea." I can hear Alex's silent nod - so attuned am I to my senses now. "You ready?" He asks. I don't know if he is talking to me or Jayde. I say nothing.

"Sure," Jayde replies. "Go for it."

I clench my hands into fists, waiting for the inevitable.

I take one final, steady breath and allow it to circulate my lungs, expanding them to their full capacity. I drink in the stale, smoke tainted air, wondering what air is like in the afterlife. Is there air? Is there even an afterlife?

I am about to find out.

I feel the gun pressing ever more firmly into my temple.

A loud bang sounds - but it is off to my left and the gun drops from my forehead. I am still alive.

I open my eyes. Colin lies prone on the floor clutching a knife in one hand and his leg in the other. Blood oozes from a gunshot wound, the red sticky goo seeping between his fingers and dripping onto the floor in an ever-increasing puddle. Jayde is clutching her left shoulder and I realise she has been stabbed. Colin managed to get to her. I see distinctive red glistening from the tip of the knife Colin still holds. The top Jayde is wearing rapidly changes colour as it soaks up her life force.

I look at Alex. His gun is pointing towards Colin.

"Nice try," he says.

Colin's eyes meet mine, and I shake my head.

"No," I mouth. "No."

Coffee Man's face contorts in pain as he begins to shuffle towards me on his bum. Like a baby learning to crawl.

"No," I implore, this time using my voice. "Please."

As he looks up at me I see his eyes dart quickly to the right. Something has captured his attention. I am just about to turn my head to find out what, when the large bulk of Rich barrels in front of me, catching Alex off guard and knocking him to the floor.

The gun fires again as the two men fall in a heap.

"Rich! No!" I scream.

Jayde shakes her head at me and then spins, aiming a kick directly at Rich's groin. It hits its mark and he doubles over, freeing Alex from his hold. In a matter of seconds Alex is back on his feet. The stray gunshot, I am relieved to see, hasn't hit anyone. It is lodged in the wall behind where Colin lies.

"These fucking men," Alex says, as he once more levels the gun in my direction.

Jayde nods. "Tell me about it. No time to waste," she says, "who knows what heroics they'll try next."

"Agreed." The chamber clicks once more. I look at Rich

writhing in agony. I look at Colin, incapacitated by a gunshot wound to his leg. Mentally I send thanks and pray they will be saved when all this is over. Whatever Alex and Jayde's beef, it is with me, not them.

"Let's count down," suggests Jayde, "you know what she's like with that counting shit."

Alex smiles. "Good call."

"I'll count," she offers. "You ready?"

Alex nods. This time I have kept my eyes open. I am not sure why.

"Three," Jayde says.

Alex steadies his stance.

"Two," she asserts a little louder.

Alex shuffles his feet as his thumb pulls back the lever to arm the gun.

"One!" Jayde shouts.

The gun fires and it takes a moment to register that I am still standing. That the gun has not been fired at me. In front I watch Alex as he begins to crumple to the ground, eyes wobbling. He turns his focus to Jayde - and so do I. She stands beside me, braced, her smoking gun pointed firmly at Alex.

"What the ...?" he mumbles before slowly falling to his knees.

I watch in horror as blood spurts from the mouth of the man I once loved. The man who killed my parents.

His body is wracked with tremors and he ends up flat on his back, jerking uncontrollably. It is morbid. It is cruel. It disgusts me to my core. Yet I cannot draw my eyes away. I continue to watch, until eventually he is still.

"He's dead," Jayde states, her voice chilling. Matter of fact.

I don't know what to say. I look at her. Am I relieved that she saved me? I think so, but I cannot compute anything right now. No part of what happened in the last few minutes makes sense.

I shake my head in confusion. "I don't understand." I say quietly.

Jayde smiles and in that split second, the years fall away. We are two fifteen-year-old girls again.

"You don't have to," she says with a sad smile. "Just know that I'm sorry."

Before I can form any reply, Jayde pulls the trigger again.

I scream, waiting for my legs to fail. Yet it is Jayde who falls to the floor. She lands haphazardly on top of Alex, her end ignominious. Blood drips from a gaping hole she has blown in the side of her own head.

I scream once more. My throat rips and tears. I carry on screaming until there is nothing left. I retch as the contents of my stomach threaten to explode. This time my legs do give way, but it is not because I have been shot. I am saved from a hard landing by Rich, whose arms I find around me, cradling me, soothing me as we fall as one to the floor.

"Fuck." I say, as I cling to him. My body is shaking. I am witnessing a scene from a horror movie. I bury my head in Rich's shoulder, hiding. I am screaming, crying, shouting, sobbing ... I am a mess.

I don't know how long I stay there.

I don't know what has happened to anyone else.

People are moving around me. Police. Paramedics. Coroners. Some are talking to me, asking questions, but I refuse to move. I refuse to leave the cocoon of Rich's arms, and Rich doesn't seem to mind.

He simply holds me carefully, reverently, soothing and stroking my hair.

"You're safe now, Ra," he repeats endlessly.

"It's okay, I promise," I hear his voice crack and break. You're safe now, Ra. I've got you. You're safe."

Chapter Twenty-Six

TWO DAYS LATER

My dearest Aurora,

Well, what a ride. I am genuinely sad that I can't be there with you, but I had no choice. My life has not been my own since the day I left you behind. This was the only way it could end. It was the only way I could protect you.

I imagine you're confused, traumatised even, and I wish I could hug you and cuddle up on the sofa watching chick-flicks like we used to. Laugh about the boys we were desperate to date - and those we'd never go anywhere near. I cannot tell you how much I miss those days. Their simplicity. The times when we thought we had forever.

Though neither of us knew it back then, our lives were always about you, Aurora. You thought you were in my shadow, but the truth is, I was in yours. You have this strength, this presence that cannot be learned or defined, and my biggest regret is that I never told you how strong you are or how incredible you are - because you are, my dearest friend - you truly are.

I know you refused to give up on me when I left and I know how much I hurt you. I could apologise - in fact, I wholeheartedly apologise - but I don't think there are enough words to adequately convey what your friendship meant to me. And, though this end play may have been brutal, the scene of horror you were forced to witness was my way of showing you just how much you meant to me. There was nothing else I could do. It had gone too far; I couldn't stop it.

It was Alex - the boy I ran away with - though you've probably realised that by now. He was so charming and handsome and I was so stupidly naive. I don't to this day know how I allowed such a screwed-up manipulative man-child into my life, but you and I were fifteen, Aurora. We didn't know what we wanted, and the excitement of having him in my world was too much to resist.

I didn't bend to his every will straight away. We'd been together a few months before he finally persuaded me to leave. I had been seeing him on the quiet, behind your back up until that point, which is why I wasn't interested in any of those other lads. I hated not being able to tell you. Especially when you began to blame yourself for holding me back.

I desperately wanted to share my relationship with Alex with you, after all, we shared everything back then, but Alex convinced me you wouldn't understand. He infantilised you, Aurora. Told me there was no way someone as immature as you could even begin to comprehend the love that he and I had. I am ashamed to admit I eventually believed he was right. After all, he was older than us. And wiser. He'd lived a life already and I was head over heels in love. He was my everything and I was too naive to see what he was really doing. I had no way of knowing his connection to you, but looking back I can see how he manipulated every part of my life, just so that he could get to you. He wanted your inheritance. His motivator was money and he was prepared to play the long game.

He moved me away from friends and family, everyone who I felt safe with and depended upon, telling me that I didn't need them anymore. He was the only one I would ever need, he said, and like the fool I was, I believed him.

Alex made his life sound so free. So exciting. I couldn't wait to be a part of it. I even dreamed of becoming his wife. It's laughable to think of now.

If I ever asked any questions, he would move the goal posts, giving me even more reasons and incentives to stay with him. That's how we ended up on Añaposta Island - although I know now that he had planned for us to live there all along. We went in a group, each coveting the dream of living our own lives with our own rules. Alex convinced us it would be perfect and we believed him. We'd leave all our negative influences behind, he said, and start our new forever in a community of people aligned with our values.

I met Yarrick on our first day there, and fell promptly into line, persuaded by the freedom and promise of a better world. It was Yarrick who convinced my parents I was in a superior place - and they took him at his word. I've often wondered what would have happened if they had been stronger - but they weren't and at the time, I was glad. I loved being a fully-entrenched member of Yarrick's community and I lived that way for many years, often singled out by Yarrick for his special attention because he would say that I was a good girl.

I laugh as I write this now. How I could have been so controlled, so naive, so stupid ... but I was. I wasn't the first and I doubt I'll be the last. So many people crave change in their lives and if they are desperate enough, they will be malleable and that is the danger point - because that is when they will believe anything.

It kills me to think you arrived at that house so soon after we left, though maybe it is better that our paths didn't cross then. Alex and I lived there, too, you see. We shared the bed in the room with the rainbow lights. Those clothes you wore - they were mine.

We had left only a few weeks before when Alex became restless. He was ready to go it alone and make his mark on the world, so he urged me to leave with him. We were going to set up our own community and Alex was to fund our lifestyle by working for Yarrick. I knew that involved drugs, but I didn't realise to what extent.

It wasn't long before we had more money than we knew what to do with, so Alex began going to events, clubs, anywhere he would meet vulnerable women, for they were easy pickings, he said.

And that's when he met you. Of course, even that was orchestrated, but I believed him when he told me it had been a chance encounter. He even acted surprised when I told him we had been school friends, you and I, and remarked on the coincidence. For that was all it was, he said. A coincidence.

It was only later, months later, as he became more preoccupied that I began to have my suspicions; and it has taken me the best part of three years to work it all out. It is Alex, not Yarrick who pulls the strings, and even Yarrick dances to Alex's tune.

I understand this is a lot, so I have taken the liberty of leaving behind recordings of conversations between Alex and I. They are located in a safety deposit box - the details of which are at the end of this letter. I hope that once you know everything, you will be free to heal.

I need you to know, Aurora, that I did try to stop this. As soon as I realised exactly who Alex was and what his intentions were, I persuaded Clarice to get you out of there.

Alex and Yarrick intended for you to rot in that cell: Alex, because it meant you were out of the way, and Yarrick, because you wanted to leave. They both had too much at stake by then and couldn't risk you talking. You weren't supposed to survive the relentless punishments but you were stronger than they bargained for - and then you got pregnant.

Yarrick has a pathological need for children because they represent the future of his message, but he doesn't care about the women who birth them. Once they have served their use, they end up in the compound, where you were. They do everything that is asked of them and more, hoping for one tiny crumb of affection from Yarrick, and I couldn't bear to see you like that, Aurora. The only reason I was saved from that fate was because of Alex. He made it clear I was his girl and, because Yarrick loved Alex like the son who would one day be his heir, I was left alone. No one was allowed to touch me. I felt so special, so loved - but I was nothing more than a pawn, too. I simply had more use than those other women because through me, Alex could get to you. I was merely a means to an end.

Alex controlled everything, he even tracked the cargo ship you returned to England on. My role was to make sure you arrived at the safe house eventually, which is why I spent time on the streets, even though I was never actually homeless. My use of Denver was calculated. His brain is so messed up that I know he will never remember the skinny woman who infiltrated his world for a while. For the record, he is the only one I used. Astrid is clean - there is no way I would ever compromise someone who meant so much to you. Rich and Colin were in the dark, too. Everything they have told you is their truth. You have my word.

In so many ways I wish it didn't have to be this way. To spend even those few hours with you was so precious, and there is still so much I don't know about the woman you have become, but that is the price I must pay for my actions and for my part in Alex's sick game. Though I know I am not to blame, I cannot help but feel that your parents' blood is on my hands, too. All those innocent lives lost for the evil and greed of a madman.

When all of this is over, you will need people you can trust, and I hope that in Astrid you have found the friend I should have been. She has a soul that is true in its beauty.

Now, though, I must close because this, my darling Aurora, is the end. I am sorry that I took the coward's way out, but I couldn't bear to see your disgust at the person I had become.

It was always about you, Aurora. I killed Alex so that you could live in freedom and enjoy the happiness you deserve.

I may have let you down in the past, but I had no intention of letting you down again.

So it's goodbye for now, my best friend. My wings will take me high above to a place where I can always watch over you. Perhaps, in another life, we'll get the chance to watch chick-flicks again.

I fucking love you, Aurora Foster.

Please be happy.

Yours always,

Jayde xx

I cry quietly as I read the letter over and over again. I have listened to the recordings and I know the whole story now.

Though I understand it, I cannot process any of it. I have lost so much and too many people have been hurt and killed. I cannot put a name to the emotion I feel. Numb perhaps.

It sickens me to think that my dad was Alex's father and that I wished to become intimate with my half-brother. That is the only thing for which I can thank, Alex. His refusal to make love has saved me from the most disgusting act of betrayal.

For now I have to try and put everything behind me. I will drive myself insane if I try to pick it all apart. Instead, I must learn to live again.

The letter was in the pocket of my jogging trousers. Jayde must have placed it there when she told Alex she was checking for weapons. In a final act of blatant defiance, she gave me the key to my freedom. It is only now I realise how lucky I was to have known her.

At the bottom of Jayde's letter there is a post-script:

PS. Don't ever forget that, like swans, true friends are mates for life.

Chapter Twenty-Seven

AÑAPOSTA ISLAND

Jim

The grave is small, barely visible. A pauper's grave. The rounded lump of earth could be mistaken for a hillock, a place created by nature rather than evil. But it is not. It is the resting place of a woman who deserved so much more. So much better.

I drop a single rose onto the mound, watching as my tears drip patterns into the dry ground. I take a moment. I close my eyes. I remember her how she used to be. Full of life and love. Standing on the dock, waving, waiting for the boat to arrive. Clarice. The love of my world.

I take a deep breath and turn back towards the village. It is eerily quiet, every ramshackle home empty now. There is nothing left except memories.

I walk through the old marketplace, the hub of Yarrick's community. Abandoned tables lay scattered, blown over by the wind that whips at my hair as I traverse the pier towards Yarrick's huts. They are a honeymoon destination no longer. No one to clean or tend to them. No one to stock them with food. Like the rest of this corner of Añaposta Island, they are deserted. Left to the laws of nature.

Finally, I make my way onto the dock and stand on its edge, a place I have stood so many times before. I breathe in the sharp salty air, knowing this is the last time I will ever stand here.

It didn't take long, once I alerted the authorities to Yarrick's activities. This is a holiday island a place of tranquillity and peace, not somewhere for a fucked-up man to reign by terror and fear. The drugs were the key. Once they had concrete evidence that he was smuggling, the rest followed in rapid succession. I wanted him dead, but I knew I wouldn't be afforded that luxury. Instead, I must be satisfied knowing he will rot in a prison far worse than the cell in which he imprisoned Aurora.

His followers are now free. Shipped back to England, or wherever their homeland is, so that they can attempt to rebuild their lives. I don't know if any of them ever will. Some left kicking and screaming, still so blinded by their manipulative master.

I feel nothing but relief now as I scan the horizon for cargo ships. They will be passing, I am sure of it, but I won't be on them anymore. Since Clarice died, I have done little except grieve, but now I am ready to move on.

It took months to turn myself in as an accessory. I knew what Yarrick was doing yet I said nothing. In my head I was protecting Clarice but the truth is, I am a coward. And I hate myself every single day for not doing anything sooner. Maybe, if I had, she would still be here today.

Sea birds swoop and dive and I watch their easy forms as they float on thermals. Endlessly seeking, searching.

Life is like that. At least in my experience.

An endless search for happiness, contentment, love.

I have known what it is to love and I know I will not experience it again.

I couldn't save her when she was here, but perhaps I have saved her now.

Perhaps her soul is looking down on me, watching as I navigate the ruined remains of her world.

And perhaps her soul is smiling.

I hope so.

With a final breath, I take two steps forward and jump into the swirling ocean below.

I am going to find out.

Chapter Twenty-Eight

EPILOGUE

SIXTEEN MONTHS LATER

We stand together, side by side, the early spring breeze jingling the bells adorning Astrid's scarf.

"How's coffee bean?" I ask.

Astrid smiles and rubs her swollen belly. "I think its father literally excretes coffee. This thing ain't stopped moving for eight hours solid."

"Ew." I reply. I love Astrid with all my heart but there are some things I just don't need to know. One of those being Colin's excretions.

"Talking about me?" he asks as he slowly approaches. His walk is lopsided, supported by an ever-present stick.

"Yep, sure am," Astrid replies. Colin's smile widens as he reaches her side and drapes an arm across her shoulders. These two are so much in love and so perfect for each other it literally makes my heart bleed. Colin is still recovering from the bullet wound in his leg. He will never walk properly and is in almost constant pain, but he never complains.

He realises how lucky we all were. Astrid nursed him day after day, supporting his recovery and attending his physiotherapy sessions and eventually, the love she held for him was reciprocated. Their bond, their connection is so beautiful and now that Astrid is only a couple of months from birthing their first child, it is a beacon of hope.

No one could have imagined the extent of Alex's depravity. Despite hours of therapy, I still shudder every time I remember that monster shared my DNA. To learn the truth about my father and Alex's mother, to understand what drove Alex to become the person he was, to realise I had a sibling who wanted me dead - that in itself was enough to fuck me up for life. Yet the hardest part to get past and the one that still gives me nightmares, is knowing that I was in love with him. That I believed he was my life, my soulmate.

When I think about my parents, my father, their loss still cuts deep, but I have been forced to face the reality of who they were, not who I thought they were. I don't know what my mother knew, and I can only assume my father had no knowledge of Alex, otherwise he wouldn't have welcomed him as my partner. I still find myself asking questions that I will never receive answers to, but I am learning to let them go, slowly. I watch Colin and Astrid and the way they have embraced their second chance and know that is what I must do, too. Because only then will I be free.

A noise to my right causes me to turn, and I smile instinctively.

"Hey, you."

Rich reaches my side, having made the short walk from the gate at the bottom of the driveway to where we are now congregated.

"Hey you, too," I reply.

I feel his warmth as he drops his arm over my shoulders in the same way Colin did with Astrid moments ago, and there we stand, the four of us, at the end of a driveway leading to a large house surrounded by fields and trees.

Rich and I are happy, though we have a long way to go. I have so many demons, and he has been crippled with the guilt he feels, knowing Alex was the person living above the warehouse all that time. He hates himself for believing Alex's story, but we all did; he conned us all, even Jayde. Colin has also struggled with his relationship with Alex. Though in his mind they were simply old friends reconnecting, the depths of Alex's obsession were revealed in Jayde's video, and Colin was sickened to know they had been boyhood friends. For his part, he had given little thought to the man living above the warehouse. Colin had no desire to rekindle any kind of friendship; they were grown men living different lives, and as far as he was concerned, their paths had simply crossed again, and he was making the man a coffee. The simplicity of Colin's understanding is so naively beautiful; it shows the truth of his nature that he sees nothing except good in everyone.

Rich is similar to an extent, although he's been forced to face his own demons and is finding it difficult to recover his self-belief. He hates how close I came to the end, and for a while wouldn't let me go anywhere without him, but we are working through it. He is a complex person, like all of us and, coming from a family who didn't communicate has made it almost impossible to get into his head. Not that I am qualified to try, far from it. We are all seeking healing in our own ways with our own support systems, but ultimately, the four of us being here now is the most precious of these supports.

It's been a difficult road since Alex. We were all forced to witness an atrocity beyond understanding. We have our moments and times when we each need solace - none more so than me - but Rich and I will get there. Every day we are opening up more, every day we are learning and trusting each other more and slowly the raw attraction has turned into a love that I am certain will keep us safe in its grasp for a long time to come.

The four of us grow silent as we look towards the incredible place we have worked so hard to create over the last sixteen months. Each of us has put blood, sweat, and tears into making this place what we know it will be, and today is the first day of the rest of our lives.

Today is the day we get to open the gates to what will be a true safe house. A place for those in need to call home. A version of Rich's safe house, but better. It will be a house filled with warmth, food and love. A home of comfort and tranquillity that extends to the four additional bedroom blocks and beyond. We can house up to fifty people in need at once and now, after sixteen long months, we are ready. The construction is complete; the rooms are furnished, the staff have been employed and trained, and we have food ... today our dream has become a reality.

What the four of us started as a project of recovery, therapy, understanding and compassion has become so much more. We are it, and it is us. It's as simple as that.

A loud bark causes me to jump as Rex bolts towards us from the front door of my childhood home. Behind him are two lanky puppies followed somewhat cautiously by their mother, another stray. She found us in the remnants of the warehouse on the day our lives changed forever. Among the police and ambulances, fire crew and crime tape, Petra appeared, and we've been stuck with her ever since. Or at least Rex has. Though none of us would have it any other way. We are an odd little family, four humans and four dogs, but we are a family, and that is something none of us thought we would ever have again.

"Are we ready," Rich asks, "now that Rex has decided to join us?"

I laugh and scratch my mutt's head as he nuzzles into my legs. I still have no idea why he picked me, but we've made a good team, he and I. We complete each other's worlds.

"Ready," I say.

The four of us turn towards the tree trunk, which depicts the boundary of my property. It stands adjacent to the gate and has been a trunk without a tree for as long as I can remember. As a child, I would climb it and hide inside its hollowed interior, but now it has its own unique purpose. Attached to the side of the trunk, the side that faces towards the road is a large hunk of wood, carefully formed into a sign. Draped over the sign is a large, black cloth, placed there by the sculpture artist this morning. None of us have seen the sign, none of us wanted to.

In addition to this sign, we have created a small memorial garden at the back of the house with a bench and two further sculptures. One of a mare and one of her foal. Clarice and Clara. I sit on that bench every day and talk to them both. I want them to know how much they were both loved. Even though I was conflicted in my feelings for Clara at first, I now realise I did love her. Very much, and I wish I could have saved her and been the mother she deserved.

A light cough brings me back to the present and I smile, indicating for Rich to go ahead and remove the cloth. He walks slowly towards the tree and grabs the corner of the black silk.

"Ready?" he asks again.

"Yep. Go for it," I reply. My nerves are screaming. This has to be perfect.

"Three!" Shouts Rich.

"Two!" We reply.

"One!" Four voices in unison.

With a flick of his wrist, Rich deftly allows the black cloth to drop from the sign to the floor, revealing its full glory for the first time. A sob escapes me, and Rich jogs back to my side, once again pulling me close and holding me as tightly as he can.

"It's okay," he whispers into my ear, "everything is going to be okay now, I promise."

I nod, as tears stream down my face.

"Shit, Ra," says Astrid. I turn to face her, unsurprised to see streaks running down her cheeks, too. "Come here, baby girl."

As one, Astrid and I move away from Colin and Rich, linking our arms together and taking a few short steps to the trunk. We reach out, fingers drawing slowly around the letters.

"Shit, Ra," she says again, "we fucking did it."

I smile through my tears, sobs building once more at the back of my throat.

"Yes, we fucking did," I say.

I feel Astrid's swollen stomach against my side as we embrace in the way only sisters of the heart can.

"It's beautiful," I whisper.

Astrid nods. "Too fucking right."

Together we read the words aloud. Slowly. Each of us knowing how much we owe to the one person who can never be here.

But we are here. Astrid and I, and Colin and Rich. And the only reason we are here is because of one incredible person.

I read it aloud one more time. Softly, almost to myself.

WELCOME TO JAYDE'S REST,

WHERE SWANS MATE FOR LIFE.

THE END

ABOUT THE AUTHOR

As a little girl, I dreamed of writing a book. With my head buried in page after page of Enid Blyton, I genuinely believed that there was a magical world at the top of the Faraway Tree, and that I would go there and one day write a book.

Later, I realised I would never write a book - because I wouldn't have the patience. I have this (annoying) habit of reading the first few pages of a book and then, if I am gripped by it, I read the end, before going back and finishing the middle. I figured that if I wrote a book, I'd probably write a great beginning and a killer ending, but I'd get bored when it came to filling in the gaps.

Fast forward to 2015, and with several challenges facing me, I discovered that I had a need to write, to fictionalise what was happening, in order to cope. On that first day of typing aimlessly into the laptop I wrote 6,000 words - and the rest, as they say, is history.

My first novel, *Twelve Days - The Beginning*, is no longer in publication. Nor is its sequel, *Twelve Days - The Future*. I made the decision to remove them from publication many years ago, simply because they didn't represent who I was as a writer anymore; however, in 2017 and 2018, I published two new books, *When Foundations Crumble* and *Resurrection* which I will be re-publishing as 2nd editions very soon. These two books are closer to who I wanted to be as a writer, though they could not be further from *The Safe House*. Now, publishing *The Safe House*, I think, as an author, I am where I want to be.

I started my business, **begin a book Writing Services and Independent Publishers** in late 2020 because I wanted to share that magical moment when you get to hold your finished book in your hands, with other aspiring authors who simply didn't know where to start. **begin a book** has gone from strength to strength which means I now get to do what I love every single day. Bonus!

I am mum to two amazing boys, 19 & 21yrs, though sadly my youngest has severe and complex needs requiring 24/7 care. He is my inspiration on the darkest of days. The man in my life is Archie - my cat.

If you enjoyed *The Safe House*, please leave me a review. Thanks!

www.ingramcontent.com/pod-product-compliance
Lightning Source LLC
Chambersburg PA
CBHW011548190726

48287CB00010B/2787